YOUR NAME IS LIGHT

TENAYA METZLER

ISBN 978-1-63814-256-0 (Paperback)
ISBN 978-1-63814-257-7 (Digital)

Covenant Books
11661 Hwy 707
Murrells Inlet, SC 29576
www.covenantbooks.com

For Nickea,
my twin sister and best friend who brings so much light into my life

ACKNOWLEDGMENTS

I would like to thank my coordinator at Covenant Books, Megan Lee, for all of the help you have given me in publishing my first book. I would have been lost without your reliable insight and advice. Also, I would like to give a big thanks to acquisitions agent Joseph Magnolia for encouraging me to submit my manuscript.

I would also like to say thank you to the editing department at Covenant Books for your patience as you helped me through the various stages of editing, and to the graphics and page design teams who brought this book to life.

A special thanks to my entire family for supporting me in my dream of writing! Firstly, thank you to my parents for reading my book in one of its earliest, roughest versions. You both read the man-uscript in its entirety, with all of its original flaws, and found a way to enjoy it while offering much-appreciated suggestions. Your early support meant so much.

Next, thank you so much to my tireless editor, Kierra. You ded-icated countless hours to edit my book and offered the blunt, con-structive feedback that only an older sister could. Most importantly, thank you so much for your medical knowledge and insight! This book would not be the same without you.

Lastly, thank you to Nickea, my twin sister and best friend, who inspired this book when it was just an accumulation of character names and plot ideas. I wrote this book for you, and you helped me to build it into the book it is today. We spent hours editing side by side, and I want to say a deepest thank-you. This was such an exciting adventure to embark on, and I was so happy to share it with you.

I would also like to give a shout-out to friends and family who encouraged me along the way. Remembering to check in and ask me how everything was going has meant the world to me, and I would like you all to know that I am so thankful.

Ultimately, I would like to thank my heavenly Father for making this entire journey a possibility. I can do nothing without You, and I certainly saw this reflected throughout my time writing this book. Your strength got me through it all. Thank You.

DISCLAIMER STATEMENT

The people and events in this book are fictional. Any resemblance to actual persons is wholly coincidental, and all references to actual institutions and locations have been creatively manipulated for the purposes of the plot.

PART

1

CHAPTER ONE

THE CHILD SAT ON A SHAGGY PINK CARPET, SOFTLY CHATTERING TO HER DOLLS.

She had just fastened the blonde doll's purple gown when tires screamed from the window.

The dolls were dropped and forgotten as the child whimpered. Then a familiar voice called, prompting the child to clamber to her feet and walk toward the door. Standing on tiptoes, she was just tall enough to grasp the handle. She toddled outside, drawn to the voice.

With a brilliant flash and burning rubber, an explosion split the air, knocking the child backward from outstretched arms. With the macadam came the blackness, and the child knew no more.

Alina bolted up from the couch with a gasp, her heart pounding. To reorient herself, she gazed around her cozy rental home, decorated with Christmas lights for the coming holiday. Her pulse soon slowed to its regular rate.

"A dream," she murmured to herself. "Always just a dream."

That same dream had haunted her from before her earliest memories.

She stared at the clock on the wall with a start.

No time to dwell on it now.

She had slightly overslept her "quick nap," and she had a shift to prepare for.

She rapidly dressed and fought her hair into a semblance of a French braid before taking a moment to regard her reflection in a full-length mirror. Her eyes took in her sea otter clogs, her navy-colored scrubs, and at last, her face. Her dark, chocolate eyes stared back sleepily at her, and she sighed, halfheartedly tugging hair free to line her face.

"Oh, well. I guess it will have to do," she murmured aloud, chuckling at her self-consciousness.

"What's so funny?" Ami asked, bounding into the room. Her brown curls bounced as she moved, and her silver-brown eyes sparkled.

"Oh, nothing," Alina replied, humor still lacing her voice. "It's just, well, I guess I wanted to look a little dressier tonight, and nothing I'm doing is helping much."

Ami walked toward her, joining her reflection in the mirror.

"I don't want to hear another word about it! You look great."

Alina smiled at the girl next to her. Ami Everly was her housemate and her best friend.

"I would like to add," Ami continued, "that you, Alina Dixon, are a beautiful and successful nurse who survives working in an emergency department, saving lives. Cute enough to stop a heart, skilled enough to restart it," she finished with a grin.

"Thanks," Alina replied, grinning in return. Then she winced.

"I just remembered that tonight's a full moon, so that vote of confidence is very much appreciated."

"Oh yeah, I know exactly what you're talking about," Ami said with a mock shudder. "I'm so glad I'm not working tonight." Ami was a dayshift nurse at the Richmond Pediatric Center, but she picked up the occasional night shift.

After a moment, Ami continued.

"I expect you to come home on time! I'll get the groceries this week, even though it's your turn."

Alina laughed. "I am forever in your debt!" she joked, happy to hear her friend laugh in return. She checked her watch. If she didn't leave soon, she would be late.

"No, seriously. Thanks, Ami. I'll make it up to you tomorrow."

"I'm holding you to that," Ami said rapidly, her eyes fastening on the clock. "Now get out of here! Your sickly patients aren't going to heal themselves."

Alina nodded and quickly grabbed her backpack, coffee thermos, and coat.

She raced out the door and climbed into her black Highlander, and she beeped the horn and waved at Ami in the doorway as she carefully backed into the street.

As she began her short commute to the hospital, the late-afternoon sun settled lazily over the city of Glen Allen, Virginia. This time of day was always beautiful; the sunlight glinting off the roofs of houses lining the street and sending shimmering reflections across the distant Echo Lake, coupled with the bright-blue sky, always seemed to take her breath away.

A tune was playing faintly, and she turned up her radio for the empowering chorus of TobyMac's "The Elements" to fill the car. Too soon, she had to turn off to reach Virginia Hospital and Healthcare Association's Emergency entrance. After parking, she closed her eyes, clasping her hands on her lap.

"Dear Lord," she prayed aloud, "please give me strength to get through this shift, give me courage to face the doctors, especially Dr. Rathberg if he is scheduled tonight, and help me to be a shining light for You. Please help my coworkers to see Your love and joy through me. In Jesus's name, amen."

With a feeling of peace descending on her, she climbed out of her vehicle and walked through the ambulance entrance of the hospital to the emergency department.

AS THE FAMILIAR CACOPHONY of shouting, cursing, and blaring bed alarms met her ears, Alina's suspicion of a busy night was confirmed.

Dr. Pridlin was in the middle of a very vocal discussion with a visibly intoxicated patient who wanted narcotics for his sprained ankle, and her favorite charge nurse, Keith, was locked in an animated conversation with an irate parent. From what Alina was hearing, the woman couldn't understand what was taking the doctor so long to come and save her son, who would "certainly die" from a superficial finger laceration. She was also furious that a nurse had told her the wait time meant her child wasn't actually dying. Yet.

Alina grimaced, but she couldn't help but smile. It was always so refreshing when someone said what everyone else was secretly thinking.

Keith looked up as Alina approached, his face wrought with annoyance. It was obvious he was quickly losing patience. She gave him her brightest, most reassuring grin.

He sighed mournfully and turned his now-intense stare on the woman, who abruptly stopped speaking in the fierceness of his piercing gaze.

Alina laughed at the transformation and continued her trek down the back hall to the locker room. As she unpacked and prepared for the long night, Sierra walked in.

"Hey you!" Sierra exclaimed, her sparkling green eyes vibrant against the soft glow of her blonde hair.

Alina considered Sierra to be an emergency veteran. She had served as Alina's preceptor when Alina started three years ago, and their bond had only strengthened through the years. Sierra always offered advice and no small number of hugs on especially rough nights. Alina lived for those hugs.

"Hey!" Alina said. "How is it out there? It looked like quite the adventure when I walked through."

"Super busy, as always," Sierra replied as she washed her hands, her glittery nails shimmering under the water. "But we've got this. We always do," she finished with a wink, meeting Alina's gaze in the mirror.

"Aww yeah!" Alina laughed. "Is Rathberg here?"

"Thankfully not. But Crulen is, and she seems to be in a pretty bad mood tonight. Anyway, holler if you need anything! I've got to get back to my constipated commando in room 12. Pretty sure he needs a soapsuds enema."

Alina laughed again at Sierra's mock gagging. "If anyone can do that efficiently, it's you!"

"I'd rather place three NG tubes than do a single enema," Sierra groaned, rolling her eyes. Alina shuddered. Nasogastric tubes had to be inserted through the nose into the stomach while the patient was awake, and patients did not like them. Or the nurse inserting them. Alina would rather do an enema.

"Anyway, I'll see you around!" Sierra said. "If you hear someone bellow, 'CODE BROWN,' you know where to find me."

Alina laughed and waved as her friend left, and she checked her reflection once more in the mirror.

"Yeah, you can do this. You are good at this. You can do this!" With her final pep talk complete, Alina left the locker room with a triumphant stride. Smiling at anyone she made eye contact with, she made her way over to Becca. Her coworker was slumped at her computer, putting the final touches on her documentation before she signed off to Alina.

"Hey, you ready to go home?" Alina asked as she sat down.

Becca merely huffed in response, and Alina surveyed the other nurse. She could tell it had been a long day. Becca's immaculate red curls from when she had taken over for Alina that morning were now a poofy mass on top of her head. Becca's curls seemed to get poofier whenever Becca was given more than her fair share of annoying patients. The greater the poof, the higher the annoyance.

Alina soon understood why as she received report on the patients she was assuming.

Alina quickly recapped the information as she signed into the computer. Room 15 was a patient with a diabetic foot ulcer and subsequent osteomyelitis receiving high-dose intravenous antibiotics, room 16 was an intoxicated woman with a blood alcohol of 320 who had passed out at a casino but was now awake and belligerent, and room 18 was a well-known drug seeker who continuously dislocated his own shoulder in order to receive sedation and IV narcotics. Studying the list further, Alina noted her last two patients: a punk in hall bed 9 who had deliberately smashed a window and a pleasantly confused elderly woman in room 19 who was being admitted after falling and lying on the floor for three days.

Alina got to her feet and headed into room 15. She always enjoyed a good foot ulcer.

THE HEAVYSET WOMAN STOOD before Alina, screaming and sobbing hysterically.

"Look, I'm sorry, Laura, but we can't send you home yet. You are still really intoxicated, so you aren't safe to leave until your blood alcohol level lowers enough—"

"Oh, you all are such—" The woman burst out a string of curses. "I called a taxi to take me back to the casino, and you can't keep me here, you…" Alina endured another rampage of cursing and yelling. She knew it was hopeless to win an argument with someone so intoxicated, so she stood there until the woman paused for breath.

Redirection was Alina's best move. "Laura, can I get you something to snack on? How about a turkey sandwich and a cookie?" At least for the moment, Alina was able to placate the woman with food, TV, and a dark room with a pillow and extra blankets. With any luck, she would doze and sleep off some of the alcohol overnight.

Just as Alina exited the room, her phone beeped obnoxiously.

"Alina, ED, how can I—"

"Code brown, code brown!" Sierra hissed through the line. "And bring reinforcements… He missed the goal of relieving his constipated self in the bedside commode."

Alina nearly laughed out loud. "Oh, Sierra, I'm coming. Anything special I need to bring?"

"How about a new pair of scrubs?" Sierra grumbled. "You'd think he had been aiming."

Alina hung up, incredulous. *Poor Sierra.* Well, that was a first.

"Hey, Keith," Alina whispered as she hurried by, "can you call the house supervisor for a new pair of scrubs for Sierra? Her patient missed the commode…"

As Alina hurried off to save Sierra, Keith's loud guffawing followed her back the hallway.

WITH AN EXASPERATED SIGH, Alina flopped down at her computer to continue charting, stealing a bite of her now-cold microwavable breakfast burrito. She checked her watch and sighed again. 2300. Only four and a half more hours until she could go home and shower.

As Alina sat, her thoughts landed on the beautiful rose bouquet that had been delivered to her the day before. Another gift from her Soter. Alina twirled her pen slowly as she traveled back through childhood memories.

Alina had grown up under the care of grandparents who had given her everything she could have wanted. Everything, that is, except what she actually needed: love and affection. Though she had never been left physically alone, she had always felt empty, deprived of love from the only family she had.

On the day she left for college, they announced that they were moving to Florida. They had claimed they would come visit, but it never seemed to work out.

The loneliness had dissipated a little, however, as an anonymous angel had taken it upon himself to send her thoughtful gifts on her birthday each year. Over time, the gifts had progressed from exotic dolls, books, and colorful candy to tuition checks, velvety roses, and luscious boxes of chocolate. Each gift arrived with a card signed, "Soter." With a quick Google search, Alina had discovered that *Soter* was the god of protection in Greek mythology.

The very idea had always filled her with warmth and joy; Alina reveled in the idea that God was looking out for her through a mysterious stranger's kindness. At times, she fantasized Soter to be one of her parents sending her gifts, though she knew that could never be. Her father had died in the military when she was four years old, and she had never even seen pictures of him. She barely remembered her mother, as Amanda Dixon had perished in a car crash just several months later.

With a start, Alina realized that Keith was right behind her chair, staring at her with his infamous ax murderer face.

"Whaaa!" Alina cried, spinning around to face him.

"Lost in your thoughts, again, Dixon?" He fixed her with his stare, and she laughed.

"Yep, sorry. Thanks for bringing me back, Keith."

"Yeah, that's me. The one who brings 'em back." Keith suddenly broke out in the chorus of "Stayin' Alive" as he walked away.

That meant he was in a good, though goofy, mood. When he was ticked off, she had often heard him sing "Another One Bites the Dust" under his breath. Quite a dark undertone, as they were both songs that could be used to keep a steady rate of chest compressions during a cardiac arrest or code.

At last, Alina finished her charting, and she stood up to check on her confused lady. The sight of a discarded gown and ripped-out IV on the floor met her eyes as soon as she walked into the room.

She spent the next twenty minutes convincing her patient that clothes are very important, that the next IV must stay in her arm, and that it is not nice to hit. After starting a new line and wrapping it, Alina finally left the room.

Her phone rang. It was Sierra again, but the seriousness in her voice made Alina freeze.

"We need you in the trauma bay, honey. Come quick."

AS ALINA NEARLY JOGGED through the bay doors, Sierra quickly pulled her aside.

"A trauma's coming in. It's bad. Sounds like a stabbing, unwitnessed. Can you be my wingman? Keith is recording, and Renée is our third set of hands."

Alina nodded, warmth flooding through her as adrenaline began pumping in her veins. The three women worked quickly to prepare the room: crash cart ready in case the patient coded, primed fluids with pressure bags to expedite fluid resuscitation, airway cart, a sheet on the floor to catch any DNA, and paper bags. Forensics would need everything.

"Don't forget these!" Sierra exclaimed, tossing Alina a plastic gown and goggles.

The ambulance lights flashed outside.

They're here. Lord, please give me strength.

Medics burst through the ambulance doors, pushing an older man on a stretcher with a bright-red stain blossoming over his entire chest through the pressure dressings that the medics had applied.

Alina inhaled sharply as he was wheeled into the trauma bay, Dr. Crulen barreling in close behind. Alina heard fragments of the report as she began prepping the man. No breath sounds on the right side. Collapsed lung. Distant heart sounds—possible cardiac tamponade. Significant blood loss.

The man was gasping weakly, his eyes glazed. Alina and Sierra locked eyes, and Alina knew. His chance of survival was slim.

Renée rapidly attached telemetry and other monitoring devices as Alina cut off his clothes with her trauma shears, careful to avoid the stab hole and other torn areas. There were fresh bruises all over his chest and abdomen, and she could see the bloody knife wound on the left side of his chest. She held all of her equipment over the sheet, placing each article of clothing in labeled paper bags as Sierra established bilateral IV access.

Dr. Crulen's sharp voice cut through the alarms and chaos as she stood over the patient with the ultrasound probe, performing a rapid trauma assessment.

Chest tube. Fentanyl. More oxygen. Pressure bags. Fluid. Emergency blood transfusion protocol.

An alarm sounding on the wall caught the attention of the room. His pulse ox saturation was 74% and rapidly declining. Alina looked at Sierra; he was already on a nonrebreather. Dr. Crulen's stethoscope was on his chest in an instant, and Alina watched with increasing panic as the man gasped, unable to draw in or exhale air.

"Tension pneumo!" Dr. Crulen barked. "Give me a large bore angiocatheter NOW!"

Without hesitation, the physician stabbed the IV angio between the man's ribs into the pleural space, and the air that had been trapped by the collapsed lung escaped through the new opening with a violent hiss.

He gasped, sucking in a desperate inhale. Alina watched his oxygen saturation slowly rise and plateau at 91%.

Everyone was ushered out of the room so he could be X-rayed, and Alina rushed back to his side as soon as she could. She felt so frantic to help him, but her looming suspicions numbed any hope she felt.

He may not make it.

The surgeon, Dr. Stagora, was already at his bedside, exploring the stab wound as the man weakly cried out. Grimness etched across her features.

Not knowing what else to do, Alina clasped his hand in an attempt to comfort him.

"Level one trauma." Dr. Stagora's voice echoed through the room as she spoke on the phone. "Confirmed cardiac tamponade. Ready the kit and tell Brad to meet us there…"

Alina lost track of her words as the surgeon rushed from the room, returning to the OR.

Alina glanced around at the emergency staff streaking around her, everything blurring and fading together. Fingers suddenly squeezed hers.

She looked down at him, and her breath caught in her throat as the man's frantic, bloodshot eyes locked on hers. Her gaze dropped to his lips as he silently breathed a word over and over again. "Lazrae," he mouthed. "Lazrae."

Alina's lips parted as she stared at the man. She repeated the word back to him slowly, looking for confirmation that she was saying it correctly. The OR team arrived, ready to rush him back for surgery.

Goose bumps trailed down Alina's arms as they left the room. The man's eyes never left her face.

When she lifted her gaze to scan the team on call that night, she felt a tangible shiver course through her as she met another pair of eyes. It only lasted a moment, but she nearly stumbled as she stepped backward.

What was that?

She slowly made her way back to her chair at the nurse's station and collapsed. She thought Sierra and Renée were still in the trauma bay, but she wasn't sure. Sierra loved teaching, so her preceptee was probably receiving a lengthy lesson on cardiac tamponades.

Alina's mind replayed the scene of the suffering man staring straight into her eyes as "Lazrae" rang repeatedly in her ears. Another shiver coursed down her spine. As the team had left the trauma bay,

Alina had seen a new OR nurse. Their eyes had met in a heart-stopping instant as she realized he had been watching her interaction with the patient.

His unflinching stare had not been one of curiosity or confusion. It had been one of cold calculation and perhaps an underlying…rage.

ALINA RELEASED A QUIET groan, massaging her forehead and leaning back in her chair as the minutes ticked by. She was extremely unsettled; she had no idea what "lazrae" meant, and she could only reason that her adrenaline had created a potential threat in the other nurse where there wasn't one. Even so, both moments felt alarmingly significant.

A full moon, indeed.

She was freaking herself out even more now.

Alina jolted upright in her chair. *What on earth am I doing?*

Her confusion must have distracted her. His final word had to carry meaning. Meaning that likely related to the circumstances of his…what would most likely be…his death. She regarded the team of policemen who had arrived shortly after the stab victim to collect the evidence and to survey the area.

Dr. Stagora walked into the ER just as Alina stood to approach them. Alina looked at her, her heart pounding. The surgeon was wearing crisp, new scrubs.

The ED around them became a blur, and Stagora simply shook her head as she walked by.

Alina slowly exhaled, her heart sinking. The man was dead, just as she feared. Now the need to tell the police what the man had told her hit her with even greater urgency. She had just taken a few steps in their direction when she heard a soft "Excuse me" behind her.

Alina whirled around. An extremely handsome, blue-eyed, sandy-haired policeman was standing behind her.

"Do you have a statement that might help us with our investigation?" he asked, concern flashing in his blue gaze.

Alina nodded, trying to ignore the butterflies in her stomach.

What on earth is wrong with me?

"Yes, I do," she replied. "The man said something to me before they took him back for surgery, and now he's dead, and, well…" Alina stopped talking. She sounded like an idiot.

"Excellent!" he exclaimed.

She was utterly entranced by his eyes. Before she could say more, the officer held up his hand.

"Might we discuss this privately?" he inquired. He leaned in close. "This man was a well-known politician operating a few hours out of Richmond. I don't even know if I can trust everyone on my team over there. Have you put any of this in your documentation yet? It would be wise to keep this quiet until I know who I can trust in this investigation. I don't want to risk the wrong person getting his hands on the man's record."

She nodded in understanding, her eyes widening and her lips parting.

"Um, yes, I believe we could use the bereavement room out in the waiting room. And in answer to your question, no, I haven't had time to chart any of it yet." He nodded in satisfaction and gave a sigh of relief. She quickly led him out to the waiting room, giving Keith a nod when he looked up with interest.

Once the two of them were safely in the bereavement room, he closed the door behind him and locked it, keeping his back turned to her. She stared at him in confusion as he turned toward her, something concealed in his hands. Her breath caught in her throat. He was staring at her in a familiar way. The cold calculation was gone from his gaze, but the rage lingered there.

"No, wait…" she began. "How could you… I thought I saw you…" She stopped, dread mounting up inside of her. "Who are you?"

She hadn't recognized him until this point, but she knew now. He was the unfamiliar OR nurse who had been staring at her, just with different hair, eyes, and perhaps even a different nose.

And she was locked in a room with him.

She took a step backward and gasped as he was on her in an instant, a tourniquet wrapping around her neck and choking off her scream. He pinned her to the floor with a knee in her back as she struggled to breathe.

Panic overtook her and she thrashed wildly, her face scraping painfully against the carpet. She scratched desperately at his hands, though her nails never found their mark.

With her remaining strength, she tried to kick upward as her hands grabbed behind her, but she met empty air.

G-God, please help...she prayed, black spots swimming in her vision. In a few more seconds, she would lose consciousness, and then...would he kill her?

Jesus! her mind screamed.

His weight was heavy on top of her, crushing her. Blackening. His breath. Hot on her bare neck. He leaned closer. Choking her. Everything fading...

A sharp intake of breath in her ear. And air suddenly filled her lungs.

All of her strength gone, she lost consciousness.

A FEW HOURS LATER, Alina sat in her own emergency room, wrapped in a warm blanket as a defense against the shock.

Five minutes after she had fainted, Keith had come to look for her. He followed her ringing pager through the ED and into the bereavement room, where he found her. Crumpled on the floor.

When she had awoken, she was in a hospital gown and cervical collar, staring up into the terrified faces of Keith and Sierra on the way for a CT angiogram of her neck. She had been vaguely aware of Sierra talking gently to her.

The bright lights were so blinding. The noises so loud.

Upon returning to the room, she had tried to speak but instead winced at her sore throat and the hoarse whisper that escaped her lips. In slow, broken words, she had attempted to explain what had... happened.

Her scrubs were gone, sent off to forensics. Sierra had performed a forensics nursing exam, taking various specimens.

All the tests had come back negative, and now Alina was alone in the room, drinking something hot, not quite sure how she was still alive. Keith had said the police needed to talk to her.

She was shivering. All over. She was scared. She kept sucking in deep breaths. Her throat hurt. She was shivering. And her brain kept repeating the same thoughts over and over and over again.

At last, the door opened, and a chubby police officer likely in his early fifties bumbled into the room. She clutched her blanket around her, pulling it tighter with icy fingers.

She was scared. She kept sucking in deep breaths. He sat down across from her. She was shivering. All over.

"Hello, m'dear," he drawled, steepling his hands on the bedside table. "I am Officer Brady."

She could only nod at him. She was scared. So scared.

"You've certainly been through a lot in the last couple of hours," he continued.

Alina sucked back a shaky sob.

"We are going to do all we can to catch that fella. If you'd rather wait to give your statement until someone can come and sit with you, that'd be fine."

His warm brown eyes were nice to look at. He had a nice, friendly face. Friendly was nice. She realized she was crying.

"No, sir," she began. "I don't want to, um, wait. I can, well, give my statement or, at least try to if I can. You look nice… So sorry, they tell me I'm in shock…" She trailed off.

He smiled at her, eyes full of concern as he pulled out a pen and pad and then turned on a recorder on the table. "All right, m'dear. I'm ready when you are."

With giant tears streaming down her face, Alina haltingly relayed the events of the night to the kind man, starting with the moment the stab victim came into the ER. She could hardly make it through the attack without dissolving into a heap of terrified misery. When she spoke of her attacker miraculously letting go of her and disappearing, the policeman raised his bushy brows.

"Did he see someone and panic?"

She sniffed and considered his question. "I am not s-sure. I didn't really notice anything other than the fact that I was able to breathe."

He nodded. "Well, m'dear, thank you. I have a few more questions for you, but I think we should take a break. Would you be willing to speak with our forensic sketch artist now? Ideally, we would have you at the station, but as you need to be monitored for the next few hours, she volunteered to join us here. Since you saw your attacker's face, we may be able to get a good sketch of him to post publicly."

Alina nodded, and soon he was guiding in a young woman with glasses and jet-black hair carrying a briefcase. Officer Brady introduced her as June. In an hour, Alina was able to describe the man to June, who sketched out the exact representation of every feature.

"I can't say which of his noses was real or what the true color of his eyes was, but everything else looks…good," Alina said, staring in terrified awe at the near-perfect sketch of her attacker.

"You did a good job, honey," June replied, squeezing Alina's hand. Officer Brady knocked and walked into the room.

"How's it going, ladies?" he asked with a smile.

"We just finished up, Brady," June told him, handing the officer her sketch.

He nodded and left the room with the rendition. He soon returned.

"Well, Alina, I handed off the sketch to our tech guys. They'll look him up in our databases and run the forensic samples. If we're lucky, he already has a criminal record."

"Okay," Alina replied. All of a sudden, exhaustion hit her. "Officer, would, would I be able to have a little coffee…with a little sugar?" she asked hesitantly.

"Of course, m'dear," he said, signaling to someone outside of the door. "Once your coworkers give the all-clear, I think it is safe for you to go home. I'll send two of my boys with you to keep you safe in case the perp attempts to make contact with you again."

Alina smiled tiredly, relishing the idea of taking a hot shower and curling up in her own fluffy bed. And Ami would be there! How she needed Ami.

"That would be wonderful, Officer Brady."

CHAPTER TWO

RICH BRADY COLLAPSED INTO HIS PADDED ARMCHAIR, SCRATCHING HIS HEAD IN BEWILDERMENT.

It was only 8:30 a.m. He had already made breakfast for his daughter, finished extensive filing for his robbery case, and completed two interviews with would-be murder victim Alina Dixon. Through it all, he had gulped down three cups of black coffee.

He blew out a breath. Despite his doctor's cutthroat orders, he knew he needed one more. With a steaming cup in his hands, he sat down heavily at his desk once again. He stared at the picture of Ms. Dixon's attacker, and a jolt went through him. He'd seen that face before.

Hmm.

Rich looked at the sketch again, his mind racing through a memorized list of the usual suspects in the area. Nope. This punk wasn't any of those unsavory characters. The man clearly had extensive resources. Not just anyone could successfully infiltrate a hospital and pass as one of the staff...or impersonate a police officer, for that matter. Rich didn't have a good feeling. He remembered the face, but he could not pinpoint it.

His computer suddenly gave a loud, jarring beep as the forensics memo came through. CSU had found blood at the scene; the perp had apparently cut himself in his hurried attempt to exit the bereavement room. Rich thought it was a sloppy move on the suspect's part, but something must have spooked him. He couldn't imagine why Ms. Dixon was still alive otherwise.

He clicked on the results and sat back in his chair, nearly spilling his coffee. The guy's DNA was in the system.

With a few clicks, Rich pulled up his file. The man's face glared back at him, a cold sneer on his face and eyes black as death. His hair was definitely a reddish-brown color.

Hmm.

The concerning thing wasn't that there were almost a hundred reports on this villain. The problem was that every last piece of information was blacked out, even his name.

Heart racing, Rich quickly picked up his phone. Nothing this huge had ever happened in Glen Allen. He first called Ms. Dixon's security detail, informing them of the new development and advising them to remain on high alert. Then he put through a second call.

"This is FBI headquarters. Where may I direct your call?" the voice on the phone asked him.

"To Intelligence. This is Officer Rich Brady."

ALINA STAYED IN THE shower until she used up all the hot water. As she dried off, she looked into the foggy mirror at her pale face and neck. She gingerly touched the ligature marks around her throat, and a hiss of pain escaped her lips.

It was a mottled combination of red and bright purple now, and she knew it would only get uglier before it would get better. She quickly donned a pair of pajamas and left the bathroom. She didn't want to see those marks anymore.

After pulling on her bathrobe and wrapping herself in her fluffy blanket, she sank on the edge of her bed. Her body felt so heavy.

As the hot tears came, she replayed the last several hours in her mind. She had finally been cleared to go home, but the dayshift doctor had recommended she take at least a week off to recuperate and to monitor for any adverse symptoms of the…attack.

When she called her manager, he graciously approved her to take a leave of absence. While she was grateful, she was also acutely aware that the time at home would leave her trapped with her thoughts with nothing to distract her from them.

She brought her hands to her eyes to wipe away the tears, but they kept flowing. Curling up with her pillow, she let them fall.

Suddenly, Ami burst into the bedroom with wide, panicked eyes.

"Oh, Alina, oh!" she cried, sprinting over to the bed and pulling Alina into a hug. Alina sniffed and smiled. She liked hugs.

"Keith called me early this morning, and they let me leave as soon as you called me and said you were going home!" Ami exclaimed, keeping Alina in her embrace.

Alina finally felt herself beginning to relax, breathing in Ami's scent of fresh lavender. After a few seconds, Alina addressed the wonderful smell. For some reason, it seemed vital to do so.

"You know, Ami," she began, "you smell really good."

Ami gave a breathless laugh and hugged Alina tighter. "Well, that's good. You smell good too. Did you use the new shampoo?"

"Yeah," Alina whispered.

A few seconds later, Ami at last released Alina from the hug. "Can I get you anything? To drink or eat?"

Alina contemplated her question before slowly nodding in affirmation. "Maybe some tea. I don't really feel hungry." As Ami stood, Alina grasped her hand. "Please hurry! I don't want to be…alone."

"Of course, Alina," Ami said, squeezing her hand. "I am not going to leave your side for a long time."

As Ami rushed to the kitchen, Alina smiled and relaxed back into her bed.

Thanks for saving me, God, she prayed. *And thank You for Ami.*

At that moment, a soothing song played in Alina's mind. Though she had no clear memory of its origin, she had always known the words by heart, and something deep inside of her knew. The song was her mother's. Now, whenever the lyrics uplifted Alina's thoughts, peace seemed to envelop her; it was like her mother was singing to her from Heaven.

Ami soon came back, interrupting Alina's thoughts and holding a steaming mug of peppermint tea in her hands. "Be careful," she began as she held it out. "It's really hot."

As Alina took some tentative sips, Ami watched with compassion in her eyes. "Are you okay to tell me what happened? All Keith said was that you had been attacked, that there were a lot of policemen, and that you had to stay at the hospital until you were cleared. The rest of my shift was absolutely awful. I just kept waiting, hoping to hear that you were headed home."

Alina took another sip of tea and then carefully sat her mug down. She hadn't noticed until now, but her hands were shaking again.

"Oh, Alina, I'm so sorry! Do you want to wait for a little and talk about it later?"

"No, no, it's okay. I want to tell you. I've already told it so many times that...it shouldn't be this hard." Alina drew in a breath.

"A stab victim came in. I was in the trauma bay with him while we got him ready for the OR. Before they took him away, he was trying to talk to me... He just kept repeating the same word over and over again. All the while, a nurse from the OR was watching us, but I didn't realize how...strange it was. He seemed so...a-angry. Later, when the doc walked out, I knew the patient was dead. The man didn't really have a chance... He had lost too much blood. I thought I should tell the police what he told me in case it was important."

Alina paused, her voice becoming shakier and shakier as she replayed the scene in her head.

"Go on," Ami said gently.

Alina cleared her throat and did her best to continue. "Before I could, one approached me and asked if there was anything I could add to their investigation. When I said yes, he asked if we could speak in private. He said he didn't trust the other officers."

Alina laughed bitterly. "I was so, so, stupid... He was really attractive, and I trusted him right off the bat. I took him to the bereavement room, but then he locked the door, and I knew something was wrong. Then he, well, I recognized him somehow as the nurse from the trauma bay, but everything was different! His hair, his eyes, and even his nose had changed. He then tried to... He... strangled me and almost killed me."

Ami gasped at this part of the story. There was a confused and panicked look in her eyes.

"How did he... How did you...get away from him?" she asked slowly, carefully.

"Other than an angel scaring him off, I have no idea." Alina gingerly touched her throat again. "Something may have startled him. He was on top of me on the floor, so I have no idea."

Ami's eyes fastened on the bruises encircling Alina's throat, and she gently moved Alina's hair to inspect the back of her neck.

"Oh, Alina," she whispered, tears glistening in her eyes.

Alina sighed, picking up her peppermint tea again. "God is so good, Ami. He's the One who saved me, I know it. That's the only explanation."

Ami smiled and stood up from the bed. For the past eight years, Alina had been trying to get Ami to open up about her faith. Whenever Alina brought it up in conversation, Ami would simply smile and nod, never truly stating her own affirmation of Alina's words. She didn't think Ami attended a church, either; Alina invited Ami to her church every Sunday, but Ami just waved her on and said she would see her when Alina got home.

"You should try to sleep now," Ami said softly. "But don't worry. I'm not leaving you. Give me one minute!"

Ami quickly went into their bathroom, and Alina heard her brushing her teeth and changing her clothes. She came back out wearing her beloved purple pajamas.

"Now scoot over!" she exclaimed, and she climbed into the bed beside Alina. The two girls shared a smile, and Alina closed her eyes.

For the first time in what felt like a lifetime, she felt completely at peace.

RICH BRADY WATCHED OUTSIDE the station window for the FBI to arrive. He honestly had no idea if he should be expecting ordinary cars or hulking SUVs. He sighed. This shouldn't be such an exciting thing for him... A poor girl had almost lost her life.

He had called the FBI. After giving his report, he was told that an investigative team would drive to the station that afternoon to meet with him and carefully review the details of the case. Everyone was very interested to find out why an assassin on Interpol's Most Wanted List would target a twenty-three-year-old nurse in Glen Allen.

Rich glanced down at his watch, smoothing his bushy mustache. Almost 3:30 p.m. Maddy would soon be getting home from swimming practice. He sighed again. His poor child still didn't understand why she and her daddy were all alone now that his wife had left them.

He had tried to spend as much time as he possibly could with his family through the years, but his job was demanding, and his wife had never been satisfied. She was always resentful and made it very clear that she hated his work for keeping him away so long. She had gotten worse the past two years, her agitation continually growing.

Then, one day, she unexpectedly became the beautiful, kind woman he had fallen in love with so many years ago again. Now he knew why: she had met *him* that day. Within the next few months, she left with the guy, and Rich and Maddy never heard another word from her. How he missed her.

Rich was startled out of his melancholy reflections as two black SUVs pulled up outside. He gave a triumphant guffaw and slapped his hand down on his desk. He *knew* they would be big black SUVs. Standing up and brushing off granola bar crumbs from his shirt, he strode outside to meet the team as the chief joined him.

An older man, probably in his early sixties with silver-gray hair and the stereotypical dark sunglasses, climbed out of the first vehicle. He was followed by a young guy with blond hair. A beautiful black woman got out of the second SUV, followed by a black-haired man with thick brows. The last member of the group was a short balding man in a crumpled suit. Silver-haired Guy was definitely the leader.

Rich realized his palms were sweating, and he subtly wiped them on his pant legs. He noticed the chief stand a little straighter than he usually did, slightly puffing out his chest. Rich followed suit.

"Welcome to Glen Allen," the chief said, shaking hands with Silver-haired Guy.

"Thank you," he replied. "I'm Joseph Moore, and this is my team."

Rich shook his hand next, taken aback by the immense strength of it. If this man wasn't careful, he could definitely break some bones with that grip.

After greeting the rest, they all went inside the police station. Rich noticed every officer's and detective's eyes glued to them as the team walked past.

Aww yeah. He was so excited to tell Maddy about Daddy's exciting day.

Once they were settled in the station's private conference room, the chief nodded to Rich: his signal to relay the events of the assault and everything they had uncovered thus far. Rich went through Ms. Dixon's statement, pausing at the end to show the sketch June had made of the criminal.

He sat back down, pleased with his little speech. Joseph Moore leaned forward and asked for the sketch with an intensity in his gaze. He had taken off his shades, and his piercing blue eyes gave him a very fierce appearance.

"Almost an exact resemblance," he rumbled, his deep voice filling the room.

Rich leaned forward in his seat.

JOSEPH MOORE LOOKED DOWN at the sketch again. *Antonov.* His mind scrolled through dozens of files stored back in Washington, some of which contained only traces of the assassin. They had never accrued enough proof to arrest the man even if they were ever smart or lucky enough to catch him. Perhaps this case would be the first nail in the killer's coffin.

Joseph stared at the man's face, feeling the steadying presence of his Glock 22 on his belt. Antonov had left this one alive. And that was what concerned him the most. Joseph looked up as a throat cleared, and he gazed at the police chief. The man had started drumming on the conference table with impatient fingertips.

"Well," the nervous-looking officer with the mustache began. Joseph locked his gaze on the man, and Officer Brady's eyes got even bigger. Joseph feared he might keel over. "I'm afraid that's all we have at the moment," Brady finished, subconsciously running his hands down his pant legs.

Joseph shifted his eyes to Owen Davies—the young man whom Joseph had personally trained; the young man he consequently trusted with his own life. Davies was already looking at him. At last Joseph spoke, breaking the palpable tension that had risen considerably within the last minute.

"The information we have on this criminal is classified," he began, his eyes scanning the room to take in the reactions of everyone present. "Though we are not at liberty to discuss details with you, I will inform you that his actions here in Glen Allen are a clear deviation from his, shall we say, usual methods of work. We would appreciate your cooperation in this investigation as we comb through every inch of that hospital and access any CCTV footage the hospital has, even though the likelihood of discovering anything is slim. We need to track every movement this man made."

Officer Brady had relaxed in his chair when Joseph had started speaking and was now rubbing his hands together, a determined look in his eye. Joseph liked him. The chief, on the other hand, just looked annoyed that his role in the investigation wouldn't be one of authority.

"We will also need to speak with all the hospital staff who possibly saw or interacted with him and the officers who had responded to the stabbing," Joseph continued. "While I am on that subject, the body of the dead man is here, yes? We will need it for our own autopsy."

The chief let out an irritated huff. Joseph nearly smiled. He loved when his team inspired action in a sleepy city of lazy policemen. Even if, in this case, the action centered around mounds of paperwork.

"Once we conclude our investigation, we will return to Washington," Joseph continued. "The criminal, unless he intends to finish the job, is already far away from here."

Officer Brady's eyes widened, and he stared at his boss. "We have two men stationed outside of Ms. Dixon's home right now, and they both checked in with the all-clear not half an hour ago."

"I know," Joseph replied, another slight smile twitching his lips. "We went there first to help secure the perimeter."

He recalled the shocked expressions on the two officers' faces when the FBI SUVs pulled up and armed agents disembarked to aid them at their post. One of the officers was so incredulous that he demanded to see the badges again to determine their authenticity.

Wise man.

"We were pleased to discover that Ms. Dixon was sleeping peacefully, and we regret that she will have to come back with us to Washington to a safe location. With her would-be killer on the loose, we will act as though a red bullseye hovers over every single part of her life. In short, we need to get her out of here...away from her known habits and schedules."

Joseph stood, and his team, Officer Brady, and at last the arrogant chief followed suit.

"Thank you, gentlemen, for your cooperation."

A few hours later, Joseph and the team's only female agent, Lily Herne, stood in the bereavement room of the Virginia Hospital and Healthcare Association.

Joseph ran his hand down his chin, contemplating every blaring detail of the scene before him. Thankfully, the local police had been smart enough to keep it taped off.

Herne spoke Joseph's thoughts aloud. "Why didn't he finish her?" she began in her soft voice, staring at the scene with her dark eyes. "This is Antonov, and he never makes mistakes. He never misses his mark, let alone aborting a mission in the middle of a strangulation. He would have broken her neck in an instant if he was interrupted and needed to escape."

"That is what worries me. And he was sloppy. He's never left any evidence behind before, let alone his own blood at the scene."

Joseph recalled the image of the stab victim's body in the coroner's examination room. Joseph and Herne had just finished there, speaking with the coroner and obtaining photos of the knife wound and victim himself. Other than the neat, professional wound, no traces of the assassin lingered on the man. The kill was clean and of military proficiency. Just like Antonov's kills always were.

The only difference this time was that the man hadn't been dumped to die in the middle of a seedy neighborhood with a missing wallet: a method of Antonov's which consistently convinced local police that the attack was a robbery gone wrong. Someone must have happened upon the scene. But that in itself didn't seem to make sense.

"The dead man, Victor Harris, fits into the picture clearly enough," Herne continued. "Big-time politicians have increasingly been on his hit list the last five years."

"True, though I am not sure why Antonov didn't kill Harris when he first stabbed him," Joseph added. "He had to follow him to the hospital, in disguise, and finish him off there. Then he failed to murder a defenseless nurse who witnessed Harris's dying words. He proceeded to flee in such a hurry that he cut himself in the process. Either he's losing his touch, a fact I doubt, or something much larger is at play here."

After a moment, Joseph spoke again. "Let's see how Donáll is getting on with the CCTV footage, and then we'll check on Davies and Rogers with their interviews of the hospital staff."

Herne gave a quick nod, and the two strode toward the security office.

Joseph let out another heavy sigh as they walked. His team didn't know Antonov. They hadn't pieced together the pattern of his kills and cover-ups. They would always be one step behind him unless... Joseph let his train of thought stop there. Herne glanced at him, and he could see the same thought was on her mind.

They couldn't finish this without... *him.*

JOSEPH AND LILY HERNE walked through the hospital until they reached the security room.

Donáll was sitting on the edge of a faded leather chair, his fingers rapidly scrolling through hours of footage from the night before. He gave a nod and cleared his throat as the two agents entered, his green eyes remaining glued to the screens in front of him.

Joseph stared at him, expecting him to say something. Soon enough, however, Donáll seemed completely sucked back into his work, with Joseph and Herne lingering obtrusively in the periphery.

Joseph looked at Herne, slowly shaking his head. She just smiled, and Joseph let out a sigh. Donáll was the best tech guy the FBI had, but he was certainly a piece of work.

At the sound of Joseph's sigh, Donáll startled, nearly spilling his cup of Dunkin' Donuts black coffee. From the dark stains running down the front of his crumpled shirt, Joseph deducted that the very event had occurred within the last hour.

Joseph didn't like jumpiness. It was a sign of a lie, of a farce destined to blow. In the case of Donáll, however, nervous antics were simply in the fabric of his nature.

Donáll turned to face them, a crooked smile on his face. "Hiya," he exclaimed. Joseph nodded again, and Herne followed suit. "The Archer is a ghost. I've never seen anything like it before. He's good. Like, freaky good. Kinda like a freaky ghost. Oh, hear what I did there?" The man suddenly broke out into song.

"Mmm, if you've had a dose of a freaky ghost, baby, you better call Ghostbusters! Ow!"

Donáll chuckled at his finale, then he turned back to his computer, completely forgetting about Joseph and Herne again.

Joseph continued staring at the jumpy little man. At last, he released a loud cough. This time, Donáll almost fell out of his chair, and his coffee, regrettably, spilled down his shirt. He quickly righted his cup before staring at Joseph and Herne accusingly.

"Hey, I don't have much left!" he burst out.

"Donáll," Joseph began, rubbing the crease between his closed eyes, "does 'ghost' imply that you've found nothing?"

"Well, yes and no." Donáll shrugged noncommittally. "How he got into the hospital was a complete materialization through the wall, if ya know what I'm saying. I have no idea what his entry and exit points were. However, our ghost does inevitably make some appearances in the hospital, though he avoids most of the obvious cameras. My facial recognition software is fooled most of the time because of his OR garb, so I have to look through all the footage myself. And it's proving to be a challenge! The one clear time I see him is when he's the police officer, but I have no idea where he changed his appearance. He's not your typical Casper, I'll tell you that. I'll keep looking."

With that, Donáll turned back to his computer, now humming his continuation of the *Ghostbusters* theme song.

Joseph looked at Herne again, and she nodded. They left the room and swiftly located Agents Davies and Rogers.

"Did you finish interviewing the staff and the officers from last night?" Joseph asked.

"Yes, sir," Davies was quick to reply, and Rogers nodded. "No one heard, saw, or suspected anything. Apparently, no one even noticed him in the OR. It's as if he just blended in to the point of being invisible." Davies's eyes held a determined look, and he ran his fingers through his blond hair.

Rogers jumped in, dark eyes glinting. "The officers here last night didn't seem to notice him either, and they *surprisingly* didn't suspect anything to be amiss even when they saw an unfamiliar officer entering a private room with a nurse."

Rogers emphasized the word, and Joseph knew the man's thinking matched his own. Some sort of bribery had been at play.

"I am confident in your suspicions, Rogers. Let them know we'll be in contact with them. At this point, we don't have much to accuse them of."

Joseph took a breath before he continued. "Back in Washington, I'll have Donáll go through their financial records, though I am certain he won't find anything. Antonov would have made any transactions untraceable, and we know that he has unlimited resources from his current employers. But he's already slipped up once this time. It seems his luck may be starting to run out."

Davies spoke up. "What's our next move, then, Boss?"

"We will visit Ms. Dixon and take her back with us to Washington. Donáll should be about finished with the security footage, so let's pack it up."

As the team got ready to leave, Joseph walked outside, his phone to his ear.

"Yes, this is Joseph Moore, FBI, Transnational Organized Crime. Vadik Antonov has shown his face in Virginia. We need Burns."

BEFORE SHE COULD REACT, he was there, choking the life out of her. She couldn't get away... His eyes...red with rage. She felt herself falling into blackness... The blackness was here.

Alina sat up in bed with a gasp, a cold sweat sending her into a fit of shivering. Her soothing dream had taken a dark turn, and she had suddenly been back in his grasp.

She hugged herself with her arms, trying to calm herself and stop the shaking. She slowly climbed out of the bed, hearing Ami moving around in the bathroom.

And then she stood. Unmoving. Goose bumps trailing down her arms. A prickling sensation at the back of her neck.

He's not here.

She was too afraid to look out of the window. She didn't know why she hadn't drawn the curtain earlier. Now she didn't want to see anything. If she did, she was not sure that she could pull herself together.

He can't be here.

"Ami," she croaked out. She could hardly take deep breaths.

Someone's watching me.

"Yes?" Ami called, rapidly opening the door and rushing into the bedroom. "What is it? Are you all ri—" She paused, taking in Alina's nearly hysterical state.

"Can you close the curtain? I am so, so sorry, but... I just can't."

In just a few seconds, Ami drew the curtain, and Alina's knees unlocked enough that she was able to sink back down on the bed.

"Thank you," she whispered.

No. Do not cry.

Ami walked over to her and sat beside her.

"He...he was here. In my dream. And he... I couldn't get away," Alina whispered shakily. "I woke up, and the feeling wasn't gone. I am afraid someone was w-watching, though it could be all in my head. Will I ever be free of this?"

Ami knelt down beside her, looking her in the eye. "It will go away in time, Alina. Everything will be okay. He will get what he deserves for trying to hurt you. And then you won't have to be afraid anymore."

Alina's stopped shivering at her finite and confident words, a certain peace settling on her again.

Suddenly, banging reverberated from the front door into the tiny house. She suppressed a cry, shocked and overwhelmed by the sudden noise.

Ami stood up quickly.

"I'll get it. It's probably just the police officers with an update. You wait here, and I'll check and be right back." With that, Ami left the room, leaving the door cracked behind her.

Alina listened carefully to Ami's footsteps in the hallway. When the front door creaked open, she jumped out of bed, too nervous, too fidgety, and too anxious to continue sitting there. She rubbed her hands nervously and continued to fidget anxiously, with repetitious thoughts racing through her mind.

She heard Ami introduce herself and then say, "Please come in," and Alina quickly ran her fingers through her cascade of tangled chocolate curls and wiped her eyes.

Ami knocked on the doorframe. "Hey, Alina?" Her voice sounded anxious. "There's some…people from the FBI here, and they would like to speak with you. Are you ready?"

Mixed feelings of shock and wonder coursed down Alina's spine.

The FBI? They want to talk to…me? Whoa…wow. Okay…wait, what?

Alina quickly licked her dry lips and straightened.

"Yep, I'm fine!" she burst out, and she widened her eyes in dismay at her blatantly false answer.

She didn't have much time for her reflections, however, as the door opened and Ami, followed by four FBI agents, walked into the room.

THE FIRST WAS AN older man with silvery hair in a military cut, and his jet-black leather jacket was slightly worn but looked well cared for. His face was clean-shaven, and she could see his bright-blue eyes flash with intelligence. The creases in his forehead and between his eyes relayed a lifetime of experience and, perhaps, a lifetime of seeing a dark and sorrowful side of the world.

He was eagerly trailed by a handsome man with blue eyes, a quirky smile, and curly blond hair, probably in his late twenties. A beautiful black woman entered next, her glossy, straightened hair reaching her petite shoulders. She was wearing a sharp white suit and matching heels that Alina could only marvel at. The fourth agent, perhaps in his late thirties, had thick black hair; dark, serious eyes; and broad shoulders and body frame. She could easily imagine him taking someone down.

Alina sucked in a breath, feeling very shabby in her fluffy pajamas and teal bathrobe.

The female agent gave Alina a kind smile, and Alina smiled back as warmth coursed through her. She seemed very nice.

His every movement emanating authority, the older man stepped forward with his hand out. He showed her his badge simultaneously.

Without thinking, she quickly rubbed her hands down her sides. Ami frequently told her about her cold and clammy hands, and Alina didn't want that to be this man's first impression of her. Following suit, the other agents each held out their badges.

As she grasped his hand, both admiring how firm the handshake was and fearing for her metacarpals, he spoke.

"Ms. Dixon," he began, "my name is Joseph Moore, and this is Owen Davies, Lily Herne, and Grant Rogers. We are part of the FBI's Transnational Crime Division."

As Agent Moore continued speaking, Alina reveled in the rich, rumbling baritone of his voice. Somehow, just being in the same room with him made her feel safe, and she had only known the agent for a minute or two.

"We are very sorry to hear what happened to you last night," he continued, "and we are relieved that you are alive and well. When we were contacted by Officer Brady, whom I believe you know, we came as quickly as we could from Washington."

Washington. Alina felt like she was in a daze that she could not shake herself from.

Agent Moore continued on. "We came here first to add to your security detail, and then we began our investigation back at the hospital."

His eyes drifted over to Ami, who was standing in the corner of the room, eyes wide and staring at each agent. Alina was certain Ami's expression mirrored her own.

"We will discuss details later," he resumed, directing his intense gaze back to Alina, "which leads me to perhaps some bad news."

Alina's heart seemed to stop, and then her pulse came back double-time, thundering in her ears.

What on earth could be more bad news? Do they think he's coming back?

She was terrified again, and her gaze flitted to Ami.

Agent Moore continued, his eyes never leaving her face. "We know who the man was who tried to harm you, but we do not know if he plans to try again."

Bile rose in Alina's throat at his words, but she took a deep breath and tried to regain her composure.

Now was as good a time as any to tell him about the sensation she had gotten only a few moments before.

"On that, uh, note, I wanted to tell you that I had gotten a strange feeling, just before you came. I felt that... I felt I was being watched."

His gaze instantly sharpened, and he nodded to the blond agent who rapidly left the room.

"Davies will secure the perimeter once more, but we must leave quickly. Pack only what you need for a few days. We should be on the road in no more than fifteen—" He suddenly stopped, taking in her panicked expression. "Ms. Dixon, it is not safe for you here. We need to move you to a safe house while we establish if there are going to be further attacks. Without saying much else, I can tell you that your attacker is highly trained, motivated, and dangerous. He is wanted in multiple countries, though no real evidence has ever come to light. Your testimony could be exactly what we need."

Alina's heart was pounding. *A wanted man—highly trained—and he wants me dead? DC? What?*

"Therefore, it is imperative for you to return with us as soon as possible." His voice gentled. "I know that it's a lot to take in, Ms. Dixon, but you will be able to come home as soon as we apprehend him. With your assistance, we will finally be able to lock this man away to prevent him from hurting anyone else. Everything has already been arranged."

Alina was gaping at Agent Moore, but she forced herself to nod. Her palms were very sweaty now.

"Waste no time. Herne," he began, rapidly turning his attention to the female agent. "Come with me for a moment, then return and remain with them. Rogers and I will check in with Davies."

The other two agents left the room, but just before Agent Moore passed through the doorway, Ami abruptly called out.

"Wait!" she began as the agent whirled around to face her. Alina couldn't help but notice that Agent Moore's hand went to a gun on his belt.

"I need to come with her," she said quickly, shifting uncomfortably under his piercing gaze. "If he comes back here, he may assume that I know something too. And I told her I wouldn't leave her."

"Of course," the agent replied, his expression softening. "We decided immediately that any family members in close proximity to Ms. Dixon must also come. The affiliation automatically makes you a target, as well."

Alina quickly interjected. "We aren't sisters, but Ami and I have been together since high school. She, uh, transferred in my freshman year. Since my parents have both…passed away and my grandparents moved to Florida, she's the only family that I have…left, and I'm her family."

The older agent's eyes darkened with something she couldn't identify. "Of course," he said slowly, his eyes fastened on Alina's for a moment. Then he turned and was gone.

Both girls faced each other.

"I'm so, so sorry, Ami," Alina said, rubbing her hands over her eyes. "I can't believe this is happening, and I am so sorry that you are being dragged into…whatever this is."

Ami replied softly, "I wouldn't have it any other way—I could not stay here while you left. You are…a light for me in darkness, and I wouldn't want to be here alone."

Ami often used that phrase, and it always made Alina feel deep sadness for her friend. How she wished Ami would open up about her faith and family, but limited words had been spoken on the matter.

At that moment, the female agent stepped back into the room, and they began to pull their suitcases from their closets.

JOSEPH MOORE WALKED QUICKLY through the tiny house after a brief conversation with Herne, almost tripping on the shaggy carpet leading to the front door. His mind raced with questions and thrilling suspicions, but he couldn't be certain.

Not yet.

Joseph was about to exit the house when his phone buzzed, and he turned on his earpiece.

"Joseph Moore."

Officer Brady answered him. "Good afternoon, Agent Moore. I, well, ahem. Excuse me."

This is not the time.

Joseph tried to wait patiently as the policeman cleared his throat, though his eyes never ceased in scanning his surroundings.

Finally, the officer was able to continue. "Sorry about that, sir. Everything is back from forensics. On both the stabbing and the strangulation. I'll send them to you promptly."

"Thank you, Officer Brady." Joseph wanted to end the call, but he knew he needed to say more. "You do extremely thorough work, and my team is grateful for that."

There was silence on the other end of the line, and Joseph feared for a second that the man had been overwhelmed by the compliment. Joseph didn't give many compliments. He hoped the man was okay.

"Oh, well, thank you, sir. I hardly know what to um, say. Oh, well, I also wanted to thank you for the selfie. My little Maddy is going to be so excited to see Daddy with an FBI agent. I know I was thrilled…" Officer Brady trailed off, probably thinking he had embarrassed himself.

Joseph didn't mind one bit. He felt a smile tugging at the corners of his mouth, remembering Officer Brady pulling him aside and asking hesitantly if they could take a quick photo together. He regretted not smiling more for the picture, but he was not a man to smile much.

"You are more than welcome, Officer. Now I must return to the task at hand."

"Oh yes, please do, and thank you so much." Joseph was about to hang up when the man suddenly spoke again. "Sorry to keep you, but will you let Ms. Dixon know I wish her luck? Maddy and I will be praying for her with all this."

Praying. That was a word that hadn't entered his mind for a long time.

"Of course. I'll let her know." Though he felt himself getting restless, he managed to keep his patient tone. "Was there anything else?"

"No, sir, thank you, sir. Safe travels back to Washington!"

"Thank you. Ciao." Joseph ended the call, and he resumed his rapid walk out of the house. His phone soon beeped as the officer's email came through, though Joseph filed the notification in the back of his mind.

He refused to open the email until they had Ms. Dixon and her friend safe in Washington.

As soon as he walked outside, Davies ran up to him with Rogers following close behind.

Rogers spoke first. "He found something." Joseph felt his stomach clench, and he locked eyes with the blond agent.

"What did you find?"

Davies held up a bag of cigarette butts in a gloved hand. "They were in the woods behind the neighbor's house. I saw a glint through the trees, but when I got there, these were the only things left behind. He must have left in a hurry when he saw me coming, but there was no evidence of which direction he fled."

"So," Rogers said slowly, putting into words what all three had concluded, "he was watching her."

Joseph stared at the surroundings, his every sense on high alert.

"Not was, Rogers. He still is. We need to get everybody out—now. Send those to forensics when we get back."

The two agents nodded grimly, and they quickly returned to the house to alert Shaw and Crewe.

It was Joseph's job to keep Ms. Dixon safe. And he was good at his job.

WITHIN FIFTEEN MINUTES OF their conversation with Agent Moore, Alina and Ami had changed and had packed their belongings.

The female agent, or Lily Herne, confiscated their phones, explaining that Agent Moore had already called their workplaces to say that Alina and Ami would be taking a leave of absence for an undetermined period of time. Phones, she had explained, would only make them more visible as targets.

Alina had smiled sadly in response, knowing that there was really no one else to call, anyway. After her grandparents had moved to Florida, they rarely returned any of her calls. It used to hurt so much, but with Ami living with her, it hardly seemed to matter anymore.

Alina snapped back into the present as the agent with them spoke.

"Are you ready, ladies?"

At their nod, she led the way out of the room.

As they walked outside, Alina stared at the sight of the five other FBI agents standing about on the tiny front lawn.

Wow.

It was surprisingly warm for a day in late December, and the bright sunlight felt like an embrace. Agent Moore walked over, a serious expression deepening the lines in his face.

"Are you ready to go?"

Alina almost lost her train of thought at the intensity of his electric gaze. "Yes, I think so, and—"

"Excellent," he interjected, glancing all around them. "This location is not secure, and we must leave as soon as possible."

Each word Agent Moore spoke sent shivers down her spine, and she unconsciously took a step closer to Ami.

This is crazy. How on earth is this happening?

"Davies, load their luggage. Rogers and I will check the vehicles." He abruptly turned around and spoke loudly to one of the other agents, striding away from them.

Alina saw that his hand was on his gun again, and she felt his commanding tone resonate in her core. It was clear that these people knew what they were doing.

The cute blond agent ran over, reaching out a hand for their luggage.

"Here, I'll get those for you." His voice was masculine and full of energy. He seemed to bounce up and down as they smiled and nodded, though she noticed his eyes continuously sweeping their surroundings, as well. He grabbed their suitcases and bounded over to the first black SUV, carefully placing their luggage inside the open trunk.

Alina's attention was drawn to Agent Moore and the other man, or Agent Rogers, as they knelt down on the asphalt to inspect the undersides of the SUVs. Soon, Agent Moore announced that his was clean, and Agent Rogers affirmed the statement for his own. Agent Moore proceeded to gesture for Alina, Ami, and the others to climb into the two vehicles.

Clean? As in, no bombs?

Trying to staunch her new onslaught of anxiety, she followed the others into the one SUV.

Agent Davies had taken the passenger seat, and Agent Herne was sitting in the back.

Agent Moore was the last one into the vehicle, and as soon as he received the go-ahead from Agent Rogers, they pulled out from the driveway and began the long drive to Washington, DC.

CHAPTER THREE

AS THEY DROVE NORTHWARD THROUGH VIRGINIA, ALINA WATCHED THE GOLDEN SUBURBS OF GLEN ALLEN TRANSFORM INTO THE COLORFUL BUSTLE OF FREDERICKSBURG.

No one spoke, and the hum of the tires on the highway lulled Alina to sleep. She startled awake as the vehicle came to an abrupt stop in a traffic jam.

Agent Davies proceeded to complain to Agent Moore. "What is this? It never gets backed up here. It's going to be at least a half hour till we're twenty minutes out from Alexandria. Do you think we could…"

Agent Moore chuckled at his unfinished question. "No, Davies, as I keep telling you, it's strict procedure to only use the vehicle lights in emergencies. Maybe you should read your manual every once in a while."

Herne laughed in the back as Davies grumbled incoherently. Alina smiled at the banter, and she saw that Ami was stirring awake.

Agent Herne spoke up in a soft but cheerful voice. "Well, now's as good a time as any to tell our ladies what's going happen when we get there. By the way, call me Lily. We're not too formal here."

The other agents spoke up in agreement.

"I'll quickly remind you of names. Joseph's driving, with Owen pouting beside him."

In response to her words, Owen grabbed at the rearview mirror and angled it so he could glare at her. Joseph aggressively yanked the mirror back into place, whacking Owen's shoulder as he once again grabbed the steering wheel.

Lily rolled her eyes as she continued. "The red-haired guy at your house all afternoon is Fred Crewe, and the man who was with him is Sam Shaw. Then there's Grant Rogers, who you met, and lastly, we have Donáll. Well, actually his full name is Lestor Donáll, but he…prefers Donáll. You haven't met him yet. He's our tech guy."

Alina and Ami locked eyes, and Alina was smiling uncontrollably. She liked these people.

"When we arrive, we'll get you set up at one of our safe houses. I'm going to be in a room attached to yours, so I'll always be nearby. If you need anything, simply holler. I'm a light sleeper."

Joseph spoke up from the front. "My room will be just down the hall, so I will also be close by. When we get there, you'll receive burner phones with the necessary numbers listed. Call if you need anything, but do not make any unnecessary phone calls to anyone else."

Alina nodded, so grateful for him and for the others. No matter what was coming, she felt that she could fully rely on them. Especially on Joseph Moore.

THE VEHICLE FELL INTO silence for a few moments, its passengers each dwelling on his or her own thoughts. Joseph glanced back to see Herne engrossed in her phone messages, likely communicating with her husband.

Lieutenant Jason Herne was returning home from military service in two weeks, and Joseph had never seen Herne in a more excited state.

Military service.

Just the words brought back a flood of memories before Joseph could staunch them, and instead of fighting, he let himself become lost in them. Soon enough, however, he was startled out of his thoughts as his phone buzzed. He immediately turned on his earpiece.

"Joseph Moore." A voice answered him on the other end. After a brief conversation, Joseph concluded the call.

"Good. We'll see him tomorrow morning, then. Ciao."

Davies asked, "Who was that, Boss?"

Joseph let out a breath he hadn't realized he was holding. "That was Gordon from the CIA. The agency's been in contact with MI5, and they found him. He's agreed to come."

"Burns?" Herne clarified. Joseph gave her an affirmational nod, and her gaze dropped. Ms. Dixon was staring at him, a curious look in her eyes.

"Blane Burns was born and reared in Scotland, and when he was thirteen years old, his mother and he moved to England. He was deployed with the British Army in Afghanistan for four years, and when he returned from service, he joined MI5, the UK's counter-intelligence agency. Though he is currently on extended leave from MI5, we need him on this case. He is one of the best trackers in the business. The man who attacked you was his mark for nearly two years."

After several interminable seconds, she asked quietly, "Why is he on extended leave from MI5?"

Davies cleared his throat beside him. "We do not know the whole story, Ms. Dixon," Joseph began, pausing to take a breath. "But we know that Burns had been hot on the pursuit of your attacker when he abruptly went on leave. Around the same time, we learned that his family had been killed in a hit-and-run. The perpetrator was never apprehended."

Joseph heard her inhale sharply.

"That's awful," she whispered. In a louder voice, she asked, "Do they think there was a connection?"

"It's only speculation, but we can assume so." He paused again. "Other than that, there's nothing else to tell. I suppose he'll…say more to us when he is ready. I am hoping that he'll be willing to help us now that the criminal has surfaced once more. He's flying in tomorrow morning."

Silence descended inside the vehicle, and Joseph returned his attention to the road. He had experienced his own share of violence and sorrow in the war and in his years at the Bureau, but nothing like that tragedy. Nothing like what Burns had endured.

Joseph stopped at a red light, rubbing the crease between his eyes. He had no idea what the days ahead would hold.

ALINA COULDN'T SLEEP FOR the rest of the journey. She hadn't even met Blane Burns, and yet her heart ached for him. She could hardly imagine how it felt to lose everyone she loved.

Both of her parents had died when she was little, but as she could barely remember them, she had never fully felt their loss. Ami, though she never completely opened up about her own family and childhood, was always interested in hearing whatever Alina did remember. She especially loved hearing about Alina's mother, Amanda Dixon.

Alina didn't remember much, but a couple of stories lingered in her memory of her mother's beautiful brown hair and a few trips to a green park. Her mother's song filtered through the clouds of her past like a beam of pure sunlight, the words filling Alina with peace. She had never shared the lyrics of the song with anyone, not even Ami. The words lifted Alina off to a beautiful memory of her mother holding her and singing in an ethereal voice. Somehow, perhaps selfishly, Alina kept it to herself.

> *Shells glitter on the shore*
> *The sea whispers you are adored.*
> *Mommy holds you near, Mommy loves you, dear.*
> *God's sea holds our love*
> *He smiles down on us from above.*
> *At the sea, you'll find me.*
> *You'll never be alone, my darling.*
> *Run along now, the sea is calling.*

The lyrics echoed through her mind as the day darkened to evening outside. *Shells glitter on the shore.*

The trees and green hills transformed to a city in the threshold of night. *The sea whispers you are adored.*

Neon lights streaked by outside in a mirage of color, and twinkling waterfalls of white light streamed down from innumerable streetlamps. Huge buildings stretched beyond Alina's vision, glittering with lights reflecting in the glass windows, and the hustle and bustle of Washington, DC, claimed her eyes as the rest of the song floated through her mind.

Run along now, the sea is calling.

Alina leaned into the window, drinking in the beautiful sight. "Wow," she breathed aloud. She looked at Ami, who was smiling at her. "Isn't it beautiful, Ami?"

"Yes," Ami replied softly, and Alina turned to look back out at the scene.

Too soon, Joseph turned into a large parking garage with a multiple-story hotel stretching up beyond it. The other SUV continued onward, no doubt returning to FBI headquarters. Wherever that was.

"We're here!" Owen announced cheerfully. Joseph pulled forward to the booth and spoke to the woman inside, showing her his badge.

Lily spoke up from the back. "As surprising as it may seem, we actually use the third floor of this hotel as a safe house. Our security team monitors everything, and the owner is one of our own."

They were eventually through, and Joseph pulled into a parking space. He let out a sigh.

"Well, everyone, we made it."

Alina nodded, and she and Ami climbed out of the vehicle. They grabbed their suitcases from the back and followed Lily and Joseph across the parking garage, returning Owen's farewell as he climbed into his own car.

As they walked, she noticed Joseph glancing around, his hand resting on his pistol again. She wondered if he ever let go of it.

Soon, they were through the double doors leading into the hotel, and the group approached the front desk.

A Hispanic woman was agitatedly typing on her keyboard, but her face broke into a smile when she looked up and saw Joseph and Lily.

"Hello again! Your floor is ready for you."

Joseph chuckled: a deep, rumbling sound. Alina really liked that sound. "Yes. Thank you, Rose. And we'll take all the keycards."

Rose nodded energetically, and she let out a short giggle as Joseph thanked her again. After some additional, rapid typing, she finished and handed Joseph and Lily the keycards as well as a card for the elevator.

"As always, enjoy your stay. Then come back soon." Rose continued typing, her attention sucked back into her work.

Joseph nodded his head toward another set of double doors leading deeper into the hotel, and the group crossed the spacious lobby and pushed their way through. A hallway of at least thirty rooms took Alina's breath away. There were fifteen floors of this hotel, with the same number of rooms on each.

This place is huge.

Alina and Ami followed Joseph into the elevator, where the older agent discretely badged in with the elevator card before pressing the button for the third floor.

This floor looked no different from the others, but Alina suspected that there was a massive security system hidden in the walls. And Joseph confirmed her suspicions.

"This is one of our most secure locations. Cameras, motion sensors, and other measures are embedded in key locations along the hall, and each room has bulletproof glass on the windows and no other points of entry. The keycards are specifically designed, and the doors are impossible to penetrate without them. No one can access this floor without a separate card to unlock the stairwell or elevator."

Alina watched the older agent as he spoke, reveling in the authority and expertise of every word. The safety she had first felt upon meeting him had not dissipated. If anything, it was only growing stronger.

"The three of us are sleeping in rooms 93 and 95, and Joseph will be further down the hall in 105," Lily said, drawing Alina's attention back. "We'll be having breakfast here at approximately 0700."

"Oh, and by the way," Joseph began, "Officer Brady wanted me to wish you luck from him and his daughter. He wanted you to know they are…praying for you. Good night."

Joseph turned and strode away, and Lily unlocked and entered the room next to them.

Pushing open their own door required almost the majority of Alina's strength, adding to the security which was steadily blanketing her.

Once they were inside, both girls blew out a breath. Alina felt exhaustion blur her racing thoughts into one fuzzy command: *sleep*. She first looked at the two beds with the fluffy white blankets draped over them, and then she glanced at Ami. With a loud guffaw, both girls dropped their suitcases and ran over to the beds. Alina and Ami kicked off their shoes and flopped on the mattresses.

After a few luxurious moments, Ami got up to take a shower. "I'll be right back, Alina," she said quietly.

"Oh, that's okay! I think I'll just get mine in the…in the morning," Alina replied with a yawn. "I'll probably be out by the time you are done, so good night, Ami." The thought crossed her mind to change into her pajamas, but the fuzzy command took over again, and Alina's eyes closed.

A heavy thud resounded in the hallway, and her eyes instantly reopened.

JOSEPH MOORE STOOD IN the hallway, leaning against the door to his room. He finally allowed himself to check his emails. To open the email that had been plaguing him throughout the entire drive. With each traffic light, his fingers had ached to grab his phone and confirm his suspicions, once and for all. And now he finally could.

With rapid movements, he scrolled through the pictures Officer Brady had sent of Ms. Dixon's wounds and the other evidence. His heart rate sped along with his progression through the pictures, and at last, he reached one of the bruises on the back of Ms. Dixon's neck.

His heart skipped a beat when he saw it. It was exactly what he had been searching for. His pulse now thundering in his ears. His senses electrifying the darkness of the hallway.

No. It couldn't possibly be…

It was. He saw it.

He staggered before grabbing at a small table sitting just outside of his room. He braced himself, not caring that he had knocked over a heavy floral arrangement that had been sitting on the table in the process.

Her name was no coincidence.

It is truly Alina.

SLOWLY, CAREFULLY, ALINA SAT up in her bed. She could feel her heart rate pick up and her palms become slick.

God. Please don't let anyone be out there. Oh, what on earth do I do? She didn't want to call Joseph or disturb Lily. The sound could have just been her traumatized mind playing a cruel trick.

For several moments, she sat still. Listening. Waiting. Hardly breathing. Just as she was working up the courage to call to Ami, she heard the shower head turn on.

Well, great. Now I can't hear anything.

Even as she strained to listen to the hallway, no other noises met her ears. She couldn't decide if that was a good thing or if it was a very bad thing.

After a few more minutes of sitting and staring, Alina carefully inched her way to the edge of her bed, her bare feet touching the floor. She then traversed the room, taking a series of slow steps until she was only a foot away from the door.

The solid, heavy, secure door. The next step in her head was to take a quick peek through the peephole out into the hallway. If something was happening, she refused to simply wait in denial while the assassins somehow broke in.

Her pulse pounded even harder as she peered through the tiny hole. As her eyes took an eternity to adjust, all she saw was blackness.

When they adjusted at last, terror seared her and she jumped back from the door. Someone was standing straight across the hallway from her room, not moving.

She darted back to her bed, fumbling for her phone.

Call Joseph. I need to call Joseph!

With shaking fingers, she rapidly tapped on her contacts and called the older agent. She waited, hardly breathing, for him to pick up. Then she stopped breathing altogether.

She took slow steps toward the door. Stared through the hole. The soft ringing had not been a figment of her imagination.

The figure across the hallway was illuminated by the light of his phone's screen as he answered the call.

AS ALINA GLANCED IN the mirror the next morning after her shower, she took in the sight of dark bags under her tired eyes. Knowing that Joseph had been the figure outside of the door last night had kept her awake for hours. Worrying. Praying. Having no idea of what to do.

He could have been standing guard as extra protection. But he had chosen to not disclose that as part of the plan. The obvious conclusion robbed her of the peace she had felt the day before in the older agent's presence: he had chosen to watch their room in secret.

Alina knew she needed to approach him before they left for the FBI building, for her own peace of mind. If she was wary of the leader of the team, she couldn't trust anyone. Alina was terrified of that thought.

She decided she would finish getting dressed, awaken Ami, and then approach Joseph Moore. If he didn't broach the subject first, she would. She needed to know.

Alina carefully regarded her outfit choices, refusing to look like a damaged victim. She was a nurse with an FBI detail. She wanted to look professional. She wanted to look like she had it all together, even if she felt like a tearful, jumbled mess on the inside.

Alina finally settled on a pair of dark jeans and a lacy hunter-green blouse. She did a single coat of mascara and pulled the hair at her temples back, letting the rest flow downward. After a final glance in the mirror, she left the bathroom to approach Ami. Her friend was still fast asleep, and Alina gently jostled her shoulder.

"Hey, Ami, it's time to get up!"

Ami's eyes opened slowly, and she pulled a pillow over her head. "Is it that time already?" her muffled voice groaned.

"I'm afraid so," Alina replied, smiling at her friend's antics. Sometimes, she wondered how Ami managed to get up for her early morning job without Alina's help. "I have to speak to Joseph for a moment, but I wanted to wake you up first."

"Thank you," Ami replied, rolling out of her bed. "I suppose I'll find a way to look presentable for the day."

Alina nodded and left the room, taking the keycard with her. She quietly closed the door to their room and turned around.

Directly into Joseph Moore.

"Well, good morning!" he said brightly.

Alina was so startled it took her a moment to catch her breath, but she finally managed a breathless "Good morning" in return. When she met his gaze, sudden chills coursed through her.

The guarded expression in his eyes was just as unreadable as it had been in her house the day before, and the force of it disarmed her. Holding her in place.

Endless seconds passed, and she eventually worked up the courage to break the suffocating silence.

"I, uh, I'm sorry. I didn't see you there."

She blinked, and the unidentifiable look in his eyes vanished.

"No, no harm done whatsoever," he replied. The new softness in his gaze did nothing to settle her nerves.

He seemed to be hesitating, and her heart was racing.

She couldn't take it anymore.

"Joseph, I tried to call you. Last night. And I… I heard your phone ringing outside my room."

His eyes widened as an uncharacteristic anxiety flashed through them. But the look disappeared so quickly—perhaps she was mistaken. He smiled at her.

"Yes, I was…making my rounds, as it were." He cleared his throat. "I apologize if I startled you or Ms. Everly. That was not my intention. I will perform a final check each night."

She forced her fears from her mind as she smiled in relief. "Thank you—that makes perfect sense. I'm so sorry. I feel so… paranoid right now with everything going on. I can't seem to think straight, and I don't know when I will…feel like myself again."

"They tell me that it will get better as time moves on, Ms. Dixon. Though I am mostly quoting therapists, others have told me the same. I have a hard time forgetting… My experiences have seemed to haunt me through the years."

He looked lost in thought, dwelling on a past darkness. Alina stood awkwardly, not knowing if she should try to comfort him or not. She felt like she should reach out and touch his shoulder, but it didn't seem appropriate.

He suddenly snapped back to the present, shaking his head. "But I do not mean to burden you with my…troubles. We are here to solve yours and get your life back in order. And we will do that."

His eyes held hers for an unending moment.

"I will not let him or anyone else harm you again. With my very life, I will keep you safe." He gave her a nod, then he turned and began to walk away.

"Finish getting ready, Ms. Dixon. We are soon leaving!" he called over his shoulder.

Alina turned on her heel and struggled to open the door with her keycard. Her thoughts were tumbling over each other and bewildering her.

I am just a witness and a target. Nothing more. And yet…

BY 0800, ALINA, AMI, Joseph, and Lily were waiting for Owen Davies to pick them up in the SUV. He soon arrived, and they were on their way into the heart of Washington, DC.

Alina was in awe of the busy city streets, her heart pounding along with blaring horns and rumbling trucks in the morning rush hour traffic. Joseph told her that this was the only time that she and Ami would come along—it was safer for them in the hotel than at the FBI building. Today, however, Joseph needed her to make her statement to the entire team. Ami was permitted to accompany her for moral support.

Within fifteen minutes, Owen pulled into the parking lot of 935 Pennsylvania Avenue NW.

Alina stared up at the massive, brown building, squinting as thousands of square windows reflected the morning sun.

After Owen parked, Alina and Ami climbed out of the SUV and walked on the sidewalk to the main entrance. Lily was behind them, wearing a sharp gray suit with matching heels. The fluffy trees on Alina's left seemed out of place, but she was glad to see them. They were a familiar sight against the unfamiliar city backdrop.

Joseph led the way through the building, nodding at other agents as he badged them through multiple secure entrances. At last, he turned down a hallway and walked through double doors.

"This is where our team works," Lily explained.

They followed Joseph inside, and Alina took in the sight of a huge office space with perhaps twenty employees working on their computers. Lily leaned closer to Alina and Ami and subtly pointed out a balding man, likely in his thirties, who at that moment jumped at something a colleague said and spilled black coffee down his shirt.

"That's Donáll. He's, as you'll soon learn, very…unique."

Alina glanced around the room and saw Grant Rogers and the two agents who had been at her house. They were each holding Styrofoam cups of coffee and sitting at their own desks. Joseph led the way to a big conference room, furnished with a long table, chairs, and a huge screen. Even this room had a coffee station, and Owen rushed straight over to it the moment they walked inside.

"This is where mission briefing takes place," Lily said. "As you both are here today, this room will probably be our main center of operations."

Owen was back, handing cups of coffee to Joseph and Lily. A few moments later, he returned again with coffee for Alina, for Ami, and finally for himself.

"I took the liberty of adding some sugar and milk to your beverages, ladies," he declared with a wink and grin. "Joseph here only drinks the stuff black, and Lily only drinks hers with creamers, but I need both milk and sugar. It's what's best. I think Joseph and Lily are nuts," he finished under his breath.

Both Alina and Ami smiled at his words.

"All right, everyone, let's all sit down. It's time to get working," Joseph announced with mock seriousness. His eyes clouded over when he glanced at Alina, and her heart rate picked up. "I'm sorry that the investigation won't be pleasant for you. But we will do our absolute best work to catch this man."

Each person sat down in the leather-backed chairs around the table, facing the front of the room. The door burst open as Rogers joined them. Joseph glanced around at everyone. "Let's begin."

AN HOUR LATER, ALINA had presented her story to the agents in the room, recalling every detail of the attack and answering each of the agents' many questions. Her palms were sweating and her voice shook as she relayed the events of that night, but she miraculously made it through to the end without breaking her resolve.

"Now that we have heard the events of Ms. Dixon's story," Joseph began as he stood, "let us discuss her attacker." He walked over to the nearest wall covered by a large tarp and suddenly pulled downward, letting the covering float to the ground.

Alina sucked in a breath at the sight of her attacker's face glaring at the room from a large photograph. Thin strands of multicolored strings stretched outward from his picture, linking to multiple other pictures, newspaper accounts, and what looked to be police and FBI reports of...murder victims.

As Alina's eyes swept over each picture of each victim, she squeezed her hands together under the table until her knuckles ached.

She felt Ami's hand on her arm, and she glanced over and saw Ami staring at the wall with fear flashing in her eyes. With a start, she realized that Joseph had started speaking.

"...covered up because our trail of this criminal had gone cold. We haven't seen action from him for about a year, but now we have a victim, Victor Harris, and an assault victim, Ms. Dixon."

Rogers stood up and handed Joseph string, pins, and a few sheets of paper. Joseph turned to the wall and tacked up the items, and Alina's heart almost stopped when a picture of the stab victim who had died in the hospital met her eyes. She looked downward to take a breath, and all she saw were her hands rubbing themselves together. She felt distant from her hands and from the entire room. She was slowly succumbing to her terror.

"The man behind each of these attacks was born in Russia, as far we know. He's former Spetsnaz, or Russian special forces." Joseph paused and tapped the picture in the center of the web. "This picture is courtesy of the Russians."

Lily stood and approached him with another paper, and Joseph pinned June's sketch from Alina's description beside his military photo. "The man before you was officially reported as being killed in action."

Alina took a few shaky breaths, confused and overwhelmed with this new onslaught of information. *Killed in action? How on earth?*

Joseph continued. "The first couple of his kills were random and well covered up. The victims were only connected by their wealth of power and influence. It was Blane Burns who pieced a pattern together and dissected each case. Soon, he established enough connections to determine where the killer would strike next. With Burns's work, we now have accumulated several dozen crimes that fit his profile, most being politicians or major business magnates here in the United States."

Joseph took a breath, his eyes sweeping over the room. "The problem was that the case fell cold. The fact that he's officially dead and buried has made him seem untouchable, and he always strikes quickly with military efficiency, never leaving any evidence behind. Until this time. This time, I believe we'll get him. With Burns arriving and with you, Ms. Dixon, we will finally apprehend this man."

Alina's mouth was dry, but she licked her lips and asked the question plaguing her mind. "What's his name?" she nearly whispered.

Joseph looked at her, seriousness in his eyes. "Antonov. Vadik Antonov."

The name sounded dark as death as it reverberated around the room. "To the criminal underworld," Joseph continued, "Antonov is known as—"

"The Archer," a heavily accented voice finished, echoing into the conference room.

CHAPTER FOUR

HER HEART POUNDING, ALINA'S EYES SWEPT ACROSS THE ROOM TO THE DOORWAY, SEARCHING FOR THE OWNER OF THE NEW VOICE.

A tall man, probably in his early thirties, walked into the room.

"Blane Burns. Thank you for coming," Joseph greeted as he half-ran to the man to shake his hand. They conversed quietly as Alina continued to drink in the sight of him.

In addition to his height, the man was muscular and well-toned underneath his pale-green dress shirt, and he had a black suit jacket swung casually over his arm. His wavy, dark brown hair was a bit long, and it was complemented by a trimmed beard. From what she could see, his eyes were midnight, and his nose and cheekbones were well-defined against his face.

Wow. This man is…so handsome. And he's Scottish. Wow.

Joseph and Mr. Burns began walking toward the table, and Alina got a better look at his face. She suddenly saw the dark circles under his eyes—eyes which seemed guarded against everything the world would throw at him.

His family… This man is suffering.

Each of the agents murmured a greeting to Mr. Burns, and Alina realized she was still staring at him. *Stop. Just stop.*

She couldn't seem to stop.

She startled as Joseph addressed her.

"This is the nurse, Alina Dixon."

She quickly rose from her chair, and she looked up into Mr. Burns's eyes. Her heart skipped a beat.

"So," Mr. Burns began, staring down at her. She couldn't get over his accent. It was deep and rich, but it was also very soft—likely due to his many years in London.

He continued. "This is the woman that Antonov left alive." His eyes bored into hers, searching out all of her secrets. With a sinking feeling, Alina realized. He didn't trust her.

His next statement confirmed her fears. "He *never* leaves them alive."

Joseph quickly interjected, "That's true, but we see it as a huge chance to finally bring him to justice. I am not quite sure what—"

"What I'm saying is that we can't trust her. The likelihood of The Archer leaving his own blood behind at the scene is infinitesimal. Perhaps you lot were meant to pick her up and bring her here. Are you sure she wasn't left alive for a reason?" His eyes cut to hers again. "Perhaps to further distract you from the truth?"

Alina's lips parted, and she stared at him with eyes wide with hurt and confusion. She had suffered the verbal abuse of patients and doctors, but this was different. This was someone doubting… everything. Her very life. She finally dropped her gaze.

He doesn't trust me… What if everyone else starts to doubt me, too? After an earth-stilling moment, Mr. Burns looked away as a new voice spoke up.

"Excuse me, Agent Burns, you're wrong," Ami began, meeting his eyes. "Just look at her. And look at her neck. You don't need a lie detector to prove she's telling the truth."

Alina watched his face as his gaze shifted to her throat, but his expression remained unchanged.

"It wouldn't be the first time I've seen someone purposefully injured to avoid suspicion," he said darkly.

Alina took a deep breath at his words, and she let herself sink back down in her chair. She sensed Ami preparing to say more beside her, but Joseph quickly resumed her defense to end the confrontation.

"I can see where your doubts may be stemming from, Burns, but she's clean. My best tech guy completed background checks on both Ms. Dixon and Ms. Everly, and I trust his work completely. Not even a parking ticket for either of them."

Alina saw Lily nod affirmatively from across the room, and she smiled a little when she saw Owen and Rogers mirror the determined expression.

Mr. Burns was still staring at Ami, his gaze intimidating and calculating.

"All I'm saying," Mr. Burns began, at last looking away, "is that this man is dangerous. Dangerous and well-connected."

He had made his way over to the Antonov wall as he spoke, and now he was pointing at her attacker's face. "With Antonov and the organization backing his movements, it's impossible to know who you can trust." His statement was heavy-laden with pain.

He's hurting. So deeply.

"That I cannot argue with, Burns," Joseph spoke up. "But just listen to Ms. Dixon's story if she is willing to share it again. Then I want to hear what you know about this organization, Antonov's assassinations, and your international work. At long last, I am certain we will get him."

Mr. Burns nodded at Joseph, lowering himself into a seat away from the others and looking expectantly at Alina.

Oh, crap. I guess I have to go through this again. Just be calm and very careful.

She looked to Joseph and found comfort in his gaze as she walked to resume her position at the front of the room. With all eyes on her, she began her story one more time.

Under Mr. Burns's scrutiny, Alina felt herself floundering. But she pressed through with as much care as she could, detailing everything she remembered about the attack and the events surrounding it.

Mr. Burns sat up straighter in his chair when she relayed the word the stab victim, or Mr. Harris, had told her.

At last, she was finishing up the attack itself. "I was almost unconscious when he sucked in a breath and was suddenly gone. I have no idea what he saw or—"

"Did you see anyone? Did he sound angry or surprised?" Mr. Burns cut in with his soft accent, eyes flashing with interest.

"Oh, well, um, I don't know. I'm so sorry I don't know. If I had to choose, I wouldn't say angry. I'd say more surprised than angry. Perhaps even a wee bit scared."

Alina abruptly stopped speaking, realizing she had accidentally slipped into a terrible Scottish accent. It was a habit of hers to mirror the accents of people in movies, and she had just done it in real life.

Oh no. Her eyes went wide, her heart pounding. *He'll think I'm mocking him. Stupid, Alina. Stupid.*

As a massive blush heated her cheeks, she glanced around the room, taking in everyone's expressions. Lily looked like she could burst out laughing, and Owen was trying to cough to cover up his chuckle. Joseph looked surprised, but mirth sparkled in his eyes.

Fearing to do so, she at last looked at Mr. Burns. He did not look impressed, but at least he did not look furious.

Well, that's a relief.

After an awkward moment passed, he broke the silence. "A little high in pitch but a fine attempt. Please proceed." He cleared his throat, and Alina finally finished her story.

Once she was done, Joseph kindly nodded at her to sit down. Mr. Burns sat for a moment, rubbing a large hand down his beard.

At last he stood.

BLANE BURNS GLANCED AROUND the room.

These Americans have no idea what they're dealing with. And they trust this Dixon lass blindly, though her story is outrageous. No one knows who we're dealing with.

His palms dampened as dark memories did their best to overtake his mind, but he buried them again. He was always burying them deep down in the darkest corners of his being.

He locked eyes with Alina Dixon, and her beautiful brown eyes widened.

It was highly possible she was a well-trained actress with the single goal of covering up Antonov's blundering attempt to murder Harris.

He would have to pretend he was growing to trust her until she became too comfortable and slipped up, which she was bound to do. If anyone would break her, it would be Blane himself.

And what was with that accent? She wouldn't dare mock me. Would she?

He also had strong misgivings about her friend. If Ms. Dixon was a plant, Ms. Everly was certainly involved. He had stared her down with as much intensity as he could muster, yet the woman hadn't flinched.

At last, he began audibly relaying the thoughts that had whirled through his head while the nurse had recounted her story.

"I think, with a little digging from your people, we will soon know why Victor Harris was Antonov's intended target. The victims on Antonov's hit list, as you lot already know, are all people with considerable power. When I was tracking him to develop his profile, he followed a clear pattern. Every one of Antonov's kills look like accidents, with his M.O. being a clean stab in the street and theft of the victim's wallet. The perfect mock robbery."

Blane took a breath, his emotions warring inside of him. The words were right there, still in his mind. Before the darkness could overtake the cold facts, he pressed onward.

"His victims are always on the verge of acquiring a vast amount of wealth or a new position of power when they die. Their companies, wealth, and positions go to their competitors or a concerned family member who had lost out to the victim years back. At times, the victim's assets completely disappear, bought out by a shell corporation which likewise vanishes. Each time that occurs, you can always expect to hear about another body being found."

Blane glanced at Ms. Dixon at his final words, gauging her reaction.

"Usually, the new victim is connected to the past murder. I suspect that, in the twenty-nine cases where such an event took place, the individual either couldn't pay up or intended to double-cross the organization backing Antonov. In either case, the person paid for the offense with his or her life."

"What do we know about this organization?" the young blond agent asked, staring at Blane with interest.

"Kratos. Its name is Kratos."

Ms. Dixon suddenly spoke. "That's one of the Greek gods of war!" When all eyes turned to her, she blushed and said quickly, "I, uh, did some research on Greek mythology once. That's one of the names I came across."

Blane stared at her for a moment. *Ms. Dixon is full of surprises. And she's beautiful.*

His brain jolted back into focus at the thought. *Now where on earth did that come from? Focus and don't trust, you fool. She's just an actress here to distract you.*

After a moment, he cleared his throat and continued.

"Ms. Dixon is correct. Kratos is a brutal god in Greek literature, known for his advocacy of violence and sovereign power. I hate to admit it, but we know very little about Kratos. You could say that it's an organization which ensures the illegal and discrete transfer of power for its…clientele. Its reach extends so far up the political ladder that it has been untouchable and nearly invisible since I began my investigation years back. I can tell you that the wealth and cutthroat power of the organization has attracted many internationally. For example, let's discuss Harris. A politician, most likely Harris's competitor, got in touch with Kratos and arranged for Harris's death."

The female agent spoke before he could go on. "If the people responsible for plotting the murders are always the obvious competitors, why hasn't a solid case been made against them? Has there never been any proof?"

"I'm afraid not. Kratos is too careful to leave loose ends. All threats are terminated swiftly and conclusively. The organization is merciless in its dealings, even being known to infiltrate and sabotage pharmaceutical companies for their competitors. With MI5, our only tangible connection to Kratos was Antonov, its lead assassin." Blane's heartbeat quickened, and he realized his mouth was going dry.

"I… I got close to him in Germany," he continued, ice flowing through his veins. "Very close."

He stared up at the photograph of The Archer. The devil's black eyes held his captive, and he nearly broke the pencil he only now realized he was clutching.

"Then I…tracked him back to London, and I, ah, I almost had him when…" Blane trailed off as the image of Isla and his child flashed in the forefront of his mind, breaking through the barriers he had built up against the pain of their memory. And the guilt that their deaths were his fault.

He was breathing hard, and he grasped at the wall.

The image of his family lying crushed in the road at last broke through. With a curt "Pardon," he fled the room, shot into the lavvy he had seen on his way in, and violently vomited into the toilet bowl.

BLANE BURNS STEADIED HIMSELF inside the stall. Hot tears seared his eyes as memories threatened to suck him back into the darkness. He had kept them buried for so long, and now they were striking him full force.

He couldn't break again. He wouldn't. Not if there was a real chance to get *him*. And he would get Antonov and make him pay for what he did. Even if he had to kill him.

Especially if he had to kill him.

The fury and vengeance rearing up stilled his racing heart, and his hands were steady as he smoothed his shirt.

Good. He needed the hatred. It was the only thing that kept him from succumbing to the pain.

All at once, an image emerged, bright in the midst of the red: Ms. Dixon's eyes, full of concern.

When he had reached toward the wall for support, she had instantly stood, hands out as if to steady him.

She would never have been able to support my weight.

A knock on the door startled him from his thoughts.

"Burns?" Agent Moore called from outside the lavvy in his rumbling voice. "Is there anything you need? Anything I can do?"

"No, thank you. I'll… I'll be right there." Blane flushed the toilet and splashed cool water on his face as he washed his hands at the sink. A mint from his endless supply was his last intervention, and he took several deep breaths as he contemplated his reflection in the mirror. The rage returned and remained, simmering under the surface. He was relieved.

He needed it.

As he left the lavvy, his mind tracked through the entirety of Ms. Dixon's story, at last focusing on one word: *lazrae.* It was Harris's dying breath, and if the nurse was telling the truth, Antonov feared the consequences of it being heard enough to kill again.

His thoughts once more centered on Ms. Dixon as he prepared to push the door to the conference room open. He shook his head and softly growled at himself.

She cannot be trusted. She must not be trusted.

ALINA STOPPED CHEWING HER nails the minute Mr. Burns pushed open the door. Joseph had asked for everyone to remain where they were until Mr. Burns returned.

Now the tall Scottish man walked steadily into the room, a hardness on his face. "I must ask you to pardon my sudden, ah, departure. I must have eaten something disagreeable on the flight over. I am quite prepared to continue." He returned to his seat, his eyes fixed coldly on Antonov's picture.

Alina glanced at Ami and saw that she too seemed agitated. Lily and Owen looked solemn, and Rogers was looking carefully at Mr. Burns, almost as if...as if he was sizing him up.

Suddenly, Rogers glanced in her direction, and she quickly turned her focus to Mr. Burns as he began to speak.

Stupidly enough, she realized she was blushing again.

The door suddenly banged open as the tech guy, Donáll, walked in and plopped down on a chair beside Rogers. Even as he sat down and placed his coffee on the table, his eyes remained glued to his laptop screen. Mr. Burns paused a moment, staring at the man before addressing the room once more.

"Returning to our discussion, this particular case is, of course, a deviation from the usual dealings of Antonov and Kratos. Firstly, Antonov left Harris alive enough to tell *lazrae* to whomever he could. Secondly, he failed to eliminate Ms. Dixon. And thirdly, he left some of his own DNA at the scene. I've tracked the man for years, and I've never, *never* seen him make such mistakes."

Owen, looking at his laptop, spoke up. "The police found where they think the attack on Harris took place. It appears Harris parked his car a distance away from his usual office complex and approached a random alley. His blood was found all over the ground in the shadows there, and his wallet was cleaned out. Just like you said, it appears to have been a brutal robbery. They questioned his staff, and no one appears to have any clue what he was doing there."

"Why would a high-stakes politician go to such a place without protection?" Lily asked, leaning forward in her seat. "If he had been elected, Harris would have initiated huge policy changes he upheld in his campaign. The polls looked to be massively in his favor. Why take such a risk?"

"Most of Antonov's victims are lured away to an isolated location," Mr. Burns replied. "Kratos could have accumulated items to blackmail him with and demanded a secret meeting in a private area. Or, a staff member could have asked for a private meeting to expose corruption in his campaign. I've even known some victims to be convinced that a family member was abducted and went secretly to pay the ransom, only to meet their end. And Antonov is masterful in his assassinations, both in the kill itself and in the art of disguise. In a blink of the eye, he can utterly transform his appearance."

Alina felt the sinking feeling in her stomach again. He had lured *her* beyond aid with a charming smile and a supposed plot. He had disoriented *her* with an utter transformation in appearance. And now she knew that all others who had met with him in such a way had ended up dead. Corpses in a morgue.

She felt like throwing up. She tried to focus as Joseph spoke to the tech man who was still engrossed in his screen.

"Donáll," Joseph began, holding up his hands in a calming manner. It was too late, however, as the jumpy man startled in his seat. Before his coffee could spill, Rogers reached over and neatly steadied the Styrofoam cup. The cup looked like it had been used and reused for the past decade.

"Donáll," Joseph tried again, "I know you've been working throughout the duration of this morning. Have you found anything about the mysterious *lazrae*? Or anything suspicious in the finances of Harris's competitors? Or anything more on the officers we suspect were paid off at Virginia Hospital?"

Donáll stared at Joseph with wide green eyes. "Would you like me to answer your inquiries chronologically, by matter of importance, or in the sequence in which you asked them?" He gave a high-pitched chuckle at his own reply, apparently unfazed by Joseph's stare and exaggerated blinking.

"How about in the order I asked them in, my friend?" Joseph replied with a controlled breath.

"Oh, right then. *Lazrae* brings up a huge number of search results, even in my filtered-for-evildoings browser. It will take time to sift through and see what the politician dude was referring to. In short, while it could hold any number of meanings, I believe it is a scrambled code for the word—"

"*Azrael*," Mr. Burns said softly, startling Donáll. Donáll proceeded to glare at the Scottish man, apparently miffed at his stolen thunder.

Mr. Burns was staring off into some unknown place. Then he spoke again, his deep, resonating voice sending goosebumps down her arms.

"That word emerged several times in my investigation with MI5. We didn't determine anything beyond its literal meaning, which is—"

"The Islamic or Jewish Angel of Death," Donáll cut in, challenging Mr. Burns with a wide-eyed stare. Mr. Burns, however, was lost in his thoughts, and Alina's mind was also reeling. In terror.

Azrael. Angel of Death.

A scan of the room told her that the others were just as apprehensive at the potential implications of such a code name. Donáll was too impatient, however, to allow the somber silence to overcome the room.

"Righto, next question. In sequence. Regarding the realm of political finance, it appears James Malkovich, the leading competitor against Victor Harris, has begun cutting corners in his campaign. He transferred a large sum in the recent hours."

"Can you trace it?" Joseph asked, staring intently at Donáll.

"Ha! Nope. It's impossible," Donáll replied, looking matter-of-factly at the now-frowning man in front of him. "I've already hacked through Malkovich's firewalls, and I can see that he transferred around one hundred thousand to another account. However, thrillingly enough, the account doesn't exist! In fact, it never has!"

"For the sakes of us all, why is that a good thing?" Owen burst out.

"Oh well, um, I suppose it gives me a bit of a challenge. The transaction is *so* clean and *so* neat that it is overtly sinister. And every online transaction has a point of weakness, and one this perfectly arranged might have a hairline fracture. I will find it, but it will take time. Now, in answer to your inquiry into our crooked officer friends back in Glen Allen, the same holds true. Once I access each of the finances of those who benefitted from Antonov's kills, in addition to these recent dealings, I will most likely discover a beautiful pattern linking them all. That pattern will point me to the firewall used to scramble each attempt to crack each individual transaction."

"Aye, but a bit of a warning, sir," Mr. Burns suddenly cut in, causing Donáll to jump. "Interpol, MI5, and other government agencies all over the world have never stopped investigating Kratos. Even the CIA got involved years back. They are all, as last I understood, compiling the transactions we know about to find a pattern, similarly to the process you just described. However, MI5 found that every time they got close, the firewall transformed itself and made all of their previous work useless. No country got through."

"Yes, yes, yes, of course, Mr. B," Donáll answered. "Mind if I call you Mr. B?" Not waiting for a reply, he continued. "But what software were MI5 and all those other agencies you mentioned using in their attempt to crack the firewall?" He stared intently at Mr. Burns.

"Oh, well, I was never closely involved with that particular side of the investigation, but I believe it was an American technology."

Alina enjoyed watching Mr. Burns think, running a hand down his chin and ending up at the end of his beard.

Okay, Alina. You must stop.

"The name of the software is *Break-Through*, Mr. B. And I happened to invent it." Donáll gave a giddy chuckle and glanced happily around the room. "It's the newest and most efficient form of hacking software since 2016. If a firewall shifts when it feels threatened, almost like it's thinking, *Break-Through* slowly but surely determines the pattern of its transformations. With the proper user, the software will eventually be able to predict how the firewall will transform before it does."

Alina had been struggling to follow the conversation for the longest time, but Donáll's announcement once again reminded her how insane…and how amazing…it all was.

She focused again, watching Mr. Burns's face to see his reaction. He looked surprised but pleased. He nodded at Donáll, murmuring a soft "Aye."

Joseph once again resumed the discussion, suggesting that a break for lunch was in order.

After eating, the hours passed quickly. Mr. Burns detailed his work tracking Antonov throughout Europe and even at times in the United States. As he spoke, Alina was in awe of his obvious skill, intelligence, and determination. She really, really liked him, even though their first interaction was frosty at best…and she had only met him that day.

I just hope I can prove myself and gain his trust.

Once questions were asked and tasks were assigned, Alina and Ami watched the FBI team break into groups to investigate their leads. One group, including Mr. Burns, began working down through the *lazrae* and *Azrael* web results as Donáll continued compiling the Kratos transactions. Alina wasn't exactly sure what the other agents were doing, but everything looked extremely important.

She sat and watched the organized chaos with Ami. Briefly, she wondered how her grandparents were faring in Florida. Their rare calls and short letters had left the matter exceedingly open-ended.

Thinking back, the lack of true affection had always filled her with a gray emptiness. She missed the vague memory of her mom and the fleeting shadow of her dad: a shadow she had never gotten the chance to meet and fill in the blanks to define.

But even then, she knew she was never alone. The gifts from her mysterious Soter always lifted her spirits, and meeting Ami the first day of her freshman year was the best thing that had ever happened to her. Through it all, her Heavenly Father was by her side, cradling her in the palm of His hand. She smiled, feeling old fears and lone-liness drift away.

Alina spoke with Ami a little, and then the two sat in silence. As the evening wore on, the room blurred into a swirl of busy color. Alina's eyelids felt heavy, and her leather chair felt especially cozy. Before she knew it, Ami was gently jostling her awake.

"Hey, Alina. Time to wake up. I think we're done for the day."

Alina sat straight up, wiping at her face in a panic in case of drool. Her neck was stiff, and she felt like she hadn't walked in a million years.

The agents were beginning to clear the room. Joseph stood talking quietly with Mr. Burns, and his face brightened when he looked over and met her eyes. When he gestured for her to come, she stood and walked drowsily over, trying to suppress a yawn.

"Were you able to sleep, Ms. Dixon?" Joseph asked. When she gave an embarrassed nod, Joseph smiled and continued. "I'm glad you did. We didn't get anywhere major in our investigation today, but we were not expecting to. One conclusion we did reach is that you are still in extreme danger."

His words brought her world into sharp focus before everything blurred, hot tears gathering in her eyes. She was so tired and confused and frustrated.

Both men were looking at her with concern, and she did her best to blink away the moisture.

"Sorry, I, um, just wish this would all be over. That we could just go back to…ordinary life again."

Mr. Burns's gaze had never been softer nor his expression gen-tler since she had first met him that morning, and she allowed herself to get lost in his midnight eyes for a moment.

When his face once again resumed a hard look, she dropped her eyes. *Idiot. Gaping at him will only make you seem more suspicious.*

"I'm so sorry, Ms. Dixon," Joseph replied. "I told Burns about your unease at your home and about the cigarettes, and he confirmed our suspicion. Without a doubt, Antonov was there."

"Antonov stalks his victims before he strikes, and we can be cer-tain he still has his eyes fixed on you. Letting you live may have been some sort of accident, and he will likely come after you again." Mr. Burns kept his hard stare as he spoke each word.

And each of his words sent shivers of horror down Alina's spine. Her knees suddenly felt wobbly—a rare sensation that she hated. She felt so weak and vulnerable.

"For this reason, I have asked Burns to stay by your side until we catch Antonov. Burns knows The Archer more than any of us, and though I will give my life…though I and my team will do everything we can to protect you, I want him with you twenty-four-seven. We *will* keep you safe, Ms. Dixon."

The gravity of the promise struck Alina, and she caught Mr. Burns giving Joseph a cautious glance.

"Please, call me Alina. And thank you. I haven't said that enough."

Joseph nodded kindly to her. "I'll pull up the SUV," he said, then he turned and walked out of the room.

Alina watched him go, then she startled as she turned and looked directly into Blane Burns's eyes.

"So it's to be you and me then, lass." His look was guarded, though his voice was light and his expression was not as severe.

"I, uh, I suppose so." Alina hated that she was floundering. Desperate to defy the onset of awkward silence, she continued. "Everything has gotten so…crazy. It doesn't even seem real," she began, hoping her comment was some sort of lead-in that would allow her to thank him again. But he interjected first.

"It is *very* real, Ms. Dixon." The harsh expression was back. "And now I'm going to explain how this is going to work. You are, during the day, never to leave my side other than of course when you need privacy. But you stick to me like…what is the expression here? Stick to me like…tape?"

"Glue?" Alina offered.

"Aye, you'll stick to me like glue. I am armed and always have my knives on me," he continued, "but in case you are ever separated from my side, I want you prepared as well."

He suddenly produced a small yet deadly looking pistol. Alina took a step backward, shocked.

How long was he holding THAT?

"I, uh, well, you see, with my faith, I don't believe in killing any-one. I could never kill someone," Alina explained, carefully watching his face. The man looked completely unfazed.

"I do not expect that you could or would. But, at times, having something to injure or at least hold up at an attacker can save your life until help arrives. You want to be a force to be reckoned with, not a helpless bairn."

Great. He thinks of me as a child.

Her eyes shifted to the pistol he was still holding out, and she reached toward it. When she hesitated, he dropped it in her hand.

Flustered, she exclaimed, "Well, where on earth should I keep it?"

"Well," he began, running a hand down his beard. He suddenly reached into his leather satchel and produced a small holster.

"It wasn't made for that pistol, but it'll do."

"Oh! Thank you." A moment passed where she couldn't think of anything else to say, and he mercifully moved on in the conversation.

"You are also going to take this." He held up a small bronze-colored wristband. He waited patiently, and she realized with a start that he was going to clip it on her wrist.

"Oh, uh, here. Sorry." She held up her wrist. As he carefully snapped it on, he pointed to a small indentation on it.

"There's a button there, and should you ever need help and I'm not with you, press it. It will activate mine." He held up his hand, and she saw a small ring of the same style and color. "And it will vibrate. The bracelet and ring also give off a signal that can be traced, much like a cell phone. Moore and I set the pieces up with the FBI's systems, so they'll be able to see where you are should you ever press the button."

Alina stared at the bracelet in awe. She felt like she was in a James Bond movie. And she had never received a piece of jewelry from a handsome man before. From any man, for that matter.

"Oh, well, uh, thank you. Thank you very much. I'll be extremely careful with it." She looked up at him and smiled brightly.

He had seemed slightly amused before, and now she thought she saw the corners of his mouth begin to lift. The look faded back into seriousness so quickly, however, that she feared she had imagined it.

"Are you both ready to go? Joseph brought the car up," Lily announced, walking up to them with Ami.

"Yes, well, I think so!" Alina said, looking at Mr. Burns. He nodded at her, and the four of them walked through the FBI building and were soon outside. Ami and Lily climbed into the SUV, and Mr. Burns motioned Alina toward a black Toyota Camry parked nearby.

As they approached his car, she noticed his tense stance and his eyes darting all around, seeking out any danger which dared to rear its head. She felt safe.

Mr. Burns held up his hand for her to wait, and he looked to be examining his car. After he had dropped down to check the underside and was apparently satisfied, he unlocked the vehicle and actually held open the door for her.

What a gentleman.

She thanked him again as she climbed in, and he just shook his head and shut the door. Loudly.

He pulled out and followed Joseph's vehicle through the busy night streets of Washington, DC. The silence was a heavy presence in the car, but at least it smelled nice. It smelled very nice, like a mix of cologne and pine needles. She allowed herself to peek at Mr. Burns at one point, and she looked immediately away when she realized he had chosen that exact moment to glance at her.

How awkward.

Soon enough, they pulled into the hotel behind Joseph. Apparently, Joseph had prearranged parking for Mr. Burns, as well, as they were able to pull right in. They walked inside, and Alina was happy to see Joseph greet Rose again. The secretary's smile was so big.

Once they entered their hallway, Joseph briefed Mr. Burns on the safety features of the hotel before handing him a keycard and saying good night.

As Alina and Ami approached their room, Mr. Burns stopped them.

"Before you turn in for the night, I am going to do a sweep of your room," he said. He seemed to be waiting, and it finally clicked that he needed her keycard.

"Oh, thank you. Here." While he unlocked and entered the room, Alina and Ami waited in the hallway.

After a moment, he rejoined them.

"The room is clear, and I agree with Moore that this will be the safest place for both of you. Call me if you need anything. My number is already programmed into your burners."

Wow. Alina had no idea how he had done that, but she was grateful.

"Thank you very much and good night," she said quickly.

"Good night then, Ms. Dixon," he replied softly. He turned away, and Alina started to follow Ami into the room.

Suddenly, she turned toward him. "Uh, Mr. Burns?" He whipped back around, his hand posed on the gun on his belt.

Does everyone here do that? One of these times, she was going to have a heart attack.

"Sorry, everything's okay. Just, I wanted to ask you to, um…to call me Alina."

He stared at her for a moment, and then he tried out her name. "Alina." He hmphed. "No, I think not. Ms. Dixon it is."

He began walking away again, and she called out one more time to him. She felt like such a pest.

"Would it be okay if I called you Blane?" She liked the way his name rolled off her tongue.

She saw his eyes close as he ran his hand down his face again. He at last held her with his eyes. "Ordinarily, I would consider the use of my first name irrelevant, unprofessional, and perhaps a bit distracting from the mission at hand. But, as I am supposed to protect…as you are under my care…well, I suppose you may do what you like. Good night."

With those words, he left her. Alina watched him for a little, and then she turned back toward her own room. After closing the door, she saw that Ami was already asleep.

As she glanced at her friend, Alina prayed that Ami would stay safe until the end of this. She couldn't bear the thought of Ami getting hurt because of her.

She gently pulled the blanket up over Ami a little more, carefully tucking it around her.

Twenty minutes later, Alina had showered and changed into her pajamas. She plugged her phone into its charger and crawled into her own bed, switching off the lamp and snuggling into her pillow.

Thank You, God, for the FBI Team. Thank You for the people who care about me. And thank You for Blane Burns.

BLANE FINISHED HIS CONVERSATION with the guards stationed in the far room of the hallway. He had requested access from Moore to speak to the security team, knowing that he would not be satisfied until he ensured the security of the "safe house" himself.

They assured him that everything was under control and that they were perfectly capable of doing their jobs.

Blane knew better. He didn't necessarily underestimate them, but he understood they were no match for The Archer if he attempted to murder Ms. Dixon again.

If he ever did in the first place.

Blane rubbed a hand down his face, his mind whirling with thoughts and emotions as he walked back to his room.

He couldn't shake the feeling that she was lying or that she had been purposefully planted to misguide them.

Yet she's so…guiltless. Everything she does seems gentle and innocent.

His mind replayed each memory of her. Every open glance. Every bright smile. And every expression of sweet and sincere compassion. She was certainly a beautiful woman.

Blane reached his door and growled at himself as he leaned his head against the frame.

She can't be trusted. You trusted in yourself once, and you failed. You. Failed. No one can ever be trusted again.

As he prepared himself for bed, Blane dwelled on the facts and confusions of the investigation. He could not understand why

Antonov hadn't killed Harris immediately. Antonov never missed his mark. *So what on earth stayed his hand?*

A thought suddenly occurred that made him hesitate as he brushed his teeth.

Time.

Antonov needed something from Harris. But he needed the man to be weak and desperate—hence all of the bruises. Harris was being tortured. That's why he didn't go straight for the kill.

Blane had no idea what Harris knew about Kratos that made him a target for both interrogation and execution. It all centered around *Azrael*.

Harris's staff declared that the politician hadn't been himself for months. He'd been paranoid and distracted, and one woman had even said he seemed "tortured in his mind."

Perhaps Harris hadn't been targeted by Malkovich, after all. The large missing sum from Malkovich's bank account could be a diversion. Perhaps Harris had been a member of Kratos itself: the only position that would explain him needing to be questioned before he was killed.

As Blane changed and sat in bed, he played out the events of that night according to his theories.

Victor Harris, a powerful and wealthy politician, was secretly a member of Kratos. One day, Kratos suspected Harris of betrayal, and maybe the organization found out that Harris contacted someone… someone in law enforcement.

Blane quickly grabbed his laptop and searched the obituaries in neighboring areas in the days leading up to Harris's murder. Blane didn't have to look far before he found what he was looking for.

Clay Jones, a private investigator based in a city on the outskirts of Harris's domain, was killed in a car accident the very same day Harris was attacked. Looking into the man's eyes knocked the air out of Blane, and he shook his head at the tragedy of it all.

He continued forward in his theory until he reached Ms. Dixon's attack.

Antonov had gone to the hospital to finish Harris off, and Ms. Dixon heard Harris's dying words, signing her death warrant. She was an easy target for someone like Antonov...his victims always were. Dark images threatened to surface in Blane's mind, and he quickly suppressed them with a growl.

The only piece of the puzzle that didn't fit was that Ms. Dixon was still alive. She said that he had "sucked in a breath" and that he was "more surprised than angry." Perhaps "even a wee bit scared."

The memory of her attempting Blane's accent and failing at it prompted another shake of his head. *That woman.*

What did Antonov see? A person coming near would have been another easy target. A group of people maybe would have been a challenge, but Donáll had checked the security footage, and no such group passed by the bereavement room the entire night.

What scared you, Antonov? Why didn't you kill her?

It didn't make any sense to Blane. The only thing he knew for certain was that Ms. Dixon could be dangerous and could never be admitted into his trust. At the same time, he had to protect her from further attempts on her life. A paradox if ever he heard one.

That was another confusing angle to all this. Even with highly trained FBI operatives nearby, Ms. Dixon would already be dead if Antonov meant to finish the job. Instead, he was watching from a distance, studying her. Blane had no idea why he hadn't gone for the kill.

But if and when Antonov changed his mind, Blane would be ready for him. Whether Ms. Dixon was false or in true danger, nothing would happen to her while Blane was around. He wouldn't lose anyone else to that devil.

Blane slammed his laptop closed at the thought, squeezing his eyes shut as the memories flooded back into his mind. Now everything seemed to trigger them to haunt him.

To bury him.

He took several shaky breaths, keeping his eyes closed. *Focus on the here and now, Burns. Focus.*

Blane laid down, his mind whirling back into his theories and suspicions. The next day, he wanted to talk to Malkovich and follow up on his lead regarding the PI who had likely been murdered by Antonov.

Azrael echoed through his mind as he closed his eyes. *Azrael. Azrael…*

THE BEAUTIFUL WOMAN STOOD in the middle of the road, cradling her two-year-old in her arms. Isla hummed softly to Olivia, stroking the child's silky curls as her own red hair flowed down her back. Blane was on the sidewalk a distance away, running toward them. Suddenly, he heard the car tires scream, and he gasped as the black vehicle barreled toward his family. He was rooted to the ground, trying to yell but gasping on air. He was paralyzed as the SUV zoomed toward them. Isla held his eyes with hers, smiling at him as the car hit them. He was there, looking down at them crushed on the road. Then Isla's face was Alina Dixon's.

Blane jerked awake, sweat pouring down his face and soaking his pillow. Gasping, he ran to the room's lavvy.

He stood in a cold shower for what may have been twenty minutes, holding his head in his hands and feeling the adrenaline fade. He used to have nightmares about the war. But that nightmare had haunted him every night since his family was killed.

And now Ms. Dixon was dead on the road, too.

"Oh, God!" he whispered. "Why?" He felt the tears well up in his eyes, though he hurriedly swiped them away with his fists.

He didn't really believe in God anymore.

Blane finally exited the shower, changed out of his wet clothes, and paced for a moment. Then he stole out of his room with his gun and his room card. In his T-shirt and jeans, he scanned the hallway, hoping for something to shoot and kill. There was nothing in the stretch of darkness.

He walked on unsteady legs to Ms. Dixon's and Ms. Everly's room, and he sank down against the wall on the opposite side of the hallway. He sat still, and after a moment, he violently rubbed away the traces of the tears which trailed defiantly down his face. He wanted the rage to come. He wanted to feel the burn of hatred inside. But he was forsaken…even of the burning.

Propped against the wall, he stayed there for hours until a fitful blackness carried him into the morning.

ALINA SAT UP IN bed gasping, her heart racing and her face on fire. Antonov had been in her dreams again, and this time she knew. She was going to die. And then she woke up.

With as much care as she could to not wake Ami, she crawled out of her bed and stumbled into the bathroom. She splashed her face with cool water and stared at her reflection. A pale face with bags perpetually under the eyes gazed back at her.

Will I ever get a hold of myself again?

Her gaze dropped to the angry bruises, a mottled combination of red, dark purple, and yellow now. She thought they looked even worse than the day before.

Alina walked back into the bedroom, and the darkness sent her heart pounding again. She was suddenly terrified of the door and the long hallway outside.

Knowing she would not sleep unless she checked, just like the night before, Alina crept over to the door and stared through the peephole. Surely it would be abandoned this time.

Dawn was breaking outside, and a little light was filtering through big windows at the end of the hallway. Terror jolted her wide awake when her eyes at last adjusted to the grayness, and she saw a figure huddled against the wall across from her.

Contrary to last night, she could distinguish who the figure was just by staring at him.

Mr. Burns. Or Blane.

A relieved sigh escaped her.

What on earth is he doing out there? Her heart twisted. He looked cold, stiff, and utterly alone in the world.

She grabbed an extra blanket, propped the door open as quietly as she could, then ventured out to the sleeping Scottish man. When she draped it over him, the cheap thing only covered the lower half of his body.

She went back into her room and grabbed the first thing she could find: her teal bathrobe.

Hopefully it won't creep him out.

Once back in the hallway, she tucked it around the front of his shoulders and chest, securing the ends against him and the wall.

He shifted and groaned softly, but his eyes remained closed. Alina thought her heart was going to pound right out of her chest.

Once she was satisfied with her work, she took in the sight of him. He looked decidedly more comfortable. And handsome. She smiled and tiptoed back to her room, shutting the door softly behind her.

BLANE BURNS AWOKE AND for a moment forgot where he was. Then he remembered the mission. He remembered the nightmare. And he remembered coming out here. The only things he didn't remember were the warm blanket and the other thing covering him. He was confused, and he was even more confused when he smelled something very…pleasant. Like fresh flowers.

Hmmm.

He sat up and a teal bathrobe fell into his lap. Glancing around and seeing no one, he held the bathrobe up to his face. *That* was where the smell was coming from.

His heart gave a strange flutter as he considered what had happened. Had Ms. Dixon…put it over him?

Suddenly, he didn't like the idea.

It angered him that she had seen him vulnerable, and it scared him that she had been out of her room. And he was furious with himself that he hadn't awoken. He didn't have much time for his musings, however, as he heard a door open and watched Joseph Moore enter the hallway.

Blane quickly stood, folding the bathrobe and hiding it under the blanket in his arms. Moore looked alarmed at his presence.

"What happened?" he asked, his hand grasping his Glock 22.

"Nothing, sir," Blane replied. "I had trouble catching some sleep, so I came out here to just, you know, to do…my job."

"Thank you, Burns. But please, I would be more than happy to take shifts with you."

"Much appreciated, sir." Moore nodded at him and stood there for a moment, checking his watch.

"We still have some time before we should leave," Moore began. "I must confess, Burns, this entire case has me in a tailspin. There's a glut of pieces to it, but they don't seem to fit together in a logical order." Blane watched Moore's hands close into fists, and he detected a hard edge to loaded words as the man continued.

"Burns, I... I can always see several moves ahead. The enemy always has a plan...an endgame. And that's when we catch them, when they're convinced they're a pawn's move away from checkmate. But a man can lose sight of that last move, can't he? When the demons come back and the control he's fought to keep for so long begins to slip away. Then nothing is clear, and he's blind and helpless to whatever the end of the game holds. That helplessness angers me beyond anything, especially now that..." Moore trailed off, staring at the door across the hallway. Ms. Dixon's door.

Blane stared at him, recognizing an onslaught of troubling thoughts on a troubled mind.

What has you in such turmoil, Moore? What demons are you hiding? No one can be trusted.

Before Blane could address him, the older agent suddenly shook his head and smiled tiredly at him.

"Wow, I didn't get much sleep. Who knew I could ramble so much so early in the morning?" He chuckled and clasped Blane's shoulder as they began walking down the hallway. "Has any of this become clearer to you since last evening?" Moore asked, drawing Blane's thoughts back to the task at hand.

Blane briefed him on his revelations from the night before, and Moore stared at him thoughtfully as he considered Blane's suspicions.

"So Harris was a member of Kratos and was planning to blow the whistle. He had already begun the process by contacting Clay Jones—a private investigator. We've had run-ins with Jones before. He was always a slippery one and wasn't afraid to break the law in order to deliver on his contract and take home big bucks."

"Ah," Blane replied. "Well, Harris needed someone outside of the law to avoid charges against himself. Kratos, however, learned of the plot and sent Antonov to kill them both. Antonov targeted Jones and Harris the same day, but he interrogated Harris after fatally wounding him in that alley. Those are what I consider to be the facts. And now for the continued theory. For some unknown reason,

Antonov is interrupted from finishing off Harris in the alley and follows him to Virginia Hospital, disguises himself as OR staff, and makes certain the job gets done there."

Moore continued the conjectured account. "Harris isn't as incapacitated as Antonov supposes, and Harris rattles off *lazra*e to Ms. Dixon. Antonov next targets Ms. Dixon and has nearly killed her when he abruptly aborts mission and disappears. We know he's been watching, but he hasn't moved to strike again yet."

"And we'll be ready for him when he does," Blane finished, locking eyes with Moore.

"Good work, Burns. Today, we'll pursue your leads on Malkovich's suspected innocence, and if your theory is correct, that man was just robbed of thousands of dollars. We'll also investigate everything we know of Clay Jones: his home, his dealings with Victor Harris, and his last hours. Hopefully, by the end of the day, we'll also know what *lazrae* refers to."

"Aye, that sounds like a good day, sir," Blane replied. He hesitated. "Am I correct in thinking Ms. Dixon and Ms. Everly will remain here?"

Joseph nodded. "I'll personally tighten our security. They'll be safe until we return."

Though Blane didn't like leaving her, he knew it was what had to be done.

CHAPTER FIVE

ALINA STARED OUT OF THE WINDOW OF THE HOTEL ROOM, SLOWLY TWIRLING THE BRACELET ON HER WRIST.

Blane's bracelet.

Ami had currently commandeered the bathroom, and the incessant hairdryer was a soothing sound. It reminded Alina of home.

Joseph had confided the day before that the safest place for her and Ami would be in their hotel room, and though she was grateful for such a haven, she felt restless.

She smiled at the realization. Her three years in the ED had made it difficult for her to sit and relax for hours at a time.

A knock suddenly sounded, and she smoothed out her cranberry dress.

"Coming!" she called, and she walked quickly to the door and looked through the peephole. When she saw Blane standing there, she rapidly ran her fingers through her hair and pinched her cheeks before opening the door.

"Good morning!" she said brightly. For some reason, she was very happy to see him.

He merely nodded at her, his eyes sweeping the room as he entered. "I wanted to tell you that Moore, Herne, and I are leaving within the next fifteen minutes. Moore and I are going to meet Rogers at Malkovich's office."

"Harris's competitor?" she clarified.

Blane nodded at her, and then he released a pent-up breath. "I apologize that I am leaving your side, Ms. Dixon. I swore yesterday that you would be stuck with me, and here we are." He shook his head, his frustrated gaze cast downward.

She desperately wanted to reassure him. "Please—it's fine. Joseph said we will be safe here, so we will be. Just come back soon."

Her final words slipped out before she registered what she was saying, and she felt a blush heat her cheeks.

He didn't even seem to notice when he locked his eyes with hers. "You can count on it," he said, his voice rumbling and sending warmth through her. "Call me the minute you need anything, though, of course, contact the team here first. You have their number."

"I will," she replied. "Thank you, and please be safe."

With a nod, he turned to leave, though he suddenly stopped and turned back around.

"Oh, uh, Ms. Dixon. I wanted to thank you for the blanket and for the, uh, the…robe. Last night."

She saw, for the first time, uncertainty written across his face.

"Oh, yes, of course!" She smiled shyly. "I was up after a bad dream, and I saw you out there in the hallway… You looked…cold and miserable, so I just thought that I would…you know what? I'm rambling. You are very welcome." She mentally smacked herself.

"Well, I plan to be sleeping out there more often than not. Moore offered to sleep in shifts, but we'll see."

She loved the way he said "Moore" with his accent.

After another pause, he nodded again and left the room, the heavy door thudding behind him.

Please keep him safe, God.

BLANE KEPT IN STEP with Joseph Moore and Grant Rogers as they entered the massive office complex belonging to James Malkovich.

There was a chance Kratos would target Malkovich next, especially if the organization learned that the FBI suspected he was being framed. Or, more appropriately, when—it was only a matter of time.

Blane felt the steadying presence of his gun on his belt as they passed through the rotating doors and entered the main lobby.

Moore immediately approached a man in a suit with large spectacles who appeared to be waiting for them.

"Joseph Moore, FBI," Moore said, flashing his badge. "My team and I are here to speak with James Malkovich."

"Yes, of course, right this way. He's been expecting you."

The man led them across the lobby, through a set of double doors, and down a hallway until they reached a large door with three armed security guards standing in front of it. Blane's eyes scanned the surroundings, his every sense on high alert.

Their guide flashed his badge to the security guards, and he proceeded to speak with them in hushed tones before turning again to address Moore.

"I am terribly sorry for the inconvenience, but I'm afraid that you will have to turn over any weapons before entering and also consent to a pat down. Security for Mr. Malkovich is rather tight at present."

"Has Mr. Malkovich's life been threatened?" Moore asked, staring intently at the man. "Does he have reason to suspect that he is at an increased risk of danger?" The man stared impassively at Moore as he replied.

"Please direct all further questions to Mr. Malkovich himself. Now these men need your identification and your weapons."

As the main security guard approached Moore, the senior FBI agent held up his hand with a brow raised.

"It is highly inadvisable to relieve myself and my team of our weapons, especially if Malkovich fears for his life. You are welcome to inspect our weapons and our badges, but then we will be taking them back. We are federal agents, and we operate under different guidelines than Mr. Malkovich's usual clientele, in case you failed to notice," he finished coolly.

As Blane held up his temporary FBI badge, he glanced at their guide. A jolt electrified him as their eyes locked, and Blane felt a tingling sensation course through his body.

However, the man's tight nod ended the interminable moment, and their guide turned a cold gaze toward Moore.

"It's against policy, but… I suppose I will relay your…requests."

With those words, he disappeared inside the room and remained for a long moment. At last, the door swung open.

"Enter," a deep voice rang out.

The weaselly guide quickly opened the door for them, and he murmured, "I'll bring some coffee for you," as they moved to enter the big room. Blane glanced back at the man as he left, his hand finding the gun on his belt. His instincts were screaming at him to be careful.

Moore posted Rogers outside to secure the room and monitor the hallway with the guards. Rogers nodded and began addressing the guards with questions.

Blane followed Moore as they walked into the modern room, dully furnished in silver and gray. The far wall was a sheet of glass, acting as one huge window to the busy city below.

A large man, probably nearing three hundred pounds, was sitting at a massive desk in the center of the room, facing them. His dark hair was streaked with gray, and he had a trimmed beard defining what was otherwise an undefinable chin.

When he glanced up, his small beady eyes studied them. After a minute, he gestured for them to approach, and he steepled his fingers on his desk as he started speaking.

"You may be wondering at the security currently in place here. They are present for the same reason that I have agreed to meet with you. I believe my life is in danger."

"Let's get straight to it, then," Moore answered. "It is because of the recent attack and murder of Victor Harris, is it not?"

Malkovich swallowed, his Adam's apple bobbing up and down.

Blane's eyes were drawn to his now incessantly drumming fingers, the sweat glistening on his forehead, the darting of his eyes.

He's nervous. Not of a potential threat—he's afraid right now. Something's here.

"I was Victor Harris's political competitor, which already puts me in a compromising position thanks to his recent murder. Now someone has stolen from me. They wired one hundred thousand dollars from my bank account into a ghost account that my best people have not been able to trace. My entire campaign was riding on the peoples' good opinion, and I have no idea how we'll get through this scandal." The man rubbed his forehead aggressively. "It's an utter nightmare, and then there's my very life to worry about."

"What alerted you to this threat?" Moore asked. "An email? A phone call?"

Malkovich kept his eyes down. "A message painted on my dining room wall. But if they killed off Harris, why am I also a target? I knew he was involved in shady dealings, but he walked on water with the public. Whoever was protecting him all that time must have finally decided to get rid of him. And now me."

The big man proceeded to let out a string of angry curses.

Blane's eyes narrowed. *He's putting on a show.*

He took a step closer to the politician, his eyes flashing with intensity. "We suspect that Harris was being protected by a shadow organization. Kratos. Do you know of it?"

Blane watched his reaction carefully, seeing Malkovich's eyes darken for an instant before he groaned aloud.

"Everyone who's anyone knows it. It's untouchable. If they've marked you, you're finished." He let out a hysterical laugh, his eyes now roving frantically around the room.

Now that was real.

Blane needed to pry as much information as he could out of the man before their time ran out. "Are you familiar with the term *lazrae*? Or *Azrael*?"

Blane noted the slight widening of Malkovich's eyes. His lips, now a thin line. His face considerably paler.

"What do you know about *Azrael*?" Blane pressed again, slowly. He took another step toward the large man.

Anger flamed in Malkovich's eyes, and he stood abruptly, pointing a meaty finger in Blane's face.

"You're starting to sound mighty accusatory." He continued with more cursing, locking eyes with Blane. Moore rapidly intervened.

"I assure you, Malkovich, it was an innocent question, pertinent to the case. We did not come here with the intention to accuse you of anything. Should we have?"

Moore's unanticipated last words turned the man's face purple, and he bellowed for the guards who had entered the room behind them.

"I will not allow these moronic fools to come in here and throw accusations at me. You made it clear that you had questions about

Harris, and I am just as much a victim as he was! Now"—he directed his gaze back to Moore and Blane—"you will be escorted from—"

Moore held up a hand. "We have a final question for you."

Blane walked toward him again, holding a picture of Ms. Dixon. The man sat down heavily, breathing hard. He glared as Blane spoke.

"This is a nurse who cared for Harris before he died," Blane began, handing him the picture, "and it is possible that she was targeted by the same—"

All at once, the big man sat up straighter in his chair, his eyes widening. "Her," he gasped, his face turning paler. He looked frantically behind them, and Blane's hand closed around his gun.

"But she's—"

His words were cut off as a bullet sliced through the air, doubling him over and shattering the wall of glass behind him. Blane and Moore fell to the ground, firing their guns in tandem.

Blane aimed for the man who had been their guide—the weasel with glasses. The one who had been staring at him. The one who had undeniably just shot the politician. And the one Blane was now convinced was Antonov.

Both of his shots missed as the man fled, but Moore's shot at the security guard who had suddenly opened fire on them hit its mark.

Moore jumped to his feet when the gunfire ceased, and he sprinted across the room toward the wounded guard. Blane was beside him in an instant, but before they could react, a bullet tore through the man's skull.

Both men leaped back in alarm, but the two shots Blane anticipated never came.

The sniper's task is done.

Moore instantly radioed for backup, his hand pressed to his earpiece, and Blane followed his gaze to James Malkovich sitting deathly still in his chair.

Blane grabbed Moore's arm and relayed his intention as a security team burst into the room and police sirens screamed in the streets below. He needed to follow the key to all this: the man who had escaped.

Moore's eyes widened, but his protest was cut short when one of the officers pulled him aside, demanding an explanation.

Blane took his moment of opportunity to slip past the rest of the law enforcement officers pouring into the room. He saw officers tending to the unconscious Grant Rogers in the hallway, but he kept moving.

Antonov would not get away. Not this time.

BLANE BURNS WALKED RAPIDLY through the maze of hallways and into the lobby. People were scrambling from their cubicles and asking what had happened and who had been shot at and who had been shooting.

His trained eyes swept over the room, looking for any calm movements among the panicked chaos. In an attempt at normalcy, Antonov would become conspicuous to anyone who knew what to look for.

Perfect.

Blane saw a familiar figure calmly weaving through the crowds toward the doors of the massive complex. It was him.

Antonov.

With adrenaline kicking in again at full force, Blane started walking after the man as inconspicuously as he could. He needed to achieve the perfect blend of panic yet purpose in his manner of movement so as to not catch Antonov's attention.

In a fluid motion, he plucked a coat from a nearby rack and slipped it on, hoping to disguise his rather overt suit.

As he took step after step, his heart thundering in his ears, Blane grasped the pistol beneath his suit jacket.

This is it.

At last, they exited the building to the sidewalk, hopefully exceeding the sniper's scope if he changed his mind and was back on the hunt.

Blane felt the assassin's gaze flicker backward, and though Blane was looking past him, he sensed Antonov's recognition. His family's killer increased his speed, and Blane increased his stride to stay on him. Antonov rapidly shifted down an alleyway, and when Blane turned, the man had vanished.

But Blane's step did not falter. The assassin's evasive maneuvers were not new to his tracker.

Eyes roving the civilians, Blane caught sight of him again. Antonov had turned on his heel and was making his way back the way he had come, this time with different hair and his suit coat inverted to a barded sweater. Usually, it was an effective way to lose a tail, as pursuers were often so focused on chasing the previous phantom that they completely missed the new one walking right past them.

But not Blane.

Blane avoided looking at him again, and he instead ducked inside a building and watched from the window as Antonov continued on his way with frequent glances over his shoulder. Blane cut across the busy store and exited out of the opposite side onto the next block, his heart pounding in his chest.

He should be coming face to face with Antonov any moment now. He wasn't sure what the man would do, but Blane's pistol was cocked in its holster. And his knife was in his hand.

Thump-thump. He was ready. *Thump-thump*. To meet the man who murdered his wife and child. *Thump-thump*. To at last avenge their deaths. *Thump-thump-thump-thump*.

Any moment now.

A heavy hand suddenly fell on his arm, and when he whirled, the steely eyes of Agent Moore met his gaze.

JOSEPH MOORE HELD EYE contact with Burns, applying pressure to his arm as he guided him toward the side of the street. The tracker's eyes blazed with fury.

Without glancing down, Joseph steadied the knife clenched in Burns's hand.

"What on earth do you think you're doing?" Burns hissed, his desperate eyes sweeping the area in front of them. Joseph glanced forward, but The Archer had vanished into the crowd.

Joseph released his grasp on Burns's arm, and the man staggered in his rage. "I almost had him. And now he's gone. What game are you playing, Moore?"

Joseph once again dug his fingers into Burns's arm. "I need you to listen to me. You've been so focused on what's ahead that you haven't taken care to look behind."

Joseph gazed over his shoulder, observing the four men who had been surgically stalking Blane Burns ever since he left the complex. They were currently situated among the street vendors, casually glancing over the assortment of offered goods.

"There are two more approaching from the south," Joseph murmured, his gaze fixed on the men. He felt Burns shift, and a quick glance at the man's face told him the full weight of the situation had finally hit the Scottish agent.

"They're all armed," Burns breathed. He was rhythmically squeezing the handle of his knife, and Moore gave a slight nod.

"They won't kill us in broad daylight—it's too public an area. But there are too many for us to take them all. We must get back. If we're lucky, one of them will get close enough that my team can grab him. But you will not engage."

Joseph held Burns's eyes for a long moment before they both turned around and started making their way back to Malkovich's complex. He could tell the Scottish man wanted to challenge his orders and face the threat head-on. Doing so would be folly—surely Burns knew that.

But Burns was still squeezing his knife's handle to death in his hand.

Almost there.

Joseph sensed that the hostiles behind them had picked up their pace, but the four men who had been trailing Burns since 17th Street had vanished.

The two men walked rapidly up the crowded street, and their pursuers matched their stride. *Maybe we'll get lucky and nab one of them.* He could tell Burns was reaching the same conclusion.

"Rogers," Joseph began, touching his earpiece in a subtle motion. "Burns and I are being followed coming up Champlain and Columbia. Two hostiles. If possible, I'm calling a code green. Track me."

Joseph heard Rogers's affirmative "Yes, sir," and his mouth quirked. Rogers had been out cold only twenty minutes before.

No matter the state, his team was ready. And each player was really, really good.

The complex was now in sight, and the men were still gaining on Joseph and Burns. Joseph looked for Rogers and officers mixed in with the crowds around them, and he saw a few of the officers he had briefed moving toward them.

Burns glanced over his shoulder, and his faltered step told Joseph all he needed to know.

"They're gone." It hadn't been a question. At Burns's nod, he shook his head. "Rogers, keep the men together and continue searching, but it appears the hostiles have cleared out."

Dejection and anger emanated from the man beside him.

Joseph had more to say, but he knew Burns wasn't ready. After a long moment of silence passed, Joseph watched as Burns shook his head and struggled to sheathe his knife, nearly dropping it on the ground in the process.

"I'm going to...check on Ms. Dixon and her friend," he said quietly. "I'll report to headquarters, but I need to check on them first."

"You do that," Joseph replied. He clapped Burns's arm before he walked back into the building to continue debriefing the officers and to get the situation in hand.

Yes...you do that, Burns.

ALINA SAT BACK WITH a sigh as the movie finished. "Good choice, Ami. That was fantastic!"

Ami smiled. "I hoped you would like it. I've wanted to watch it together for a long time, but we've been so busy lately."

"Yet now when we suddenly have free time, I feel so restless," Alina said with a laugh.

Ami leaned forward, looking at her with searching eyes.

"You did a little extra makeup today, didn't you."

Alina felt herself blush. "Oh no, I hope it isn't too obvious."

"No, not at all! It's very natural." Ami grinned. "Are you dressing up for...someone in particular?"

Alina groaned, holding her hands to her face to cool it down. "Maybe. I feel so stupid. We've only just met, but I—"

"Like him? Might have a crush?" Ami cut in. "I don't blame you. He's very attractive. And sincere. And don't feel stupid," she continued. "He seems like he cares a lot about you."

Alina snorted, looking down at her bottled water. "I mean, that's his job right now. But when all of this is over, he'll be off again to Europe. It's silly of me to even think that..." She trailed off, realizing that Ami's eyes were full of...what she could only describe as deep sadness.

"Ami?" she asked cautiously. "Are you okay?"

"Yes!" Ami said with a quick shake of her head and a forced smile. "I'm sorry, Alina. I... I think I got carried away in my thoughts. I think you're right to be cautious. It might be a good idea to not get too attached, after all."

Before Alina could say a word in reply, a knock suddenly sounded on their door. "I'll get it!" Ami exclaimed, jumping up and brushing roughly at her cheeks.

Ami reached the door and opened it wide. Without looking through the peephole. Before Alina could warn her.

Alina was on her feet, praying Blane Burns would walk through the door. But no one was there.

Crap.

"Ami," she breathed. "Shut the door. Shut the door right now!"

Her eyes wide, Ami grabbed the door and started pushing it closed, but it suddenly swung open with enough force that it threw her into the wall.

Alina screamed as Ami crumpled to the floor and a figure darted into the room.

God. Help me!

It was the man who had attacked her. The Archer.

She backed away from him, fumbling at her back for the holstered pistol that Blane had given her. A desperate gleam lit his eye, but instead of pulling out a gun, he held a cloth in his hand.

She finally loosed the pistol from its holster and held it out, but he rushed at her before she could even aim. She jumped back and screamed again, and suddenly Blane Burns was in the room.

With a bellow and yell for backup, the Scottish man charged at the assassin, knocking into him with his full weight.

Both men crashed to the ground, and Alina watched in horror as Blane slammed Antonov's head into the ground. Blane moved to land another blow, but Antonov slid away and kicked, striking Blane directly in his chest.

Before Blane could catch his breath, Antonov was on his feet. Alina paused, her heart racing and adrenaline pumping through her. She had to do *something* if he tried to attack Blane again.

To her utter shock, the assassin just stared at her, his eyes crazed. Her breath caught in her throat, and she brought the pistol up in both of her hands. Aiming it at him. But her shaking finger never reaching for the trigger.

Suddenly, shouts resounded in the hallway, and his eyes darted back and forth. Between her and the door. Within a split second, he rushed from the room.

She sank to the ground as Blane charged out after him.

Her mind reeling, she crawled toward Ami and was relieved that she was conscious, holding her head and groaning. Alina got to her feet and grabbed an ice pack from the mini freezer, and she wrapped it in a towel before dropping again at her friend's side.

Alina helped her hold the cold compress to her head, and at that moment, Blane came back into the room, breathing heavily.

"Are you okay, lass?" he asked, his eyes full of concern as he analyzed every inch of her. His gaze dropped to Ami, and he was on his knees, gently checking the bruise on her head.

In answer to his question, Ami softly replied, "My head just hurts, but that's all."

Alina was relieved to hear Ami's words, and she likewise saw relief spread across Blane's features.

She finally worked up the courage to ask. "Did you get him?" Blane locked eyes with her and shook his head as two guards walked rapidly into the room.

"Agent Burns, we just found one of ours unconscious in the landing. That guy must have grabbed his key card to reach this floor. Then he was in and out in literally sixty seconds—he knew the exact layout, which room…and we only got him on the motion sensors. We have no idea how he got in so fast without being picked up on our cameras right away or how he managed to elude us all so quickly in his escape."

Blane's eyes closed, and Alina feared he was balancing on a very thin line. "He's the best of the best. You did all you could," Blane said with a slow exhale. The men nodded and left the room, calling in the incident to headquarters.

Blane got to his feet, and together, he and Alina helped Ami onto her bed. "You're a nurse," he said to Alina quietly. "Should we get a medical team in here?"

Alina checked her friend's pupils and did a few neurological assessments before shaking her head. "I think she just needs to rest. I'll keep monitoring for any signs of head trauma."

With the immediate danger over, Alina suddenly felt the terror she had been holding off course through her, and she sat down hard on her own bed.

Blane looked at her, weariness and concern battling each other in his bloodshot eyes.

He looks like he needs to sit for a very long time, too.

Instead, he spoke softly. "How did he get into the room?" he asked, rubbing his hands over his eyes.

"Ami was distracted and opened the door before she checked," Alina replied. "I'm so sorry that I didn't do anything—"

"No!" he interrupted, his voice raised. Glancing at Ami, he lowered his tone once again. "I should have been here." He suddenly gave a sharp exhale.

"We tried to question Malkovich, and he was killed. Right in front of us."

Alina gasped at his words.

"It was Antonov, and I didn't realize it in time. I pursued him, but… I had to lose him. There were others, and I…" He stopped, his

98

voice sounding strained and dropping even lower into a whisper. He sank down beside her, sitting on the edge of her bed.

"And now he almost hurt you, and I lost him again."

He looked defeated. Alone. Her heart went out to him, and without thinking, she gently clasped his big hand.

He never looked at her, but his warm, firm fingers slowly squeezed hers.

"But you did get here," she said softly. He looked at her then, and the vulnerable gratitude in his eyes made her squeeze his hand back.

His ringing phone broke the silent moment, and he gently pulled his hand away as he answered. Her fingers felt so cold.

She could hear Joseph on the other end of the line, but Blane stood up and walked into the bathroom so he didn't disturb Ami. Alina was glad to see that she was resting.

When he returned, he quietly relayed that Joseph had sent Lily Herne on her way back to the hotel as soon as he heard what had happened. Lily would sleep in their room tonight, and the hallway would be placed on lockdown and fortified with more agents. Blane said that Joseph was furious at how the situation was handled and that he was relieved that she and Ami were all right.

"He wants me to come back in, as soon as you and Ami are... settled," Blane finished.

"All right," Alina said slowly, suddenly panicked at the idea of him leaving. Just then, Lily's commanding voice in the hallway drew her attention, and she felt a little more at peace with the idea.

Blane rose to open the door, and after he and Alina explained what had happened and Lily had hugged Alina so tightly Alina struggled to breathe, Blane said goodbye and left the room.

Lily reported that she had personally overseen the security changes being made and that there was no possible way Antonov could get back inside. She next ordered Alina to get ready for bed before going over to check on Ami.

As Alina closed and locked the bathroom door, she heard Lily admitting a new team of agents to inspect the scene and to collect any evidence Antonov had left behind.

Alina showered, brushed her teeth, and was about to crawl into bed to face a night of almost-certain nightmares when a thought crossed her mind. Grabbing her bathrobe, she crossed the room to where Lily was setting up a sleeping bag on the floor.

"Would you be willing to set this out in the hallway, or just toss it out there?" Alina asked, heat spreading over her face. When Lily's expression of utter confusion demanded that Alina be more specific, she quickly clarified. "It's just in case Blane sleeps out there again—he did last night—and needs it."

Lily arched an eyebrow before a small smile tweaked the corner of her mouth. She nodded, and soon the bathrobe was in a dignified pile of fluff on the floor in the hallway.

Alina collapsed on her bed in a heap, more exhausted and horrified each time she relived Antonov bursting into the room. And Ami crashing into the wall.

When she closed her eyes, mercifully the image of the sleeping Scottish man from the night before filled her mind, and him squeezing her hand elevated her thoughts from her seemingly inescapable fear.

With a prayer, she closed her eyes. As her mother's lullaby drifted through her mind, sleep took her.

BLANE DROVE TOWARD THE FBI building.

He was shaking.

You missed him. Twice.

His palms were sweating.

She could have been killed.

His heart racing.

Burns, you fool.

He knew he could have been captured or killed earlier that day. His obsession with getting Antonov had completely blinded him to his surroundings. He had lost his touch within the last few years, and it had nearly cost him his life. Then, had he waited just five minutes more before checking on the two women under his protection, they could have both been murdered.

And there would have been two more lives lost under his care to add to his count.

Maybe they were wrong to bring me in.

He strangled the steering wheel, remembering.

Remembering. His family on the road. Rage transforming him, blinding him, burning him.

He always felt like he was burning.

Running to his handler at MI5. Being told that their deaths were because of him...because of his lack of caution and his reck-lessness. Being informed that he was suspended from active duty. Realizing everything of any worth in his life was gone.

Then there was the blind rage. The punch. The assault. The blackness.

By some stroke of luck, he had not touched alcohol after that. Alcohol had made his dad a monster and had claimed his very life in the end, and Blane had promised his mum he would never touch the stuff. And he hadn't. But oh, had he been close.

Blane slammed on his brakes as he nearly ran a red light, earning himself a chorus of horns and rude gestures from surrounding cars.

Focus, Burns. Focus.

Soon enough, Blane was parked at the FBI building, his head resting on the steering wheel. The burning and despair were choking him again as he relived the last few hours.

He dragged himself from the car and walked toward the building.

Before he knew it, Blane came face-to-face with Joseph Moore.

"Moore," Blane began, sucking in a breath. "I just came from the—"

Moore abruptly cut him off, his voice strained past the point of breaking. "How? The security was foolproof. There was no way in—I organized it myself. There was no way."

Blane answered him quickly. "He knocked out one of the circu-lating guards and stole his card to reach the floor, but he didn't even bother to disable the cameras and other obvious security measures. Then Ms. Everly opened the door. That's how he got in their room. He was in and out so fast, running like a madman, as I heard said."

Moore stared at him, a calculating look in his eyes. "So. He didn't even have a plan. He just saw a chance to kill her and took it."

"There's more," Blane rumbled quietly. "He knew exactly where to go—down to the right room. He had the blueprint of our entire floor in his head. When I was leaving, I saw the entire team of guards being replaced... I assume on your orders."

"Yes. In case any of them were compromised. I just can hardly believe..." The older agent trailed off as his phone beeped, and he rapidly whipped it out. Blane stared at him in alarm as the expression on his face became one of absolute confusion.

"Antonov left something behind—a cloth on the floor," Moore began. "The lab just finished. It was soaked with chloroform."

"Chloroform!" Blane exclaimed. His mind reeled in shock. "He was planning to take her?"

"It certainly looks that way," Moore replied grimly. Both men were silent for a moment, lost in an onslaught of thoughts.

"That doesn't make any sense," Blane said finally, forcefully rubbing his forehead in his frustration.

"We'll figure this out, Burns," Moore responded, briefly clasping his shoulder. "But we need to keep our heads. And we must work as a team if we hope to keep her safe."

Blane fell silent as they began walking to the conference room, knowing to what the agent was referring. After a painstaking moment, he couldn't put it off any longer.

"Sir, I know that my behavior earlier today was...reckless. I apologize. It won't happen again. And...thank you for watching my back."

Moore was silent, as if he knew Blane was not finished.

"And I did not mention this before, but thanks for bringing me in after...everything. I'm sure you've heard the rumors."

Moore stopped walking and looked at him, a knowing look in his piercing eyes.

"If anyone is going to violently lash out at a superior, it's a man who went through the horrors you did. In fact, I wouldn't be sure I could trust you now if you hadn't." Moore gave him a nod, and they continued walking. "You do anything for those you care about, no matter the consequences. You…do what needs done. And you cannot falter in your next move. You must not, Burns. Or else that will multiply your failures and bury you even deeper in the ground."

Moore's words left Blane's thoughts in even greater turmoil. Each word was loaded with…a cold regret, with a hardness. Blane knew the older agent was purposefully keeping something from him, and whether that secret dealt with Moore's true loyalties, Blane had no idea.

No one can be trusted.

At last, the two men reached the conference room, and after debriefing the rest of the team, Blane collapsed in his chair. Exhaustion hit him like a brick wall.

Silence descended, heavy in the room. Then the tech man drummed his fingers on the table, and he abruptly spoke.

"Well, I for one had success today!" With that, he began briefing the agents on what he termed his "inevitable and super cool breakthrough that would in fact change the game."

As he rattled off words like a machine gun, Blane sat forward in his chair. He was suddenly very focused, and he felt a burst of energy surge through him.

"So, as you know, *lazrae* and *Azrael* were giving us problems. It is clearly a codename of some sort. But it isn't in any encrypted government, military, terrorist, or civilian databases, and all searches in every possible nook and cranny of the Web were turning up nothing at all relevant."

Donáll straightened his tie and licked his lips. Blane was surprised to see that he did not have a cup of coffee beside him. He thought the man breathed the stuff.

"And, though I am beginning to peel back the layers, the Kratos database is still closed to me. I will continue in my efforts."

With this last declaration, Donáll immediately began clicking things on his laptop, and he even started humming as he chewed his gum.

Blane stared at the tech man. He glanced around the room. Moore was rubbing the crease between his eyes and slowly shaking his head, Davies was doing his best to stay calm, and Rogers was giving Donáll an unpleasant stare. Before anyone could say a word, Moore held up a hand. The older agent stood, and, after he had given everyone a knowing nod, he approached the jumpy man.

Moore got within a few feet of him, and Donáll didn't seem to care or notice. He just kept rapidly typing. And clicking things. And incessantly chewing his gum.

This is infuriating.

Moore leaned down close to Donáll, and Blane heard a snort. He glanced over to see Davies suppressing a laugh. Rogers was still glaring.

With a merry twinkle in his eye, Moore spoke, his voice only a soft murmur. "Donáll?"

The tech man almost fell out of his seat, and from the cessation of his obnoxious chewing, it was clear that he had accidentally swallowed his gum. Donáll stared at Moore accusingly.

"WHAT?" he demanded.

"The breakthrough, my friend? WHAT'S THE BREAKTHROUGH?"

Donáll jumped at the intensity of Moore's question, but then he smiled and rapidly stood up.

"Right, the breakthrough. Yes. Uh-huh. Let's begin."

Within a few minutes, Donáll had shared his findings with the room. Once he had heard Malkovich had been killed, Donáll had meticulously combed through both the politician's phone records and online presence. Numerous "shady" calls and encrypted communications proved that Malkovich's role in Kratos had been greater than just being a victim of its game.

With this new angle, Donáll had hacked through Malkovich's "high school-level firewalls" and had found records of massive funding for the US HAARP Research Facility based in Alaska.

Moore spoke up. "The High Frequency Active Auroral Research Program is run by the US military, specifically the Air Force and Navy, and its public purpose is to study the ionosphere. Lots of controversy has surrounded HAARP in recent months, and it was even in danger of being shut down."

A thrill coursed through Blane, and he jumped into the conversation. "HAARP is very familiar to MI5. When we had been working to crack Kratos, its name came up many times. There were rumors that Kratos had been funding secret militant research there—a weapon that is undetectable and lethal with even the briefest contact."

"Why was the investigation closed?" Davies spoke up. "Nothing ever stuck?"

Blane continued. "Aye. It is a stronghold. Several HAARP officials we spoke to were clearly corrupt, but they were well-protected. Various agencies tried—MI5, the CIA, and others—all with different angles of attack. But no one could touch them or even get close to the facility. With that level of invincibility, we were certain Kratos was protecting them. We could never get close enough. By that point in our investigation, I had just pieced together Antonov's identity. With me tracking him across Europe and my team focusing on a potential Kratos attack in London, HAARP was placed on file for later investigation."

Moore was nodding. "And then Antonov happened, and here we are."

Blane nodded back, all of his energy directed into one mental command.

Focus.

Rogers spoke up. "What has changed? Won't HAARP be as impenetrable now as it was five years ago?"

Donáll replied, "Now HAARP just lost one of its primary donors. Malkovich may also have been Kratos's direct contact to HAARP, overseeing the facility's operations and reporting back. At this time, HAARP will be looking to fill the hole. They'll be distracted."

"Hang on," Davies cut in. "I see a problem here. Why would Kratos take out their main man, especially without having a replacement? Shooting him in broad daylight with FBI present at the scene moved him to the top of our priority list. And we only now uncovered his connection to both Kratos and HAARP. This looks like a setup."

Moore answered slowly. "I agree. It seems too easy. The connection was too carefully preserved for us."

Blane spoke up. "Aye, unless Malkovich's assassination was not part of the plan."

Everyone looked at him in surprise, and Blane cleared his throat before continuing. "One part of this equation that continues to not fit is Ms. Dixon's involvement. Antonov never misses his mark. Never. Even when interrupted with Harris's interrogation, he still finished him off quickly and efficiently. Ms. Dixon was his final target that night, yet he didn't kill her. She saw his face, she heard *lazrae*...and yet he never finished the job. What scared him? And why did he come to the safe house this afternoon with the intent to abduct and not to kill her? That strays even further from his usual methods. It doesn't make any sense."

"But what does the girl have to do with Malkovich's murder?" Rogers challenged. "You still haven't addressed that."

Blane stared at him. "What if Kratos had Antonov kill Malkovich because of Ms. Dixon?" He turned to look at Moore. "You heard what he said right before he was shot. He recognized her. He knew her. Maybe Antonov was there in case Malkovich lost his nerve and slipped up. And the exact moment he was killed was when he recognized Ms. Dixon and likely deviated from Kratos's script."

Moore spoke, a hardness in his voice. "Why is Ms. Dixon such a major player here?"

Rogers interjected. "Whatever the reason, she must remain with us. Today proved that she is not safe alone, even in one of our most secure locations."

"I agree," Davies replied. "And I think she should come with us when we look into this HAARP business. Fred and I finished up at Clay Jones's house this afternoon. But get this, the place was too neat, almost sterile. Kratos must have been there to remove anything that the PI dug up for Harris. However," Davies paused, a twinkle in his eye, "they were too quick, and they missed something big. You know the rain we had last night? It uncovered a package Jones buried in his garden, and there was a small flash drive inside. As you could probably guess by this point, HAARP research was the featured content on the drive. Looks like Harris had a change of heart and had Jones trying to find a weakness in the facility that he could use to expose Kratos."

"So we know for a fact that HAARP is an integral part of Kratos's web, or at least one of its many webs," Blane said. "I would wager that *Azrael* is a code name for some operation or for someone there."

"Exactly," Davies affirmed.

"All right then, folks," Moore said in a commanding voice, drawing all eyes to himself. "This somewhat extends past our reach, as the CIA would normally handle hostile organizations with a global presence. However, I am going to present our case to some select higher-ups and see if we can't make some travel plans. And I'd like to add that my trust doesn't have a far reach outside of the people in this room. Kratos could be anywhere and anyone, so we must be as... independent in this as possible."

Blane agreed with him completely. The less people involved and knowledgeable of their plans, the better.

"I believe that is all. Get some sleep. I intend for us to fly out tomorrow if this thing gets approved." Moore left the room, his hand up at his earpiece.

Davies was grinning widely. "Aww yeah, guys, we're going to Alaska!" The energetic blond man was trying and failing to fist pump the ever-serious Rogers. He then leaned toward Blane. Blane obediently raised his fist, and Davies winced at the impact.

Blane's smile immediately fled. "Sorry, I forgot that we don't actually... Is your hand okay?"

Davies stared at him. "Yeah, dude, you really went for it there. That's solid. Nice." Davies grinned again and walked out of the room with a wave. Rogers soon followed without a backward glance.

Blane sat in the empty room for a moment, his warring emotions colliding with each other. He was thrilled that they were getting close to Kratos, but he was afraid. After the day's events, he felt utterly unprepared to keep Ms. Dixon safe.

And he couldn't let anyone else die on his watch. He wouldn't be able to bear it.

Blane drove back to the hotel and made his way through the building to reach the security room. The new agents said all had been quiet, and Blane quickly checked in with the additional men posted around the hotel. He finally made it to their floor, but he froze when something out of place in the hallway caught his eye.

The hammering of his heart slowed when he recognized Ms. Dixon's robe.

That's nice.

Blane readied himself for the night then made his way into the hallway with his pillow, his scratchy hotel blanket, and his gun. He positioned himself across from the girls' room once again, being sure to wave at the security camera so that the now trigger-eager team would be aware of his presence. If Antonov somehow got in again, Blane would be waiting.

Minutes passed, and Blane stared awkwardly at the robe beside him.

Is it appropriate to use it? Would it be rude to not?

He sat, debating. Finally, he pulled it across his lap. *Okay. Fine. That'll work fine.*

Soon, with Ms. Dixon's smile lightening the dark thoughts lingering in his mind, sleep took him.

CHAPTER SIX

ALASKA?

Alina was embarrassed, but she was bursting with excitement at the thought. She looked briefly away from Blane to Ami, who was giving her a knowing smile. She could feel a massive smile spreading across her face.

Snap out of it. This is not a holiday. This is a serious development in the case… Stop being so excited!

But she had only known anxiety and fear for the past four days, and she was grateful for the physical and mental relief the joy procured.

At the sound of her name, she startled and glanced sheepishly into the intense gaze of the Scottish man in front of her.

"Ms. Dixon. Are you listening to me?"

She stuttered around for a moment before giving up. "No. I'm sorry."

She flinched at her inattentiveness as he took a deep, calming breath. "We have no idea what we will find there, and it will be danger-ous." His voice suddenly dropped lower, and his eyes took on a differ-ent look that momentarily took her breath away. "But this time, I am not going to leave your side. As I said before, we'll be stuck together."

"Like glue?" she offered with a smile.

"Aye," he replied. Though his mouth was set in a grim line, she saw a twinkle in his eyes.

Then Joseph was walking toward them.

"If everybody is packed, let's head out. I have a buddy who's got a plane. Name's Clyde Henry, but we call him Hawk. He's waiting at a remote little takeoff strip out of the city. Only a few of us are going—Donáll, Davies, Rogers, myself, and you three. We cannot risk large numbers on this…mission."

Joseph's eyes were wide, his expression very serious. He was rubbing his hand over his jaw. Then his attention was once again focused on the three of them. "Well, let's get going—" he began, starting to walk away.

"Hold on, Moore," Blane cut him off, studying him with careful curiosity. "This mission has been sanctioned by your director, right?"

Alina turned her attention back to Joseph, who couldn't quite meet Blane's eye and instead focused his attention on the wall behind them.

He cleared his throat. "Uh, well, let's just say that I do not have good standing with the FBI director. Name of Turne. He would never sanction this mission. In fact, he would probably just hand it over to the CIA, anyway. I don't think I fully trust him." Joseph was suddenly staring at Blane. "In fact, I do not believe I trust him at all." With that, he began walking away again.

"So what trick did you pull to allow us to take a team to Alaska?" Blane pressed, studying his retreating back.

"We're all due for some well-earned holiday," Joseph called over his shoulder. "Let's move!" He was gone.

Alina and Ami traded a glance before Alina peeked at Blane. Annoyance, stress, and amusement were flitting across his face all at once. He turned to them, signaling them to grab their luggage, and they were off.

Glancing back down the hallway, she felt a shudder course through her. She was relieved they were leaving.

She would never forget the horror of Ami slamming into the wall. Or the desperate and wild gleam in Antonov's eye when he leaped at her.

BLANE SAT IN THE aisle seat with Ms. Dixon beside him, staring out the window. He felt very cramped. His years of flying had always involved bigger planes with seats made for bigger people. He was practically folded in on himself to fit in the tight space.

The pilot was old and too cheerful, but he looked capable. At least Blane thought so. And Moore seemed to trust him. So Blane decided he would have to trust him as well and be done with it.

And he was getting the impression that Ms. Dixon had never flown before. During takeoff, she had been clutching the sides of her seat like her life depended on it, and her foot had been continuously tapping.

What she assumed was the floor as she tapped was actually the top of his left foot, but he kept it to himself. He could ignore the tapping, and he did not want to cause unnecessary embarrassment.

Now, glancing at her out of the corner of his eye, she seemed entranced by the wing of the jet cutting through the golden-lined clouds.

He was enchanted by her nervous wonder. Something mundane to him was magical to her, and he found himself smiling. Isla had always loved flying. Isla. His wife.

And Blane was lost in memories.

He was remembering her smile, her laugh, his wee child's toothy grin. They were so real to him he thought he could reach out and touch them. He wanted to smell her hair. Isla always washed it with shampoo that smelled of lilacs, and it always dried in shimmering red waves.

Blane relished each memory as it played across his mind's eye, warming him in a way he had not known for so long.

It was a golden, sunny day. He was throwing his daughter up in the air and catching her—over and over again as she giggled and called him Da-da. He was hugging and kissing both of them.

And then he was cradling their dead bodies and sobbing into their bloodstained hair.

Despite his best efforts, he couldn't hold back a harsh gasp. He was on his feet, his face turned away before Ms. Dixon could look into his eyes. He didn't want her to see him like this. So broken and raw. Goodness knew she had seen too much of that already.

Mercifully, she did not say anything, though he knew.

She knew.

He mumbled something about the lavvy and moved toward the back of the plane, his hand violently rubbing his head to force out the memories as best he could.

But sweet Olivia remained. His poor child. His poor little girl.

His heart was crying out for something…anything…to hold on to. But God had abandoned him long ago. Shaking, he reached for the door to the toilet and stopped, realizing it was occupied.

He leaned against a row of seats, slowly regaining his composure and fighting for the slow, life-sustaining burn. The rhythm and heartbeat of his existence.

His attention snapped to the present as the tiny door of the lavvy swung open and Ms. Everly emerged.

She started at his unexpected presence, alarm flashing through her wide eyes.

"Oh, I'm sorry, Ms. Everly," Blane began quickly. "I did not mean to be startling you. I just was, uh, waiting for…"

"No, you're fine," she responded brightly—a sharp contrast to the tears that shimmered in her eyes. She attempted to scurry around him, but he reached out and touched her arm.

Her eyes widened again, but something else flashed in them this time. Fear.

"Are you okay, lass?" he asked as gently as he could.

"Yes, thank you. I just do not think I'm completely over what happened at…at the hotel. I don't know if I ever was able to thank you for rescuing us. So thank you, Blane."

She held his gaze for a moment more, and then she was carefully making her way back down the aisle toward Davies and her seat.

Blane could not shake the sadness and the fear that had burdened her gaze. There was a hopelessness there.

Just like the hopelessness he saw in his own eyes every time he looked in a mirror.

Blane rapidly ducked into the lavvy, secured the door behind him, and took deep breaths as he locked his hands on the tiny sink.

Only a moment. A breath. Then another. And finally, HAARP was central in his mind.

The mission.

Good. Focus on the mission.

A quick glance in the mirror told him the weakness was gone. All he saw in his eyes now was fierce, burning determination.

They were closer than ever to breaching the fortifications locking Kratos away from their reach. And once they stripped down its walls, everyone inside would be exposed.

Blane took a breath. Antonov would be exposed. And that's when Blane would take him down. Once and for all.

Exiting the lavvy, Blane walked a few paces to Moore and reviewed the plan for once they touched down near Chitina.

They would land in a remote field to avoid as much attention as possible. From there, they would meet two of Moore's retired FBI mates who would take them to a safe house. Then the team would strategize how to best infiltrate HAARP.

It was not much of a plan. But it was something. Something for Blane to mull over, to consider every possible angle, every potential situation.

Giving Moore a rapid nod, he returned to Ms. Dixon's side.

As he sat, he noticed her straighten in her seat.

As he turned toward her, his eyes met hers. She was looking at him, smiling that gentle smile. That beautiful smile that promised she understood everything and held blame for nothing. Blane was afraid of getting lost in it.

Rapidly, he pulled out his phone. He needed a distraction. Anything.

Then he heard her hesitant voice, breaking through his scattered concentration.

"I was wondering…if you wanted to talk. To tell me about them. I would love to know what they were like."

She continued to look out the window as she spoke, as if she was afraid she would startle him. She only turned to face him when she finished speaking.

For a reason unknown to him, he knew exactly what she meant. She wanted to hear about his wife. She wanted to know about Olivia. And he had no idea why, but he wanted to tell her.

"My wife. Isla. She was the most beautiful woman I've ever seen. Her eyes were so bright and green, and her skin was like ivory. Her hair was…like ripe strawberries brought in on a warm summer day."

Blane expected his voice to break with emotion, but with a strength he didn't know he had left, he pressed onward. He wanted to tell this woman everything about them.

"She was so...full of life. And faith. She wanted everyone around her to be as joyful as she was. And my...my child. A girl. We named her Olivia. She had my eyes and her mother's hair. And I..." He trailed off, his voice breaking at last.

"And I loved them both so much," he finally whispered. He couldn't look up to meet her gaze. He just cradled his head in his hands.

Ms. Dixon sat without a word, but after a moment, he felt her hand warm his arm. And the warmth spread through him, softening the grief. He felt his own hand reach to cover hers, and they sat for an endless moment.

Him remembering. And her just near him, silently supporting him. And he suddenly felt himself turning toward her.

When his eyes finally met hers, his heart leaped into his throat.

He was afraid he could kiss her. This caring lass. Those eyes.

What am I doing?

He quickly cleared his throat and sat up straight, releasing his hold on her hand. She gently removed hers from his arm, and she sank back against her seat.

"Thank you for...for telling me about them, Blane."

He could only manage a quiet "Aye."

He was acutely aware that this woman had broken through every barrier of mistrust he had initially held against her. Innocence radiated from her like beams of light, and Blane was shocked at how quickly his doubts had dissipated. That smile seemed to melt every-thing away. And he had almost kissed her.

Blane rubbed a hand down his beard, his thoughts drifting into his past once more. Sudden shame overwhelmed him as Isla centered in his mind. Gritting his teeth, he forced himself to obliterate Ms. Dixon's smile from his thoughts.

Isla was his wife.

He knew one thing for certain. He could not be distracted with these debilitating thoughts if he hoped to succeed in protecting Ms. Dixon. Her and everyone else.

Hawk's voice mercifully rescued him from his manic mind as it resounded over the intercom, alerting the passengers that they would soon be landing.

Blane was relieved. *Take a deep breath.*

Let it out.

At last, they were close. To action. And close to making Kratos bleed, starting with ripping out whatever was hidden in the back rooms of HAARP.

FOR THE REMAINDER OF the flight, Alina relived the moment. She was sure that Blane had almost kissed her. Then she cringed through the moment he didn't and instead seemed to cut himself off from her. As well he should—he had just told her about his wife. She never wanted to come between him and his memory of her.

Even though she feared she was falling in love with him.

Overwhelmed by her thoughts, she was relieved when Hawk finally brought the taxiing plane to a halt in an open field.

As soon as she stepped out into the alpine air, she was captivated by the mountainous landscape.

The earth beneath her fur-topped boots was a patchwork of frozen ground and white snow, and the sunlight glittered on icy crystals as far as her eyes could see.

Even as a little girl, she had always dreamt of coming here. And Alaska was just as beautiful in person as she had imagined it.

Pulling her chocolate-colored coat around her and relishing the softness of the fur trim on her skin, Alina glanced at her best friend.

Ami's eyes were full of wonder as she stared at their surroundings. Like Alina, Ami had never traveled so far before. This was a new and wonderful experience for both of them.

Alaska.

One of the reasons this state was so magical to her was that it was native to her favorite animal—sea otters. She absolutely loved the unique bond the mothers had with their pups.

Ami had always endured the countless sea otter videos Alina found with such patience, and the frivolous thought made Alina smile.

She hoped that, at some point, they would be able to see one. But she scolded herself, recognizing that that should be the last thing on her mind in the days to come.

Just then, two big SUVs pulled up. Joseph's retired friend, nicknamed Patch due to an eye-patch covering his left eye, jumped out of one. Another man, most likely the Pete character Joseph had described, clambered out of the other.

She smiled as she watched Joseph, Hawk, and the two new men embrace and clap each other on the back. Then she laughed out loud as the three men grabbed Joseph and attempted to lift him off the ground. She had never heard the older agent laugh so loudly.

Alina, Blane, Ami, and Owen climbed into the first SUV that Patch was driving, and Alina was glad to see Joseph slide into the passenger's seat. With Blane beside her and Joseph within her line of vision, Alina felt simply and wholly safe.

She watched the pine-studded land out of the window as the vehicles drove down the lonely road. The mountains in the distance caught and held her gaze, with their peaks jutting into the sky like glittering tips of ice-topped spears. As she stared in awe, she felt the tension and the terror of the last week rise and drift away in the sparkling, crystal wind.

She clasped her hands.

Thank You, God. All of this is beautiful. And I know Your hands made it all. Thank You for the beauty. And for the peace.

Her thoughts and prayers lingered for a moment before Owen abruptly snagged her attention.

"Ms. Dixon, I, uh, well, let's see here." His brows were furrowed in concentration, and she was certain he was trying to think up something...anything...to say. He was sitting in the seat in front of her, his neck craned back in order to make eye contact. "Do you... uh, like...um, uh...board games?"

Owen didn't make eye contact when he asked the question, but as soon as he finished, he looked back at her, a hesitant and hopeful smile on his face.

Alina laughed at his expression, and her own eyebrows knit together. It was a completely random question, and it had caught her off guard.

"Uh, well, yes, but I am often so lazy that Ami and I choose to watch movies instead when we can relax. But I have always liked the game *Clue*."

His face brightened. "I usually get a little restless during movies, but I love that game too!" He paused. "And *Battleship*. Always loved that one. Except one time I was playing with my little brother and I got so mad when he—"

Alina loved listening to Owen's rampage about his little brother's antics, but a sudden movement to her left caught her eye. Blane was leaning forward toward the seat in front of him where Ami was sitting. But then Owen asked her a question about hide-and-seek as a childhood game, and she was back, fully invested in the conversation.

"Well, good to know. Maybe when all this is over, we can spend some well-earned time playing group games," Owen said at last, giving her his boyish grin. Alina couldn't resist smiling back. His upbeat everything was contagious.

As she settled back, she saw Owen slightly turn his head toward Ami, and Ami turned to him and gave him a grateful smile.

And did he just wink in return?

It was a weird situation. She glanced at Blane, but he was sitting, stone-faced, staring at his phone.

Huh. Well, whatever that was.

The rest of the drive passed uneventfully, and they were soon in the small Alaskan town of Chitina. Approximately two hours from HAARP, according to Joseph.

Patch pulled up to an unassuming gray building set a distance away from the center of the town and punched a button on a remote, opening massive garage doors. He pulled the vehicle in one side of the garage, and Pete soon pulled beside them.

As soon as the team climbed out of the vehicles, the two retired FBI agents ushered everyone inside the living portion of the safe house.

Alina's eyes explored what she assumed to be some sort of living room. There was a worn table with dirty coffee mugs perched in the center, three sumptuous-looking couches pushed over against the far wall, a few folding chairs, an old television set, a radio, and absolutely no windows. There appeared to be lots of dirty dishes scattered around the place too. Lots and lots of dirty dishes.

Joseph raised an eyebrow. "Really, guys? I gave you a full day's notice we were coming. You two are such slobs."

Deep chuckles resonated throughout the room, and Joseph ducked as Pete chucked a pillow at his head.

"Merry Christmas, by the way. Sorry, we didn't think ahead to get you all presents!" Patch announced.

Shock descended on Alina as she suddenly realized that December 25 had come without her realizing it.

"Don't worry about it, guys. And thanks for the reminder," Joseph responded, smiling at Patch. "I think we all forgot what time of the year it is, especially with everything…everything that has happened. Merry Christmas, everyone."

Alina joined in with the resounding "Merry Christmas!" from around the room, warmth flowing through her.

Thank You for Your Son, Lord.

"Oh, all is not lost! I think we have some of that there ginger-snap coffee from last Christmas, Patch!" Pete exclaimed jollily.

An hour later, they were all sitting at the kitchen table. Alina glanced at the coffee in her cup, and she risked another tentative sniff.

Nope. Something was off with the stuff. *Uh-uh. Gingersnap, yeah right. More like gingercrap.*

They were seated and waiting for the first of many planning sessions where they would strategize their best plan for infiltrating HAARP. But they were waiting for Patch, who apparently had to prepare a load of laundry which had been a long time in starting.

Gross.

She peeked at Ami, and she could see that Ami wasn't touching the coffee, either. Their eyes met, and they both tried to hide their smiles.

Just then, Patch arrived carrying a sleek remote in his hand. Alina stared at him and then at the remote. It didn't seem to fit with the dated television set in the living room or anything else in the safe house that they had seen so far.

Suddenly, Patch aimed the remote at the counter and shelves lining the wall in front of them. Alina stared in awe as the whole structure swung inward, spinning around to reveal a wall of advanced-looking computers, camera systems, and other technology.

Joseph whistled. "Looks like some money went into this place since I was last here."

Pete chuckled. "Only the finest for two gents surveying one of the most highly secretive and corrupt federal research facilities in the United States."

Alina felt a terrifying thrill course through her, and her eyes locked with Blane's. They were here.

Really here.

One step closer to understanding everything. And one step closer to taking down the organization that had killed Blane's family and that had almost killed her.

BLANE FINALLY SAT BACK in his seat as the briefing process began.

He had been stewing over his brief conversation with Ms. Everly on the plane for hours. He had also been mulling over the odd request she had asked of him during the drive.

But now, as they were starting to plot their plan of attack, Blane devoted every ounce of his focus to the task.

The pilot had left the safe house for the ambiguous purpose of "plane maintenance," and Moore had finished filling in Patch and Pete about the case thus far.

Patch stood. "Well, if you have good reason and the proper authorization to get into HAARP, then that will be just peachy. So, Joey, are you authorized for this?"

Moore looked a bit uncomfortable, though whether the discomfort came from the obvious lack of authorization their team had or from the use of "Joey" as a nickname, Blane was not sure.

"Well, guys," Moore began, "when I told you we were coming for HAARP, I didn't quite tell you everything. Our presence here, in fact, is quite unauthorized and quite secretive. I did not want to worr—"

Pete abruptly let loose a raucous laugh. "Of course, we knew that this was a secret mission. Me old mate there was simply trying to get a rise out o' you."

Blane was a little taken aback by what he could only assume was a failed attempt at a Scottish accent. *What is this?*

Patch resumed. "In preparation for your arrival, we actually began monitoring the facility even more closely than we already had been. You see," he began, addressing Ms. Dixon and Ms. Everly with a wink, "us old fogies have permanently retired here to keep tabs on this group of shady scientists. You're all in luck."

Pete picked up where Patch left off. "As you are undoubtedly aware, I work quite legally there as a janitor. It's an excellent way to monitor all sorts of things up close and personal, to see the new faces, and to get very detailed layouts of the floor plans. Yeah, that's right—there's not just rows of antennas here. There's a whole facility, though its presence is not publicly known. While I'm inside, my man Patch here monitors all the feeds that I've secretly placed during my more…thorough cleaning jobs. All this techy stuff is actually his." The man paused for a breath before he resumed.

"Anyway, HAARP just got some new jumpy kid in management. It seems something—probably that politician's death Joey was telling us about—sped along his initiation. He is still very out of his element. Perfect time to strike."

Donáll burst out laughing, and Blane and the others stared at him. "That was great! You know, HAARP is a very chemistry-based facility, and he said 'element,' so, yeah. It was funny."

Donáll did not seem at all bothered by the lack of a reaction his explanation generated, but he did seem to be waiting for some sort of response.

"Um, yes, Donáll, thank you for your…dazzling insight," Moore said finally, his eyebrows raised and an amused smile playing across his face.

"Truly a hardcore intellect there, man," Davies joined in.

"Okay, everybody focus!" Pete barked out, and the room was silent once again. "Our time to get inside is during one of the nights when this new guy is in place. His name is Fred Montage. Anyway, we'll work with your tech man to tell him where he needs to mess with footage and cameras inside HAARP. Now we haven't been able to access all of the inside cameras, so we don't have a solid idea where any of the truly incriminating stuff is."

"Actually, Lestor Donáll here, my 'tech man,' knows HAARP like the inside of his ancient, recycled, Styrofoam coffee cup," Moore said with an obvious shudder. "He actually trained and completed research there before coming to work in the Transnational Unit with me."

"It's true!" Donáll piped up, his attention still arrested by whatever was doing a jig across his laptop screen.

Patch and Pete both looked impressed. "That's neat," Pete said finally. "Well, sonny, you had best get working on accessing the cameras—"

"Already done," Donáll sang. "I got every one of them."

The two retired agents glanced at each other, then at Moore, and then at Donáll again. After a long moment passed, Patch resumed the session.

"Joey, you need to get in contact with someone back home. This visit will need to appear official, so someone currently in Washington will need to confirm that the inspection is sanctioned."

"'Already done,'" Moore said, quoting Donáll. "I contacted an agent we trust, Lily Herne. While Director Turne was conveniently out, Herne processed our HAARP request, and we—Davies, Rogers, and I—are listed in the system for the inspection—"

"How is Turne going to react when he sees the unauthorized inspection in the records?" Pete asked, staring at Moore.

"Well, he might, or he might not… Let's just say that the request will be…delayed a little, or that it will be a bit glitchy. It will not fully enter the system until our little tour is underway, and it will not upload itself to the official record until Herne takes care of it manually. Turne won't ever see an acknowledgment prompt due to other unforeseen technological issues…thanks to Donáll. And finally, when HAARP inevitably makes the confirmation call to the FBI, Donáll arranged that it will be transferred directly to Herne's office line."

Moore took a breath, glancing carefully around the room. "Ultimately, we should get in and out without any interference from my superiors. Our spontaneous visit will not remain undetected for long, especially if HAARP is Kratos and Kratos has infiltrated the FBI as I suspect. But"—Moore's eyes brightened, and he steepled his hands on the table—"by then, it will be too late for them. If this is one of Kratos's laboratories, we will have already found what we are looking for."

Patch spoke up. "I agree with you on that one, Joey. That's why I suggest we have Pete go in for his janitorial shift. But he'll need a partner in order to get into the records room."

"Records room?" Davies asked, an incredulous expression on his face. "With all of their resources and oodles of money, why on earth would one of the most powerful organizations in the world keep a physical records room? That's so last century!"

"Because, inevitably, everything online can be hacked by brilliant, skilled, and constantly improving individuals," Donáll chimed in. "Take me, for example."

Blane was unamused, but Davies's eye roll quirked up the side of his mouth. He glanced at Ms. Dixon, and he could see her struggling to hide her grin.

This bloke is too much. And he's still talking.

"Someone with my unmatchable talents and abilities would break their firewalls eventually. So HAARP took precautions even before fraternizing with Kratos by pulling all of their records offline. Obviously, this was before Kratos, because if anyone would have noticed Kratos while I was there, it would have been me—"

Donáll broke off at an intense stare from Moore. "Anyway, since HAARP stored everything in a secure records room, it can be assumed that they are still utilizing the same methods with Kratos's involvement."

"AS I WAS SAYING," Patch roared, "we need to get access to these records in case Kratos has been storing transactions and supply lists among them, and Pete here knows how to break in undetected. But he'll need an accomplice who can keep watch."

Pete suddenly interjected. "My usual janitor buddy will be conveniently ill the night of our raid, which will provide the perfect opportunity for my partner to accompany me in. With a few well-placed facial prosthetics and some makeup, no one will know the difference. After all, no one really notices the janitor," he finished proudly.

He paused for a moment. "The only slight problem with this whole thing is that my fellow janitor is a woman."

The old man winked at Ms. Dixon, and Blane stiffened. He felt he needed to make it clear that she was not leaving Blane's side, but Moore beat him to the punch.

"Ms. Dixon is not going inside at all," Moore said firmly. Blane looked around the room to see which agent could possibly dress up as a believable woman when Ms. Everly spoke.

"I'll go with him," she said, her voice full of strength.

"Absolutely not," Moore replied. "You are in as much danger as—"

"I know, I know," Ms. Everly interrupted quickly. "But we don't have anyone else, and I'm willing to go in."

"Will you be able to pick a lock, missy?" Pete chimed in. "There's one in particular we'll need to crack, and my hands are a little too bumbly nowadays. I was thinking I needed one of the agents here to do the trick—"

"I can do that. If you walk me through it, I definitely can." She didn't meet anyone's gaze as she spoke.

There was a soft look of concern in Moore's eyes as he looked at Ms. Everly. "Only if you are comfortable," he said after a moment. "I would never have you do something you do not want to do."

Ms. Everly attempted to muster a brave smile, and she dipped her head in a barely perceptible nod.

Ms. Dixon stared at Ms. Everly, and then she turned to Blane. She looked terrified.

Moore continued. "Donáll will be our eyes and ears. He will monitor all cameras and communication inside the complex while Rogers, Davies, and myself go on the official tour."

A question had been gnawing away at Blane since the conversation began, and he finally put it into words. "I see a bit of a problem here. This mission is not authorized. We have no warrant. We will have no backing from the FBI. If we are caught by innocent people, we will be arrested. If we are caught by Kratos, we will be killed."

Blane took a breath, his mind racing through the endless ways the mission could fail. "Any evidence confiscated will be inadmissible in court. We would perhaps root Kratos out of HAARP, but we would not shed any public light on whatever they are doing."

The room was silent for a moment. Then Moore spoke. "Each of your concerns has been weighing heavily on my mind as well, Burns. This move is, from a practical view, absolutely insane."

Moore's eyes locked on Blane's, fixing him with a stare of burning intensity. "But in order to crack Kratos's armor, we need to meet insanity with a little of our own. I have deliberated over every possible scenario that could go wrong, and despite the endless list I've compiled, I am afraid we do not have another choice. As you all know," he said, turning his attention back to the room, "going through proper channels would only alert Kratos to our intentions, and they would quickly succeed in stopping us before we started."

After a moment, Moore resumed. "There is only one way to do this. We need to see or hear something incriminating on the official tour—something that would give us a valid excuse to investigate. Blood, a scream, a gunshot. Then if we were to find something, anything of value, we would have enough grounds for a raid."

A small smile spread across the older agent's face. "We already have the attention of the FBI in Anchorage, and we have quick accessibility to state troopers."

Rogers spoke up. "How did you manage that, Moore?"

"Donáll's NASA friends alerted him to some rather interesting heat signatures at HAARP in an old section of labs adjacent to the original structure," Moore answered. "They were already deemed structurally compromised, and a chemical spill several decades ago supposedly sealed them off from the rest of the facility for good. The signatures are nothing concrete, but they certainly piqued the interest of several vital agencies. Donáll will be in direct contact with the Bureau, and if we get something during our scouting mission, federal agents and troopers on standby will charge in."

Moore let out a chuckle. "It sounds like these guys are biting at the bit to see some action. And it will be a relief for us, especially if something was to go south and backup would be our saving grace."

"Do they know that this is unauthorized?" Davies asked.

Moore pursed his lips. "Well…not all of them. Most have only been told that something suspicious may be going down and that backup may be needed. I know a guy in the Bureau here by the name of Erik, and he told me he would deal with any backlash if our involvement was to be discovered."

How many mates does Moore have?

A thoughtful look came over Moore's face. "Actually, this whole mission is riding on discretion and a need-to-know basis. If anyone other than Erik was to discover that we are here unsanctioned, the mission would fall apart." He took a deep breath. "Something solid against Kratos—that's all we need."

Every ounce of sanity in Blane's mind was screaming at him that this was crazy. And Moore had never addressed Blane's role in this operation. He needed to act, to be a part of something, to do something in this attack on the organization that had murdered his family. Blane looked down and saw his hands squeezing each other. He was tense. He was stressed.

But he knew that Moore was right…it would be now or never. Blane's thoughts raced over and over. Every potential pitfall. Every inevitable disaster. But one clear thought searing through his head.

Now or never.

JOSEPH WAITED. IT WAS dark, but he could clearly make out the form standing down at the fence. He could clearly see the puff of exhaled air in the freezing night. A quick glance behind him, and

Joseph began to silently make his way down the hill at the rear of the safe house to reach the figure.

Now how to avoid startling him so he doesn't break my face...

Joseph wasn't sure how the man would react, but he needed to speak to him. It was now or never.

Joseph took a few more steps, and his heart nearly leaped from his chest when something under his foot snapped. The man in front of him whirled around, and Joseph found himself gasping on the ground, the breath knocked out of him. But at least his nose was intact.

Blane Burns was staring down at him, his eyes blazing.

"Moore?" he thundered. "What do you think you're doing, creeping—"

Joseph quickly grabbed his arm and let out a rapid "Shush!" He swiftly continued. "Please keep your voice low. I came to talk to you privately." Joseph was breathing hard, but in a second, the Scottish agent had set him back up on his feet.

Burns was now looking at him with what Joseph could only hope was a mild expression. Perhaps it was to his benefit that he could not see Burns's face.

"Kratos has people everywhere, and there are very few people in this world that I trust. Especially now." Joseph took another breath and continued. "I want to believe in my people with every fiber of my being. But due to the gravity of this mission, I have decided to keep its most vital players under the radar...just in case."

Joseph hoped that Burns was handling this well. He couldn't be sure, but Burns's whole stature looked a little...tense.

"Beyond all doubt, I am certain that I can trust Ms. Dixon. And I trust Patch with my very life." A beat. "And I trust you, Burns. I trust your judgment, your skill, and your intentions. You have more reason than anyone to hate Kratos."

Without warning, a series of images flashed through Joseph's mind. Smoke. Soft hair smeared with blood. Tiny hands. An innocent and beautiful face. The world black.

Joseph cleared his throat. "We all have reasons to...hate Kratos." Joseph sensed that Burns was tensing up for some question, so he plowed ahead. "As such, I want you on the inside. With Ms. Dixon and with Patch. Donáll is the only other who knows about this." Joseph was almost certain that his words had relaxed the man in front of him.

"Donáll told me that the records room is a good start, but he recommends having someone do a sweep of the abandoned labs before we send in the cavalry. Especially if we don't happen upon any opportunities that validate our need to investigate and call in reinforcements, I don't want to leave empty handed. That's why I want you on the inside gathering whatever evidence you can. Photos, recordings, samples—I want it all. I want to know what Kratos is up to." Joseph paused for a breath before he continued.

"I know anything you acquire will be inadmissible, but if you were to draw us to you with, say gunfire, while we are on the tour, we will have an opportunity. And if something goes wrong, we'll still have gotten what we need. Then we'll bring the place to life with Alaskan law enforcement."

Silence stretched on. And Joseph was suddenly angry that his knees were acting up in the cold. The shrapnel was perpetually there, waiting to hurt him. Always reminding him.

Ignoring the pain, he focused on Blane Burns. "I know a lot could go wrong. But I also know this could be a huge break in the case. And it will be a complete secret. No one else will know except the five of us if all goes well."

The silence was deafening, and Joseph nervously ran a hand down the newly grown stubble on his chin. He hadn't realized he needed a shave so badly.

At last, the Scottish man answered.

"I think it is a good move, Moore. I was hoping you would have something for me to do in there. I'll organize what we need as discreetly as I can."

Relief flooded through Joseph at Burns's competence and his willingness. "Excellent, my man. We are heading out at 1800 hours. I already briefed Patch on this. You, Ms. Dixon, and Patch will be following along a more obscure road that Patch and Pete have been using to approach HAARP undetected for years. Donáll will have a private comms unit between only him and you three."

"One question, sir. Why have Ms. Dixon go in with us? I don't like Ms. Everly's involvement, and Ms. Dixon will be in even greater danger."

Joseph took a breath, his heart racing. His mind clouding in unrelenting worry.

"As Pete said, he needs a woman, and she said she will be able to pick the lock with his instruction. I don't like Ms. Everly going in either, but I just do not see another way. And Ms. Dixon? Where on earth should I send her if not with you? She'll be safer with you than with Donáll or alone in the safe house. And you and Patch will need more eyes in there."

Joseph ran his hands through his hair. "The uncertainty of it all has me nearly stretched beyond…breaking, Burns. But I just can't see any other moves to get us ahead in this game. And we must." He stared at Burns.

"I need your…your support." Silence between them. But only for a moment.

"You have it, sir. I'll get moving."

There was one more thing Joseph needed to say. He quickly stopped the man as he turned to leave.

"Oh, and, ah, Burns," he began. "If all else fails, there is one vital outcome that cannot. I want his name."

"The head of Kratos, sir?"

Joseph affirmed Burns's thought in as steely a voice as he could muster. "The head of Kratos. The master moving all of the pieces. We need his name. Or at least how to find him."

"We never got close to a name or even a description at MI5," Burns said, his voice laced with frustration. "We came to the conclusion that he lives in plain sight, somewhere that most people wouldn't think to look. Protected by his organization and by his clients, not a ghost operating without an identity. Our theory was that he has built up unbreachable defenses and, as a result, chooses to live in the open. Seemingly vulnerable but virtually untouchable."

"But not for long," Joseph replied grimly. "Not if we can pull this off. But ensuring Ms. Dixon's safety and the safety of everyone else, of course, must be paramount." Joseph let out a low chuckle. "I tend to get so caught up in all the action that I sometimes forget to protect the ones closest to…well, the ones I am responsible…for."

Dark memories reared their ugly heads in his mind's eye. He stopped talking and rubbed his hand over his chin again. Silence. And then Burns spoke.

"You know I understand, Moore. But the disconnect is that you know all of my secrets. And I don't know any of yours."

Joseph closed his eyes.

Not now. No. Not the right time.

"Well, a man's secrets are…you know, I am simply quoting crap from some bygone age. Let's get some sleep, Burns."

Blane Burns stood there a second longer, studying Joseph in the dim light of the rosy dawn just spreading over the distant mountains. Then he turned and disappeared into the darkness that was still clinging to the safe house and surrounding landscape.

Joseph leaned against the fence, taking in the sight of the Alaskan horizon. In the midst of the pandemonium in his mind, Burns's unspoken accusation disturbed him.

But Joseph could not tell Burns of his past. His mission. He could not. He needed to focus on the present. The present nightmare.

So much danger. I could be leading everyone to their deaths.

A wave of nausea hit Joseph, and he clutched the fence.

Again.

The word resonated throughout his being, and he squeezed the life out of the frozen metal. *And if she dies? You will have failed.*

A breath, then two.

Again.

The tears gathering in his eyes blurred the sunrise and sapped him of strength. Another breath. And another. And Joseph opened his eyes, angrily rubbing away the wet trails slowly freezing on his face.

You won't screw this up. Even if he doesn't trust me, Burns will protect her. And then, well, then everything should fall into place. For better or for worse.

His phone buzzed, and Joseph answered a confirmation call from a protected line. "Everything is as planned," Joseph said slowly. "We'll be there at 2000 hours. Get everyone ready."

Joseph hung up, and he began his trek up the hill to the safe house.

Get ready.

CHAPTER SEVEN

THE VAN WAS SILENT AS PATCH DROVE BLANE AND MS.
DIXON ON A PATH THROUGH THE WOODS.

They were getting closer.

Blane kept mulling over his unexpected meeting with Moore
in the early morning. The man had seemed so unsettled...so full of
regret for the past and terror for the future. Moore was undeniably
hiding something. Blane had been suspicious of that ever since that
first exchange back at the hotel.

How much more does he know?

A hand grasped his, and he rapidly turned to see Ms. Dixon
staring at him with wide eyes.

"I'm sorry," she murmured, dropping her eyes and then releasing his hand. "I think I'm just... Well, this seems like something out
of a movie and not real life. I do not know what I am supposed to do.
I think I'm... I'm a little... I'm just..."

"Terrified?" Blane offered. He reached down, squeezing her
hand as gently as he could. "I know, lass. I know."

"And Ami? I know Pete needs another person, but I'm so worried about her. I just wish I knew she was somewhere safe. I feel
responsible for her, and I..."

Blane sensed where she was heading with this, and he rapidly
built a roadblock. "I'll be putting a stop to that, Ms. Dixon. Nothing
that has happened thus far has been your fault. Nothing. And we are
all responsible for her safety. Not just you."

She smiled so beautifully it took his breath away. "Thank you...
it's so hard, but I do know that. But do...do you know that?"

Her question was soft, careful, searching. It was searching his
very heart, rooting out all the darkness.

He was not responsible. For anything.

The gravity of her question settled on him, and he almost gasped to take his next breath.

Blane could only manage a forced smile, and he released her hand with a final squeeze.

She doesn't understand. She doesn't know. How could she?

He had been the object of his own hatred and burning blame for so long. Every mistake and regret was a dagger digging in his chest, destroying what was left of his heart. His own family. Dead.

Because of me.

ALINA SAT BACK IN her seat, succumbing to the silence once again. The suffocating silence.

She watched as Blane took out his phone and rapidly scrolled through it until he apparently found what he had been searching for.

It looked like he was studying complicated blueprints. Turning back to the window, she stared at the dark trees flashing by in time with her racing heartbeat.

Soon enough, Patch broke the stagnant air.

"We're here, folks."

Their hands found each other in the dark, clasping tightly together on contact. Hers trembling. His strong.

Then their eyes met, and they climbed out of the van.

Alina sucked in the biting air as she stared down over the bank into the dense forest—the forest that would shield their approach toward the secluded north end of the HAARP complex.

She fumbled with her gloves as she looked around at the others. The three of them were dressed in black from head to toe. They even had thin breathable masks to pull up over their faces. Blane had assured them that blending in with the shadows would be their best move to avoid detection.

Under their tactical jackets, they had on professional lab attire as a last resort in case "slinking through the halls in black ninja suits no longer became an option," as Donáll put it.

Carefully and methodically, Blane pulled out the three lab badges Donáll had designed for them.

Alina was Beauty Belle, Patch was Blackie Beard, and Blane was Lucky Charms. Alina thought the Irish-themed name was a little insulting in its inaccuracy to his Scottish origins, but Blane didn't seem to care.

Donáll had explained over and over again that, if they reached the point where someone inspected their badges up close, they would already be dead, anyway.

She hadn't liked his blatancy.

The badges and lab coats under their black layers would be a final cover if they had to abort their covert operation for any reason, though Alina was praying that it wouldn't come to that. She wanted to stay in the shadows instead of going out into the open, as Kratos already knew what she and Blane looked like.

And if we are discovered...

She killed the line of thought before she could finish it.

Blane produced three pairs of waterproof boots for them to don. Their comms units came next, and Donáll assured them that their line of communication was strong and secure after they had turned them on.

Lastly, Blane pulled out three pistols, each with a silencer on the barrel. Patch took his immediately, but Alina stared at him, slowly shaking her head.

"I can't. I'm sorry. I never could."

Patch was staring at her, but Blane nodded. She was relieved he wouldn't force her to take it. She still had the small pistol he had given her, anyway.

Alina took a breath and closed her eyes. She knew that, when they opened, she would be as ready as she would ever be. She heard Donáll talking in her ear, and Blane was beside her.

Please keep everyone safe.

With her prayer, her mind cleared. She opened her eyes and pulled her mask over her face.

JOSEPH GAVE THE GLARING, seemingly prepubescent man in front of him his most dazzling grin. He knew that Montage didn't trust them. But he also knew the man would have to let them in. It had been part of his rigorous training, after all.

"And you are sure that you got the correct day for this inspection?" he asked. "This is highly unorthodox, and I can assure you, this facility does not appreciate visitation without proper appointment. Our work is very delicate."

Joseph almost winced at his high-pitched voice, which once again caused him to question if Montage truly was the thirty-year-old manager Patch had been studying for months. The man pushed up his glasses, and he glared at the three FBI agents in front of him.

At Joseph's nod, he resumed in a snide tone. "Well, I will have my assistant place a call to Washington. For your sakes, I hope your director will confirm this appointment. If not, you three will be on your way shortly, facing a thorough investigation and likely severe disciplinary action for your impudence. Unannounced visit, indeed. Quite unorthodox."

"Copy that," Donáll said in his ear, and Joseph was relieved to know that Herne would be alerted to get into position to receive the call and confirm the meeting. Joseph smiled at how well the plan was working so far, and the manager's glare narrowed even more. Joseph responded by only grinning wider at him.

Fred Montage phoned his assistant and remained on the line as she called Herne. Still glaring. And still sweating, apparently. He kept mopping his face, and he was careful to keep his arms down.

Apparently, his assistant was satisfied with the phone call, and Montage stood there, running his handkerchief over his face. This time forgetting to hide his pit stains. Joseph could feel Davies tensing up beside him like a boxer in the ring.

Joseph spoke at last. "Well, if that satisfies you, then we can begin the inspection, Fred. Is it okay if I call you Fred? See, my cousin had a little goldfish named Fred, and it, therefore, has sentimental value to me—"

"Just give me your badges," Montage interrupted. He grabbed each of their FBI badges, scanned them into his computer, and confirmed that they were three agents in the Transnational Division of the FBI.

"I'm seeing everything this oaf is seeing, and it all looks good," Donáll said in Joseph's ear.

Excellent.

Joseph smiled again at Montage.

"Please come with me, gentlemen," the man said at length, resignation dripping from his voice.

"Lead the way, Fred," Joseph said, and the four men started making their way down one of the hallways. One of the long, white hallways.

Joseph tried to quell his racing heartbeat. He had his Glock 22. And two of his best guys. And his best nerd in his ear.

This is going to work.

PETE WALKED CALMLY DOWN the long corridor, his scratchy janitorial uniform extra irritating tonight.

Soon enough, he found what he had been looking for. With a quick scan of his surroundings, he knelt down with a screwdriver to loosen the hinges of the ancient service hatch between the supplies room and the kitchen.

The guy in his ear had told him that the cameras and other security in this area would be disabled for a full two minutes, so he took his time to ensure he wouldn't drop the door once he detached it. He didn't have time to try to pick this one's lock.

At last, he caught the heavy door with an "Oof," and the shivering girl on the other side was able to slide through to join him. Working together, they resituated the door, and Pete stuck the hinges back in place with his tools.

"I'm sorry it was so cold, waiting in there," he murmured. The supplies room had exceedingly easier access to the outside than the closely monitored employee entrances, so his partner had to join him a different way. Once they were inside, it would be much easier for her to pass as Glenda, his janitorial counterpart.

And he was relieved it had worked, though she looked cold and miserable.

With a burst of insight, he slipped off and held his sweater out to her. She stared at it in alarm, but then she took it from him with a grateful smile and slipped it over the janitorial uniform Pete had been able to secure for her.

As they walked down the hall, with him pushing his janitorial cart in front of him, he felt even worse than he had before for the young woman beside him. Stress and worry poured off of her in waves, and he keenly felt her fear.

What is her name again? Alina? No, that's the other one. Abby? No… Amanda?

He gave up and spoke in a low voice. "Lookie here…missy. We're going to be fine. If you just stay close to me, we'll make it. I've been in here more times than I care to name, and let me tell you, I know these halls like the back of my hand."

They arrived at the stretch of lockers, and Pete told her that her task was up. He glanced down the hallway as he took a breath, preparing to talk his partner through picking the lock.

"Okay, now this is going to be a little diffi—"

His attention snapped to the girl beside him as the tiny lock fell to the ground. He gaped at her as the locker swung open.

Wow. She's good.

He praised her efforts as he grabbed the keycard from a hidden slot located on the door. She tried to smile at him, but her eyes were wide. And frightened.

"Ah, another step complete. And we're almost to the records room. Just down this length of hallway yet, then a duck to the left, a smidge to the right, and then down some stairs. To the left is the door we need."

She looked at him with an unasked question, and he already knew what she was thinking. Before his wife had died, he had always known what was on her mind. He had an uncanny knack for always guessing what people wanted, and he was happy to learn that he had not unlearned that skill during the six months he had spent cooped up with Patch in the stuffy safe house.

"You just did the most stressful thing you have to do. You're simply my extra pair of eyes now. You just stay close to me, and I'll deal with any extra security measures as we get to them."

Pete was also a master security-system dismantler. He didn't know what the proper term actually was—he just knew he was renowned for it back when he worked at the FBI. Back in the glory days. Back when his Janet was still alive.

He smiled, reliving memories of her chasing him with the watering hose, singing opera in the shower just to annoy him, allowing him to step on her toes and to nearly drop her as he attempted to dance with her.

Those were some glory days.

He suddenly heard talking up ahead, and his mind refocused in the current day. In the current danger. He rapidly grabbed his cart and gave the girl beside him towels to carry over her arm. Making eye contact with her, he intimated that they should walk.

Just stay natural. And keep walking.

He felt her terror within himself, and he wished he could promise her that everything would be all right.

Trust me, his eyes pleaded with her. *Just keep walking.*

ALINA, BLANE, AND PATCH moved through the black water, their boots making hideous squelching sounds as they walked through the underground storm drain. They were radio-silent for the time being—there was no reception.

The dripping ceiling was so low that Alina's black beanie kept brushing against it, and she shuddered, doing her best to hunch down.

Poor Blane and Patch looked even more uncomfortable as they walked, their heads and shoulders considerably stooped. Alina wrapped her arms around herself, the biting, winter air choosing at that moment to flow through the passage. She watched her breath billowing out in front of her, white against the gray and black. At the very least, the mask insulated her face a little. Just then, she stepped on something that moved, and she squeaked, biting back a scream. Blane whirled, striking his head against the ceiling.

"Are you...are you all right?" Blane managed, rubbing his hand hard over his head. As she relayed that she was, she watched his sudden tension dissipate.

Patch glanced over his shoulder, and she could imagine she saw mirth in his eyes. As they continued walking with Blane in the lead, Patch leaned toward her. "I knew he was going to hit his head at some point. He's just too tall for his own good."

A soft "I heard that" floated back through the heavy air, and Alina nearly laughed. After interminable minutes of sloshing through the darkness with noxious smells bombarding their senses, they reached a sharp incline. At the top, there was a ladder leading to what looked to be a manhole. A welded shut manhole.

Donáll had assured them that this would bring them out under a hallway which would connect to the hall leading to the old labs. Once they made it through, he had reiterated, they would have to climb up through a floor vent and then walk downward and to the left until they reached their destination: the entrance to the labyrinth of abandoned labs.

They paused once they reached the manhole, and Blane produced a small tool from the pocket of his leather jacket. Donáll had explained that it was some sort of high-powered laser which could cut through metal in a number of seconds. Apparently, no one from the original building contract was still alive, so the manhole and other key features of the original HAARP structure had since been forgotten. The original blueprints to the complex were also exceedingly rare to come by, as Pete and Patch claimed that almost all of them had mysteriously disappeared. As such, their copy of the original blueprints was one of their greatest acquirements.

Her focus snapped to Blane as he aimed the tool at the borders of the hatch, sending orange sparks flying. Alina blinked against the sudden, harsh light.

Donáll's "number of seconds" estimate proved to be highly inaccurate, as it instead took Blane a total of three minutes until he was able to force the weakened hatch open. Their next task proved to be even more of a struggle once they had shimmied their way up to floor vent, with Patch in the lead and Blane taking up the rear. For approximately five minutes, Patch unsuccessfully tried to unscrew the vent cover so that they could enter the hallway.

Make that six minutes.

Her respirations began to quicken as she watched the seconds hand on the lit screen of her watch. Still no success. Only passing time. And a greater chance of getting caught—likely by the bad guys. All of a sudden, Donáll was back in range, yelling that they needed to make better time. Poor Patch reacted very badly.

"Listen," he hissed back at the voice sounding in his ear. "Pete's better at this kinda stuff than I am, okay? I admit it! You're just a tech guy like me! I bet you wouldn't know what to do—"

Alina turned to Blane as he sighed behind her, and she watched him rub his hand down his face as he interrupted Patch.

"Okay, okay," the Scottish man said finally. "I don't know if this will draw too much attention or not, but we're out of options. I'm coming through."

Alina tried to plaster herself against the tight space to allow Blane to pass, but he got stuck between her and the wall.

"Oh, oh, I'm sorry," she said breathlessly, his nearness sending shivers and warmth through her simultaneously.

"No, uh, pardon me," he responded as he desperately tried to crawl past her.

She couldn't help but feel the solid muscle of his arm. Of his chest as he lifted his arm over her. She couldn't help but feel the warmth of his body against hers as he at last pushed himself through. She was blushing now.

Oh my goodness. How awkward.

Patch mumbled something incoherent as he made himself as small as he could. Then he proceeded to verbally abuse Blane as the large Scottish agent wedged him against the wall to make room. In about five seconds, Blane's laser cut through the vent cover. Then they froze in horror as a loud screech resounded, the metal protesting as Blane tentatively pushed the loosened cover out of the way. After a breathless moment of silence, Patch let out a long sigh. "Well, why didn't you do that five minutes ago, Lucky Charms?"

Alina saw Blane shake his head, and the three of them climbed up through the vent and took cautious steps out into the hallway. Dim light pooled on the floor from the ceiling—a sharp contrast to the fiery sky bathing the walls in a sickly red glow through a wall of windows.

"Gorgeous," Donáll breathed into her ear. Blane looked uncomfortable, but Donáll quickly continued. "No, not your vandalism. Look up. The mass of dipole antennas. Major part of HAARP's auroral research. I designed some of those myself."

Through another window, Alina thought that the tangle of white antennas glinting ominously against the blood-red Alaskan sky was more terrifying than it was beautiful. It looked like something out of a science fiction movie. And she hated those. Without conscious thought, she took a step closer to Blane and actually stepped on his foot as he had taken a step toward her at the same time. She felt melty feelings blend with the terror. And then she just kind of felt sick.

As the three of them walked deeper into the complex through the flickering hallway, Donáll suddenly spoke again.

"By the way, I wanted to let you know that I'm restarting the feeds of all the cameras and controlling what the security room sees as you move forward. Just FYI. Not bragging here, just educating. And oh, yep, keep your eyes peeled for that lab."

It all sounded like some bizarre dream she would soon wake up from. A shiver coursed through her as she remembered. Last night in her dream, she had been playing with the dolls on the carpet. The voice sounded and she ran toward it, but Antonov was suddenly there. Waiting for her as she tore open the door. As he grabbed her, she had awakened. Her nightmares weren't as frequent anymore, but they still managed to obliterate her peace and suck her down into inescapable depths.

"The first lab is coming up." Blane's gentle voice cut through the darkness, drawing her back into the freezing hallway.

Donáll was talking in her ear, directing them toward the proper door, saying he was shutting down the cameras but that they had to hurry. Blane was going for his tools and approaching the door, but it swung open the minute he applied a little weight to it.

Eyes wide, he rapidly stepped back from the door. The three of them stared at one of the cameras, listening to Donáll cackle at his own little joke.

"Of course, inner security is the tightest. All cloak and dagger algorithms. I see Kratos written all over this thing. Actually, get inside now. Everything will come crashing back in three seconds if I don't restore the system. Quick!"

Blane shoved Patch and Alina through the door and dove after them, closing the door rapidly behind him. A single red light had stopped flashing the minute the door closed, and now they were in complete darkness. Alina had to slow her breathing so she wouldn't hyperventilate.

They got to their feet and began moving through the blackness, Donáll guiding them in the correct direction until they reached a lit hallway.

"Alrighty! Up ahead should be the door to the allegedly abandoned labs, if these blueprints are serving me correctly...oh, to your right!" Donáll exclaimed.

They all froze, slowly turning in the named direction. Alina's heart sank in her chest. The old door there was completely cemented shut. There was no way in.

"Were...were we wrong?" she asked, despair creeping into her voice.

"I do not think so," Blane murmured quietly, his eyes scanning the surrounding hall. "They need that there for show when conducting official tours. I'd wager there's another way in."

He proceeded to turn to the walls around them, with Patch following suit.

"Donáll, any insight?" Blane asked, reaching out to fiddle with a nearby lighting fixture. A beat of silence. Then another. "Donáll?"

Alina's breath caught in her throat. Her comms was silent. And from the look on Blane's face, his was too. His eyes locked on hers for a long moment.

Something's wrong.

Their heads whipped to the right in unison as laughter echoed down the hall. Patch and Alina both looked to Blane in horror. These labs were abandoned. No one was supposed to be here. The only people who would be were...definitely the bad guys.

God, please no.

No one else from the team was looped into their system. Without Donáll, they were completely cut off. Blind. With no one to control the cameras. They were radio-silent and alone inside one of Kratos's most impenetrable strongholds.

Without wasting another second, Blane once again turned his attention to the walls surrounding them. Patch jumped in, tapping and listening while Alina desperately scanned the hallway. Another bout of laughter. Echoing down the hallway toward them. Getting closer.

Oh, please, God. Please help us find this door and get through.

The laughter was getting closer.

PETE BREATHED A SIGH of relief as he and Ami—*Ah, that's it!*—slipped into the records room. The keycard had worked.

He murmured, "Worst part is over. Now let's get to work. All of these files are HAARP and HAARP only. Patch and I determined that HAARP and Kratos are, indeed, separate entities. But the kicker is that someone inside HAARP gave Kratos permission to utilize all of the resources of this facility."

Pacing around the massive room, he continued. "Therefore, I believe Kratos records are here yet kept separate from the HAARP research. If we can find tangible proof of some sort of underhanded dealings, we can somehow bring it to Joey's attention, and then the troopers and other federal agents will sweep in. Let's find the needle in this field of hay!"

Pete actually felt happy. He liked this young lady, and he was glad to spend time with her. Even if it was during an extremely risky endeavor with no assurance of a backup team. As Ami scouted the other room, he traced his finger along the wooden paneling above the wallpaper. He was hoping to press some button and open up a secret compartment amongst the rows and rows of filing cabinets in the immense room.

No cigar. And he could not even say that he had been close.

Next, he was army crawling his way over the floor, looking for hidden caches or other mechanisms along the base of the cabinets.

Nope. Now you're dusty. And you must look stupid, flopping about like a fish.

Pete righted himself, and he turned his attention to higher places. No Kratos employee would crawl around on the floor to grab a file. The files would be stored in something much more slick-looking. Like one of them fancy safety deposit boxes.

Janet had always been asking if they could get one, just so they could say they had it. Even though they had had absolutely nothing to put in it.

Instead of distracting him, Pete's new flood of memories only served to heighten his senses. He surveyed the room carefully, certain he would find what he was looking for.

And there it was. Just like Kratos to flaunt its invincibility.

"Hey, Annie, come here!" he whispered loudly. "I think I found it." It was a single shield, like a coat of arms, and it featured a telling "K" along its top banner.

She came toward him from the other end of the room, her eyes wide, her mouth in a grim line. Pete braced himself on top of a conveniently placed chair, and he tried pushing in the whole shield. When that failed, he tried to twist the shield. When that likewise failed, he tried one more offensive avenue. He simply reached out and pressed the "K" engraving in the banner. A keyboard immediately swung out, nearly causing him to lose his balance.

"Hey, Angie, look in my bag there. I need some of that stuff labeled 'powder' and one of them little brushes in there. Both should be tacked into the inner pockets."

Once the girl had handed up his supplies, Pete got to work dusting the keyboard for prints. Some idiot must have used it last— the prints were only slightly wiped off. He rapidly determined the letters with slight smudges on them: *L, E, A, R,* and *Z*. Pete's mind went to work, crunching numbers and the possible chances he would have to guess at the word before setting off some sort of alarm.

And then that'll be that.

Suddenly, Pete had a lightbulb moment. Joey had been mentioning something about some Angel of Death business. What had that word been? *Ezral...no. Azrel?* Then all at once, Pete got it.

"Azrael. The *A* key gets pressed twice."

He rapidly typed in the word, and a light shake and rumble behind Amelia echoed throughout the room. A fancy, sleek-looking safe had emerged from behind a panel that had been covered over with wallpaper. Pete jumped down from his perch, favoring his left knee. He sidled up to the safe and grinned at the girl next to him.

"Would you like to do the honors... Andi? No, excuse me, what was it? I've been calling you so many different *A* names in my head that you wouldn't believe it."

He chuckled, but she simply whispered, "Ami," in response.

He felt sorry for her. Her fear struck him deeply—he could remember how afraid he had been his first time in the field.

"Okay, Amy. I'll open this safe, but we will have to work—"

Suddenly, the FBI tech man's voice was in his ear. "Hey, guys, I'm back to helping you. Our three friends on the official tour are doing okay for the moment. Looks like you will have approximately five seconds to open the door before the tiny biometric cameras aimed at your face recognize that you are not in the system."

"Well, thank you for letting me know, Mr. Right-on-Time. Me and Amy here would have crashed and burned right under your supervision."

"But you didn't. You didn't. Now five seconds. I'll try to hold it off a little longer, but this system is more advanced than I have dealt with before. Give yourself approximately five seconds."

Pete looked at her, the question in his eyes clear. And she nodded. In that instant, he ripped open the door to the safe. With lightning speed, his fingers pulled out...absolutely nothing. He desperately felt around inside the safe...but nothing. He slammed the door shut just as the tech guy in his ear finished his countdown.

"What'd you find, Gramps?" the tech guy inquired.

Pete was in shock. Something wasn't right. He glanced up, but she wasn't there. He had been so distracted with the safe that he hadn't heard them come.

"What in the—" Patch began. "Tech man, do you see my partner?" He jogged through the records room, checking behind everything in sight. "Dude, where are you? Ally was taken. She's gone! Do you hear me?"

He paused, his heart racing, the taste in his mouth souring. "Tech man?" He switched channels. "Joey?"

Silence. And pure desperation. Pete turned to run back out of the records room when something smashed over his head. He fell to the ground, the world going black.

"BAD, BAD, BAD," DONÁLL was repeating over and over again, driving Joseph insane.

Party Boy Montage was distracted talking to one of his security guards, and Joseph took a precious moment to hiss, "What's bad? SPEAK, MAN!"

He saw both Davies and Rogers flinch at the feedback, and Donáll finally explained himself.

"Our records team! Old man and little woman! I lost 'em. Their signal, my visuals in their area, everything. I think my stuff is slowly being hacked!" Donáll was on the verge of hysterics.

"Keep a clear head now, do you hear me? Slowly shut down. Only leave open your communication with me and with the Bureau. Let Erik know we may have a situation."

"But, Boss, they can't do anything to help them. Only your friend knows the whole truth, and everything will fall through if we expose all this espionage we've been hiding," Donáll rambled desperately.

Joseph clutched a hand to his head. His worst fears were coming true. Montage whipped around at the movement.

"What are you whispering about? I said give me a minute, and I feel like you all are plotting a mutiny!"

Joseph didn't have a reply, but Davies jumped in.

"We were just commenting on how solid this place has been so far. Perfect for top-notch research. And very secure. Like those biometric scanners you have in the…"

Joseph glanced at Rogers to ensure that he was focused on Davies's conversation with Party Boy. Then with ice in his veins, he murmured his greatest fear and his heaviest question to Donáll after switching to a private channel.

"If you're hacked, Kratos can see everything. They can see… everyone. Do you still have them in sight?"

"No, no. I disconnected from them the minute I realized something was up. But I'm dark now, Boss. Useless. If I try to challenge the hackers, they will pinpoint my exact location out here. And then they will come, and then they will kill me."

"Stay dark, Donáll. You're more useful to me alive than dead. Just keep me updated."

Joseph glanced up to offer up his million-dollar smile to Montage again, but he instead locked eyes directly with Rogers. The look in his eyes was as searching as Joseph's was desperate. But Joseph nodded at him, relaying a sense of confidence that he did not feel.

"Anyway, gentlemen, come along. This is the final stretch of our little tour. As you see out of the window in the gathering night, our expanse of dipole antenna structures is quite impressive. It stretches all the way down, past the old labs, until it reaches our southern end…"

"Where do you house the records for all of HAARP's transactions, Fred?" Joseph asked, not quite knowing if he was making a grave error or an intelligent move for his team. Montage paused to stare at Joseph, his gaze probing.

"The FBI we normally get here never ask such specific questions, Agent Moore. But I suppose that our private transactions should be subjected to random and quite frankly frustrating government searches whenever the government chooses. Come with me," he huffed.

Fred Montage led the way, and the three agents fell in step behind him.

I need them all to stay alive. If You are out there, God, I need You to make sure that they are and will stay safe. Oh, please keep everyone safe.

ALINA GLANCED WILDLY AT Blane, the pale lighting illuminating the three of them like spotlights. Searching for the hidden door. Any door. No word from Donáll. And the footsteps getting closer. Her knees turning to jelly. And then she was falling. But she was in Blane's arms before she hit the floor, and he desperately dragged her along with him down the hallway, away from the voices. Blane must have heard something that she didn't, as he whirled around after a few steps. Patch was peering out of and gesturing to them from a narrow opening in the wall.

The voices and footsteps just around the corner. Blane half-carried Alina and shoved her into Patch's arms. In a single motion, he ripped off his mask and spun out of his tactical jacket as he whipped around to face the thunderous laughter.

The door slid closed silently behind him. Alina's breath was coming in short gasps as she stood, her hands on the door.

Oh, Blane. He didn't get in.

He didn't get in.

She turned to Patch with panicked eyes, but he grabbed her arm and shoved her to the ground behind a stack of storage boxes as the narrow door swung open with an electric hiss. Two scientists walked in, both holding briefcases and glancing carefully over the room. Right over their hiding place.

They know. It's over. We'll be caught.

But then one of them laughed, and they kept walking.

Alina had never been more grateful for their black clothing. She took the moment to finally glance around the secret room. And all of her hopes fled. Everything was in disrepair, and shelves as far as the eye could see were completely empty. If this was the abandoned lab, it was clearly unused, and it cut her to the heart. Nothing in the room pointed to Kratos—it was as abandoned as it could be.

Alina's attention was drawn back to the pair as they approached a series of cabinets. She watched the female scientist deftly press in a corner of a shelf, causing a hidden keypad to swing out from the wall. The woman's fingers proceeded to punch in a series of numbers, sending musical notes from the different keys echoing across the empty room.

A light humming Alina had not heard up until that point was rapidly silenced, and Patch mouthed "trip lasers" to her.

She tried to concentrate as the two scientists stood near the middle of the room, continuing to talk. Then a stillness ensued, broken only when the male scientist reached beneath a cluster of valves and the entrance to an inner chamber materialized in the far wall.

Kratos. It has to be.

Walking slowly, the two scientists disappeared inside. And Alina's pulse at last resumed a safe rate. As soon as the scientists left, they would have time and opportunity to see what Kratos was doing here. But, even now, Alina couldn't fully focus on the task at hand.

God, please let Blane be okay.

Eventually, the two scientists came back through the door, and their animated gestures and frustrated expressions instantly alerted her.

Something was wrong.

The female scientist looked…terrified. They rapidly left the room through the door from which they had entered. Patch, apparently starved for action, immediately stood.

"Well, Alina, looks like we lucked out. I know the code to turn off all the security. And now we know where the innermost stronghold is. Let's go."

Alina had a sick feeling of dread in her stomach, and she yanked him back down beside her with all of her strength. In that instant, the door to the inner chamber swung open as three men entered the room.

Alina felt herself shaking. *That was close again. Too close. Oh Blane, I wish you were here!*

Alina tried to study the three people, but some force of new terror seemed to limit the scope of her gaze. There were two men flanking the man in the middle. The man in the middle. A big man, with silver hair and a silver beard. A huge scar on his face, running from his right ear to the corner of his mouth. Everything about him commanded an unyielding sense of power. Authority. And some presence of what Alina could only describe as…blackness. A level of alarm amplified with every step he took toward their hiding place, sounding in her ears and filling her with dread.

Just as the men were passing directly by them, the man in the middle stopped. Immediately, the other men stopped beside him.

Horror coursed through her as an ugly smile wormed its way across his face. Then her breath caught as he slowly turned his face toward their hiding spot.

Ducking her head. Praying the mask concealed her face and helped her melt into the shadows.

Paralyzed.

She couldn't breathe. She was powerless. And he was still standing there, smiling in their direction.

He knows. Oh, God, please help us!

He suddenly chuckled, and the spell was broken as he began to walk again. His two guards, like clockwork, moved effortlessly forward as if they had never stopped in the first place.

Alina pulled her mask off, desperate to take a breath. Patch did the same.

The man had sucked the very life out of her. Pure evil emanated from him. She and Patch glanced at each other as the men disappeared through the outer door, but Patch rapidly held up a hand and cocked his head to the side. He heard something out in the hall.

Alina heard it, too.

The voices of the two scientists they had nearly encountered were back, and they were blending in a nauseating cacophony with a single reedy voice—a voice undoubtedly belonging to the man in the middle. Their conversation was soft yet laced with the dread of the unsaid, and Alina clamped both hands over her mouth as a silenced gunshot sounded just outside the door. A body thudded to the ground.

She squeezed her eyes shut. Then the voice again. She could only make out his last couple of words. "…again. Do you understand? Ahh, I thought so. Thank you. And get this cleaned up."

God, You're more powerful. Please help.

She opened her eyes, making direct eye contact with Patch. He looked grimmer than she had ever seen him. Their eyes locked, he offered his hand and helped her stand. His attempt at a brave smile froze on his face, however. A snap of fingers had resounded in the outside hallway. Before Alina or Patch could react, two new guards burst through the door, their guns trained on them.

Oh, God. Oh no.

They were gesturing for Alina and Patch to move into the center of the room. Her head felt light…her steps floaty. Everything bright, sharp, narrowing, in focus. They were being called to the middle of the room. She had seen enough movies to know what that meant. Alina almost threw up, but she kept her hands in the air. She had never felt so trapped.

Trapped.

So helpless.

Helpless.

Oh, God. Please.

Patch looked so old. So tired and resigned. At their violent gesturing, he helplessly tossed his gun to the floor and raised his hands.

God, where's Blane? Where's Blane?

Thump-thump. The guards cocked their guns and placed their fingers on the triggers. *Thump-thump.* Raised the guns. *Thump-thump-thump-thump.* Both straight at Patch, one aimed at his head and one at his heart. *Thump-thump-thump-thump.* Then they would shoot her.

She felt a cry rearing up inside of her, and without thinking, she channeled all of her terror, anger, and desperation into one name.

"BLANE!"

FRED MONTAGE WAS STARING at them carefully as they inspected the records room. Joseph knew one of his best friends and Ms. Everly had been here. And he knew they both had been taken. He was only hoping and praying that they were still alive.

Joseph crushed the temporary HAARP badge in his hand, utterly furious with the situation. The records plan had failed. Which meant that Kratos had been fully aware of it from the beginning.

They were wasting their time here. He was about to suggest moving on when Donáll was suddenly yammering in his ear.

"Boss, Boss, Boss! A shot fired in No Man's Land! You gotta get over there! GET OVER THERE NOW!"

Joseph never thought he would be overjoyed to hear those words. Now for the supersonic hearing abilities.

"What was that?" Joseph asked.

Montage stared at him with sudden stress etched across every one of his weak features. "What?" he asked, concentrating on a conversation in his own ear.

Which was all the distraction Joseph Moore needed. "A silenced gunshot, if my ears are not failing me! And they never do!" Joseph rapidly took off running, Davies and Rogers racing along beside him. Montage gave a high-pitched yell and started shouting in barely coherent sentences that his party was running away without supervision.

Hold on. We're coming!

With Donáll reciting the pathway to the abandoned lab from memory, Joseph, Davies, and Rogers quickly gained ground in that direction. Montage was chasing them and calling for more guards.

Now only two questions remained. Would they make it to the abandoned lab region before being shot or dragged out? And was the gunshot enough for Donáll to bring in their backup?

Hold on. We're coming.

A SILENCED GUNSHOT RESONATED in the room, but it was not Patch who fell. One of the guards had been hit in the leg, and he collapsed, crying out in pain. Before the other guard could react, his gun was actually shot out of his hand.

Alina searched frantically for the source of the shots. Blane Burns was springing on top of the guard who had just lost his gun, cutting off his cry with a hold around his neck before he slammed the guard's head against the ground, stunning him. Another blow to the head, and the man lost consciousness.

While Blane was taking out the one guard, the one who had been shot had crawled toward his own gun, but Patch was on him in a matter of seconds. A well-placed blow to the head, and he was out too.

Alina slowly sank to the ground, shock and relief depleting any strength left in her. But Blane quickly pulled Patch to his feet, and he dragged Alina along with him through the innermost door. The one that he had emerged from, following what Alina could only assume was the same pathway that the man and his bodyguards had taken.

"We have to be quick and quiet," Blane was saying between breaths. "There are camera feeds in here, and I saw Moore and the others standing outside the labs right before I joined you. I hope the shots are enough to get the reinforcements in. But the three of us? We cannot get caught."

Alina was hanging onto his every word. He had come. Just like at the hotel. She had called out to him now, and he had come and rescued them. She had watched him effortlessly incapacitate two guards rather than killing them.

Thank You, God, for this man.

But Patch interrupted her reflections of awe with a forceful "Burns! Did you see this?"

Alina turned her attention to where Patch was gesturing. Rows and rows of glass bottles, situated behind enforced glass cabinetry as far as she could see in the laboratory sanctum. Maybe thousands of them. Maybe millions. And over half of them were filled with a crystal-clear fluid. Biohazard machinery and pharmaceutical equipment were also organized in purposeful stations around the room. Alina's blood turned to ice in her veins, however, at the sight of endless military gas masks lining the wall, illuminated by biohazard signs and flashing red lights.

"What is all this..." Patch murmured.

Blane's expression was dark. "I think Kratos has been creating some sort of...biological warfare. I was able to take some pictures for evidence before I heard Alina call my name."

Patch nodded, and they all ran toward an exit on the other side of the lab. But Alina's mind was not ready to leave the moment.

Alina... He called me Alina.

JOSEPH, DAVIES, AND ROGERS all tensed as they heard a woman yell. Joseph was terrified he knew to whom it belonged. They paused outside a cemented-shut door that Donáll confirmed was the main door to the abandoned labs.

"HEY! You three are not authorized to be down here! And I don't know what distress sounds you imagined you heard, but there were none."

When the three men didn't move, Montage's face turned beet red. "You three will leave now, or I will have my men here forcibly remove you from the premises."

Come on, Burns. Help us get inside.

Suddenly, two silenced gunshots and cries from inside the wall wiped the smug look off Party Boy's face.

"Will you provide entry to the other side of this door, or will you force my colleague to resort to destructive measures...Freddie?" Joseph asked. He nodded his head toward Davies, who began slowly rolling up his sleeves. Montage was glaring at them. He eventually gestured to one of his men, and Joseph watched in amazement as a concealed entrance suddenly materialized in the wall.

"Donáll," Joseph murmured. "Are they coming? Are the reinforcements coming?"

Joseph never heard an answer, and he forced himself to focus on the hidden electric door slowly opening in front of them. Montage, a resigned look on his face, gestured for Joseph and his team to go down into the lab first. Joseph's fingers closed around his Glock 22.

Two guards were unconscious and bleeding on the floor. A trail of blood lead through another door which had been left open by... someone.

"And here you were telling us that the labs down here are completely abandoned!" Joseph scoffed. "Two armed guards and a... secret room."

The three men walked into the inner sanctum of Kratos's Alaskan stronghold. Joseph's breath fled him as the sight of millions of glass bottles met his eyes. Bioterrorism.

Davies appeared to be just as shell shocked, and Rogers's eyes hardened. Somehow, this seemed bigger and more catastrophic than what they had been anticipating.

Azrael, indeed.

Joseph could only imagine the destructive capabilities of whatever he was staring at. He did not have a long time for reflections, however, as he abruptly heard the sound of five guns cocking. With their hands in the air, they slowly turned to face Montage and his armed guards.

"There. Are you three happy now?" Montage demanded with an ugly sneer. "You have given me absolutely no choice. You invited death in, and now it's here. You simply have seen too much."

Montage took a couple of steps toward Joseph and purred through his next words.

"Before I have you killed, I want to know. Who beat down my guards? I'll easily find out who I communicated with back in Washington, and that woman will soon be killed. But who was in here?"

Joseph refused to meet the questioning glances of Davies and Rogers. He was simply listening for Donáll. To confirm that the place was surrounded. To confirm that this execution would be stopped cold before a single shot was fired.

"You seem to be at a loss for words, old man," Montage snapped, anger clouding his features.

Joseph met his gaze. And then he answered. He couldn't help himself.

"'Old man?' You should learn to respect your elders, runt. You would have had much to learn."

Montage's face turned a furious shade of red. "'Would have had?'" he sputtered. "I don't think that you understand the gravity of the situation. I am going to have my men shoot you—"

"Yes, yes, we know," Davies interrupted. "But it isn't that simple."

Fred Montage raised a brow. "Oh? Do you even know who you are—"

"If you and your guards want to live to see tomorrow, we suggest you put your weapons down and raise your hands," Rogers cut in with a voice of ice.

"Or don't," Davies goaded. "And we'll take bets on how long you have left."

Joseph smiled, pleased at how easily this inept fool had become unsettled. But the dread in his stomach was growing. It grew in fact, for an additional three seconds of silence.

Three.

Excruciating.

Seconds.

He felt Davies's eyes on him.

Montage breathed out in relief, a smirk once again spreading over his face. Just as he opened his mouth, a voice sounded over the sound system that extended throughout the entire complex.

"This is the FBI! We have you surrounded. Place your weapons on the ground and put your hands on your heads!"

Joseph, Davies, and Rogers took the moment of panic to swiftly take down the five operatives. Joseph knocked Montage's gun from his hand and kicked his feet out from underneath him. He confiscated the gun then met another guard head-on. With a few blows, Joseph had him on the ground, groaning in pain. Joseph stepped back to survey the quick work he and his team had made of the room as Rogers and Davies kept their pistols trained on the men in front of them.

Joseph shouted, "In here!" and a team of Alaskan Federal agents swiftly located the concealed door and entered the room, their guns trained on the prisoners.

Erik walked in just then, nodding to Joseph. "Howdy, brother."

Joseph let out a breath he hadn't realized he had been holding, and he clapped his old buddy on the back. "We are certainly glad to see you and your boys. Have a look," Joseph said, inviting the seasoned FBI agent into the adjoining room housing the thousands of bottles. "This is what Kratos's Alaskan venture has been. I think we should lock this area down, at least until we can get your forensics team in here to survey the stuff. I want to know what we are dealing with."

Erik whistled. "Kratos. They kinda fell off our radar for a while, and I was shocked when you called and said they may be operating at HAARP. Right under our very noses. And it looks like they have been busy."

"If it's safe to transport, I want a few bottles shipped to Washington, and every bottle must be thoroughly accounted for," Joseph replied. "Whatever this is, I have a feeling it…well, I hate to use the cliché phrase, but it undoubtedly was manufactured as a weapon of mass destruction."

"I have to agree that that's the appropriate term for it, pal." Erik paused, his expression darkening. "And we have no idea how many bottles have already been distributed."

"Nor why they paused production," Joseph added, running his hand down his chin.

"Okay, next steps," the other agent began. "I'm bringing in reinforcements from Washington, and we'll clean this place out and confiscate all of the equipment. We'll run tests on it and see if there's any way we can trace it. We'll lay traps for potential black-market buyers and for companies that already may have their hands on it, and we'll ultimately shut this place down. It'll take time to distinguish true HAARP researchers from turned Kratos operatives."

"Try to keep this as contained as possible," Joseph said. He glanced out toward Montage. The man's eyes were glued to the floor in shock as he was being handcuffed.

Joseph lowered his voice to a murmur. "Though Kratos undoubtedly already knows what happened here, this will root them out. We have to watch them make their next move carefully. I'm afraid punishment will be thoroughly attempted for all failures made tonight, starting with Fred Montage." Joseph locked eyes with his friend. "As much as that guy makes me want to shoot him, we need him alive. Keep him safe."

"Understood." As both men turned and walked back to the main laboratory, a state trooper began reporting to Erik.

"We got men at all the exits, and most people, namely the HAARP scientists, are assembling peacefully in the main lobby for questioning. We rounded up all the hostiles we found, and your agents and mine are still looking…"

While the trooper continued, Joseph nodded to Davies and Rogers and made his way out of the lab.

DAVIES AND ROGERS RUSHED to catch up to Joseph as he walked rapidly down the hallway.

"What on earth just happened?" Davies asked. "How did we get in there? Who took out those guards? Boss?"

"I would like to know the same thing, Moore," Rogers affirmed coolly, staring at Joseph.

"The records room was not enough," Joseph murmured. "But I can only tell you more back at the safe house."

They began making their way down the hallway, heading for the main doors. All of a sudden, the men cringed as Donáll's shrill voice trilled over their comms.

"FELLOWS! You're still alive. How exciting."

Joseph squeezed his fists together, slowly, steadily, taking a deep breath. "Yes, we are still alive. No thanks to you, Donáll. Why didn't you give the confirmation that the agents and troopers were in position?"

Davies and Rogers both stared at Joseph, their mouths hanging open.

"You antagonized Montage back there before you knew we had backup?" Davies asked.

"I seem to recall you calling Montage a 'runt,' Moore," Rogers added.

Joseph simply let loose a nervous laugh. Then he was shouting.

"DONÁLL! I'm still waiting for an explanation."

Annoyance laced the tech man's voice as he answered. "I was a bit distracted. I needed to make sure that the others were out, and I still do not have a visual on them."

"Burns, Alina, and Patch?" he asked, fear dripping from each word.

Before Davies or Rogers could say a word, he held up a hand. "Donáll? Is it them?" Joseph repeated.

"No, her friend and Pete. They were opening the Kratos safe in the records room when I unexpectedly lost contact with them. All my feeds went black, remember? I still haven't found them, even though I brought everything back up."

His team looked at him. "We need to find them," Davies said slowly.

Joseph nodded gravely. "Yes. But their presence here needs to be a secret. We cannot have everyone looking—"

"Sir, they could be dead—" Rogers interrupted, but his words were stopped short as Joseph slammed his fist against the wall.

"I KNOW! I know..." Joseph trailed off wearily. "He's one of my best friends. But we can't risk them being found. If charged for trespassing on federal grounds, it will land them in jail. And incarceration would make them sitting ducks for Kratos. DONÁLL! Please tell me you've got something. I'm going to go talk to Erik, but I think we need someone still inside and under the radar to search for them."

"'Someone still inside,' Boss?" Davies asked.

"Yes. Donáll. Is Burns still in the complex?"

"Affirmative. And... I...yes, I found Pete and Ms. Everly!"

BLANE, MS. DIXON, AND Patch were hiding in the vent system just outside of the abandoned laboratories. He had remembered the accessible structure from Donáll's blueprints, and they had sheltered here at the last moment before the lab doors opened and Moore and the others came in.

Blane was relieved to hear the sounds of the reinforcements streaming into the labs. He knew this would be a major setback for Kratos. A voice suddenly screeched over his comms unit, and he felt Ms. Dixon and Patch cringe beside him in the darkness.

"Hey! Hey, guys. Are you all okay?"

In as low a whisper as Blane could muster, he began to answer Donáll. "The three of us are safe for the time—"

"Great, great. Fantastic. Except we have a problem."

Dread uncurled in Blane's stomach.

"Pete and Ms. Everly are trapped a distance from where you are. I can only see their heat signatures, so I can't accurately determine their current state of being."

Blane felt a hand latch on to his, squeezing hard.

Ms. Dixon.

"According to my blueprints, it actually looks like they are in one of the conference rooms. They were undoubtedly taken when their feeds went dark and I lost contact when they opened the safe in the records room and they were talking to me but I lost them—"

"Donáll!" Blane hissed. "They need to be extracted without the Feds and troopers finding out, yes?"

"Yes, that's actually why the boss had me talk to you, Mr. B. Very delicate matter."

Blane blew out a breath, his mind racing.

Aye. That is one way to put it.

He squeezed Ms. Dixon's hand back as he replied. "Okay. Okay, I'll get there. And Patch and Ms. Dixon?"

"They should just sit tight, right where they are. You going alone will draw way less attention. Moore will make sure they are told when the coast is clear, and then they can go back out the way they came. The sooner we all get back to the safe house, the better."

"Understood," Blane replied. "The hallway?"

"A couple of agents running by, but if you head out in the next twenty seconds, you should be clear. Then you'll head to your right. I'll direct you."

Blane took a breath, released Ms. Dixon's hand, then slid over to the opening in the vent.

Once twenty seconds had passed on his mental clock, he silently dropped down into the semi-lit hallway. He hit the floor running, keeping his breathing steady.

Silence in the interminable hall. His heartbeat thundering in his ears. Shouts far away...some distant firing. Heavy footsteps, and he hid amongst the shadows, trusting that his newly-donned black clothes would conceal him. Silence again. A sigh of relief. And the adrenaline pumping through his entire being.

"Okay, I'm heading right. How far away?" he murmured.

"Keep going right. Then you'll make a left. And then you'll go straight." Blane followed his instructions, silently jogging down the hallways. Pausing to get his bearings.

Left. Then straight.

"Keep going straight. Then cut right. And then you'll want to go up that flight of stairs, and then you'll be right there. They'll be to your left—"

"I'm there," Blane interrupted, bending over to catch his breath. "To my left, you say?"

Silence on the other end. "Yes. Yes, the left. Wow."

Blane searched the wall to his left, but no doorway met his eye. "I see nothing. It must be a secret room of some sort. You said it was a conference room?"

"Yes, well, it used to be. And from this camera view, it still looks that way. They must have just disguised the outside. Maybe they have lots of good stuff in there! Besides our friends, I mean."

"Aye. Exactly the thought that crossed my mind," Blane said softly.

He tapped the wall, listening, breathing. He didn't think he could risk some light, but he had no idea how he would find the concealed opening. "Are they incapacitated? Or are they awake and mobile?"

"Well, I can't tell with just the heat signatures, can I? But actually, one of them moved a little when you tapped on the wall. I think one is…yep, one is coming close to you."

Blane's heart leaped. This would perhaps be easier than he had been thinking. "Ms. Everly?" he murmured, his voice conspicuously rumbling in the darkness. "Pete? Can you hear me?"

He heard a voice through the wall. "Who are you?" It was Ms. Everly's voice.

"Blane. Blane Burns. Are you both all right? I'm here to help you, but I can't seem to find the door. Is there a way to open it up from in there, lass? Can you see anything…" He trailed off, thinking he heard soft crying.

"I don't know… I just, I don't know…" she said, her voice weak with tired despair. "It's just so dark, and my hands are all slippery, and I—" She stopped, her cries becoming more and more debilitating.

Burning dread once again took up residence in his stomach at her words. "Don't worry, lass. I'll get in. I'll get you out. I'll get you both out."

Blane's voice sounded calmer than he truly felt. Dropping to his knees, he started searching along the bottom of the wall for some sort of catch or gap he could get his fingers in. "Are you hurt?"

"I'm fine," she murmured. "But Pete, he's...he's bleeding so much..."

"Okay, okay, we're going to get him out. Don't you worry yourself. We'll get him out together." He suddenly caught hold of something that gave a little as he pulled.

He pulled harder until a door opened in the wall with an ominous, echoing creak. Blane froze, holding his breath as he awaited heavy footfalls on the stairs. But all was silence.

Blane gently eased the door open further, and he crept through. And collided into what he could only assume was Ms. Everly. He started to step back when the girl wrapped her arms around him and began sobbing into his chest. He stood completely still for a moment. Then he gently put his arms around her. Once her sobs subsided, he pulled back, rubbing her freezing arms with his warm hands.

"Let's get out of here, all right, lass?" he asked. In the dim light coming from the hall, he could see her give a small nod. "Donáll? Anyone nearby?"

"Nope. You should be good. For a little while."

"Okay, okay. I'm going to risk some light, yes? Let's see what we have," Blane said softly, pulling out his phone. He turned his flashlight on its lowest setting, and he breathed out in relief as he surveyed her. Aside from drying blood on her forearms and hands, he didn't see any active bleeding or gaping wounds. He turned his attention to the soft moans he only now noticed were coming from the other end of the room, and his flashlight revealed the crumpled form of Pete. A sweater was wrapped around his head, but the fabric was soaked through with blood.

Acting quickly, Blane knelt down next to him and spoke to the old man. "Pete? Can you hear me?"

"Someone struck him on the back of the head," she said shakily. "The wound has been bleeding pretty badly. May I have your phone?"

She proceeded to shine the light carefully in each of Pete's eyes. "His pupils are reacting okay, so I think he might just have a mild concussion, but we'll need to watch him...after we..."

"Get out of here," Blane finished for her.

She helped Blane lift Pete over his shoulder, but the man weighed more than Blane had anticipated. Gritting his teeth, he readjusted his grip as carefully as he could. As Ms. Everly beamed the light around Kratos's hidden room, Blane finally took time to survey the interior. The circle of light illuminated a series of graphics on the walls, with a glass case embedded in the midst of them. The command fired off before he truly had time to process it.

"Shine the light on that case again!"

He knew they could not lose this chance. Holding tightly to the man slowly sapping his arms of strength, he appealed to her again.

"Please, lass. Just for a second. That's all I need."

A few seconds were all he got as voices suddenly amplified in the nearby hallways.

"Let's go," he said, and she led the way out of the room. As she turned off his light and the area plunged into near-blackness again, he assumed the lead, whispering to her to hold his loose-hanging hood so she would not lose them.

Listening to Donáll, they moved quickly down the opposite hallway, avoiding the stairs he had used to initially reach the room. Any energy he had felt draining away from him had been restored with full force, and he practically flew down the hall, all the while ensuring that Ms. Everly never lost her grip.

Earlier that night, he had heard a name. And now he knew a place.

ALINA QUICKLY WIPED AWAY her tears in the back of the van. Terror and doubt were working in tandem, destroying what was left of her sanity.

Oh, God, please keep Pete and Ami safe. And Blane. Please be with them. Bring them all safely back to me. Please.

She looked up and made eye contact with Patch, and he gave her a gentle smile. She could see his hands clasped in prayer, and he soon closed his eyes again, his lips moving silently.

A sense of peace filled Alina, and she leaned back against her seat.

Then she rapidly sat up as one of the van doors opened, and Joseph and Blane carefully lifted Pete into the vehicle. The old man was breathing.

Oh, thank You, God. Thank You.

Patch released a sigh of hearty relief at the sight of his friend.

Alina strained to look out of the tinted windows, the unasked question nearly bursting from her. But then she looked back to the men laying Pete on the floor.

Blane's eyes met hers, and she saw all the tension in them immediately melt into a dark-blue softness. He answered her with a strong voice.

"Ms. Everly is safe and well, right beside me. She tended to Pete's injuries while they were…inside."

Relief filled Alina at his words, and she continued to pray silent prayers of thanks as Blane moved aside and Ami stepped up to the van. Other than the dried blood on her hands and clothes and the exhaustion keeping her barely upright, Ami looked okay.

Her best friend was alive. And well. It was too much to ask for.

Blane helped Ami crawl into the van, and Alina saw that his arms were shaking.

He must have carried Pete all the way out here.

Joseph was addressing the van, relaying that they would leave immediately and meet the others at the safe house. His gaze shifted toward Pete as he spoke, and he then looked at both Alina and Ami.

His eyes conveyed that he fully trusted them to take care of his friend.

Monitor neuro status and neuromotor responses. Cleanse it. Stitch it. Bandage it. Monitor for bleeding. Frequent neuro checks. Yes. We can take care of him.

She stilled at the sudden intensity of his gaze. There was something there…something else. She had nearly forgotten the night he had been standing outside of her room. She had nearly forgotten his panicked expression, his rushed response to placate her.

But she refused to dwell on those doubts. She refused to doubt him—the man who was giving so much to solve this. To protect her and Ami. The man whose support mirrored the kindness of Soter—the faceless man who had loved her through cards and exotic gifts over the years.

Joseph climbed into the driver's seat, and Blane sat in the passenger's side.

"Let's get out of here, team," Joseph rumbled, his blue eyes bright and piercing in the rearview mirror.

As they drove away, Patch switched seats with Ami in the middle of the van to be closer to his friend, and Ami slowly moved back to sit beside Alina. Alina wrapped her arms around her best friend, and Ami sank against her.

Wetness on Alina's shirt. Holding her. Smoothing her hair as she cried. Holding her as tightly as she could.

Hold her, Jesus. She needs You right now.

Suddenly, Ami's breath hitched, and she shuddered violently in Alina's arms. Alina followed her gaze out the back of the van, and her eyes landed on a man, standing in the exact place their van had been not a minute before. He was slowly disappearing in the darkness, yet she knew exactly who he was.

It was the man in the middle, the man whose smile had since haunted her mind and invaded her thoughts. The man who had mercilessly orchestrated murder, calmly, without any feeling in his voice.

And he was smiling that same smile, so far away. Sociopathic. Inhuman.

Alina stared harder, but he had vaporized, vanishing in the snow and surrounding trees.

Dread filled Alina, and she hugged Ami with all the strength she had left. Soon, Ami was breathing soft constant breaths, and Alina just held her. All the way back to the safe house.

Just hold her, Jesus. Please hold her.

CHAPTER EIGHT

BLANE BURNS WAS SITTING STIFFLY ON A HARDBACK CHAIR AT THE SAFE HOUSE, HIS ARMS CROSSED UNCOMFORTABLY.

Ms. Dixon had just massaged his shoulders. He was afraid of how much it had meant to him. He could have lost her so many times within the last seven hours, and he had to keep reminding himself that he hadn't.

And that he had gotten what they needed.

The name he had heard echoed throughout his mind, searching fruitlessly for a foothold in some memory, some case from MI5 long ago…it was all a bottomless chasm he couldn't grasp. But he had a name. And he had a place. *Austria.*

His attention snapped to the present as Ms. Dixon, Ms. Everly, Moore, Davies, Rogers, and Donáll entered the room. Patch was still sitting with Pete in one of the bedrooms. The old man was resting comfortably after the two nurses had masterfully stitched up his head. All except Moore sat down, preparing for a quick debrief before moving into the next phase. A phase that Blane was thoroughly looking forward to having, despite his exhaustion.

Moore blew out a long breath, and Blane only now noticed dark circles under his eyes and tense lines burdening the older agent's face. He knew the mission had weighed more heavily on Moore than perhaps anyone realized.

Moore spoke, his commanding voice demanding the attention of the room. "I am so, so proud of everyone here. We made it in there, we did what we had to do, and we…we are all still alive. And going to stay that way, thanks to our skilled nurses."

He dipped his head in gratitude toward the two women, and smiles spread over both of their faces.

"Erik called. Twenty-six suspected Kratos operatives were taken into custody, but it is clear that many escaped as the raid got underway. And Fred Montage"—Moore sighed, his head hanging lower with each word—"was somehow killed. Staged like a suicide right under the noses of the Feds who had him in custody. He knew more than any of the muscle caught. They claim he hung himself in his cell before he could be questioned…but we all know better." Raising his head up once more, the weary older agent continued.

"I do have some concrete news regarding the bottles we found. The lab discovered that the liquid inside is, as far as they can tell, a potent mutation of the Marburg virus. Kratos must have isolated strains of it from animal hosts and synthesized virulence factors in the lab to cultivate its mortality."

"What is the Marburg virus?" Ms. Dixon asked. "That is not something that I remember hearing about," she said, turning to her friend for confirmation.

As Ms. Everly shook her head, Moore answered. "Essentially, it is a hemorrhagic virus that comes from fruit bats in a very specific part of Africa. It causes high fevers, severe vomiting and diarrhea, and disrupts normal clotting capabilities in the blood, causing the person to hemorrhage. This results in hemorrhagic shock and organ failure. The original virus has a high mortality rate—it was already deemed a category A bioterrorism agent. Kratos seems to have streamlined it. Their efforts have not only decreased the incubation period, but they also have exponentiated the hemorrhagic factor."

Moore took a deep breath. "The lab thinks it could now be fatal in a matter of hours. The victim would just bleed out."

Blane felt coldness spread down his arms to his fingertips.

"The people at the lab are very…concerned. It apparently undergoes escape variance almost instantaneously when threatened. We have nothing in the world that could even be manipulated to start working on a cure. They said that an antidote for this kind of virus would be valuable beyond measure."

The room took a collective breath.

"MI5, CIA, the FBI from Washington, and a few Interpol agents are flying out to get their hands on this case. It's so huge that everyone wants a piece of it for their respective top research facilities. And there will be a task force assigned to tracing the mutated strain to determine if any samples were sold or if any cases have been reported."

The tension was palpable as Moore continued.

"I am nearly convinced that we may still be okay—as Kratos stopped production, we can only hope that they stopped distribution. But, thankfully, our team here will not have to worry about that. We need to focus our attention in a forward trajectory."

Moore glanced at each member of the team as he continued. "As a positive note, Erik has assured me that no one will be privy to the actual events that led up to the official raid. That should answer at least one concern that I'm sure you all have. I'll now stop talking and open the floor for questions."

The agent collapsed on a couch, though his eyes and expression remained alert. Davies jumped up immediately.

"Alrighty. Boss, I know you said earlier that you had Blane, Alina, and Patch on an even more secretive mission than the rest of us. You wanted them to get to the labs, and then you wanted them to provide us with reasonable cause to investigate. And it worked. And we're all still alive." Davies proceeded to finish his line of thought, staring thoughtfully at Moore the whole time.

"And it was a great move because Kratos was somehow aware of our plan to infiltrate the records room."

"You are correct," Moore replied. "I knew we needed another hand in this, and only Donáll, myself, and those directly involved were aware of the plan. And somehow, we avoided Kratos to get them in there without problems."

"Actually, sir, we did have a situation," Blane spoke up, and all eyes settled on him. "I was separated from them when we discovered the decoy lab."

"What happened?" Moore asked carefully.

Blane replayed the events in his head, reminding himself that he was surrounded by people he trusted.

For the most part.

"I circled back but couldn't get close enough to get in. I was almost blown by a group of three men, but I was able to discreetly tail them at a distance. My instincts told me that they would lead me to that lab a different way. And they did."

Blane placed his hands on the table, feeling the solid surface beneath.

"The three men entered through the opposite hall using another concealed door, which led to a similar abandoned decoy lab. It opened directly into another section which I now believe housed the fruit bats. There were rows and rows of empty cages and chemical equipment."

Blane glanced at the team as he spoke. "I slipped in before the door sealed, and the men moved on into the one containing the virus itself. I followed when I heard them pass into the next decoy lab— the lab where I was certain Patch and Ms. Dixon were hiding. I was gathering evidence when I heard Ms. Dixon call my name. I made it over there and saw the two guards, and I...well. I intervened." Blane took a deep breath, steeling his nerves.

"So, we were discovered. But you lot came in next, so, well, here we are."

Ms. Dixon spoke up, her voice shaking slightly. "Before those guards came in, we heard someone get shot out in the hallway."

Moore addressed her. "They never did find the body, but they found traces of blood in that area. Whatever happened, that shot is what Donáll heard to get us running in your direction."

"How did Kratos learn of the records plan?" Rogers was on his feet, and he took a seat beside Ms. Everly. "Do you remember what happened?" he asked quietly.

"Pete was o-opening the safe," she began, her voice quivering. "I was walking toward the back of the room, as I had...heard a noise." Her eyes were locked on the table as she relived everything.

"Someone grabbed me and dragged me out of the room, and I didn't have time to scream before something was put over my head. I heard the safe open, and I heard Pete searching for me...and then...

I was in that black room somehow, and Pete was dropped beside me, and I was trying to stop the bleeding..." She trailed off.

The room plunged into silence, and at last Moore stood. "I am truly sorry for what happened. You should have never been in a position of such danger, and I can never apologize enough for that. But I am afraid the only thing we can do now is keep moving forward. Which I am completely at a loss of how to do." The agent released a long breath. "We rooted Kratos out of HAARP, but I'm afraid we learned nothing of the spider in the center of the web."

The silence was suffocating, heavy with disappointment. Then Blane heard his own voice beaming through the midst of it. "Actually, sir, I think I can help with that."

All eyes turned toward him.

"I followed those men, as I said, and I was sure that the one was the commanding presence. They walked in perfect synchrony with him, and they flawlessly responded to his every word. One of them said his name."

Blane took a breath.

"Black. Mr. Black."

Thundering. Electrifying. Dread mixed with equal doses of fear and thrill.

The stillness was broken as Donáll's fingers flew across his keyboard, beginning to sift through every piece of online data, government file, and dark web association for the name.

Ms. Dixon's voice joined the ceaseless tapping.

"I saw him...he turned and smiled at Patch and me. And I saw him as we were leaving HAARP this morning. He was...st-standing there, just smiling again."

She took a shuddering breath, and Blane wanted nothing more in the world than to find the man and destroy him. For Isla and Olivia. For Ms. Dixon. For every single person in the room.

It had been Blane's purpose for so long. Find and finish Antonov, then find the man responsible for ordering the hit. Then Blane would finish him, too.

Burning, slowly spreading through Blane again. It was like a friend that had abandoned him for the last few days. And Blane could only attribute its loss to the woman in his charge.

He could wait no longer. "I think I know where to find him." All eyes on him once more. Some shocked, others cold. Others filled with fear.

Ms. Everly was looking at him, her eyes wide, her lips slightly parted. He knew she remembered. The glass case.

It had been enough time.

"When I extracted Pete and Ms. Everly, I saw something in that room—"

Donáll, who had been silent up to that point, jumped in. "Yes! It had been completely remodeled on the outside, so I knew it was a big room of Kratos's secrets."

"There was a wall filled with blueprints, maps, and other detailed plans," Blane continued, "but only one thing drew my attention. A glass case with a special event featured inside. I could only make out the name, which was German for 'Imperial Ball.' I can only assume that it was referring to—"

"The New Year's Eve Ball at the Hofburg Palace in Vienna, Austria," Moore said slowly. "Excellent work, Burns. Perhaps Mr. Black has a penchant for the debutantes. Donáll, I want you on this immediately. See if you can find any online proof of this idea, and I'll get in contact with Interpol to get some backup over there. Excellent, Burns. Exactly what we needed…"

Blane lost track of Moore's words in the busy excitement of the room. He felt a sudden chill, a dagger of hatred from some gaze, yet the only eyes he met as a he glanced around the room were full of fear.

Ms. Everly. Her brown eyes wide. Shining with tears. Pure, desperate fear.

Blane could only hold that gaze. He couldn't look away. The world around him felt dull, slow. Her fear engraving itself, deep in his mind. Ms. Dixon soon drew her attention, and she looked away.

What happened, truly, in that room?

He was so shaken by her gaze that he had to leave, crossing through the safe house to reach the porch. The early morning sunshine did nothing to relieve his pounding head, his thundering heart.

He lifted shaking hands.

Vulnerable.

He shook his head, locked his hands into fists. But there was nothing he could do. The memories were coming.

A startled crow suddenly flew past him, and Blane turned to see Rogers behind him. The agent was standing a few paces away, concern clouding his gaze.

"Hey, man," Rogers said quietly as he closed the distance between them. "I saw you come out here."

As they stood in silence, staring at the distant mountains, the agent grasped Blane's shoulder. "No matter what is consuming you right now, we need you to focus. We all need to. If we do, we can get these guys. You hear me?"

"Aye," Blane responded softly.

Rogers nodded, and he left Blane standing there.

A deep breath. The memories reburied. And the burning restored.

Antonov had been strangely absent from this whole affair. Where was his part in all of this? Blane would find him. In Austria, halfway across the world, anywhere. He would track him down. He was good at that. He was ready.

Suddenly, Ms. Dixon's laugh—a sound he had not heard in many days—resounded in his ears. And a memory from before HAARP cooled his rampant, boiling thoughts. It was a simple request that Ms. Every had asked of him concerning Ms. Dixon. He had completely forgotten about it. Blane shook his head, a sigh escaping his lips. He didn't like it. But he knew he at least had to try to get it done. As he made his way back inside, he was startled out of his thoughts by a triumphant shout from Donáll.

"GOTCHA!"

The man stood smirking at his computer, holding his cold cup of black coffee. He finally looked around the room.

"I found our spider. It took a lot of work, like always. But I beat it. And I got it." The man paused, drawing out the suspense even as everyone stared at him.

"Draven. It's Draven Black," he announced finally.

The room exploded with activity as Moore, Davies, and Rogers swarmed Donáll. Blane watched from a distance, his heart pounding. *Well, well, well. Draven Black. Finally.*

They had the man's full name. Now it would only be a matter of time. But first, there was Ms. Everly's request. He waited until Moore looked up at him, and then he gestured for the older agent to join him in the hallway. Once the man stood before him, Blane addressed him.

"Sir," he began slowly, "I have a peculiar favor to ask of you…"

ALINA'S HEART WAS POUNDING. She didn't know where they were going. Or why Blane was being secretive. They were sitting in one of Hawk's tiny helicopters, which he had somehow acquisitioned for this trip. They were somewhere south from where the safe house had been, but Blane was keeping their destination a secret from her.

He was looking at her, his gaze soft. She couldn't be certain, but she thought she felt something different in the air between them. He had come to her rescue back in that laboratory. She had called for him, not knowing if he could even hear her. And he had come, and he had saved her.

She was embarrassed by how desperately she wanted to kiss him. But Alina was still afraid of the haggard despair she caught glimpses of in his eyes. That loss…that unrelenting pain. It seemed to strike him out of nowhere, and then it slowly ate away at him.

In those moments, he seemed so lost, so full of guilt…and then the look in his eyes would darken to one of hate and revenge. And that was what she was even more afraid of. He needed help, but she knew she did not have the power to give it. Only God could. Blane needed to see that.

The minutes ticked by faster than she realized, and Hawk was soon landing the plane on an open stretch of concrete.

"Let's go, lass," Blane said.

He stood and, crouching so his head wouldn't scrape across the top of the tiny aircraft, he opened his door and jumped down to the concrete below. He came around the side of the helicopter, waited for her to open her door, and held out his hand to help her down. She had a flashback of Blane opening the door of his car for her back in Washington.

So long ago. Much had happened since then.

As her feet hit the pavement, salty sea air assailed her, and all of her senses became fine-tuned to her surroundings. The crash of ocean waves…the cry of gulls. A touch of warm sunshine beaming down. Deep blue ocean water, spanning as far as her eyes could see.

"The Gulf of Alaska," Blane said, looking at her.

"It's beautiful," she breathed.

Blane offered her his arm, and she took it as they began walking toward a tiny complex near the water.

Could it be?

They entered the building, and Blane exchanged vague words with the woman behind the counter as he subtly passed her several large bills. Soon Alina found herself sitting on the concrete outside by the water, with a towel-wrapped bundle lying contentedly in her arms.

There was a tiny sea otter pup sleeping inside, its little flippers sticking out. She just stared at it, happiness flooding through her. The woman stayed nearby, but Alina and Blane were able to sit side by side for a few silent, precious moments.

Alina stared into the sea otter's adorable face, and she gently caressed the soft fur of its head. This had always been one of her dreams. Yet she had never imagined that it would involve the most handsome man in the world sitting beside her.

She kept stroking the sea otter's head, and after several moments, she gave in to the urge to gently lift up one of its tiny flippers. Now it was awake, and the pup did not like it. It started letting out a series of squeaks, and it stared at her with wide eyes. Alina frantically tried stroking the little sea otter back to sleep, and even Blane tried speaking to it in the gentlest voice she had ever heard from him. But the pup had had enough. She and Blane locked eyes, both panicked, both filled with mirth.

"Uh…ma'am?" Blane managed, and he and Alina burst out laughing.

The smiling trainer took the sea otter from Alina, telling them that they could leave the way they had come in. Once they were outside, Alina broke the growing silence with the question that had been on her mind ever since the sea otter had been placed in her arms.

"Did Ami put you up to this?"

Blane gave her a sideways smile. "Aye, Ms. Everly. That she did. When Davies was trying to distract you by talking about board games."

"Blane?" Alina asked.

"Mm-hmm?"

"I think she would like it if you called her Ami. You can always ask her, of course, but I think she would like that."

"I'll…keep that in mind," he replied, still staring out at the sea.

"And Blane?" Alina asked again, still feeling the warm little sea otter in her arms. "You just made one of my dreams come true. I… I'm just so… Well, I can't put it into words."

He peeked at her from the corner of his eye.

"May I…just…uh…" She trailed off, but at the soft look in his eyes, she went for it. She wrapped her arms around him and held on tight. She felt like some huge, burdening weight was lifting off her, even though his touch on her back was light. He was silent. And she had one more request of him.

"Blane?"

BLANE LIGHTLY EMBRACED THE woman in front of him, a tumult of emotions throwing his brain into a frenzy. The one clear sensation coming through was the smell of her hair. It was that same flowery scent he had smelled on her bathrobe that lonely night in the hallway. With a start, he realized he needed to answer her.

"Yes, Ms. Dixon?" he replied with difficulty. Every one of his senses felt electrified.

"You have saved my life twice now. I know I am hardly in a position to ask for anything more," she mumbled, her voice muffled against his coat. "But could you call me Alina? You did once, and I've wanted to hear you say it again ever since."

She pulled back from him, and her beautiful brown eyes stared up searchingly into his. He was absolutely mesmerized by those eyes. Colors swirled into a masterpiece...like rich chocolate and a touch of red velvet. Sparkling.

And waiting for his answer.

"Aye," he replied softly.

His entire world glowed to life, shadows dissipating in the air as a smile lit up her beautiful face and she wrapped her arms around him once more. He was smelling her hair again. He tried her name out, mouthing it silently to himself.

Alina. Alina. Aye, Alina it is.

And he hugged her back.

JOSEPH LEANED AGAINST THE side of the safe house, slowly shaking his head to clear his mind. He was exhausted. Patch approached him, saying that Pete was awake and wanting to talk.

Joseph hurried into the room, checking his watch for the hundredth time to see if Burns and Alina would return soon. Burns had updated him fifteen minutes ago, and Hawk's coordinates revealed that they were only a few minutes out.

Perfect. They would leave for Austria in approximately two hours.

Joseph observed his friend, who was sitting comfortably on the bed, glaring at him.

"What?" Joseph asked, unsettled. "What did I do?"

Three painstaking seconds of glaring and confusion. And then Pete broke the silence with raucous laughter.

"Nah, you're fine!" Pete guffawed. "You're too easy to frazzle, ya know that?"

Joseph smiled and sat on the chair beside Pete's bed.

"Patch said you wanted to talk, buddy."

"Yes, siree! I want to know what happened back there. Somebody knew that Angie and I were coming. She disappeared first, and the next thing I remember is waking up in the arms of that Scot. Kratos knew, Joey. Do we have a mole?"

Joseph let out a long sigh, running his hand over his stubble as his face darkened. "I don't know. Kratos has eyes and ears everywhere. The whole team knew about the records room plan with you and Ami, but some of them didn't know about the lab infiltration plan. And Kratos didn't seem to know about it, either."

Joseph leaned forward, his eyes burning with intensity. "I trust my team. I have to. But instances like this make me wary. My doubts are like these little gnats I just can't kill. Kratos has been a move ahead of us almost this whole time…and they nearly were again. This was our first major score, but I'm afraid Austria may end up being a dead end. If this Draven Black is indeed our spider, he undoubtedly will know we're coming."

"You say 'dead end,' Joey, but I say trap," Pete said, locking eyes with Joseph. "They knew we were coming. And all that stuff in the room where we were held makes me suspicious. Feels like planted evidence to me."

"And you may very well be correct, friend. I've certainly reached the same conclusion. But I just do not see another way to go about this. It's the only lead we've got."

A new voice cut into the room. "Boss?" Davies asked, poking his head in. "Blane and Alina are almost back. We're packing up."

"Thank you, Davies." Joseph stood to leave.

"I wish me and Patch could come with you," Pete said mournfully. His face brightened. "You're still the reckless Joey I served with all them years."

"Yes, still the same 'reckless Joey.' And you're the same wise ol' Pete," Joseph replied with a grin.

Pete's loud chortle warmed Joseph's heart, and he shook hands with his friend. "You need to stay here and recover. Patch assured me he is going to take excellent care of you."

"That's right!" Patch spoke up, coming into the room. "I've got loads of hot chocolate and reruns of *Gilligan's Island* on the agenda."

"Save me?" Pete asked Joseph with a mock expression of misery, earning a thump on the shoulder from Patch.

Joseph laughed and left his two buddies, going back out into the main room. He was just in time to see Hawk land the helicopter outside.

Excellent. Good.

He watched Burns and Alina disembark, and he felt a smile quirk up the side of his mouth as he noticed their nearness. But his smile faded as the Scottish man suddenly locked eyes with him. The man's gaze was searching. Severe.

When Burns had inquired about taking Alina away, Joseph had not reacted well. He saw it only as a risk to her safety—a risk he was not willing to take.

Though Burns had ultimately convinced him that he would keep her safe, Joseph was certain the agent had seen his panic at the idea of her leaving. And he was certain Burns remembered Joseph's secrecy that freezing night. Down by the fence.

Joseph turned away, reentering the safe house with slow steps. He knew Blane Burns didn't trust him, and Joseph was nervous that the man wouldn't wait in silence for much longer. Something would have to be done, but Joseph couldn't think about that now. He needed to focus on Austria, and he hoped that Burns would as well.

Austria. Vienna. The Hofburg Palace. The New Year's Eve Imperial Ball. Draven Black.

Joseph's heart rate sped up with each consecutive thought, and he watched as his entire team entered the house.

Forget about Burns. You must focus, Moore. Focus. And address your team.

"Welcome back, everyone. Now get packed up. Hawk's taking us to Europe."

Everyone scattered to their respective living areas in the tiny safe house, and Joseph checked his phone for messages from his Interpol contact.

Another unauthorized mission. But now they had some backing. And some powerful friends. And no matter what happened over there, Joseph knew what he had to do. What he could never fail again. And what he could not reveal to Blane Burns.

As everyone headed out to the vans with their belongings, Joseph bade farewell to Patch and Pete. Then he left the safe house, joining his team outside.

Austria. It's now or never.

PART

2

CHAPTER NINE

BLANE BURNS STARED DOWN FROM THE WINDOW OF
THE SACHER HOTEL INTO THE SNOWY STREETS OF
VIENNA.

He was extremely uneasy. He knew something was going to
happen tonight.

So much at stake. Again.

He wanted them to have more federal support. HAARP had
only been a success because of their element of surprise, but he was
certain that, tonight, they would be fully on Kratos's radar.

*Seeing the ball advertised in the glass case—obvious. Coming here
immediately—obvious. They're waiting for us. This has to be a trap.*

Blane sighed heavily, rubbing his hands over his eyes. He had
seen his family die in his dreams again, and the sorrow and guilt had
stolen away any clarity of his mind. Rather than reviving him, the
inevitable, burning hatred that followed served only to stretch his
already raw nerves beyond a point he kept forgetting he was capable
of bearing.

And then there was the other issue plaguing him.

Joseph Moore.

After everything they had been through at HAARP, Blane
wanted to trust the man with his very life. But the tiny shards of
doubt that had troubled him in the past had begun poking through
once more.

Just that morning, Grant Rogers had pulled Blane aside, inquiring if he was aware of any other surprises Moore was hiding from
the team. Underneath Rogers's composed exterior, Blane knew that
the agent had not moved past Moore's deception at HAARP. Rogers

could not accept that Moore had hidden the mission Blane had been a part of from the rest of the team.

At the time, Blane had defended Moore's actions, but Rogers's words had fueled all of Blane's doubts about their leader. As Blane donned his tux, his paranoia began dragging every questionable facet of Agent Joseph Moore from the shadows into the blinding light.

The man had secrets. A past burdening him, much like Blane. Yet the older agent refused to confide in him, despite the efforts Blane had made.

Blane wasn't certain, but he was afraid the secret centered around the woman under his care.

Alina.

Moore's behavior at the hotel. His outburst in Alaska concerning their trip. The consistent intensity of the agent's words toward her, with her, concerning her. It was a secret. And secrets were dangerous. Secrets were wild cards that risked their chance to end this.

Blane liked the older agent. But he was also acutely aware that someone on the inside was undoubtedly a Kratos agent. Kratos always managed to stay one step ahead of them, and though his instincts did not point Blane toward Joseph Moore, the secrecy surrounding the seasoned FBI agent was not a vote of confidence in his favor.

Before the team dove any deeper, Blane wanted Moore to tell him everything. No more secrets. At long last, he planned to confront him. *Tonight.* He glanced down at the note.

1700. Blane Bar. Come alone.
—Burns

But before Blane could concentrate on the upcoming meeting, he had an Imperial New Year's Eve Ball to prepare for. He ran a hand over his beard and checked that his gun was secured in the holster on his belt. He didn't like the absence of his knife in his usual boots; the wardrobe requirement had made dress shoes, infuriatingly enough, his only option. And, perhaps foolishly, he didn't like his tux. He had never liked tuxes. Blane blew out a breath and shook his head.

Focus. Keep your head about you. Draven Black will be there tonight, and you'll need to spot him. You'll need to find him before he can hurt anyone again. You cannot let them down.

Blane drew a deep breath and smoothed his hair back. He stole a final glance of himself in the mirror, dubbed his appearance to be satisfactory, left his room, and headed straight for Moore's. With a subtle flick of his wrist and discreet knock, the note disappeared under the door. Blane continued moving.

He will come. He has to.

JOSEPH MOORE TOOK SLOW, cautious steps toward the Blaue Bar. Burns's note was clenched in his fist, nothing more than a sweaty, disintegrated ball now. He didn't like this. *A deep breath.* It was a deviation—a distraction from the mission so close at hand. *Another breath.*

Joseph was fooling only himself. He was not frustrated at the repercussions of this meeting. He was afraid.

He was in front of the closed French doors, and before he let himself think twice, he pushed them open. The sight before him chilled him. The room, adorned with oil paintings on royal blue walls and illuminated with a glowing chandelier, was completely devoid of human life. The golden designs trailing the walls and swirling along the floor circled empty chairs at abandoned tables. Empty barstools, spanning the length of a polished drinking bar. Save one.

Blane Burns was sitting at the furthest end, two full glasses sitting on the bar in front of him. The man hadn't even turned when the doors slammed against the walls. He was simply sitting there. Waiting.

Joseph took tentative steps in his direction, saying nothing. Doing nothing. Until at last he found himself seated beside the Scottish agent.

Silence stretched on between them. Burns slowly swirling the untouched bourbon in his glass—the only movement. Joseph sniffed at the whiskey in the glass in front of him before tasting it. The alcohol did nothing to silence the blood pounding in his head, rushing in his ears. Just when Joseph feared he could bear the silence no longer, the man spoke.

"Trust. Trust is vital. Without it, the team crumbles. The mission fails. And the game is lost."

Burns's eyes were still downcast, but Joseph could see them flashing. Dangerously.

"Secrecy, Moore. There is too much of it. And I will not be risking the lives of everyone on this team with secrets. This mission is undoubtedly a trap."

Joseph was mesmerized by the swirling amber liquid in the man's glass as Burns continued.

"I need to know that I can trust you with my life. So now, you come clean. No more hidden pieces, hidden moves. No more secrets, Moore."

Joseph jumped as Burns suddenly slammed his glass on the bar. At that moment, Burns locked his gaze on Joseph. His eyes were hot coals, burning through Joseph.

"Are you the mole?"

Joseph went still at Burns's question, and he watched the man beside him with cautious eyes.

A gun cocked underneath the bar.

"My job is to protect Alina, no matter the cost." Burns took a breath. "And I will continue to do so. Even if that means protecting her from you."

The man's voice dropped an octave, his tone hard. Searching.

"I need to trust you, Moore. But you must be honest with me." His eyes, flashing and sparking.

"Be. Honest. With. Me." Burns was waging war with Joseph with that locked stare, and Joseph's heartbeat accelerated.

"Are you Kratos?"

Joseph shook his head. Slowly. Weakly.

Thump-thump. "Then what is it…"

Thump-thump. "That you aren't…"

Thump-thump-thump-thump. "Telling me?"

Joseph abruptly held up his hands. Surrendering. Even as the unanticipated movement nearly caused the Scottish man to bring the gun into view.

"All right, all right," Joseph said quickly. He took a slow, deep breath before downing the rest of his whiskey in a single shot.

He would need it.

It was time to tell Burns the truth. The man deserved at least that much.

THE HUSTLE AND BUSTLE of the streets outside the window blended in gentle harmony as Alina looked into the full-length mirror in front of her.

Wow.

She gently trailed a finger down the cool velvet of her ball gown. The sapphire fabric shimmered under her touch, and the embroidered beads and pearls adorning the neckline and bodice sparkled in the pale light of the room. She twirled slowly, enjoying the gentle swish as the layers of the gown spun and settled back into place. She could hardly believe she and Ami would be going to an actual ball. Another dream she had once thought was unattainable. Alina glanced at Ami, and the joy in her friend's eyes lit up the room.

"You look beautiful, Alina," Ami said, gazing at her.

Alina felt her smile spread across her entire face. "Thank you. I can't believe it—it's even my favorite color. How on earth do you think they found these?"

A knowing look came over Ami's face. "Well," she began, "maybe Joseph had some help."

"Oh, Ami, thank you! I had no idea!" Giddy and smiling, she swished over in an attempt to wrap Ami in a thankful hug, but they both dissolved into giggles as the poofs of their gowns made the task difficult. Once the giggles subsided, they stepped back and straightened their gowns.

"You look stunning, Ami."

Ami's eyes practically sparkled against the soft lavender of her gown. Deep purple flowers trailed in embroidered waves along the trumpet sleeves and scalloped hem. It fit her perfectly.

"Thank you," Ami replied, blushing.

Ami always seemed shy and a little awkward whenever she received a compliment, and Alina had never discovered why. There were so many mysteries surrounding her, but there were also so many knowns. Ami was her closest friend—the only family Alina truly had.

Thank You, God, for Ami.

"Hey, you need your gloves!" Ami announced, startling Alina from her prayer.

Ami grabbed a pair of white opera-length gloves, and Alina slowly pulled them on. They felt cool and smooth against her skin. She repositioned the bracelet that Blane had given her over her wrist.

"And here's the final touch," Ami said softly, pulling out something from an unopened box sitting on the bed. Alina gasped at the silver headpiece in her hand, the sapphire rosebuds and white pearls twinkling in the soft light.

Ami gently nestled the piece amongst the curls piled on Alina's head—the perfect complement to the tiny pearl hairpins holding up the hairdo.

"Oh, where's yours?" Alina cried.

Ami laughed and pulled out a delicate tiara entwined with an array of purple and silver flowers, and Alina helped Ami place it on the top of her head. Ami's soft brown curls were carefully pinned to cascade down her back, and the tiara was the perfect addition.

She looks like a princess.

As Ami slipped into her heels, Alina quietly regarded her friend. Flashbacks of Alaska had been haunting her thoughts, reminding her of the terror she had felt when she thought she had lost Ami. Now she simply looked at her, seeing how alive she was. How precious she was. Both in Alina's eyes and, more importantly, in God's eyes. Alina felt she needed to say something.

"You have always been there for me, Ami. These last few weeks have been a nightmare, yet you stayed with me every step of the way. You have been a better friend than I could have ever asked for, and I don't know how I can ever make it up to you," Alina whispered, her eyes bright with tears. She didn't know why, but this moment felt huge and fleeting all at once.

A wave of sadness flitted across Ami's face for the briefest of seconds, disappearing as quickly as it appeared. She proceeded to determinedly squish their gowns together until she reached Alina and could wrap her in a hug.

"I'm sorry this happened to you, Alina. To both of us. I'm so, so sorry. But… I want you to know that you have given me so much over the last years that we have been together," she said, her voice faltering. "These last years have been the happiest of my life."

A moment of silence passed before Ami spoke again. "Your friendship is more than enough," she whispered in conclusion, releasing Alina with a final squeeze.

They turned to face the window, quietly drinking in the fairytale skyline of Vienna. They stood for endless moments in nostalgic reverie, reliving memories of happier times. Early moonlight streamed through the glass windows of their room, painting the two friends in muted, white light. It felt like a beautiful dream one would soon awake from. And Alina wished it would last forever.

All too soon, a knock reverberated on the heavy door, and the beautiful moment became a beautiful memory. Alina would never forget it.

Joseph's voice filled the room though he was still on the other side of the door, and the two girls smiled at each other in anticipation.

"Are you ladies ready?" he asked. "The ball begins in half an hour, and we should be leaving. Vienna is extremely busy at this time of evening."

"Yes, we're ready!" Alina said, and she and Ami quickly grabbed their clutches.

"Don't forget your wrap, Alina!" Ami said with a smile. Her smile suddenly widened. "Or you could…" She lowered her voice conspiratorially. "And Mr. Burns would be duty bound to protect you from the cold."

Ami finished her sentence with a wink, and Alina blushed as her eyes dropped to the tiny bronze-colored band Blane had given her. In truth, out of all the beautiful things she was wearing, the band made her feel the most like a princess. The blush continued to warm her cheeks as she followed Ami into the hallway.

"Now as you ladies know," Joseph was saying, his back turned to them as he surveyed the city below them from the window, "this may turn out to be an extremely dangerous meeting. We have only our Interpol contact and a few other resources to pull from for this occasion, but other than that, we are on our own. It is almost a certainty that Draven Black will be present this evening." He drew a deep breath, and then he straightened to his full height. "But I want you to know that I will do everything in my power to protect both of—" His breath whooshed out as he turned around, his eyes softening as he looked at Ami, then Alina. "Beautiful. Absolutely beautiful."

The older agent cleared his throat and turned back toward the window, blinking rapidly.

"There is every possibility that Black is expecting and planning on our attendance this evening. However, Rogers thinks that you will be safer with us, in a public setting, than you would be back here with a skeleton security crew. And I agree with him. Ami, Davies will remain with you throughout the evening, and Burns will be with you, Alina. Rogers and I will be scouting the area, and all of the exits will be covered by Austrian BVT agents. Donáll will once again be heading communications."

Joseph's eyes steeled again as he turned, making eye contact with both of them.

"If he is there, we will get him. But apprehending Black will not come at the risk of your safety." His voice gentled as he finished.

Alina smiled at him, hoping to relay a sense of assurance she was not quite certain she felt.

She remembered Black's face. That terrifying smile. And the possibility of seeing him again filled every fiber of her being with dread. Her hands were sweating in her gloves, and Ami had tensed beside her.

God, please help us tonight.

As if in direct answer to her prayer, Blane appeared, walking toward them from around the corner.

Oh my goodness. Well hello there, handsome.

BLANE STALKED DOWN THE grand hallway, tumultuous thoughts reeling in his head from Moore's confession earlier that evening. He had felt cruel, but he needed to be sure of Moore's intentions before he led a team into a probable Kratos ambush. Then his thoughts shifted.

Alina.

The poor woman had been through so much already.

How on earth can she bear this, too?

Without realizing yet another transition in his thoughts, Blane was back in that afternoon along the Alaskan Gulf. His thoughts had been returning there more often than Blane cared to admit.

The scene replayed again. Slowly. Preciously.

Alina, staring up at him, hugging him, her eyes pleading with him to call her by her first name. Her beautiful eyes. Her beautiful name.

Alina.

Warmth spread through him as the memories soothed the tension overshadowing him. He was quite lost in that afternoon when he rounded the corner and his eyes lighted on the lass herself.

His thoughts came in. Slowly. Individually.

Alina.

She...is...so...beautiful.

So, so beautiful.

Alina.

He could suddenly think again, yet still he stared at her. Her gown. A deep blue, accenting the fairness of her slender neck and shoulders. Her hair. Tendrils wisping from her bun and falling in a waterfall of curls, gracing her neck and caressing her face. Her face. Dark eyelashes framing her chocolate eyes. A tantalizing shade of rose on her lips.

His gaze slowly fell to the bronze band adorning her gloved wrist. All the jewelry in the world, and she only wore the simple piece he had given her.

She was delicate and lovely. Radiant. For the first time since he had met her, he allowed himself to drink in the sight of her. He had not seen anyone as beautiful since he had held Isla and wee Olivia in his arms. Somehow, she reminded him of both of them; she was the picture of Isla's grace and Olivia's innocence. In the midst of his reflections, a new realization struck him. Hard.

Alina also had the unwavering faith his wife had before she had been taken from him. That faith he had walked away from so long ago.

Embarrassingly enough, he must have stared at Alina for at least thirty seconds while his thoughts coursed through his mind. At last, Moore broke the spell and cleared his throat. Blane cleared his throat in turn, feeling heat creep up his neck.

Get it together, Burns. FOCUS!

But she is so beautiful.

Blane shook his head, and when he glanced at Alina again, she was smiling nervously at him. Blane felt himself smiling back. Then he made eye contact with Moore, and a brief nod passed between them. They understood each other—Moore would tell her in his own time.

The older agent's voice filled the hallway. "Let's go."

Soon, Moore, Davies, Ami, Alina, Grant Rogers, Donáll, and Blane himself were headed to Vienna's Hofburg Imperial Palace for the New Year's Eve Ball. Blane felt his palms sweating, though he wasn't sure if it was at the prospect of finding Black, encountering Antonov, or dancing…with Alina.

He glanced around at the others in the car. Alina's nerves were only somewhat masked by her excitement, Grant Rogers looked tense as he drove, and Ami looked…frightened.

He feared that she hadn't been fully rescued from that dark room in HAARP. From the dread that still haunted her features, he was convinced that some part of her mind was still trapped there. He wanted to say something…anything…that would reassure her.

Without thinking, he glanced at Alina, and a jolt electrified him as their eyes met. He looked from her to Ami. He wanted her to know that his intention was to only encourage her friend. He then looked to Ami, and he nodded at her as they made eye contact.

"Everything is going to be all right, lass. Don't you worry. We're going to get him, and we will do everything to protect you and Alina," Blane said softly.

She gave him a small smile. The smile grew much larger as Alina slipped her arm through Ami's. Soon enough, their vehicles arrived at the Hofburg Imperial Palace.

CHAPTER TEN

ALINA STARED IN AWE AS THE GLORIOUS BUILDING LOOMED IN FRONT OF HER.

The vast symmetrical walls towered heavenward, ensconced in golden light. They met in the center to form a majestic entryway flanked by pillars and arches, overlooked by an intricate balcony. Each grand arch and glass window sparkled against the black night blanketing the landscape beyond.

She sighed aloud at the breathtaking sight, and as Blane helped her out of the car, pure happiness filled her. If she would have looked at him, she would have realized that the Scottish man only had eyes for her.

Owen quickly bounded toward them, eagerly offering his arm to Ami. Alina's heart swelled at the sight. She had suspected the handsome agent had liked Ami since he met them so many weeks ago, and the scene before her now confirmed her suspicions. The look of awe in his eyes as he stared at her friend said it all.

Joseph and Grant Rogers took the lead, followed by Ami and Owen. Blane offered his arm to Alina, and the two of them brought up the rear. Donáll was somewhere off-site, hidden away in a van to run communications. He was their eyes and ears.

Alina barely felt the chilled air through her silk wrap; touching Blane's arm sent warm tingles up and down every inch of her.

The six of them slowly ascended the stairs and at last entered the fairytale palace.

Seamlessly, the group dissolved. Blane and Alina glided toward the end of the foyer, Owen and Ami moved in another direction, and the others blended through the crowd. Then Blane was softly talking to her. "Donáll is soon activating our comms. Is yours on?"

Alina nodded, a thrill coursing through her.

As they watched hundreds of guests swirl about them in a rippling mass of colors, the full weight of their mission—the full weight of possibly meeting Draven Black again—hit Alina, and she took a calming breath.

Blane squeezed her hand. Her heart melted, and she felt strength and courage course through her again.

"By the way, I... I wanted to thank you for everything you have done for Ami. Not only for rescuing her in Alaska but also for...all of your kindness toward her. I do not think that lots of people have shown her kindness in her life, and by the way she looks at you, I know that you mean a lot to her. Thank you."

Blane glanced down at her. "I, well...you are very welcome, lass. I am glad to hear it. I keep feeling like I am making a bumbling mess of things."

As she began to reply, a white-gloved waiter appeared at her elbow with a tray of crystal glasses filled with sparkling beverages. She graciously smiled and accepted the offered glass before looking questioningly at Blane.

He studied the liquid before shrugging, and she tipped the glass to her lips. She sputtered as a bitter, burning taste filled her mouth. Blane immediately swiped the glass from her, suspicion transforming his features as he took a whiff. Apparently satisfied, he took a small sip. A grin overtook his face, and he glanced at her in amusement.

"It's just sparkling wine, lass. Not battery acid."

She sniffed indignantly. "Well, alcohol is disgusting. It never tastes as nice as it looks."

His reply was drowned out by the chiming of eight o'clock reverberating throughout the room, followed by the call for dinner. She took Blane's arm as they walked toward the massive, gorgeous dining room.

Alina's eyes drank in the golden accents sparkling along the cream walls, complemented perfectly by gold candlesticks placed throughout the dining room. The deep red cushions on the decadent chairs contrasted brilliantly with the pale whites and golds of the long table, and thousands of crystals in the candlelit chandeliers bathed the space in a shimmering light.

It's so beautiful.

As they took their seats, Joseph's voice came over their comms. Alina jumped at the sudden noise. She had forgotten how disconcerting it was.

"All right, people, remember to keep your eyes peeled. We all know what he looks like." There was a brief pause, and then Joseph continued. "And Antonov may very well be here too." Alina saw Blane stiffen at the reference. "Alert the rest of us the instant anything happens."

"Reading you loud and clear." Donáll's voice came on.

Alina blew out a slow breath, trying to focus her thoughts on the task at hand rather than the beauty around her.

Faces blurred together as waiters presented the first course of the evening, which was a savory beef and dumpling soup. As the buttery dough and vegetables melted in her mouth, she had to control her breathing. Every time a startling laugh or clash of silverware resounded, a million butterflies took flight in her chest.

The second course of Martinigans soon appeared in front of her. Dried plums and chestnuts flavored the seasoned meat, and Alina was careful to avoid dripping the sauce on her gown. As she slowly ate the main course, she perused the room with her eyes.

Relief filled her at the absence of any familiar faces.

Before she had finished her roasted goose, the waiters placed a silver bowl of spicy potato goulash before her. She finally allowed herself to fully drink in the gorgeous scene as she tasted the Austrian delicacy.

Breathtaking floral arrangements brought the room to life with brilliant greens and reds, and glistening ice sculptures gracing the periphery of the hall caught her eye. Deep purples, greens, and blues of the satin and silk gowns of the other guests blended together in a glimmering galaxy, and the soft strings of the orchestra merged with the gentle hum of conversation and clinking silverware.

A raucous laugh close to her abruptly captured her attention, and she turned to her date of the evening. Poor Blane had become engaged in grudging conversation with a boisterous tourist during the first course, and he had been unable to escape the man's endless questions ever since.

At the tourist's laugh, Blane's helping of Martinigans underwent an exceedingly harsh cutting job, and Alina almost laughed herself. Suddenly, Alina was startled by gentle tapping on her shoulder. When she turned, a waiter wordlessly presented her with a crisp envelope on a small platter before seamlessly melting back into the crowd of servers. Alina lowered her eyes discreetly as she withdrew the note, expecting to see Ami's familiar script.

Alina,

> *I trust that you are enjoying a magical New Year's Eve. Imagine my surprise and utter delight when I saw you arrive this evening, my little Alina, at the very same New Year's Eve Ball as myself, halfway across the world. How fortunate it is that we will at last be able to meet. I cannot wait to introduce myself after these many years.*
> *I will be on the balcony overlooking Heldenplatz Square at the conclusion of the third waltz for the guests. I dearly hope you will come.*

> *Soter*

Her heart was racing. Alina couldn't believe it.
Soter is here!
Alina glanced around at the other seated guests, hoping to meet someone's gaze. Whoever the man was, Alina had always considered him to be her guardian angel. She quickly slipped the note into her clutch. The matter felt exceedingly private to her, and she didn't want to risk losing the magic of the moment by sharing the note with Blane. At least not yet.

Soter was the only link to the parents she had lost long ago… A few of his notes had even referenced the beauty of her mother. Their connection meant the world to her.

Immeasurable excitement coursed through Alina at the prospect of talking to someone about the family she had never known.

She hadn't thought about her mother for so long with everything that had happened, and now all of her questions and wonderings struck her with full force. She simply wanted to know everything about Amanda Dixon…what her work had been, if she liked chocolate or vanilla, what she smelled like… The thoughts brought tears to Alina's eyes.

Blane was finally free of the tourist, and he looked at her with a mock, pained expression. His midnight eyes were at once filled with concern.

"Are you all right, Alina?"

She nodded, a smile spreading over her face. *It sounds so nice when he says my name.*

He nodded back then directed his attention to the room around them as he wolfed down the raspberry sorbet palate cleanser in a single gulp. She bit back a smile as he winced, pain scrunching up his face.

Even as he blinked away the tears gathering in his eyes, she could tell he was observing and absorbing everything…every conversation, every face, every clang of silverware around him. It was all filing through his mind as he sorted through the details.

Wow.

Alina directed her gaze about the room as well, even as another course was presented to them. This time, it included a variety of specialty mini-sandwiches which were collectively called belegte brote. Alina selected one and tried to take a small bite, but she didn't know if she could eat much more.

She eventually caught sight of Ami and Owen sitting several tables away, their backs facing her. Owen's arm was draped protectively over the back of Ami's chair. She didn't see Joseph or Grant Rogers. Her eyes trailed the room. A breath, then two.

She didn't see the man she had been terrified of at HAARP or the face of the man who had attacked and had tried to kidnap her. Goose bumps climbed up her arms at the possibility of seeing either of them again.

YOUR NAME IS LIGHT

A number of delectable strudels were placed on the table. Determined to at least taste one, she bit into a cream cheese strudel drizzled with sweet vanilla sauce.

Blane practically inhaled his apple strudel as guests rose from their seats around them. At his nod, they stood in tandem, and he offered her his arm as they joined the others assembling for the debutante dances. Alina was thrilled at the prospect of dancing in the beautiful chandelier-lit ballroom. The massive glass windows allowed light from the moon and stars to filter in, and the room sparkled with a magical glow. Alina was relieved that she and Ami had taken ballroom dancing lessons years ago. She could only pray that everything would come flooding back now.

She started at the sound of Joseph's voice in her ear. "Twenty-two hundred hours. Time for the debutante dances. Keep watching."

Alina gave a soft gasp of delight as the debutantes glided to the center of the ballroom, each wearing glimmering white dresses. Excited murmurs from the spectators were soon quieted by the live orchestra, and Alina watched in awe as the debutantes met their partners and began to dance in perfect synchrony.

Before she knew it, the debutantes and their partners were curtsying and bowing to the polite clapping that resonated throughout the hall.

"Alles Walzer!" suddenly echoed through the room, and all of the guests around them paired off, joining the debutantes on the ballroom floor.

"No one get too distracted." Joseph's voice had a teasing tone. Blane looked at Alina, a questioning look in his eyes. Though her stomach plummeted, Alina nodded with a smile.

The Scottish man held out his hand.

BLANE'S HEART HAMMERED AS he led Alina onto the floor. He was extremely nervous; he hadn't danced in a very, very long time. He was also extremely uneasy that Black had thus far gone undetected. The man was here, waiting unseen yet ready to strike. And Blane was certain that Antonov was also lurking in the shadows of the room. No matter what happened, Blane would ensure that Alina was kept safe. He had no idea if Antonov still intended to kidnap her or if his plans had regressed to killing her, but Blane wouldn't allow either to happen.

He looked at her then, and all thoughts fled.

Every nerve was practically electrified at the prospect of dancing with the beautiful woman in front of him. Her eyes were wide, and a blend of nervous excitement lit up her features. He gave her what he hoped was a reassuring smile, though it was mostly for his own benefit.

He took her dainty gloved hand in his, and they began to dance the waltz as the music drifted in. Relief chased away his nerves as the steps quickly came back to him.

Despite a few missed steps from his partner, Alina was utterly graceful. He knew he shouldn't let himself become distracted, but she was making it…difficult. Extremely so. She was beautiful and just so…radiant. Like Isla.

Isla.

Blane's breath caught in his throat as a memory clawed into his consciousness without warning.

The last time he had danced was with his wife.

They had just put Olivia in bed. He had swept Isla into his arms and twirled her around their tiny living room. Her red hair, flowing freely in shimmering waves. Her soft laughter, musical and golden.

Then Blane was there. The road. The black SUV. And the utter helplessness as Blane watched the vehicle crush the lives of his wife and child in front of his eyes.

Blane stumbled, his breathing increasing tenfold as he fought to suppress his rising nausea. Alina's dark eyes widened with concern, and without a word, she led him off the floor and through the crowd. As they moved toward a quiet corner of the room, Blane's eyes were so blurred with tears that he could see nothing. Nothing but Isla's face, then her body on the road.

Alina stood quietly beside him, saying nothing yet silently lending him strength.

He knew he had to try.

"Alina, I am sorry… The last time I danced, it was…it was with my…with my…" He trailed off, emotion strangling his voice.

"With your wife. With Isla," she finished for him.

He met her eyes. There was no pity in that gaze. Her eyes promised only that she would do anything in the world to release him from his prison.

"It's not weakness to grieve, Blane," she said softly. "It's the only way you can begin to heal."

His eyes dropped. He was ashamed—ashamed of his loss of control, ashamed of his failures, ashamed of everything inside him that was clearly laid before her.

"I'm saying a prayer for you," she whispered.

Blane could only manage to nod at her. Her faith was inexplicably strong.

And she's praying for me.

Before he could think of anything to say, Rogers was with them.

"Something the matter, Burns?" Rogers's tone was a blend of concern and curiosity. He was holding two drinks, and he started to hand one to Blane. Blane shook his head in answer as he reached for the glass, but Alina abruptly grabbed his hand, squeezing hard. She looked into his eyes, seeing the hurricane of emotions rising and threatening to overcome him.

"Blane needs to…to take care of something for a moment," she said to Rogers. "Will you stay with me until he comes back?"

Blane stared at her, then at the strong and competent Rogers. He could only nod. The lass knew exactly what he needed—even before Blane knew himself.

At Rogers's nod in return, Blane squeezed her hand back and fled the crowds, desperately searching for a door that would lead him to nothing.

JOSEPH MOORE LEANED FORWARD from his position against the wall on the upper level of the ballroom. He had been watching Burns and Alina dancing with a lightness in his heart, but they had unexpectedly left the dance and stopped in the periphery of the ballroom. Now Burns was gone, and Alina was with Rogers. Joseph trained his gaze around the room, but he couldn't locate Burns.

He must have found something.

"Burns, have you got something?" Silence answered Joseph's question. "Burns?"

Joseph startled as Alina's voice came privately over his comms. "Blane had to step away for a moment. I think he'll be back soon." Joseph didn't like the worry lacing her words.

"Well, he better make it quick," Joseph replied gruffly. "He needs to be by your side at all times." He paused for a beat. "Is everything all right?"

"Yes," she said. He heard her hesitate. "Just…memories of the past. But don't worry—Grant Rogers is with me."

Satisfied, he murmured a reply and then checked in with their Interpol contact, Bauer, on their private line.

Nothing from the agents at the doors.

He then checked in with Donáll.

All quiet.

Black's here. He must be.

BLANE SUCKED IN THE crisp, winter air, his chest heaving. The French doors closed behind him, and he found himself in a private garden.

Dark trees on the periphery. Complete silence. Alone but for the light of the moon, trembling on the snow-dusted cobblestones beneath his feet.

A few more steps and Blane sank down on a solitary stone bench. He pulled off his comms unit with a shaking hand. As his eyes closed, Isla, Olivia, and the black SUV filled his mind. But this time, Alina's soft voice echoed through the burning.

"It's not weakness to grieve, Blane."

The screams of the tires were muted by her words, and the scene transformed to a single, beautiful picture of his wife and his daughter.

"It's the only way you can begin to heal."

With that, Blane released the bitter torrent of tears that he had locked inside. Head in his hands. The cries tearing out from his chest, howling out from him. The stars cold and pale, then blurring as more tears distorted the world around him. He sobbed harder than he had ever let himself before. He sobbed until his throat was raw and his lungs were freezing from the icy air. And still the tears came.

I'm sorry I couldn't save you! his mind screamed into the night. He cried for what was lost, for what could have been.

"Forgive me, Isla. Oliva, forgive me," he whispered.

As the tears fell, he felt the burning hatred and rage that had filled him for so long billow out from him with every frozen exhale. In the void that remained, there was the warmth of calming peace. Filling him. Upholding him. His tears were gone, now only wet trails glistening on his face.

What is this…this peace? Where is the revenge? The rage that has carried me all this time?

A final thought stilled his thoughts and froze any tears that still remained in his eyes.

Perhaps this has been Alina's prayer all along.

THANK YOU, GOD—THE dance is finally over.

Alina had not enjoyed dancing with Grant Rogers. She felt guilty, but his palms had been clammy, and he wasn't at all as graceful as Blane. As they had moved about the dance floor, her eyes had searched for Blane and also for Ami and Owen, but none of them were nearby. She hoped with all her being that Blane was all right. *Please draw near to him, God.*

Alina was now standing by herself as Agent Rogers had excused himself to bring her some water when the dance had concluded. She was grateful—she had had enough of sparkling wine for one night.

The strings began filling the air with an enchanting melody for the third waltz of the evening, and Alina's heart rate picked up as she recalled the letter from Soter.

After the third waltz.

Glancing around, she did not recognize a single face. She wanted to relay her intention to Rogers, but she was unable to locate him in the crowd. Alina grabbed her voluminous skirt, and being careful to not slip in her silver heels, she began to ascend the grand staircase. At each step, questions flew through her mind.

What does Soter look like? Step.

Was he a friend of my mother? My father? Step.

Why haven't we met before now? Step.

How can I possibly thank whoever he is for all the ways he has blessed me over the years? Step and almost trip.

Alina grabbed the banister to steady herself. After a deep breath, she glanced around once again, hoping to see Blane, Rogers, or Joseph. Seeing no one, she was at least relieved that she saw no sinister glares or faces from her nightmares. As far as she could tell, she would be able to meet Soter without endangering herself or him.

As she resumed her careful trudge up the staircase, she wished that Blane would have been able to come with her; she would have loved to have him by her side to meet the person who had made her lonely childhood so…magical. She was nearing the balcony as a thought struck her, and she subtly touched her earpiece. At least she hoped it was subtle.

"This is Alina reporting in. I'm going to be out on the upper balcony for a moment."

She heard only static in response, and a sense of unease filled her. She pressed the button on the earpiece and spoke again, but the same silence followed. Her pulse began to pound, and she tried to slow her breathing.

Maybe I'm too far out of reach?

Alina was now at the balcony doors, and she hesitated for a long painstaking moment, glancing around for Blane or Joseph. No familiar eyes met her gaze. Thoughts running rampant through her head, arguing and fighting to be heard.

No one knows where I am.

A moment out there with him is safer than being alone in here.

What if this meeting makes both of us targets?

Joseph said that he and Rogers are keeping watch.

Find Blane and get out of here.

Soter is like the father I never knew.

I might never get this chance again. I must meet him.

I must.

Taking a deep breath, she pushed through the doors.

He knew my parents, and he cares about me. I have to meet him. For them. For my mom.

Pure delight swirled away her doubts as she saw delicate snowflakes floating downward from the starry sky. The Vienna cityscape beyond the balcony was breathtaking.

And there, standing along the banister, was a lone figure staring out at the view. *So that's him. My guardian angel.* Alina took a few tentative steps toward him and eventually worked up the courage to call out a nervous greeting.

"G-good evening."

The figure turned toward her, but she couldn't make out his face in the shadows. She took a few more steps toward him through the falling snow.

He was speaking to her. His voice was higher than she expected. It also sounded a bit…familiar, though she had no idea from where she recognized the voice.

"Alina. Thank you for coming. I have anticipated this moment for many, many years now."

She spoke through the ominous feelings beginning to compress her on all sides. *For Mom.* "I have wanted to meet you—"

"Would you come a little closer, Alina? I want to be able to look at you."

Alina took a few more steps toward the figure. She continued walking toward him as if in a dream, drawn to the man who had cared for her throughout the worst moments of her childhood. With every step, beautiful memories flooded her mind. Finally, he held up a hand. She stopped.

The voice resumed. "What a beautiful child you are. Oh, what am I saying, you are all grown up now. Absolutely lovely."

"Thank you," she faltered. "I cannot see you. The shadows are too strong. Could you…"

She heard him chuckle as she trailed off—a very light, strange sound. She definitely knew that laugh. Her world slowed down.

"Of course." He slowly stepped into the light.

That face. *Oh.*

That smile. *No.*

That familiar, reedy voice. *God.*

Light-headed. Knees going weak. *Help me.*

She became aware of a presence behind her.

The man's silver beard did little to hide the scar running down his face, from his right ear to the corner of his smiling mouth. It was the man from Alaska. The new face in her nightmares.

Draven Black.

BLANE LEANED AGAINST THE bench, his breaths slowly returning to a normal rate. He finally felt composed enough to return to the ball. To Alina.

The last thought made him smile.

As he put on his comms unit, the smile froze on his face.

Static.

He changed channels. *Static.*

He changed to Alina's channel. *More static.*

Blane was on his feet in an instant, sprinting out of the garden and back into the palace.

There are no guards at this door. Where are the guards?

Something was wrong. Very wrong.

Blane walked hurriedly through the hallways, following the weak strains of violins toward the ballroom. Adrenaline pumping through him. He was climbing the stairs in the ballroom now, his eyes probing the crowd.

She stood out vividly, yet he couldn't see her. Where on earth was Grant Rogers?

Blane Burns, you find Alina right now. YOU FIND HER RIGHT NOW!

He shouldn't have left her side. He had known better. *God, what have I done?*

Focus, Blane. Keep your head and focus.

His hand was on his gun, his eyes were searching. The dining room. He ran, his hand on his gun and his eyes searching. Frantically. He tapped into his comms, switching to her private channel.

"Alina, come in. Where are you?" All he heard was static. His hand was on his gun, and his eyes were searching. Everywhere. He switched back to the common channel.

"Does anyone have eyes on Alina?" Static. Hand on his gun. Eyes searching. The dread and fear beating his sanity nearly to death.

What have I done?

A man suddenly bumped into him, and by the time Blane regained his balance, he was gone. But he had left something behind. A note.

Blane's pulse pounded in his ears as he read the scrawled words.

I have your girl.
Parking lot.

His heart, thundering in his ears. His blood, freezing to ice in his veins.

No. No, Burns, you fool. No!

It was Antonov's hand. He would know it anywhere.

Blane started running. Fury and panic creating an epiphany of red. His hand was on his gun. He tried his comms again. Nothing.

As he ran, new thoughts ravaged his mind.

I have your girl. My girl. Parking lot. Alina. Save her. My girl.

Blane was outside, his gun out. The parking lot abandoned. Blane circled the luxury cars slowly, his gun out and every nerve in his body electrified. Antonov didn't reveal himself.

Blane sucked in a breath, preparing to yell the monster's name. He didn't have to.

An arm circled Blane's neck, and Blane twisted out, trying to dislocate Antonov's arm in the process. He lost his grip, and a blow to the side of his face had him seeing stars. But only for approximately two and a half seconds. Blane caught the fist before it landed a second blow, and he kicked at Antonov's knee to take him down. Antonov was anticipating the move, and he took advantage of Blane's momentum to shove him to the ground. He knocked the gun out of Blane's hand and drove his fist into Blane's stomach.

Blane grunted but was on his feet in an instant, grabbing at the arms circling his throat. Using his size as an asset, he threw them both backward, slamming Antonov into the Aston Martin behind him. He landed one good blow into the side of Antonov's head and reached down, fumbling for his gun. If only he still had his knife.

Blane didn't get the chance to grab it before Antonov jumped him again, trying to force him downward. Blane's rage strengthened him, and he kicked backward. This time, his heel hit its mark, and Antonov grunted with pain as his knee crunched. Blane took the moment to punch his face again, and then he had the assassin shoved up against the same luxury import. And Blane was choking the life out of him.

The black eyes. The red hair. No disguises this time.

Blane didn't know what he was doing. Didn't know anything except Isla's and Olivia's faces. Flashing through his mind. He was gasping. If he didn't let off, he would kill this man.

But then, Alina's face filled his mind, and Blane loosened his grip. He kept Antonov firmly shoved up against the vehicle. The devil was gasping too.

"Where is she?" Blane demanded, shaking the assassin violently. "If you have hurt her—"

Blane suddenly felt a sharp, stinging pain in his side as Antonov slashed him with a concealed knife. Antonov took advantage of Blane's loosened grip and shoved Blane backward into the wall behind them. Blane's vision blackened for a moment as his head slammed into the wall, and the punch he threw missed his attacker completely.

Antonov now had him by the throat, and he was using his body weight to increase the crushing pressure. Blane was afraid that his time would soon run out. Suddenly, the chokehold loosened, and his head was slammed against the wall again.

"Listen to me. She's not here. I only wanted you to come. Stop fighting and listen."

Another head slam rendered Blane completely disoriented and helpless against the murderer of his family. As he tried to consider what options he had left, he felt the cold blade of the knife against his throat.

"I need you to listen to me. I am not your enemy here."

Not my enemy? NOT MY ENEMY? Blane gave a dark laugh. "You're not my enemy? You murdered my wife and my daughter and you are not my enemy? I'm going to kill you as soon as you tell me where Alina is."

Antonov leaned into his face. "We are men of war. I had my orders. I am not the one who made that call. You know that. You're just like me, Burns. Following orders."

Blane stared into the assassin's eyes. He didn't really have a choice.

"Now listen. You'll get your wish soon enough. I don't know how many hours I've got left."

Confusion overwhelmed Blane.

"Yes, I'm dying." Antonov's eyes were wild. Frantic. "Poisoned, somehow. By the same people I've devoted my life to. To him."

"Draven Black?"

Antonov increased the pressure of the knife against Blane's throat. Blane tried very hard not to swallow.

"No questions. Just listen. Harris didn't die like he should have. I was interrupted while interrogating him. And then I tried to kill the girl. But it was a mistake. And now I must die for my attempt on her life."

He locked eyes with Blane, seeing the questions Blane was dying to ask.

"I couldn't kill her because of who she is. Who her mother was. That night in the hospital. It was a mistake. I didn't see her birth-mark until it was too late."

Antonov gave a low chuckle, but Blane could see the pain in his eyes. The poison was already working.

"He's obsessed. He's been watching her for her entire life. Any attempt on her life is a death sentence. Though I realized my error and left her alive, it was…too late. No matter my ranking in Kratos. No one touches that girl."

He grimaced again.

"Then he sent me to kill Malkovich. He told me it would be my chance at r-redemption. But it was a…a lie. They tried to kill me after I shot him. I evaded the sniper, but I knew my only hope was to get the girl. She would have been my bargaining chip. But, of course, you came when I had my only chance to take her. I couldn't hide for very long. He found me. And he had me p-poisoned."

All the pieces clicked into place. Antonov's rapid escape from Malkovich's building. His desperate attempt to kidnap her from the hotel.

"Why are you telling me all this?" Blane asked, bracing for death.

"To take down the man who has discarded my life. And to give you the chance to end it."

Antonov suddenly released him, and Blane jumped away from him, his eyes searching for his gun. It was in Antonov's hand, and he was holding it out to Blane.

"You're my equal, Burns. If I'm going to die by anyone's hand, it's yours."

Blane stared at it. Then at him.

"Before you kill me, you should know that the key to all this is the girl's mother. She stole something from him. And he wants it back. Now make it quick."

Blane took the gun and trained it on him. The man who had mercilessly killed his wife and daughter on the road. The man who had destroyed everything Blane had loved. The man who had set Blane's world on fire.

Blane's whole body trembled as he warred with himself. He could have pulled the trigger. Months earlier, even days earlier, he would have. Without a second thought.

But things were different now.

Blane knew he could never live with himself if he did. Alina filled his mind, and he lowered the gun.

"I can't."

His vision cleared. The red dissipated.

"And I won't."

Antonov just stared at him, confusion transforming his face.

Blane shook his head, his breath coming out in short gasps. "Tell me. Who…who is Alina's mother to Kratos?"

Antonov opened his mouth and began to speak when fireworks lit up the sky behind them. Blane's gaze returned to Antonov, but the assassin was crumpled on the ground, eyes wide open and a clean gunshot wound in his forehead. Blane sucked in a breath and dropped to the pavement.

He's dead. Oh, God, he's dead.

He laid perfectly still between the cars, anticipating a second shot. He tried his comms again. Nothing. He knew his only hope would be getting inside the palace. He knew a moving target would be no problem for a trained sniper, but it was his only option.

With a prayer he didn't even realize he prayed, Blane leaped up, sprinting across the parking lot. A huge black van roared up beside him, and three men were jumping at him before he could react. His gun was knocked from his hand, a blow to his stomach doubled him over, and the men threw him inside. His head smashed against the side of the vehicle, and everything went black.

ALINA TOOK A COWERING step backward from Draven Black, but two men materialized on either side of her. She didn't need to look to realize two more were directly behind her. Her whole world. Standing still. Then crashing down.

"Don't worry, Alina. I am not going to hurt you or spirit you away. I just wanted to meet with you."

"S-so…you, you're my…guardian angel?" she whispered. She felt a wave of nausea rising up within her, and lightheadedness threatened to take her to the ground. The notes, the gifts, everything…had all been from *him*?

"'Guardian angel?' I'm flattered. *Soter* is the Greek god of deliverance and safety." He gave a soft laugh, and it filled Alina with an overpowering dread. Her knees so weak. Everything so sharp and blinding. "Yes, child, I am Soter. I only wish you were more pleased to see me. I've known you all your life. You are quite the special… well, woman now." He took a step toward her, and her fear paralyzed her.

Oh, God. Oh, God. Oh, God, please help me!

He was right in front of her now.

"May I?" He lifted his hand. Alina could only look downward as he traced his finger down her cheek. He was suddenly lifting her chin so that their eyes met. She felt sick and cold. All over. The look in his eyes was distant; it was like he was reliving a memory and dream from long ago.

"You look so much like her," he whispered. He finally released her, and Alina realized tears were trailing down her face. His eyes regained their strange, cold look. "This all must be very confusing for you. See, with my line of work, one must never be too careful. That is why the two of us could only meet now." He sighed. "While I do not wish to overwhelm you, dear child, there is something I must have you do for me. Time is of the essence."

He touched his ear, communicating with someone through what Alina could only assume was another comms unit. She was suddenly speaking to him. "I, I have n-no idea what y-you could possibly want from me. But I will tell you this. There is nothing that I would ever do to help you. Nothing."

Fireworks exploded in the sky above them. Then Draven Black was holding her face again. Less gently this time. "I think you will with the proper motivation." He smiled about something being said in his ear. She thought she was going to throw up. *That would take him by surprise.*

He stood there, staring into her eyes. Then he looked annoyed. A bullet sliced through the air, crumpling the man standing on her right. Another shot came and wounded one of the men behind her. Alina screamed and jerked away from him. Without another thought, she fled back toward the doors. No one stopped her. She heard the roaring sound of a helicopter and more gunshots, but she didn't look back. Arms encircled her.

JOSEPH MOORE HELD ALINA as she struggled against him.

"Alina, Alina, hey, Alina! Stop. It's me! You're safe!" She looked up at him, fear potent in her eyes. "You're staying with me, and I'm not letting you out of my sight."

The poor girl nodded at him, and he hugged her fiercely.

"Is he still there?" she whispered hoarsely, wetting his suit jacket with her tears. Rogers came in, shaking his head.

He answered Joseph's unasked question. "Yes, the two operatives you wounded are dead. Black's men must have finished them off as they fled in the chopper." Joseph nodded and continued to hold the shaking girl.

"And, sir, I am so, so sorry for leaving her side. I alerted you to the two potential hostiles I saw when I was getting her water, but when I returned, she was gone. I thought Donáll… I mean, I'm so sorry I didn't—"

Joseph cut off the agent's apology. "No, stop right there. Though I lost the two men you told me about, we found her. She is safe. We need to focus on what to do next, not what we didn't do."

Rogers nodded gratefully, and Joseph began to guide Alina down the stairs to the lower levels of the palace. The guests were clearing out in a panic at the sound of the gunshots and the helicopter, and the palace's security were frantically calling in reinforcements.

Their Interpol contact, Tobias Bauer, was striding toward them.

"Moore," he began. "I called in a chopper, but I'm afraid he's long gone by now. And my boys found one of yours."

Joseph's heart thundered in his ears. "Dead? Who? Burns? Davies?"

"No, no, and yes, Owen Davies. He received a severe beating and was knocked unconscious, but he will live."

Alina lifted her head, her eyes wide with panic. "Ami?" she asked, clutching Joseph's arm.

"Was a woman with him? In a purple dress?"

Bauer shook his head.

"Oh no," Alina gasped. Her face was pale. "Ami. Oh no. Ami…" she whimpered. Joseph caught her as her knees gave out, and he guided her to the nearest chaise lounge.

"Don't worry. We'll find her. If she's not here, they have her. But we'll find her."

Joseph remembered the tracking device he had given Ami Everly after her capture at HAARP. He could only hope she had it with her. He glanced at Alina again, and he could see she was silently repeating her friend's name over and over again.

Joseph looked Bauer in the eye. "I need medical attention for Davies and for my tech man, Donáll. Our comms were down, and when I checked the van in my search for Alina earlier, he was out cold. Our systems were wiped and destroyed. Thankfully, we didn't have anything crucial to our investigation on those servers. Also, I need new computers. We have a tracking system in place for Ami, but I need computers. And lastly, I need Burns. Where is he?"

Rogers suddenly returned. Joseph hadn't even noticed that he had left. "Burns is gone. I found his gun out in the parking lot. And I found Antonov's body. He's dead—bullet in the head."

Joseph barely suppressed a growl at Rogers to shut up. Alina had been a shaking, crying mess on the chaise, but this news elevated her to a shaking, sobbing mess.

"Get Antonov's body. Take some Austrian agents with you. And then bring Donáll and Davies along when the medics are finished with them. There is much to be done."

Bauer escorted Joseph and Alina out of the palace to waiting vans, and they rapidly traveled to a nearby safe house. Joseph's mind was violently beating his sanity.

The doubts were justified. His darkest fears were manifested. He had gotten lucky at HAARP.

But that luck had run out.

The nausea returned, roiling and twisting and unforgiving.

If they die, the blood is on your hands. In Iraq. And here. It has always been.

Joseph tried to breathe, but he felt every error and every loss he had ever been responsible for loom in front of and blow up in his face, crushing him, burying him alive.

He squeezed his eyes shut against the accusations and failures driving him beyond all reason, and he just supported the girl beside him as they walked into the safe house.

"We'll get them all back, Alina. We will."

She glanced at him with tears streaming down her face. "I'm praying that we will," she whispered. Her words struck something inside of him.

If You are out there, God, I pray we'll get them back. For her sake.

CHAPTER ELEVEN

BLANE AWOKE IN DARKNESS, A FIERCE HEADACHE RIPPING HIS JUMBLED THOUGHTS IN TWO.

He was shirtless, and his hands were cuffed behind a chair. A chair he now realized he was sitting in.

He was cold.

He grunted in pain as he shifted, his muscles screaming.

Why am I still alive?

He was so cold.

His first clear thought was that of Alina. He frantically glanced around and was relieved to see that he was alone.

I hope she's safe.

Thoughts of his confrontation with Antonov, Antonov's murder, and the screeching van abruptly overwhelmed him, and he tried to suppress his rising panic.

He forced his brain to think clearly, and he remembered his ring. The ring that he had synced with Alina's bracelet and with the FBI's tracking systems. By some miracle, it was still on his finger.

Thank You, God.

He didn't even know when he had started praying. But somehow, after the prayer left his lips, he didn't feel quite so alone.

Blane knew he didn't have much time before they would realize he was awake. He concentrated, biting back the pain as he fumbled his hands together as best he could, twisting the ring around his finger to press the button.

There.

The door slammed open.

Just in time.

Three men came through, all Austrian and all much larger than Blane. They were staring at him, and he stared right back. No one would see Blane Burns's fear.

Suddenly, the tall bearded man Blane recognized from the HAARP laboratories walked through the door. The scar running down the right side of his face identified him as Draven Black, head of Kratos. The mastermind behind the brutal killing of his family.

The fiery hatred that had sustained Blane for so long had slowly cooled in that courtyard, and it had died altogether as Antonov had handed him the gun and Blane lowered it. Now he felt only a freezing dread slowly spread through his entire being as he stared at the man in front of him. Blane knew that his own death was an inevitable end to whatever Black's purpose was.

It's only a matter of time.

Blane felt a stab of grief as he realized he would never see Alina again.

Black was studying him, and Blane held his gaze. After an eternity, Black spoke.

"Welcome, Mr. Burns. I meant to have you brought here in a more…quiet manner. A little something in your drink. But your surprise tête-à-tête with Antonov necessitated your more…dramatic procurement."

Black took several steps toward him, continuing to speak.

"In any case, I am glad to finally meet with you face-to-face. We have been aware of you for a much longer time than I care to admit, and I am simply glad that we can at last address your…involvement here."

Blane continued to hold his gaze.

"You may be wondering why you are here now and why you are not dead. I'll make this brief, as my time is very…precious to me. Firstly, I want to know what you discovered during the HAARP invasion. You must tell me everything that you saw. Everything that you heard. I did not appreciate the breach of my Alaskan facilities. You were quite undetected. And quite…invasive."

Every muscle in Blane's body tensed. The underlying anger in the man's reedy voice was terrifying, even to Blane. "Secondly, I intend to use you, or your body, at the very least, for a greater purpose."

Blane felt his stomach plummet, and his breath escaped him at the violence in the man's eyes as he spoke. "I will get right to it. I need my vial. I know dear Alina knows where it is, but she will require some…persuasion. I am aware that she will only get it for me if I have a bargaining chip. At this point, I have two." Blane was utterly confused, and his tumultuous thoughts must have clearly appeared on his face.

"Such a stupid man." Black sighed, quickly closing the remaining distance between them. Blane didn't flinch, even when Black reached toward his face and gave it a good slap.

"Ow," Blane responded flatly, his eyes shooting Black with daggers. Then came a punch that had him seeing stars.

"Let us stop wasting time, shall we? You are going to die—it's only a matter of how long you have yet to live. So tell me what I want to know."

"Before I tell you a single thing," Blane began, staring directly into the contemptuous depths of Black's eyes, "I want to know. Who is Alina's mother to Kratos?"

Black nodded to one of his men, and the agent walked over to Blane and grabbed his throat.

Blane was losing air. Rapidly. Focusing all of his remaining energy into keeping his composure and not panicking. A moment later. Desperation. He was straining against the cuffs, straining for air, lungs straining, lungs screaming. With a nod from Black, he was released, though a severe punch to his stomach depleted the air he had been suddenly able to suck in.

"Antonov always told me that you are a man more easily persuaded through…mental manipulation, Mr. Burns."

Black continued as Blane's vision blurred, the room spinning.

"He was right, of course, but the effectiveness of your family's deaths appears to have expired. If you do not start talking, I will become more…creative in my methods now."

Blane followed the man's eyes to the table beside his chair, and he saw an assortment of blades and surgical tools.

Black selected a blade with a jagged edge, and he tenderly fingered the teeth. "Talk. Quickly now."

"Truly," Blane began, despising the shakiness he heard in his own voice. "I only heard your name. Then I saw all of the bottles, and I stayed behind to accumulate evidence. But that was all. Nothing else learned. Nothing else reported."

Blane knew this last statement was key, and he said it in order to direct all of the man's anger onto himself and away from the American team.

Away from Alina.

Black gazed at him. Apparently satisfied, the man swiftly straightened and took a step back.

"Thank you for your cooperation, Mr. Burns. I believe you in how little you achieved in your botched invasion. I simply wanted to hear it for myself." He sighed in what seemed like a strange kind of self-gratified relief, and then he pierced Blane with his eyes.

"Now then. On to the more important matter. Your demise."

Blane continued to stare at him, though his thunderous heartbeat filled his ears.

I pressed the button. Someone must be coming.

"I've got a little surprise for you. I will accomplish your death, motivate Alina, and gain a successful test of loyalty simultaneously in these next few moments."

Ice flowed through Blane's veins. *What on earth is this devil talking about?*

"Oh, darling! Come in."

Blane's heart was in his mouth, and his palms were slick. His worst fears were confirmed.

Ami Everly walked into the room.

ALINA WAS PRAYING, OVER and over again.

Oh, God, please help Ami. Please help Blane. I can't lose Ami. I just can't. She means everything in the whole world to me. You know that. Oh, please help her.

Alina was crying again. Or maybe she hadn't ever stopped.

And I can't say goodbye to Blane yet. I'm in love with him, God. Please help them.

She was sitting in a room, surrounded by agents in the safe house, yet she felt so alone. Without Ami. And without Blane.

Oh, please be with them and help them.

Her only source of comfort was Joseph Moore sitting at the row of computers, furiously typing and pulling up tracking software. Apparently, he had given Ami some sort of tracking device after she had been imprisoned in HAARP, and if she had it with her somehow, he would be able to find her.

Alina heard Joseph curse under his breath, and dread filled her.

He looked to her first, his eyebrows furrowed in confusion. "It looks like she never turned it on. We can't track her."

Alina's blood went cold.

"But don't worry. This is only a minor setback. We have their pictures out to all the local stations, and we are working on contacting the television networks."

Joseph got up and walked over to Donáll, who was frantically typing. The tech man looked tired and bruised. But even with his mild concussion, his fingers never slowed.

"This guy will find them in no time." Joseph was smiling at his tech man, and he gently patted Donáll's shoulder.

But Alina saw it.

It was a shaky smile. One liable to break if kept up for too much longer.

Alina wrapped her arms around herself, feeling chilled. She was still in her ball gown, though Joseph had given her his suit jacket to ward off the shock and the cold. She simply kept praying, over and over again.

God, please. Let them live through this. And please let us find them.

Owen Davies was sitting in the corner of the room, holding a pack of ice against his head and looking utterly miserable. She knew he blamed himself for losing Ami. Much like she blamed herself.

God, please. Please.

A vibration on her wrist startled her, reverberating through her entire being and causing her to almost fall out of her chair. Her bracelet! Blane had activated it! Joy coursed through her, and she leaped to her feet.

Joseph was looking at her with concern. "What happen—"

"Blane!" Alina cut in. "He pressed his button! The one on his ring! Track him! QUICK!"

Alina held up her wrist to Joseph, showing him her vibrating bracelet. Relief transformed Joseph's haggard face. Wasting no time, he and Donáll pulled up the appropriate tracking system.

"We got him!" Joseph and Donáll yelled in tandem. Alina collapsed back into her chair.

Thank You, God. Thank You.

The next few moments were a blur as the room exploded with activity.

Joseph was ordering Owen to stay at the safe house and recover. The Austrian agents, the Interpol agent, and Grant Rogers were suiting up with Kevlar vests and firepower. Then Joseph was physically pushing Owen down into his seat. Alina was standing up again. The agents were pouring out of the safe house. Joseph was suddenly in front of her. And, somehow, she was sitting back down.

"Alina, you may not come. It is far too dangerous." He grabbed her hand. "Please...trust me," he whispered. "I'll let you know as soon as we have them." His eyes were pleading with her. They were pleading with her to give him a chance. A chance to make everything right again. She knew he was tortured, holding himself responsible. For everything. And the weight of it all was crushing him.

For his sake, she put on her bravest smile. "I do."

She locked eyes with him as agents streaked all around them, just holding his eyes with her own.

"Joseph, I do. I believe in you."

She squeezed his hand, and she watched the guilt haunting his eyes transform into a fierce determination. He nodded at her, and she knew her words had meant everything to him. He then grabbed his own equipment and ran out of the safe house.

Alina rushed to the window and watched as the three vans sped away, her hands clasped in prayer.

Please keep them safe. Let Ami and Blane be alive.

BLANE STARED AT AMI, his world slowing down and sharpening. His ever-increasing heartbeat a deafening roar.

The girl's hair had tumbled down, and the hem of her dress was ripped and dirty. She refused to meet his eyes.

Draven Black slowly walked over to her and put his hand on her shoulder, smiling at her. The way she shied away from him filled Blane with rage, and he strained against the cuffs.

She's so afraid of him.

Blane couldn't take it. "Stop touching her," he ground out in fury.

Black nodded to one of his men, and the man came over and punched Blane in the mouth. This time, the stars lasted for much longer. While Blane was blinking and trying to clear his vision, Black addressed him again.

"Ever the gentleman, Mr. Burns. You find out this girl has been betraying you, working for and reporting to me, and you are still trying to defend her."

Blane refused to believe that Ami was purposefully betraying them. Her fear of Black proved as much.

His cynicism must have shown in his face, as Black was suddenly next to him, pulling his hair back to force Blane to look up at him.

"How do you think I found out so quickly what you fools were doing in Alaska? Though you did manage to evade her with your little stunt of sneaking in, she revealed everything else when we pretended to imprison her and her partner. Her partner who, by the way, we would have killed if she hadn't felt the…need to aid him."

Blane was taking small measured breaths, his brain a mass of confusion.

When I rescued her and Pete…she had been one of them all along.

Blane couldn't think…couldn't reason through her betrayal.

But then he remembered when he had found her. Her tears. Her falling into him, sobbing and hugging him in that dark room.

She was desperate. There was so much more than that room that she couldn't escape from.

Black was still talking. "How did you think I knew that you were looking to find me at the ball? How do you think I've been able to stay one step ahead of you all this time?" He released Blane, and Blane just sat in his chair, staring at Ami.

Look at me. Just look at me, lass.

"Yes, yes, Ms. Ami Everly has been working with me since she was sixteen years old. I saved her from a rather nasty foster situation, and in turn, she has been loyal to me ever since."

At this, Black walked back over to Ami and cupped her chin to meet his eyes.

"She was the perfect plant to get close to Alina. They made quick friends, and she has been an integral part of my efforts to monitor Alina ever since. I'm so proud of her." Black's smile was disgusting and despicable.

Blane was still trying to meet Ami's eyes. He wanted her to know that he didn't hate her.

Black hadn't saved her like she had hoped; he had distorted her life beyond all recognition, and he was forcing her to betray the only friend she had ever known. And doing so was destroying her from the inside out. All those secret tears. All the overwhelming fear in her eyes.

Oh, Ami, look at me!

"But we never did find my vial, did we, Ami?" Black murmured, his eyes calculating. "And now both of you are very valuable to me. You two appear to be the brightest points of Alina's life, poor girl. Both of you, damaged and ugly."

Ami finally met Blane's eyes, but her look of sorrow froze the cold dread within him. He knew what was coming.

"The only problem with Ami here is that the lines between her artificial life and who she really is seem to be blurring together." Black grabbed her face again and squeezed.

Blane started to strain against his cuffs when another blow to his face knocked his head back.

"I would like to make those lines dark and distinct again, and you, Mr. Burns, are going to help me do it."

Blane wasn't feeling well. He understood that his limited time was approaching its inevitable end.

"I am going to have Ms. Everly here take that ring from your finger. If you make any more intrusive comments or decide to struggle, I'll have her take the whole finger. Then she is going to shoot you."

Blane blinked and glanced at Ami as Black released her. The look in her eyes was one of resigned defeat.

He knew he was going to die.

God, please look after Alina.

"I am going to send the ring to Alina. With it, I will also send pictures, or pieces, of your corpse. I haven't committed to either option yet. I will then inform her that she must give me what I want, or I will kill Ami here, too. Her choice." Black laughed, his reedy voice echoing throughout the room.

My Isla and sweet Olivia, I'm coming.

"All right, quickly now. Get the ring, Ami dear."

Blane tried to make eye contact with her as she walked toward him, but her eyes were cast downward. When she was finally in front of him, she met his eyes. There was a small smile on her face, and as she went behind him to take his ring off his finger, he felt cool metal against his palm.

The key.

Blane's face didn't change even as a glimmer of hope coursed through his entire being. But he was terrified for her.

What on earth is she going to do?

Ami slowly walked back to Black and held out the ring. In exchange, Black gave her a small pistol, and then he guided her to stand directly in front of Blane.

He slowly and carefully tried to unlock his cuffs.

There! One hand free.

But the other one was stuck. The key just wouldn't turn.

"Go ahead, Ami. Shoot him."

Her hand shaking, Ami aimed the gun straight at Blane's chest. Her eyes were wide, and he desperately tried to remove his other cuff.

She placed her finger on the trigger.

Blane met her eyes. *Thump-thump.* He tried to tell her it was okay. *Thump-thump.* He forgave her for everything. *Thump-thump-thump-thump.*

Big tears rolled down her face, and she just stood there, seconds away from pulling the trigger.

Thump-thump-thump-thump.

A feeling of peace washed over Blane as he imagined holding his family again.

Black began rolling the ring agitatedly in his hand. "Ami, I am growing impat—" He suddenly stopped and flipped the ring over.

Oh well. That's that.

He met Blane's eyes, a cold gleam of rage in his stare. "You pressed it, didn't you. They're coming. We're out of time. Ami, shoot him. Now."

The shot never came. As Black began to speak again, Ami kept her eyes locked on Blane's.

"So. You have chosen your side." Black snapped his fingers in a sudden motion, and a shot rang out.

Blane braced for death, expecting to feel it rip through him. Instead, Ami fell to the ground, gasping. Blood pooled on the floor around her.

"NO!" Blane roared.

He tried the key again, panic and desperation threatening his consciousness.

"Finish her. And bring him." With a flourish, Draven Black left the room with the other man.

The lock suddenly gave, and as the agent raised his gun to deliver the final shot, Blane dove from his chair and shielded her body with his. He heard the gunfire, but the cry of pain wasn't his own. He looked up to see armed men streaming into the room, with Joseph Moore in the lead. They quickly took down the other Austrian.

Oh, thank You, God. Thank You.

Blane quickly lifted himself off the gasping girl beneath him. He tried to remain calm as he surveyed the extent of the damage the bullet had done.

No.

It was a single shot to her torso, but she was losing too much blood. He pressed his hands to her abdomen, not knowing what else to do to stop the bleeding.

"Help me!" he cried. "She's shot! HELP ME!"

Moore was beside him, and the older agent ripped off his jacket and pressed it to the wound.

"Get a medic in here now," Moore ground out to the others, a desperate yet determined look in his eyes.

Blane could only sit on the floor and watch as a medical team burst into the room. He watched as they grabbed gauze to stop the bleeding. He watched as they loaded her onto the stretcher. He watched the somber glances they shared between themselves. He watched Ami's eyes. She was crying and gasping in pain.

But then her eyes met his.

Blane struggled to his feet, even as a wave of pain blackened the world for a moment. He heard Moore's orders to stay down echoing through the room, but he made his way to her side. Someone grabbed his arm, but he needed to stay with her.

He hardly had the energy to shake off Moore's grasp, but he did. He followed the team outside to an ambulance. He was noticed and thoroughly examined for injuries, and soon he was being strapped down in a stretcher too. He was close to Ami's stretcher and reached out his hand to grab hers, but all of his energy had left him. The world was going black again. He was carted up into an ambulance, and Moore appeared beside him. Blane tried to speak.

"G-get Alina here. She needs to be here..." He trailed off, unable to continue. Everything was darkening.

"She's on her way to the hospital to meet us," Moore replied softly. "I'll see you there soon. I'm going to ride with Ami."

Blane watched the agent leave and climb into the other ambulance. Ami wouldn't be alone.

Good. That's good.

Then the world was black.

SHE'S BEEN SHOT. LOSING lots of blood. *Ami's been shot. God, please let her live. Please let her live.*

Alina was sitting with Owen Davies in the car. *Please.* They were on their way to the hospital. *Please, God.* To meet Ami. *Oh, please.* Who had lost a lot of blood. *God, please help her!*

After an eternity, they arrived at the hospital. Alina jumped out of the car and ran through the emergency doors, with Owen close behind her.

I hope I've made it before they take her to surgery.

Alina's thoughts finally calmed enough to recognize Grant Rogers standing in the waiting room, and she and Owen followed him down the hallway to one of the ED rooms.

Ami was in a bed, covered in wires and tubes. She was too pale. The nurses and a doctor were all frantically rushing around, preparing her for surgery.

Joseph was suddenly by Alina's side. His face somber. His eyes full of anguish. "While they're getting her ready, the doctor says to… talk to her. Just in…in case."

Alina stared up at him, tears flowing down her face.

No.

She approached her. Her best friend in the whole world.

Ami's eyes opened, and though she didn't have the strength to smile, her eyes were smiling at her.

"Alina," she whispered, and her face crumpled in pain.

"I'm here. I'm here, Ami," Alina said softly, grasping her hand.

"I w-want to s-say that I'm sorry for everything. Y-you were the only g-good thing in my life. I-I never wanted to…to h-hurt you. P-please forgive me."

"Hush, Ami. Of course I forgive you. For anything. Anything." Alina was sobbing now, and she squeezed her best friend's hand. She knew she had to say something else.

She didn't know if Ami was ready, but the time was now. Alina might not get another chance.

"Ami, I don't know what's going to h-happen. But God does. And I want you to know where you're going if…" Alina trailed off, the tears and emotion strangling her voice.

Ami finally found the strength to smile. "I w-would like that. I w-would like Him. H-He always h-has been there for…for you."

The doctor was saying they were almost ready.

"Pray with me, then, Ami. If you can't say the words, think them. Jesus, I believe that you are the Son of God. I admit that I am a sinner, and I accept Your gift of salvation. I would like to spend eternity with You."

Alina watched Ami mouth the words, and the look of pain on her face transformed into one of peace.

"T-thank you. Oh, Alina, I can see Him. I love you, A-Alina."

"I love you too, Ami."

Alina kissed her forehead, but Ami's eyes were already glazed over, staring at something in the distance that Alina couldn't see. And then Ami was gone, off to the OR, a place where Alina couldn't follow.

Then she was sitting. And waiting. Praying. And praying. Joseph was there beside her. He was praying too. Then Blane was coming into the room. He looked awful. She was crying in his arms. Then the three of them were sitting. And praying.

The hours passed. Slowly. Then the doctor came. And Alina's world came crashing down.

The words were there, swirling around the room. Alina didn't want to reach out and grab them. She didn't want reality. She wanted her best friend.

She sank to her knees, sobbing. Joseph was wrapping her in his arms, and she was sobbing into his shoulder.

"She can't be gone," she cried. "She just can't." Her world went colorless and empty. The brightness gone from it. "She was my whole world," she whispered.

Joseph just hugged her. And Blane was standing there, raking his hands through his hair. Rubbing his hands together. Joseph eventually let her go, and she looked up at Blane.

When her eyes met his, he wrapped his arms around her.

CHAPTER TWELVE

THE ROOM WAS SILENT IN THE AUSTRIAN SAFE HOUSE.

Blane, Joseph Moore, Grant Rogers, Owen Davies, Lestor Donáll, and Tobias Bauer were sitting at a long table.

The silence. It was so heavy. So suffocating. Blane just twisted his hands back and forth.

It should have been me. I should be dead. Not her. Oh, God, why couldn't I do anything?

It felt just like that night, years ago, on that street.

I should have saved them. I should have saved her.

The silence. The deafening silence. The dead silence.

No.

Blane couldn't take it anymore. He stood, his chair screeching backward and startling everyone. All except Moore.

Before Blane could speak, the older agent was on his feet.

"Before anyone moves, I am going to speak. We will not accomplish anything if we each blame ourselves for this...tragedy. Ami's death." Moore's breath hitched, and Blane knew he was punishing himself just as much as Blane was.

But he was trying. Trying to keep them moving forward.

"I know each of you is replaying events, wondering what we could have done differently... I know I am. But that will drive any man to insanity." Moore fixed Davies with a hard look, and the young agent looked downward. Moore then turned his intense gaze to Blane.

"Sit down, please. We need to move forward, not back into the past. For her sake." Blane felt himself sitting down.

"Now, Burns, tell us what happened tonight. Every detail you provide will help us destroy Draven Black. We have no one else. The two men we captured during the raid were assassinated before we could question them. Someone was there, waiting for the perfect moment to kill them. And then they took it." Moore growled these last words.

Rogers spoke. "Antonov's body was gone after other agents and I returned to the scene."

Everyone in the room took a collective breath, and then everyone turned to stare at Blane. Waiting for him to relive his nightmare.

Blane released the breath he had been holding. Slowly. "While I was looking for Alina, someone gave me a note: "I have your girl—parking lot." I recognized Antonov's writing. He was waiting for me as I suspected, and we fought. Could have killed me. But he wanted to talk. He'd been poisoned for his attempt on Alina's life, even though he had let her go after he had realized who she was. He said Black is obsessed with Alina and that his error was unforgivable."

Blane paused, remembering the assassin's panicked eyes. His desperation and resignation while waiting for death.

"He said the key to this is Alina's mother." He gave Moore a weighted look. "Apparently, she took something from him, and Black has been monitoring Alina all her life, searching for it."

Blane closed his eyes for a moment, wringing his hands under the table. "Then he gave me his gun. He wanted me to kill him. But I… I…couldn't." Blane took another breath and let it out, the sound echoing throughout the room.

"Then he was shot right in front of me before he could answer who Alina's mother was to Kratos. Who Alina is to Kratos. Antonov was dead. I tried getting back to the palace, but a van came up beside me, and well, that was that."

Blane's palms were sweating, but he pushed onward.

For her sake. And for Alina's sake.

ALINA WAS SITTING IN the blackness of one of the safe house rooms. Her body was being flown home to be buried.

Her body. Ami's body.

Alina sucked in another breath and hugged herself, feeling new tears trailing down her face.

Her mother's voice floated into her lifeless thoughts, lifting the grayness and fog for a brief moment.

Shells glitter on the shore
The sea whispers you are adored.

Alina wished she could be at that sea. Wherever it had been. She wished she and Ami were there right now.

Mommy holds you near, Mommy loves you, dear.

Alina wished with all her heart her mom was here. Her heart was so empty. Lifeless.

God's sea holds our love
He smiles down on us from above.

Alina tried to find peace in that promise, but it was so hard. She didn't understand.

Why, God? Why did You take her from me?

Alina wished she knew. Wished she could understand.

Everything was dark and cold. And the room was too black. Alina couldn't stand it any longer.

She peered in the dark at the pile of clothes Joseph had left for her on the bed. She slipped off her silver shoes. She pulled off her gloves, letting them fall to the floor in a shimmering pile of white. Working slowly and methodically, she unzipped the back of her gown, letting it fall down around her. She slowly pulled on the T-shirt, black pants, and black jacket. Her hands felt around in her hair, pulling out the pearl pins studding her bun. Letting the curls fall. Pulling them back into a ponytail. Lastly, her fingers traced the rosebuds and pearls on the headpiece. The last thing Ami had touched. Alina pressed it to her cheek, the metal cool against her hot tears.

I wish she was here. Oh, how I wish Ami wasn't gone.

The only thing giving Alina peace was that Ami had met Jesus before she died. Alina knew her best friend was in Heaven, meeting God. Alina smiled at the scene in her mind, knowing her friend would never be hurt or shed a tear again. She would live among the angels now.

And I will see her again.

With a renewed sense of hope and peace flowing through her, Alina gently placed the headpiece in her bag and left the room, closing the door softly behind her. She was walking down the hallway. Blane was speaking in the large room, his voice quiet but steady through the wall.

Step.

Blane's voice. "And then he was saying he would test someone's loyalty, motivate Alina to give up whatever she knew about this vial, and accomplish my death all at once."

What vial? Whose loyalty?

Step. Increase in heart rate.

"And then he called for her to come in."

Who?

Step. Heart hammering. Mouth dry.

Blane paused, then stopped her dead in her tracks. "Then Ami walked into the room."

Alina's steps faltered as she heard muttered words coming from the other room.

What?

She reached the door. Grabbed the handle. Started to turn it.

"Ami's been working for Black all this time. He placed her in Alina's life. She's been working with him since the beginning."

Alina thought she was going to throw up.

And the door swung open.

BLANE STOPPED MIDSENTENCE AS Alina stumbled into the room. Her eyes wide. Her movements agitated. He was on his feet in an instant. As was Moore.

"Alina," Blane began, and he saw her lips open and close.

"Ami was...you must be wrong... She—" the lass began, and then her eyes were rolling backward. Blane leaped across the room and caught her as she fell in a dead faint.

He stared in a panic at Moore.

"It's all right, it's all right. Just take her back to her bed," Moore said, sadness overshadowing each word. Blane lifted and carried her to the tiny bedroom, ignoring the burning pain in his side from Antonov's knife wound.

As gently as he could, he laid her on the bed. He pulled the extra sheet from the foot of the bed and tucked it around her. *There. Wait.* One last thing.

A strand of hair had fallen over her cheek. He reached out and moved the soft curl to the side of her face. Her beautiful face.

Moore had followed them in, and Blane looked at him.

"I should be here when she wakes up."

Moore nodded, and Blane continued. "Ami may have been working for Black, but he had been forcing her. He had found her in what I can only assume was some abusive foster home, and in return he made her spy on Alina for him. God only knows what he did to her."

Blane's voice was choking with rage. He felt hot tears well up in his eyes.

"She…she gave me the key to the cuffs. Black was going to have her take my ring to send to Alina as a threat. Her final task was to shoot me, to reprove her loyalty, he had said. But she gave me the key. She wanted me to escape."

"What happened?" Moore asked softly.

Blane took a deep breath and cleared his throat. It didn't clear away his grief. Nothing could.

"I couldn't unlock the second cuff. She waited, hoping I would move. When Black realized my ring was a tracking device, he gave her one more chance to kill me before they fled. She didn't, and… and one of the men shot her. It happened so fast." Blane closed his eyes against the scene. The scene which had been replaying over and over again in his mind.

"I finally got free and reached her before the agent killed her, and then you came in and…well. You know the rest."

Moore sighed and shook his head.

"You…you cannot blame yourself." Moore took a shaky breath before he continued. "I take full responsibility for everything. For your capture, Ami's death, everything. If I had only seen, I…" He trailed off, his voice nearly breaking.

Clearing his throat, the older agent at last pressed onward. "Ami…she did what was right in the end. I only wish that I had seen…only wish that I had known…and helped her somehow."

"Aye. There was always a deep sadness hanging on her, but I should have pressed. I should have done more to understand…" Blane paused. "I just wish she had trusted us. I wish she had confided what had happened. We would have protected her with our lives."

A hard look came into Moore's eyes, and he stared at Blane. "Maybe…maybe she couldn't," he said slowly. Realization dawned in his eyes. "Maybe she wasn't the only plant. She knew someone else is here, always watching, making sure she didn't stray. She didn't know who to trust." His words were bitter. Biting.

"This confirms my long-held suspicion, Burns. We have a mole. Ami could not have assassinated our prisoners, and Kratos had inside knowledge of our operations long before Ami became involved. She couldn't have given them all of the information they knew…" Moore trailed off, rubbing a hand tiredly over his face.

"I'll think of our next move. In the meantime, you must stay with her, Burns. You are the only person I trust, and I need you by her side. Especially when she wakes up."

Blane looked at her sleeping face.

"She will blame herself for what happened," Blane murmured. "I just hope I can help her before her guilt sucks her down and… ruins…her. Like us."

"You will. I have faith that you will, Burns." Moore rubbed his hands together, taking another deep breath. "I am going to round up the team. I'll put Donáll on any records we have of Alina's mother. I've had him look before, but we may have more to go on now. The rest of us will be trying to find out what vial Black was talking about. And we will pinpoint his next move."

Moore started to walk out of the room, and then he hesitated.

"Alina met Black face-to-face while you were with Antonov."

Blane's mouth went dry, and he looked to Alina in a panic.

"What?" Blane asked slowly.

Moore stared steadily at him. "He had her surrounded. Then he touched her face, and from what Alina told me, he said that she looked like her."

"Her mother?" Blane asked. His hands were white in tight fists.

"I can only assume so. As you know, Black has always been a ruthless, cold-blooded killer. Amanda Hart must have been close to him to merit this much emotion."

Blane was nodding. "Some old friend?" He dared to ask the next question.

"Some...lover?"

Moore immediately shook his head. "No—never. Jack and Amanda were the most faithful, God-fearing couple that ever lived. I could never figure out how two people could love each other like they did. She would never have been involved with someone else. No, my gut tells me this is a family matter."

Blane felt a wave of nausea rush through him at the idea. At the idea that Alina was somehow tied by blood to the monster. He took a breath and braced himself on the bedpost.

Moore was watching him.

"I'll have Donáll look into it. We will crack this. And Burns," Moore began, holding eye contact. The words looked to be unbearably painful for him to get out. "We need to...to see if Alina knows about this vial. Whatever it is."

Blane could only manage a nod. He hated to pressure her after all that had happened. But they didn't have a choice. For Ami's sake, they didn't have a choice.

Moore left the room, and Blane wanted to do one thing before he sat down to wait for her to awaken. He looked around the tiny room, feeling like a hulking intruder. He peered into the closet and was about to give up when he saw it sticking out of her suitcase. He pulled out her bathrobe and inhaled, hoping he would smell the same scent that had greeted him so long ago in that hallway in the hotel in Washington, DC.

Aye. It was the same flowery smell.

Blane tucked it around her before sinking into a nearby chair. Every muscle in his body was screaming at him, and the bruises that had overtaken his face throbbed with every movement. He didn't want to frighten her, so he stared downward instead of staring at her. Didn't work. He stared at his hands as he rubbed them together. Still his gaze was drawn to her. He eventually got up and checked outside the window for signs of danger. *Nope.*

He needed to sit down or else he would fall over. Once settled in his chair again, he started playing with the zipper on his jacket. *Nope.*

He hated himself, but she was so beautiful. He was still struggling to tear his eyes away from her face when her dark-brown eyes fluttered open and met his.

ALINA SAT UP WITH a start as she awakened to find Blane Burns staring at her. He was on his feet, staring at her with a kind of sheepish concern. She smiled. Then everything came flooding back.

"I fainted," she said miserably, her hands absently twisting the covers. She noticed her teal bathrobe was covering her. She looked at Blane, and her smile returned as he quickly avoided eye contact. Then she remembered the last words he had been saying, and she sank back in the bed.

"Before you say anything," Blane began softly, "I want to tell you that Ami was the good person you always believed she was. And you were the brightest light in her life."

Hope dawned in the midst of the turmoil of her thoughts, and her eyes pleaded for Blane to explain. He continued. "Black found her when she was only sixteen. She was in such a horrible situation that going with him must have felt like a rescue. But soon enough, he revealed his purpose: she was meant to enter your life as a plant. Her one purpose was to report back to him."

Alina felt dizzy. *Poor Ami. Poor, poor Ami.*

"I always wondered where she came from," Alina murmured softly. "One day in ninth grade, she was suddenly there, taking all the same classes as me. We became friends. We are…or w-were best friends." Alina quickly wiped her tears away.

"She never told me of her life before I met her. And she was always asking questions about me. About my mother."

She was hugging her bathrobe. It smelled a little like Blane.

After a moment, she took a shuddering breath. "What happened last night?" she finally whispered. "Joseph only told me she saved you. But he wanted you to tell me."

She watched grief cloud Blane's eyes.

"Black was going to have her shoot me. To prove her loyalty. He said she was having trouble differentiating between her fake identity and real life. She slipped me the key to my handcuffs, but I couldn't get free, and she waited. Black realized a team was coming, and he gave her a final chance. She didn't take it. Then he had one of his men, well…one of them…" He trailed off. He was reliving the nightmare.

She was living it too.

When he could finally continue, she watched his fists tighten. "I am so, so sorry. I did get free and was able to get to her before they killed her, and then Moore and the team came in, but it was too late. I am so, so sorry." His pain sliced into her heart.

She knew Ami's was another death that he blamed himself for… another death for which he would never forgive himself. She got up and walked over to him, taking tiny steps. Then she wrapped her arms around him as he wept. She held him for a long time, crying too.

At long last, Blane stepped back, rapidly brushing at his eyes. "I meant to console you through this. And now it's just the opposite."

He sighed, and she looked into his eyes.

"Thank you, lass."

Strangely enough, she wanted him to kiss her. In that moment, all she wanted was to kiss him back. His eyes shifted to her lips. Her heart almost stopped. Then he cleared his throat, and the moment was gone.

"Alina, Moore told me that Black talked to you about doing something for him. We know it has something to do with a vial. One that your mother took from him."

Alina's mouth went dry at his words, and she sank into the nearest chair.

"Wha-what?" she finally managed. "My mother?" Nothing made sense. She felt so overwhelmed and afraid. And she missed Ami. So much.

"We think Black and your mother were connected years ago, possibly family. Something went wrong, and she took a vial from him. Other than that, we...we don't know much. And we are not sure how much of your past was real."

Alina's eyes roamed the room as she tried to concentrate on the memories...on a past she had never known, trying to remember. She dwelt on his conclusion—that her entire life was a lie. As her known world threatened to shrink and collapse inward on her, the unknown stretched before her in a dangerous, gaping chasm. And all these questions were pulling her toward the edge.

"I never truly knew my grandparents," she finally remarked. "They always held me at arm's length, never really let me love them, and they certainly never loved me. And when I grew up, they retired to Florida and have seldom answered when I've tried contacting them."

Pieces were at last falling into place in her jumbled mind. She feared the final picture they would collectively form.

"So maybe they weren't even my real grandparents. Some sort of actors. And Ami, placed in my life to get to know me and to become my...my f-friend."

She pressed onward, wiping away more tears.

"So everyone around me was constantly watching and reporting to Black—like I was a...a specimen under a microscope. Someone always watching. And he personally reached out to me every year," she finished with a shudder.

At Blane's look of surprise, she took a trembling breath.

"On my birthday, I would always get a card and some sort of exotic gift from... Soter."

"Greek god of protection," Blane mused aloud.

"Yes," she replied bitterly. "I always thought of him as my guardian angel. I was so stupid."

She hadn't noticed until now, but at some point, Blane had knelt in front of her, clasping her hand. She liked the way his hand felt. It was so big and warm, calloused yet gentle. Then one of Blane's first statements returned to the forefront of her mind.

"So my mother and Black were connected somehow? And she stole a vial from him and Black thinks that I know where she hid it?"

Blane nodded.

"That's why Antonov let you go that night. I think that all Kratos operatives knew to only watch you and to never, under any circumstances, approach you, let alone attempt to harm you. Maybe because of who your mother was to him, or maybe solely because you may be the only person alive who knows where she hid this vial. Antonov's murder of Harris, that politician working with the private investigator, went wrong, and when Antonov tried to kill you to clean everything up and then recognized your birthmark...well, he was too late. Once he realized his life was forfeit, he tried to kidnap you from the hotel as leverage. Soon after he failed, he was poisoned."

Alina sat in a shocked silence, remembering. Remembering the kidnapping attempt. Remembering his initial attack.

"He had gasped when he saw something," she said finally. "The birthmark on my neck. The way I could always be identified."

Blane was nodding, and she shut her eyes against the memory.

"And what on earth is in this vial?" she asked at last. She realized she was squeezing his hand extremely tightly. She looked up into his eyes. His gentle, midnight eyes.

"I've been asking myself the same question. All Antonov said was that having the vial is necessary before Kratos can accomplish its plans."

"Plans...concerning the virus from the HAARP laboratory?" Alina asked, dread settling in her stomach. "What could my mother have stolen that could halt the mass production and distribution?"

"Maybe a certain irreplaceable strain of it?" Blane offered. "Maybe an early prototype? Maybe..."

Joseph walked into the room. "How about an antidote for it? I'm sorry to interrupt you both... I wanted to see how you are doing, Alina."

She glanced at him, her eyes soft and sad. "Thank you. It's just...all so overwhelming." His previous words suddenly hit her. "Did you just say this vial is an antidote for the virus?"

Joseph nodded at her.

She caught a sudden look between Blane and Joseph, though a slight shake of Joseph's head seemed to break whatever unspoken communication they were sharing. She glanced at Blane, but he was looking at the floor.

Suddenly, Joseph was addressing her again.

"Are you able to come out to the main room, Alina? I think Donáll has been having some success with what he's been looking into. And what we need right now from you," he began, fixing her with his gentle gaze, "is to try to remember anything about your mother. Anything at all. I am certain she would have communicated the location of this vial to you somehow."

Joseph reached down to help her stand, and Blane hovered by her side.

The weight of the responsibility she held was overwhelming. Their entire endeavor rested on her.

And she was terrified that she wouldn't remember.

JOSEPH MOORE WALKED OUT to the briefing room, Alina and Burns trailing behind him. He was so sorry for the loss of Ami. So sorry for everything Alina had endured. And he was desperately trying to suppress his own guilt that was rising up and threatening to drag him under.

His men. Jack. And now Ami.

Burns's stare had shaken him, but he convinced himself that now was not the time. He would tell her. But now simply wasn't the time.

There were lots of things on his mind, but first and foremost was the issue of a Kratos plant still among them.

Joseph was certain that Black wanted them to believe that Ami Everly was the only leak. Surely, she had been feeding Kratos the specifics of their mission since she joined the team.

Yet there were other inexplicable incidents that didn't fit with her as the only Kratos plant. Namely that she should have told them everything, as she was an unwilling pawn in Black's game. He thought back to his conversation with Burns. There had to be another traitor in their midst, someone always watching and keeping her in line. In truth, they had been one step behind Kratos well before Ami Everly joined them. There was another mole—he could feel it. And Joseph feared the mole was one of his own.

Joseph sighed, rubbing a hand down his face. If his worst fears were confirmed and one of his team had been compromised, he knew the individual wouldn't show his hand yet. Not until they found the vial. Then…well, Joseph didn't know what the traitor would do then.

He felt a cold chill run down his body as he entered the room, but no eyes were watching him as he scanned those around him. Joseph took a breath and pulled out a chair at the long table for Alina, and then he sat at the head. Everyone was present and everyone was silent.

"Okay, everyone. I'm going to go over what we know. Then what we are going to do."

With a nod at Bauer, Joseph flashed up his shared screen.

"What we know so far. Politician Victor Harris is a member of Kratos, he goes soft, and he intends to blow the whistle. He hires Clay Jones, a private investigator, to carry out the investigation and gather evidence against the organization. Kratos takes care of the problem, and Antonov murders Harris and Jones. Antonov can't kill Harris after interrogating him, so Antonov finishes him off in the hospital. Harris says *lazrae* to Alina. Antonov tries to kill her too but stops once he recognizes her birthmark."

Joseph glanced around to make sure everyone was still following. Burns had an intense look, Alina looked overwhelmed, and the rest of his team appeared tired but focused. Joseph took a deep breath and continued.

"Next, we focus on James Malkovich—another politician who we know is going to be targeted. He recognizes Alina's picture, but he is killed before he can say anything compromising. Again by Antonov. This event, when coupled with Donáll's investigation into

Malkovich's personal and business accounts, proves that he wasn't just a victim of Kratos—he was a member."

Burns spoke up. "And we know there were others there in addition to Antonov. For one, the sniper. He picked off the operative we captured, and I now know he attempted to finish Antonov. Secondly, Moore and I tailed Antonov after the shooting, and...well, there were other Kratos agents. Antonov himself told me that he had been assigned the hit to earn the chance of redemption, but Black intended for him to be killed in the crossfire all along. When he wasn't, Antonov tried to kidnap Alina as a bargaining chip against Black. He failed, and at some point afterward, Kratos managed to poison him."

Joseph nodded and continued. "Next, Davies's discovery of HAARP research at the investigator's house linked Kratos to the facility, and Donáll's breach of Malkovich's firewalls solidified the connection. We go to Alaska and uncover that Kratos has been mass-producing biological warfare, now identified as a mutated strain of the Marburg virus. As a current note, I heard from my old FBI friend, Erik Singer, and he says every agency involved is taking huge strides in the case to stop any future distribution."

Joseph glanced carefully around the room. "At this point, we also learn that the leader of Kratos, Draven Black, is going to be at the New Year's Eve Ball at the Hofburg Palace."

Joseph took another breath, feeling the recent events too sharply to continue. "Well, we...we all know what happened. And from that night, we learned two things: Black needs a vial that Alina's mother took from him long ago and Black's headquarters are in Norway."

Everyone except Donáll reacted in shock.

Davies glanced sharply at Joseph as Rogers interjected. "How do we know that?" Joseph could tell both men were extremely tense.

"Donáll, would you take the—" Joseph began, but the little man was already on his feet. He had also somehow hijacked Joseph's screen and began flashing up his own...stuff.

Joseph still didn't understand everything his jumpy nerd did. But he was thankful for him.

"Hi, everybody," Donáll began excitedly. "This is probably the coolest thing I have ever done. Not that I never did stuff like it before, but—Boss, if you glare at me like that again and I spill my coffee, we're going to have some problemos."

Donáll sputtered a little and then continued, purposefully ignoring Joseph.

"Okay, so this whole time I've been slowly trying to crack through Kratos's main database. The first breakthrough I had was when we learned Malkovich was a bad guy. His firewalls were weaker than they should have been, but I realized his system mirrored the same mega-firewall locking me out of Kratos. By pulling his security apart, code by code, I better understood the Kratos beast."

The man took a long sip of cold black coffee. Joseph looked around the room at impatient faces.

"Once I broke through the outer walls of Kratos's system, I needed to get through the inner firewall. I compiled and cross-checked everything we and every other country in the world has ever known about Kratos, and I was at last able to break through the inner firewall. How specifically did I do this, you may ask? Well, I first accumulated all of the metadata and sifted through codes of attempted hacks from every other country—"

"Just move on, Donáll!" Rogers ground out.

Donáll cleared his throat. "Well, when I reached the innermost point of the system, it demanded a password. From everything we had learned at the ball, I got it."

Donáll looked in Alina's direction, but then he dropped his eyes.

"You usually expect a password to be something random that no one could ever guess. But this Black character—well, everything he does is purposeful, and he thinks he's invincible. He's also obsessive, and we know what matters most in the world to him. Therein lie the chinks in his armor. And in this case, we know Black's weak points are this missing vial, Alina, and… Alina's mother."

He paused, and the resulting silence ricocheted off the walls.

"The password could only be five characters. I had two attempts. Obviously, 'antidote' was out. So, of course, I tried 'Alina.'

The warning flashes were enough to give someone seizures. Then I tried 'Mandy'...and I got in."

Donáll took a deep breath, glancing quickly at Alina before continuing.

"I knew I only had two minutes tops to comb through as much information as I could before the system recognized that I had broken through. Turns out I had fifteen seconds. But it was still enough. There was a digital web of contacts, locations, neutralized targets, and open targets. And in the middle? Tromsø, Norway."

"Where?" Davies exclaimed.

Donáll looked impatient. "It's a small village. In Norway. The center of the Kratos web is Tromsø, Norway. We can only assume Black's headquarters are there. And before anyone panics that Kratos was able to hack and destroy the FBI's server upon recognizing it as a threat, I would like to clarify that I created my own ghost server. Just FYI."

Joseph quickly stood.

"All right. We know where Black is going to be. His plans to... force Alina to give up the vial's location fell through. I imagine he is heading back to his lair to lick his wounds and regroup. Before we go in with the entire Norwegian Armed Forces and perhaps agencies all over the world who want to see Black either behind bars or dead, we need leverage. His weak point is his missing vial. Without it, he cannot unleash *Azrael*. We must find it."

Joseph took another breath before slowly turning to lock eyes with Alina.

"I feel callous having to pressure you after...everything that has happened. I hate to do it. But I am afraid I have no choice. I need you to try to recall any memory that could possibly lead to the vial's location. Please take some time, and just...really think about it. Any little detail could be a breakthrough."

He gave her his best reassuring nod.

She looked so vulnerable. So afraid.

EVERYONE WAS STARING AT her. Everyone.

Everything right now is hanging on me.

I can't do this.

I can't remember.

She took shaky breaths. A hand squeezed hers. Blane was looking at her, supporting her with his eyes and with his smile. He apparently saw her panic, and when he glanced around the room, he lost his composure.

"Okay, you idiots, stop staring at her. The poor lass can't be pressured into remembering on the spot. Moore said she should take her time, and then she will share it with the rest of us." Alina just looked at Blane, and then she looked down at the table.

Joseph cleared his throat before speaking up.

"Yes, yes, I'm sorry. Everyone, get to work. I want eyes in this Norwegian town. Research the area. I want to know where the base is."

"Alina," Blane said softly as the room became a bustle of activity. "Do you think that you would be able to think better somewhere that's a little less…chaotic?" She nodded and slowly rose from her seat.

"I think I'll retreat back to the bedroom." She paused and met his gaze, wondering if he could read her fear. She felt so alone.

Blane spoke, his voice a deep rumble. "If you do not want to be alone, lass, then I—" He was cut off as she grabbed his hand.

He smiled. "Alrighty, then." Together, they walked through the safe house.

They sat on the bed, side by side. Silence between them. And Alina was thinking. Then she was thinking out loud.

"I don't understand this. Ami was always asking me about my mom and my memories of her. I always thought she didn't have any of her own memories and wanted to treasure mine, but now, well…" She trailed off. Blane nodded at her, and she pushed on.

"I told her snippets of what I remember. Barely anything besides the smell of her hair and trips to a green park. But that's about it."

Blane's eyebrows shot up at her mention of a park, and Alina quickly continued her thoughts.

"But if it was hidden in that park, wouldn't Black have found it by now? I'm sure he learned of it almost as soon as I told Ami, so he likely exhausted that avenue long ago."

Blane nodded, trying to hide the disappointment in his eyes. Alina hated to disappoint him. To disappoint Joseph. And everybody else.

"Is that the extent of your memories of her? Anything else? Anything could be significant."

Everything was blurred, distorting into one black hole of a past that was taunting her.

Faces. Places. Home. Just the watery outlines of a childhood that was lost. Hopelessness. And everything muddling into and intensifying in a dull roar.

Alina covered her ears against the roar of her failure. Blane must have been looking at her, but she squeezed her eyes shut.

God. Please help me to remember. Something...anything. Please.

Hot tears of frustration wetting her cheeks. Blane's hand resting timidly on her shoulder.

"Oh, Mom," she cried aloud, "where on earth can I find you?"

Then breathlessness. That sweet, ethereal voice in her mind. Her mother.

"At the sea, you'll find me," Alina whispered, repeating the line of the song playing in her head.

Alina turned to Blane, eyes wide. She must have startled him, as he quickly withdrew his hand.

"At the sea, you'll find me," Alina repeated excitedly. "Oh, Blane. Her song. Mom's song."

"You'll never be alone, my darling. Run along now. The sea is calling."

Alina spoke the words, her emotions clamoring with hope and overwhelming every fiber of her being.

"What if the vial is hidden at the sea? It was the only song I remember my mom singing... She must have made sure I would never forget it. And I... I never told A-Ami about it. It was one small piece of my mom that was so... I mean it was so special that I just wanted to keep it...for me."

Alina took a deep breath, and Blane squeezed her hand.

"Excellent work, Alina. Grand. Now we can't tell anyone this yet. Truly, the only other person here that I trust is Moore."

Blane glanced toward the door and then leaned in close. His next words a whisper, his breath hot on her ear.

"Somehow, Black has countered every move we've made against him. And it couldn't have solely been because of Ami. Someone was always there to kill captured Kratos agents before we could interrogate them, and Kratos has been aware of things that we discussed when Ami wasn't present. This suspicion would also explain why Ami never confided in us. She didn't know which of us she could trust."

His words filled Alina with bitter sadness. She had been asking herself the same question over and over again—of why Ami had never told her. His explanation hardly filled her with peace, however, and it took her a moment to finally voice the question that had settled in her mind.

"Do you know who it is?" she asked.

Blane's eyes now burned with intensity. "No. But we have a plan."

As he whispered to her what the night would hold, Alina leaned in even closer. She realized it was difficult to breathe. But it wasn't listening nervously to his every word that made her breathless.

It was being so close to him.

JOSEPH MOORE WAS STARING at the figure concealed in the shadows behind the safe house. They had dangled the bait. Now he was waiting to see who would bite. Joseph rested his hand on his gun, his heart rate steadily increasing. He was waiting for one move. One move from one of his own agents. One he had trusted with his very life. Joseph couldn't believe any of them could betray him. Betray the team. Then the figure placed the phone to his ear, and the voice that spoke cut Joseph to his very core.

Grant Rogers.

Joseph stepped slowly out of the shadows, gun in hand, adrenaline pumping, heart sinking. Rogers looked up, expression unchanging as he ended his call and just stood. Waiting. And Joseph walking. Slowly. Gun in his hand. His hand steady.

"Moore." Rogers locked eyes with him as Joseph approached.

"Rogers," Joseph replied. His voice steady.

"What are you doing out here?" Rogers continued, holding his gaze. Joseph saw his hands discretely handling his phone. Most likely clearing his calls and correspondence with Kratos.

"Let's cut the crap, Rogers." Joseph was now a few feet from him.

Steady now.

"Donáll traced your call. Kratos."

A small, strange smile flitted across Rogers's face as realization dawned.

"Her story was fake. She didn't remember the vial being in some cabin in the woods."

Joseph nodded. "We needed to set a trap for the rat. And you took the bait." Joseph couldn't prevent the pain at Rogers's betrayal from bleeding into his voice.

"You need to come with me. And I am not going to let some random Kratos marksman shoot you until I've questioned you. Let's go."

Joseph's gun was trained on his agent, eyes scanning everything.

"I'm not worried for my life, old man. Drop the gun. And I'm afraid you're coming with me." In a flash, Rogers had his pistol trained on Joseph even as Joseph cocked his own gun.

Rogers grinned. "I know you won't shoot. But I will."

Joseph merely stared at him. The pain was a debilitating presence.

"Nineteen years. Nineteen years we've served together, Rogers."

No contrition on the man's face. Only an ugly smile, spreading slowly, surely.

Joseph's pain transformed to a simmering rage. "When? When did they turn you?"

"Enough talk, old man. You have three seconds to drop the gun."

Steady.

Before Rogers could begin his countdown, Blane Burns had a pistol at his temple.

"Moore may not shoot you. But don't think for a second that I won't." To prove his point, Burns cocked his gun.

At that moment, Bauer and five Austrian agents stepped out of the shadows, weapons trained on Grant Rogers. Rogers scanned these newest additions to his confrontation. His smile only grew. And Joseph's blood ran cold.

Kratos is already here.

Joseph locked eyes with Burns as Rogers spoke again.

"You know why you'll never beat us? We're smarter than you. We were here before you, and we will be here after. We're everywhere. And now this is your end."

At his final word, he fired. Burns struck Rogers's hand, causing the bullet to rip into Joseph's leg instead of his heart. Joseph fell, his yell of pain lost as a shower of bullets hit them from the air. Through the haze of fiery agony, he raised the gun still clutched in his hand.

Burns and the others fired upward toward the source of the gunfire. Two of the Austrians with them suddenly focused their shots on Bauer and Burns, but they collapsed as Joseph and the Scottish agent returned fire. When the smoke cleared, one of the remaining Austrian agents was not moving. And it looked like Bauer had been hit. Joseph heard his own sniper returning fire to the Kratos marksman, and all was still in a moment. Davies came running, his sniping equipment abandoned. Joseph glanced up, and it took all his remaining strength to suppress his fury.

Rogers was gone.

A shirtless Davies dropped down to compress Joseph's bleeding wound with his newfound bandage.

"No, no, no—I'm fine!" he growled at Davies. "Check the others!" His head sank down to the earth beneath him. A hot iron poker was stabbing his leg over and over.

Joseph's world began blacking around the edges, but he slapped his own face and shook his head to clear away the fog. Suddenly, Burns was beside him, reapplying pressure to his leg. Joseph growled and was in the process of ordering the Scottish man away when Burns interrupted him.

"Be quiet. You're bleeding too much. You must stop moving."

Joseph settled back but tried to remain alert for the return of the others who had initially fanned out to secure the perimeter. The few men were now walking toward their group, shaking their heads. Joseph swore—though whether it was for Rogers escaping or for the burning pain, he wasn't sure. Soon enough, he and the other wounded were helped back inside the safe house.

Joseph was furious that his plan C to back up plans A and B had also failed. And he was enraged about the pain hazing his thoughts.

He was sitting down, and Alina was beside him, applying his newly removed belt as a tourniquet above the wound on his leg. She was assertive now, scouring the room and barking out orders for clean bandages and something to use as a disinfectant.

Joseph admired this side of Alina: the ED nurse from Glen Allen. She was purposeful. She was composed. She knew what she was doing.

Ambulances pulled up outside, and Bauer and one of the men were loaded in. The medical team came after Joseph, and despite Alina's agreement that Joseph needed medical examination, he growled them away. It had been a clean shot. Through and through. And Alina had been able to request a wound kit from one of the ambulances before they left.

He had been through worse before. Alina could cleanse and pack the wound, stitch him up, and he would survive. He had to. Now with Rogers gone, they had to regroup.

Joseph shifted in his chair, grunting softly at the pain shooting down his leg. They could finally finish this. Joseph, Alina, Burns, Davies, and Donáll. They knew where the vial was. Now they just had to find it.

CHAPTER THIRTEEN

ALINA TOOK SLOW AND STEADY BREATHS AS SHE WATCHED THE WING OF THE JET CUT THROUGH THE CLOUDS OUTSIDE THE WINDOW, LEAVING PATCHES OF GRAY SKY IN ITS WAKE.

They had been in the air for hours now. She did not know exactly where they were headed, but she felt too exhausted, too drained, to care. She knew only that they were flying to reach a specific beach in New Jersey—a beach Donáll had pinpointed as the location in her mother's song.

Alina glanced at Blane in the seat across the aisle from her. He seemed lost in his thoughts, staring out of the window at the ashen, shapeless clouds. His fists—slowly clenching and unclenching. Eventually, he rose from his seat and walked back through the plane. Maybe he was thinking about Afghanistan. Maybe he was reliving the grief of his past. Maybe he was thinking about Ami.

Alina was.

She had hardly slept the night before… She had just cried for hours, missing her best friend. She was exhausted, and she knew she looked it. But everyone else with her in the plane—Blane, Joseph, Owen, and Donáll—looked it too.

Blane, Joseph, Owen, and Donáll. She started again. *Blane, Joseph, Owen, and Donáll. Blane, Joseph, Owen, and Donáll.*

Alina stilled her thoughts, rubbing her forehead with the palm of her hand. She forced herself to keep her eyes glued to the leaden sky outside her window, straining her mind to remember.

Something.

Anything.

The four names repeated again. *Blane, Joseph, Owen, and Donáll.*

Maybe I'm going insane.

Just then, she was startled out of her brooding thoughts as Joseph Moore sat heavily in the seat Blane had vacated, his face drawn. Alina was struck by how old and tired he looked, and she could see his gunshot wound was paining him a great deal. He ran his hand down his face for a few moments, saying nothing. Alina sat patiently, waiting.

Finally, he turned to face her, though his eyes were focused on some minute speck of dust on the back of her seat or on her small suitcase perched on the floor. Anywhere but on hers. He took a shuddering breath, and then he was speaking to her.

"Alina, there is something that I should have told you a long time ago. Soon after I met you, in fact. It is something I have kept hidden from you, only because I didn't want to…to hurt you."

She stared at him, concern in her eyes. His still refusing to meet hers.

"It's about your…your father."

Hope blossomed within her at his unexpected words. "You… you knew my father?" She searched his face, her next words only a whisper. "Why didn't you tell me?"

Remorse contorted his face as he at last drug his gaze from the carpeted floor to meet hers.

"Because I'm the one who killed him."

JOSEPH WATCHED AS A blend of horror and confusion marred Alina's features, and guilt washed over him anew.

Her lips opened and closed a few times before she finally managed a whispered reply. "What? I… I don't understand, Joseph."

He closed his eyes, the pain and shame coursing through him, crushing him. But he had to tell her. He needed to stop being a coward and tell her.

"Your father was my closest friend."

He pressed on, her shock raking through his heart like daggers. "He was closer to me than anyone, closer even than Pete and Patch. His name was Jack. Jack Hart."

Her eyes revealed that she had millions of questions. Her lips seemed to be trying out her father's name, repeating it silently. He continued onward. "We served together in Iraq. It was 2003. We were in the same platoon, though I was his...his captain. We had each other's backs. He saved my life several times, and I saved his." Joseph took a deep breath, suppressing the waver in his voice.

"It was April 6, the final day of deployment for your father and some of the other boys. We had one final scouting mission that day, and Jack volunteered to come. He was so excited to go home, and he thought coming would make the time pass faster." Heat crawled up Joseph's neck, spreading over him. The nausea rose with it.

"It was a route we had scouted numerous times before, and it had always been clean. Every time. Jack thought we should change up our pattern anyway and go a different way. Going the shortcut we always used made us too predictable, he said. But I was so eager to get him and the boys back that I... I took us anyway. It was the fastest route."

Joseph paused, the pain tightening his throat along with the nausea. He couldn't bear to look at Alina now. "He sensed it before I did, and Jack...he shoved me off the trail a second before the world exploded. Somehow, the enemy had come and laid landmines there, right under our noses. Shrapnel in my knees—a few pieces are still there, but that was the only lasting damage thanks to...to him. The others...weren't as...they..." He trailed off, the hardness of his face breaking with emotion. He had to gasp to breathe.

"All fifteen of my men were killed instantly, except Jack. He was...dying. He sustained injuries that I... I knew he could never survive." A violent shiver wracked his body, tears now coursing down his face. The red-hot flame of his guilt was searing him from the inside out, and he quailed from it.

He shamefully met her eyes, and he realized with a start that Burns had joined them. Whether the man had returned to support Joseph or to comfort Alina, Joseph didn't know.

"Jack could still speak, and I did everything I could to save him. In our...last moments together, he gave me his final request. He wanted me to find his wife and child. He wanted me to tell them he loved them, and he wanted me to do everything in my power to protect them. And then my best friend died, along with the rest of my men. Because of me."

He was sobbing. Each breath a struggle, any energy left wrenched away as he shook and cried.

After a few, endless minutes, Joseph rubbed his hands up and down his face, trying and failing to remove the tears there. A hand clasped his, and he looked up in shock as Alina clutched his hand, her eyes bright with her own tears.

But what took his breath away was that he didn't see hatred or contempt in her gaze. What he had feared to see for so long. Instead, he saw something that he hadn't seen for a long, long time. Forgiveness. Maybe even love.

He had made it this far. He needed to finish for her. And this time, he held her gaze with his.

"Protecting his family became my purpose. I had connections in high places, and I was able to request emergency leave. I went directly to Pennsylvania to find his wife and child. When I…when I turned onto the street where Jack and his family lived, I saw smoke. I found the big white house that Jack had always bragged about building with his own two hands, and there was a…a burning car. There had been an explosion, and I saw hundreds of bullet casings on the ground."

Joseph could hardly take a breath. His head hanging lower and lower. "I was too late," he whispered. "There was someone in the driver's seat…and I was certain it was Jack's wife. But then I saw a toddler on the ground, not moving. I rushed to her and held her, and I thanked whatever God is out there that she was still breathing. She had the tiniest little birthmark on the back of her neck, shaped like a crescent moon."

Joseph gave a soft chuckle. "Jack had told me about that birthmark. It was one of the things that helped them finally decide on her name."

He once again locked his eyes with the gaze of the girl sitting across from him. "Alina," he said slowly. "They named her Alina."

He continued on. "Suddenly, as I held her, everything went black. The next thing I knew, I was in an ambulance, being told that I had been knocked out in a car collision. I got back to that street as soon as I could. But the neighbors told me that Amanda was childless and that she had been the victim of a car explosion earlier that day. She was already in the ground. And I couldn't find the child anywhere—she was gone."

Joseph was agitatedly rubbing his hand down his chin, lost in the desperation of the memories. "I tried everything I could. I went to the police. Investigators. No one would listen. They said I was confused from my head injury, and they even dug up my military record and claimed I was suffering from PTSD from Iraq. They said I must have been hallucinating about the toddler, and they claimed that no casings were found at the scene. I could not find the casings, though I searched and searched."

Joseph shook his head at the madness of it all. "Kratos was there and gone. A perfect accident."

"What did you do?" Alina asked, her eyes still wide with shock.

Joseph looked at her, his expression gentling.

"I received an honorable discharge from the military as soon as I could, and then I got into law enforcement. I have been trying to find that child ever since. And now that I have, I must keep her safe at all costs."

He paused for a long moment.

"Alina, I'm so sorry that I have kept this from you. Everything has come full circle, it seems. Antonov only recognized you because of the birthmark on your neck, and Grant Rogers may have been initially assigned to me to monitor me all these years. Because of what I saw that day and my determination to find you."

He took a deep breath, his eyes searching hers. "I had to tell Burns about my connection to you—back at the Sacher Hotel. He wanted me to tell you then, and I should have. But I was so afraid. I didn't know when or how. I didn't know how to tell you that your life has been a lie. To tell you that we are fighting against the people who killed your mother and that you are working with me—the man who killed your father."

He needed to finish this. "But after everything that has happened, I knew I could never forgive myself if I didn't tell you now. Ultimately, it is your past. And you deserve to know…to know about your family."

With a breath, he sank back in his seat, his demons exposed at last. He was utterly exhausted. And utterly terrified that she hated him, despite the look in her eyes earlier.

But since he told her, he felt as though a heavy, debilitating burden had lifted from his chest. He had been keeping this secret from her since that night he had stood outside of her room, knowing that the toddler he had lost so many years ago was inside. Now he could only hope she would find it in her heart to forgive him.

Moments of silence, dismantling Joseph's peace. She wasn't saying anything. And fear overwhelmed him again; he was certain. She hated him. By telling her everything, he had lost everything.

ALINA STARED AT JOSEPH now in wonder. He was one of the many phantoms of her past with his connections to her father. And to her mother. She studied everything about him with new eyes: the silver in his hair, those intense blue eyes that always softened when he was looking at her. She thought back to after she had first met him, remembering. *That's why he was always staring, always watching. That's why he was standing outside of my hotel room that night. He knew who I was.*

And he wanted to protect me.

All at once, she realized his expression had changed. His position had shifted. Her eyebrows furrowed in confusion as she realized he was almost cowering away from her now, his hands clasped in front of him and his eyes averted.

Understanding dawned, shining through the shock still clouding her mind.

He thinks I hate him. That I blame him. For everything that had happened and for everything that has happened since.

She reached out a hand to him again, and her heart broke as he flinched. "Joseph, I do not blame you. For anything. My father died in a tragic attack in the war. And my mother died because of something she did to…to stand up against Kratos. Not because you didn't get there in time." She felt tears welling in her eyes again as his desperate eyes met hers. She clasped his hand once more.

"I meant what I said in that safe house, Joseph," she whispered. "I trust you. I believe in you. And now I'm telling you, I do not blame you."

She reached out her other hand and wiped away a tear trailing down his face. "And you must not blame yourself, either."

She squeezed his hand, and then she gently pulled away. The relief that had transformed his features filled her with joy. "Now, Joseph, you must tell me," she began. "What was my father like? I've wanted to know about him for so long."

A small smile lit up the older agent's face, and he had to clear his throat before he managed to answer her. "What was Jack like? Well."

He began describing a wonderful father she had never known. Her father's courage, funny laugh, messiness, and failure at cooking made her laugh as Joseph told her stories.

She painted her father's face in her mind as Joseph described him. Strong chin and nose. Dark-brown eyes. Thick and curly brown hair. Clean-shaven.

A thought seemed to flit across Joseph's mind, and he pulled out a small photograph from his wallet. There were several moments of comfortable silence as she stared at the picture of Jack Hart. Her dad.

"May I...may I keep this?" she finally asked, her soft voice breaking the still air.

"Of course," Joseph replied.

After a moment or two, Hawk's voice boomed over the cabin speakers, and all three of them jumped.

"Please fasten your seatbelts, folks. We are approaching Newark, New Jersey, and will begin our descent momentarily."

She finally asked the question that had been pushed to the back of her mind.

"So, where are we going once we land?"

Joseph locked eyes with her. "Lavallette Beach."

THE SANDY GRAVEL AND spiney trees dotting the landscape stretched on and on as they drove. An interminable, isolated sandiness.

Alina sat back in her seat. Lavallette Beach. A sleepy little beach town along the Atlantic Coast. One that could very well hold memories of her past, if Donáll had found the correct location. She prayed that he had.

She took the time to study the others in the vehicle with her. She had been so consumed with Joseph's revelation on the plane that she had forgotten that she needed to monitor their wounds. She began with Blane, studying his visible bruises. She had changed the bandage on his knife wound before they had begun the drive, and she was relieved to find that it was healing nicely.

Taking in the sight of each of Blane's injuries had brought back the onslaught of memories from Austria. Her conversation with Joseph had held them at bay for a time, but now they struck her with a vengeance. She had come so close to losing Blane in Austria, too.

The thought terrified her.

She shifted her attention to Joseph, watching him flinch every time he tapped on the brakes. She had checked on his gunshot wound, and she had been satisfied with the healing process. But no matter how many times she attempted to reassure herself, no matter how many times she took out the picture of her father to lighten her spirits, she felt the grief of Austria blend with her fear of the present, and she felt like she was suffocating. Once again, her fears constricted into the needlepoint concern that she wouldn't know what they were looking for even if they found the right beach house.

God, please let all this not be for nothing. Please help it to be over soon.

Alina drifted away with scattered thoughts until Joseph's voice jolted her back into the present, announcing that they had arrived. At least, they had arrived probably close to where they wanted to be. Hopefully, with all of Joseph's precautions, they were still undetected.

Everyone slowly unloaded from the incredibly cramped van, stretching and tentatively ensuring that their leg muscles were still functioning.

Alina knew her legs were not working properly as she stumbled out of the vehicle. Blane caught her at the last second and helped her regain her footing.

"Sorry," Alina said breathlessly. "My legs are being stupid... They fell asleep during the ride."

Blane looked at her, a small smile on his face.

"Well, until your legs decide to cooperate, I'll be here to catch you."

Alina's heart fluttered, and she felt a sudden warmth spread through her. Just the sound of his voice gave her a soothing calm; it made her feel like there was a chance everything would be okay.

After Joseph had returned to his seat on the plane, Blane had spoken to her. Gently. Softly. Asking her if she was all right, knowing that everything Joseph told her had utterly overwhelmed her.

His question had meant more to her than she suspected Blane would ever know. The man had just been through a living nightmare himself, and he was concerned about her. In the midst of everything else, he had wanted to know if she was all right.

As Blane now turned to discuss their next move with Joseph, Alina stared at him. His thick, dark hair. His broad shoulders and muscle-bound back. His big, strong hands. His accent. His kind smile and sparkling eyes. That gentleness that sometimes emanated from him. So rare. And always for her.

Alina clasped her hands nervously and tore her gaze away, hoping no one else would catch her staring at him. She couldn't help it.

She was in love with Blane Burns.

Alina smiled to herself, knowing that she had loved him long before.

Soon enough, Joseph briefed them on the plan. He was emphasizing all of the details concerning their search for the beach house Alina's family may have stayed in years ago. Alina finally stopped her internal musings of Blane in order to better focus on Joseph's words.

They would travel in pairs and communicate with burner phones every half hour. Donáll unzipped his backpack and handed out the phones.

Alina and Blane would start at the northern side of the town, knocking on doors and inquiring after the possible location of the Hart's beach residence. They would pretend to be family members who were using the residence for a short vacation in the early days of freezing January. Donáll and Davies would start on the southern end, going house to house as IRS agents searching for the elusive Hart family. Donáll even had premade badges for that cover. Joseph's angle would focus on the rental agencies, inquiring after a beautiful residence, formerly the Harts' many years ago. He had always admired the haven his coworker had talked about, and Joseph wanted to find out where it was so he could bring his own family to the same place years later.

Joseph didn't feel great about any of their covers. But it was the best they could do with the time and resources they had.

An hour later, Alina was becoming more and more disheartened with every confused glance and slammed door. Having people to talk to was a luxury, however, as most of the beach houses they came across were locked and vacant. A check-in with the rest of the team mirrored similar defeat.

No one seemed to know her parents. Not one friendly face lifted her spirits with a memory of her family. There was nothing. She felt Blane squeeze her hand, and when she looked at him, his encouraging smile melted away her fears. She squeezed back, and to her utter delight, their hands stayed clasped together.

They were coming up to the last line of beach houses along the northern side of Lavallette Beach. These were abandoned, and they were just a few yards away from the lolling waves of the Atlantic Ocean.

Alina started to approach the first house with heavy steps in the sand when Blane suddenly paused. Alina glanced at him in alarm but he was simply staring out at the slate-blue, white-capped horizon. Still holding his hand, Alina stood next to him, allowing her eyes to drink in the same sight. They stood in silence for a few minutes, listening to the waves and seagulls as the salty air blew gently across their faces.

Eventually, Alina spoke. "It looks so desolate and sad out there," she said quietly.

"Even so," Blane replied. "Absolutely beautiful."

Alina's heart hammered as she peeked at him and saw him looking at her.

She didn't even have to ask the question on her mind as his arms gently wrapped around her. Her arms slowly encircled him, and they stood for a long time, each lost in thought and enjoying the precious moment of their embrace.

Blane eventually spoke, his breath warming her face.

"Everything is going to be okay. These are the last houses, but there are plenty more heading inland that we haven't checked ye—" He suddenly choked off as she tightly squeezed him, cutting off his air.

"Alina?" he wheezed. "Can't breathe, lass."

Alina was staring ahead at the last, tiny beach house a few paces from the others. There was something about it. Her muscles tensed as adrenaline coursed through her. It seemed familiar.

The sun glinting off the white sideboards. *This house!* The smell of petunias growing in the window boxes that were emptied long ago. *Maybe!* Riding on top of broad shoulders, staring out at the same ocean under a pink-and-purple-streaked sky. *MAYBE!*

Poor Blane's plea suddenly registered in her mind, and she rapidly released him. He took a few deep breaths, staring at her. "Have you remembered something?" he asked. He whirled around. "One of these houses?"

"That white one on the very end with the dark-blue trim? Something about it…yes, I think so!" Alina practically yelled. Blane's huge smile rapidly transformed into a look of seriousness.

"I'll call the others," he said, his eyes sweeping the area. "We have to be very careful. We don't have much time—I'm sure that Kratos has already pinpointed our general location. Let's get inside."

Alina's eyes were wide as she also stared in every direction, expecting to see helicopters approaching with men jumping down to come after them. She nodded at Blane, and they ran down the beach until they reached the back door of the little house.

"How are we going to get—" Alina started to ask, but Blane had already picked the lock with some little tool he had swiftly produced from his pocket. *Wow.*

He ushered the two of them inside.

As Alina looked around the beach house, faint memories materialized and swirled in her mind, overwhelming her with emotion. Her eyes drank in every detail of the house. Her house.

The tiny kitchen, the stairs leading up to a little loft with the quilt on the bed, the blue couches with embroidered seashells—all memories from a distant dream. A different, faintly familiar world. But one that Alina had once been a part of. She slowly nodded, confirming that this was, indeed, the place they had been searching for. Blane whipped out his burner phone.

Alina wandered through the beach house. They had sipped hot chocolate in those kitchen chairs. Mommy had braided her hair in that little bathroom. Daddy had read her stories in that fluffy armchair. Alina sank into the chair, hoping she would get a whiff of some familiar cologne or aftershave. She smelled only mothballs, however, and she coughed at the large plume of dust that rose as she sat down. No one had been here for many years.

She stood from the chair and continued her journey in the living room, trailing her finger over the colorful seashells inlaid in the table and brushing dust off a small collection of books on a nearby shelf. Her eyes lit upon a dust-covered trunk sitting in one of the bedrooms.

As if in a movie, Alina watched her own hands open the lid. Those same hands sorted through the items, finding an old blanket she thought she recognized, candlesticks, a tablecloth. She could just imagine sitting on a couch and snuggling with the blanket or eating by candlelight. Then her hand closed on a small rectangular frame. She froze. *Could it be...?*

Hesitantly, she turned the frame over, and her eyes drank in the sight of the couple behind the glass. The familiar face of the beautiful woman practically glowed back at her. *Mom.*

Her focus shifted to the man beside her mother: his face the mirror reflection of the photo that Joseph had given her. *Dad.*

They were laughing together in the picture.

Alina watched as a teardrop splashed against the glass, and she quickly wiped it dry.

These are my parents. Lord, thank You.

After a minute, Alina slowly put the items back in the trunk, closed the lid, and stood. Gently, she placed the framed picture on the fireplace mantle, and she turned to see Blane lowering the blinds of the windows.

If the vial was anywhere, Alina was certain it would be here. *Now to find it.*

As she softly brought her mother's song to life once more, her voice echoed through the little house. For a moment, her words seemed to be suspended with the dust in the air before eventually fading downward amongst the dappled light on the wooden floor.

> "Shells glitter on the shore
> The sea whispers you are adored."

Alina's heart raced with excitement, and she rapidly approached the table inlaid with shells, shimmering in the sunlight. She attempted to press them inward, hoping one would open a compartment somewhere.

Nope. They were all solid.

Alina bit back her disappointment and resumed her mother's song.

> "Mommy holds you near. Mommy loves you,
> dear.
> God's sea holds our love
> He smiles down on us from above."

She glanced around, hoping to see some picture of herself in her mother's arms or a Bible or a portrait or a painting... *Maybe a painting.*

And Alina's eyes saw it. *A painting.* It was positioned high up on the wall. She didn't even hear Blane quietly stand a few feet behind her as she walked over to it and stared.

It was a gorgeous piece. A stretch of white sand, with colorful shells sparkling amongst several white-headed seagulls. Turquoise water capped with white foam approaching the sand in gentle waves. A bright, heavenly sunlight adding a golden glow to the entire scene.

Alina's heart was racing. Then it almost stopped as she read the cursive of the artist's initials: "*A. H.*"

"At the sea, you'll find me."

She had. She had found her mother.

Alina stood up on her tiptoes and gently tugged at the painting. It wouldn't budge.

That's a good sign.

Blane was beside her in an instant, and she could practically feel waves of intensity radiating from him.

"Is it—" he started to ask but stopped sharply. His eyes narrowed and focused outside the window. In an instant, he grabbed her hand and pulled her to the floor, a finger to his lips.

Alina's eyes widened, and a slow terror spread through her being. She wanted to ask what he had seen or what he had heard, but she remained silent. *Thump-thump.* The silence was suffocating her. Her pulse thundering in her ears. *Thump-thump. Thump-thump. Thump-thump.*

Blane was slowly pulling out his pistol, and he was training his phone on the painting before placing it to his ear. Then a sudden panic transformed his face, and he was frantically covering his nose and mouth with his shirt, shouting at her to do the same.

She saw it. A white fog rapidly seeping underneath the doors. Before they could react, the room was filled with it. Blane was crawling toward the back of the house, pulling her with him. But Alina could already feel her limbs growing heavy and her thoughts clouding. Cloudy brain, cloudy consciousness, cloudy thoughts.

Fluffy clouds. Pretty clouds.

Blane was desperately trying to get them out of the house or at least hidden, but Alina was just cloudy. She didn't feel frantic. Just felt clouds. Fluffy like her bathrobe. That smelled like Blane.

Then she was out.

BLANE FELT THE INCAPACITATING agent slowly wrenching the reins of his consciousness from him.

No, no, no!

Alina was out cold. He just needed to get them out of here. He tried to keep pulling her. But he couldn't. Maybe if he could just open a window and get some air…but he didn't have the strength to even stand. Couldn't pull himself up. And he couldn't even hold his gun anymore.

With a final burst of strength, he threw himself back toward Alina. Everything detached. Couldn't think. His phone and gun clattered on the wooden floor. Black boots slowly walked into his line of vision. And his world went black.

JOSEPH MOORE WAS WALKING with Davies and Donáll toward the northern end of the beach, his eyes searching for the beach house that Burns had called about. As they neared the last line of houses, Joseph felt a sense of unease take hold. He wasn't sure why, but his hand flew to his Glock 22.

A sudden ringing fried his nerves, and he noticed the others jump at the sound of the incoming call from Burns. *This is new.* It was a video call. Joseph didn't even know burner phones could do that. He answered, but all he saw was a painting and then a ceiling.

"What is it, Boss?" Davies trailed off, staring at the phone.

Joseph stared at the screen in confusion and the others leaned in as they walked, picking up their pace.

They still couldn't see the end of the houses lining the northern side.

Suddenly, all three men yelled as a gas mask loomed over the phone, and a heavy boot blackened the screen as the phone was undoubtedly crushed.

"What the what?" Donáll cried, his voice higher pitched than normal.

"Kratos," Joseph ground out. "They found them." He broke out into a desperate run. He didn't know when he had ever run faster.

The sand picking up in a sudden wind stung them as they ran, and the waves roared like an enormous, shapeless beast. At last

Joseph spied the final beach house, and he increased his pace even more. That was the house.

No! The front door of the house was swinging loosely in the wind. The whole area looked abandoned.

No, God, please, no! Please, let them be there still.

But Joseph was lying to himself. This whole thing could be a trap. Alina and Burns would be gone. Burns could even be dead.

They had developed a plan in case something would happen to any of them on this mission. Joseph was not going to let Vienna happen all over again.

They had been taken. Now to find them. The world slowed for a moment.

Before it's too late.

And Joseph could only pray that Alina and Burns had been ambushed before they had located the vial.

They were within twenty feet of the beach house. As a tight unit, they inched along the last few dwellings, guns drawn. Poor Donáll looked extremely afraid. But he was steady.

Am I?

Joseph shook his head and tightened his trembling hand on his gun. They would find them before it was too late. But if the vial had been taken…

Joseph forced himself to focus. A deep breath. Slow exhale. A nod at Davies. Solid eye contact. Then Joseph charged into the house.

He came face-to-face with five Kratos agents. Joseph immediately noted the gas masks and the faint remnants of white fumes quickly dissipating through open windows. But no time for thinking now. He and his men fired while the element of surprise was on their side.

All five were down. Still alive but no longer a threat.

Finally. They would have some living proof of Kratos's operatives. At least for as long as they could keep them that way.

Joseph suddenly felt light-headed, and his attention snapped back to those white fumes. Some sort of incapacitating agent.

Burns and Alina.

Wasting no time, the three of them restrained all of the agents to the solid maple table that was conveniently bolted to the floor. Joseph called the local precinct to request backup, but he was met with an infuriatingly unconcerned, disrespectful, gum-smacking 911 operator.

"And the name's Joseph Moore, yeah?" the young woman asked. She sounded…bored.

"Yes, ma'am," Joseph replied, trying to keep his cool against the *smack, smack, smack* of her gum.

"And you said you're FBI?" she continued, sounding as thrilled as if she were filing his taxes for him.

"Yes, ma'am, the Transnational Unit. But the point of the matter is—"

"Yeah, I'll bet you are," she interjected, her voice dripping with a sort of sarcasm that made Joseph's blood boil.

"Look, I can connect you with my superiors, or you can connect me with yours. But I don't have *time* for that, so send out two armed units to the northernmost point of the Lavallette coastline, and you send them RIGHT NOW!"

There it was. He had lost his cool. But he could hear her sharp intake of breath and brief coughing episode. Hopefully she had swallowed her gum. He closed his eyes for a brief moment to regain his composure.

After being on hold for what felt like a hundred years but couldn't have been more than thirty seconds, he was connected to the police chief of Lavallette who assured him that reinforcements were en route.

Hanging up, he turned to Davies, who was making quick work of the painting in the living room. The beach scene painted by Amanda Hart that Burns had shown them in the video call before they lost contact. Either the vial itself or another clue to its location had to be behind it. A sudden thought stole Joseph's breath and made him break into a cold sweat. *If Kratos had only been one minute later…*

What if Kratos had *meant* for Joseph to find the painting?

Shaking his head and speed-dialing Herne, he gave a reassuring nod in Donáll's direction. The man was visibly shaking as he held their five prisoners at gunpoint.

She picked up instantly. "Yes, shall I activate Operation Find and Recover in One Piece?" she asked.

"Yes, and only send an FBI unit you completely trust out here. We have prisoners, and these ones are actually alive."

"You got it. I'll send my husband and his boys. To…?"

"Local precinct in Lavallette. Do you see Alina and Burns?" he asked, praying that their plans had not been compromised.

"No, wait yes! Yes, yes, YES!" she exclaimed. "They are definitely in the air. But it's too soon for me to tell where they are headed. They are flying over the Atlantic."

Joseph could have hugged her. "Excellent."

Davies called out, "I found it, Boss!"

Joseph nearly stumbled as relief and fear seared him. But he resumed his call.

"We'll obviously need a jet. Hawk had to leave. And we'll need any others that can be spared, maybe Crewe or Shaw if they have both been cleared."

"May I make this a code red, sir?" she asked.

"Yes. We will be storming the Kratos complex—of that I have no doubt. Send word to MI5, Interpol, and even the CIA. Get everyone you trust. We need as much backup as possible. Keep them on standby."

Joseph ended the call, and he finally allowed himself to take in the sight around him. He was certain this was the beach house Jack had always been talking about. Just like his own home, Jack had built this one from the ground up.

Joseph's eyes were drawn to a framed picture sitting on the fireplace mantle. Upon closer inspection, he took a sharp intake of breath as he recognized his best friend and his wife. He knew he couldn't leave it there, and he grabbed it just as the local police arrived on the scene. They were collectively impressed at the FBI badges and at the scene before their eyes.

An hour later, the Kratos operatives were being loaded into the large SUVs taking them back to the local precinct. And then to Washington.

Meanwhile, Joseph, Davies, and Donáll headed to the airport to wait for whatever transportation Herne had been able to obtain on such short notice.

Davies was the first to spot the aircraft.

The three of them climbed the steps of the small jet, and Joseph was shocked at the empty interior of the plane. He approached the cockpit, expecting it to be empty too. His hand flew to his gun at the sudden thought that the jet could be a trap. The vial, wrapped in layer after layer of paper inside a manila envelope, was burning a hole in his jacket. But then he saw Lily Herne herself in the cockpit, grinning at him. He felt a strange mix of joy and resigned dread.

"So. No one else in the FBI—"

She cut him off. "That we can trust. I'm afraid this one is on us. Maybe other agencies will come, maybe they won't."

Her eyes lit up, and Joseph didn't have to turn around to realize that her husband, Jason Herne, had joined their little group. He was trailed by Crewe and Shaw. The three of them must have stepped out of the plane just before Joseph, Davies, and Donáll had approached it.

"Well, I trust everyone on this plane completely. Good work, Herne."

She nodded in response. "They have about a four-hour lead, but I can say with relative certainty that they are headed to northern Europe. Possibly to the main Kratos base Donáll pinpointed in Norway. I'll reach out again to the other agencies once we know for certain where Alina and Blane land. We'll see if they come through. In the meantime, buckle up, boys!"

Joseph quickly rejoined Davies and Donáll as Jason Herne sat with his wife up front.

And they were soon in the air.

Joseph finally allowed himself to register the throbbing pain in his thigh, and he gingerly rubbed it as he leaned back in his seat. The vial was heavy on his mind. If it fell into Kratos's hands… He closed his eyes against such a terrifying outcome.

With a breath, he opened his eyes and concentrated on watching the progress of Burns and Alina across the Atlantic. The fact that their trackers were still sending out strong signals was good. It proved that Donáll's tracking implants had gone undetected. For now.

He felt old fears surfacing, but he suppressed them with a shake of his head and a silent growl. No time for that.

Hang in there. We're coming.

CHAPTER FOURTEEN

ALINA AWOKE TO A BLACK WORLD, AND SHE WAS MOMENTARILY DISORIENTED.

Where am I?

And then it all came flooding back to her. The beach house. Her parents. Her mother's painting. The white gas. Blane's desperate look.

She gasped at the terror that struck her, and her fears transformed to full-on panic as she realized her hands were tied to the armrests of her seat and that there was a hood over her head. Her own labored breathing and rushing blood filled her ears.

I need Blane. Where is Blane? Please, God.

She feared she was going to black out. It was hard to breathe. She almost screamed as something touched her foot, but relief coursed through her as she realized that it was another foot. By the way it tapped hers, she knew it was Blane's.

He's alive. Thank You, God. Thank You.

She didn't want to make a sound. Better to keep Kratos thinking she was still unconscious. Better to go back to sleep. Better to block out everything. She just wanted to be back home with Ami. Just wanted to…block out…home… Ami.

Oh, please, God.

Her terror was paralyzing. And she was crying. She must have been shaking, though no one approached her. Then they were landing. Alina couldn't tell if minutes or hours had passed since she had first woken up.

As soon as the plane came to an abrupt halt, she heard zip ties being cut, and suddenly her hands were free. She didn't have time to rub feeling into them, however, as strong arms roughly yanked her from her seat. She suppressed a scream but couldn't hold back a gasp as she was hustled down the aisle. Her legs were so weak. She gasped again as she was lifted down the airplane stairs. More hands pushed her along until someone cuffed her own behind her back, and she was forced into what she could only assume was a car. She heard Blane grunt behind her, and she was terrified that he had been hurt. She was so afraid.

Another body, presumably Blane's, was shoved beside her. Then the car was driving. And Alina was crying again. The suffocating hood was unbearable.

She felt him lean into her.

Blane was trying to keep her calm. To let her know he was still here. She wasn't alone.

Alina knew that Joseph had had a plan in case any of them were taken, and she knew that the team was likely tracking and coming after them. Unless Joseph, Owen, and Donáll had been ambushed, too. She shuddered violently at the thought.

She had no idea how long they had been in the car when it skidded to a stop. Before she could react, a car door was opening, and she was being yanked out of the car. She almost fell over, and she was half-carried as she was led up a flight of stairs into what was probably a building.

Alina was hyperventilating now. Their footsteps were echoing on some polished floor for several paces. Then Alina heard a door creak open. The hood was yanked off her head, and she was falling, shoved through a doorway. Stars circled for a moment as she smacked her face on the floor.

Before she could get oriented, Blane was suddenly thrown beside her. He was also handcuffed and still had a hood over his face. Then the door was pulled closed, and a heavy lock clicked. She was relieved they were alone.

"Alina?" Blane asked, his voice muffled. "Lass, are you in here?" She heard his barely suppressed panic as he struggled to his feet.

"Yes, yes, I'm here. We're alone." She took a few steps toward him and told him to kneel. Once he complied, she twisted to the side, wrapped her fingers around the hood, and gently pulled it off his head. He blinked against the sudden light, and when his eyes rested on hers, they were bright with unshed tears.

"Well, that's good news," he whispered, offering a weak smile. She saw his eyes fasten on her cheek, blossoming red from where it had hit the floor.

The concern in his eyes rapidly transformed to rage. He shakily got to his feet once more, and she watched him study their surroundings. Both of them cuffed. Both of them disoriented.

Or so she thought.

Blane walked over to her and, as well as he could with his arms fastened behind him, leaned in and rested his cheek against hers.

"I see only one camera, well-hidden," he murmured.

She felt goosebumps run up and down her arms as his warm breath tickled her cheek.

"From this angle, my left side is hidden. Grab the pack on the inside of my belt, if you can."

A thrill of hope coursed through her.

She threaded her fingers through his belt, and they closed around a small leather pouch. She struggled against the leather and breathed a sigh of relief when she finally tugged it free. But her heart lurched as the pouch nearly slipped through her fingers.

Don't drop it, you clumsy idiot. DON'T DROP IT!

Alina finally had it held loosely in her hand, and at her nod, Blane continued to whisper. "You need to open it carefully. There's a lock-picking tool inside. You need to keep it hidden in your hand. We can't take off the cuffs now, or we'll lose the element of surprise."

Alina nodded, her eyes wide. A panicked thought entered her mind. "What about you?"

He looked deep into her eyes just then, holding her captive. Even in the midst of this nightmare, she got lost in the depths of those deep blue eyes. She had never noticed the pale flecks before.

"They'll be expecting me to try something. But not you. Besides," he murmured, leaning in even closer, "this time they didn't strip me down." He wiggled his eyebrows in an attempt to lighten the situation, and she felt herself blushing.

Stop it, Alina!

Blane smiled roguishly at her response. "I meant that I still have what I need on me."

Embarrassed at the warmth spreading through her, she nodded and started to take the tool out of the pouch. It was slow going with her cuffed hands. When she glanced up, seriousness had overtaken Blane's face, and the moment between them ended. She felt the weight of the situation crushing down on her once more.

"You remember how I taught you to unlock the cuffs?" he asked, and she nodded. Though her hands were so slippery with sweat that she wasn't sure she'd have the grip required to do so.

Just then, he stiffened and locked eyes with her as the door slammed open.

THE SKY AROUND THEM was darkening rapidly. They had been in the air for about eleven hours now.

Joseph was getting more and more restless.

He was up. He was down. He was checking his aim with his pistol. He was testing his wounded leg. Gritting his teeth against the pain. He was checking in with Herne. He was obsessively tracking their progress against the movements of the two tiny green dots. He resorted to angrily chewing gum as he watched Alina and Burns finally reach Norway. *Just as Herne had predicted.* By the speed of their movement, Donáll thought they were now in a vehicle.

How much time do they have left? He looked at his watch for what must have been the hundredth time. *Four hours to go. Only four. Four.* He checked in with Herne and her husband again, who explained for the third time that the government agencies Herne had contacted had responded and that agents were en route to Tromsø, Norway, to meet them.

He then attempted to brief Donáll and Davies again of the plan. Donáll barely heard him, and when Joseph stole a look at his tech man's laptop, he could see Donáll was also locked on the tracking screen.

Davies just nodded, fiddling with his gun. Joseph knew he was just as agitated as Joseph was.

"Careful, Davies," he said as lightly as he could, trying to make eye contact with his agent. "You may shoot someone prematurely."

Davies eventually just stared at him, not fully registering Joseph's words. He nodded with a "Yes, Boss," then got back to staring and fiddling.

The guy was stressed. And Joseph knew he was thinking about Ami. Joseph simply clasped his shoulder gently before returning to his seat. He wanted to call in the entire Norwegian Army, but he was certain it had been infiltrated by Kratos to the highest level. He wouldn't expect anything less from the country of Black's headquarters.

No, their mission had to be completely in the dark. Or else Burns would be killed, and Alina…well, he actually had no idea of Black's plan for Alina. The very thought petrified him, and images flashed through his mind in an overwhelming sequence, catching him unawares.

All of his men, dying. Jack's desperate eyes as they darkened forever. The few agents he had lost before heading his team at the FBI. Ami. His failures swirling about him, blinding him in a snowstorm and threatening to bury him alive.

Joseph shook his head, his hand tightening on his gun. *Not this time.* A sense of peace.

Three more hours. Only three. Three.

BLANE PREPARED HIMSELF FOR anything as the door to their cell burst open and three men came in. He even recognized one of them. And then he truly started to feel afraid. More for Alina's sake than his own. He knew there was a slight chance he could get them out of this, but he also knew there was a greater chance he could fail. And he didn't want her to have to watch. And that was exactly what he believed Black would have her do.

For her sake, he kept a neutral facial expression. Then the men grabbed him and forcibly walked him out of the room. He craned his head to look back at Alina. It looked like the other agent was leading her out too, though she was being taken in a different direction.

Blane could only hope that she hadn't dropped his lock pick.

They rounded a corner as more men joined them, and he was thrown to the ground before he could register what was happening. His head struck the floor, and the world went black for a moment. When his vision cleared, his hands were uncuffed, and his shirt was being cut off. His concealed knife clattered to the floor.

As two men held his arms, his boots were the next to go, and both knives and his second pistol fell out. Then lastly, his belt was removed, and it was flung away with the rest of his weapons.

Well, that's that then.

He needed to try something while he was still able.

Blane slumped his dead weight against the hands of his captors, and the moment of surprise was all he needed. He headbutted the agent on his right while shoving back into the man on his left. Both men grunted and released him for the briefest of seconds.

With adrenaline pumping through his veins, Blane dodged an incoming blow and landed one of his own, feeling a satisfying crack against the operative's cheekbone. He ducked to the side as another blow came, and he took a few steps toward his gun.

At that moment, one of them got the back of his head with something heavy, and his world blacked out again.

He had been so close.

He slumped down as someone kicked behind his knees, and he tried to crawl toward his discarded weapons until he was grabbed backward. Something twisted his shoulder at an unnatural angle, and he gasped in pain as he felt his shoulder pop. His arm fell awkwardly at his side. Then he was crying out as a kick connected with his ribs. Then the blows began landing on his head. His face. Heavy boots from all sides, striking every inch of him.

They're going to beat me to death.

He was picked up and thrown down again, and his head thoroughly slammed into the concrete. He knew he wouldn't be conscious for much longer. No fight was left in him as the onslaught continued. The room was dark and white, black and blinding all at once. He tried to lie very still, hoping they would cease once they saw he was unconscious. They suddenly yanked him upward, and he couldn't suppress a groan of agony as they reattached the cuffs. As he was held, a fuzzy figure approached him from the front.

"Always the nuisance, Burns. Finally, we have you right where we want you."

The figure leaned in close, and his face slowly came into view.

Grant Rogers was smiling at him.

Then something slammed into the back of his head again, and the world went black. And it stayed black.

ALINA WAS SITTING IN a chair, her arms still securely handcuffed behind her back. Miraculously, they hadn't found the lock-picking thing. She was alone except for the two other guards who had forced her into the massive room. It looked like the interior of a cathedral, remodeled to be a huge empty space. Except for the chair she was sitting in, the room was empty. And very echoey. The ceiling above was striped with large, rectangular windows which streamed dull light onto the floor.

She was terrified. She didn't want to try unlocking her cuffs until something was happening. She didn't want to blow their only chance of escape if the guards discovered the tool. Her palms were sweaty, and she was hot, cold, and shivering all at once. She was so overwhelmed with her thoughts that she screamed at a sudden shout. Heavy footsteps resounded outside of the door.

Blane.

Fear coiled around her, suffocating her. *God, please be with him. Please, Jesus. Please.*

The door at the opposite end of the huge room suddenly opened. It opened slowly, and the creak reverberated around the room, bouncing off the walls and thundering in Alina's ears. A single figure, flanked by two others, slowly entered through the open doorway. He was in shadow, but Alina knew. It was Draven Black. The man who had fed her childish imaginations with perfect lies. The man who had orchestrated so much pain and loss. The monster who had taken Ami from her.

She watched him move underneath the beams of dull sun. Watching him disappear in shadow and reemerge in the garish light.

Watching a nightmare unfold. Unable to move. Unable to look away. Alina felt paralyzed as he closed the distance between them, his two guards lurking behind him. He was standing right in front of her.

"Welcome to Norway, Alina." His reedy voice echoed through the room and shook Alina to the core.

He hesitated, waiting for her to say something. But she just stared at him. Then he cleared his throat and continued. "I must apologize at the way you have arrived with us. But I am glad to have you here. Your face, so like your mother..." His voice faded, and Alina was shocked to see such emotion from him. She hadn't believed he could feel anything at all.

She felt furious words bubbling up inside of her, threatening to spew out. *THEN WHY DID YOU KILL HER!*

But she kept silent.

Black shook his head and refocused on Alina. His pale eyes glinted strangely at her.

"I'm afraid this conversation will have to be brief. My rash agents in Lavallette made a grave error in capturing both you and Mr. Burns before you had a chance to reveal the vial's location. And then they had the decency to stay behind and search...where they were soon picked up by that old man and his ragtime team of imbeciles."

Alina's heart hammered in her chest at the mention of Joseph.

Black resumed. "That issue will be dealt with swiftly. But that is not a polite topic of conversation for us, dear."

He leaned in close as if to touch her cheek, and she, repulsed, leaned away from him. A hard look entered his gaze, and she feared for a moment that he would slap her.

Well, do it. Go ahead and do it! She wanted to scream the words at him, but he took a deep breath and straightened again. He was fighting to keep his composure.

"Back to the matter at hand. My vial. It is of dearest importance to me, as I cannot move forward in a direction I have been planning for a very, very long time without it. And, as I have made clear to you already, your mother took it from me."

At this point, Alina dared to question him. She needed to know. "Who was my mother to you?" Her voice sounded stronger than she felt, fueled by her hatred toward him.

He actually looked pleased to hear her speak, and the soft look returned to his eyes at the mention of her mother. "Well, dear, your mother was, my...well, my little sister."

The room blurred in and out of focus while nausea overwhelmed her senses. She had been well aware that such a reality was possible, but hearing him say the words...her world was shattering.

He's my uncle.

"Well, don't look so thrilled, dear." He chuckled, staring at her. "Now that we have that pretty fact established, let us move forward to matters of business as family." He whispered something to one of his men, and then he turned his pale eyes back on Alina. "I know that the vial has been found. I know that Joseph Moore and his team are coming, though my men are unaware of when. He really is doing a most excellent job of hiding from me." He chuckled again, and Alina wanted nothing more in the world than to wake up and realize this was all a horrible dream. But there he was, still talking to her.

"This is where you come in, Alina. You will need to get the vial from them and bring it to me. It will be very, very easy. The alternative is I kill your friend."

A sudden snap from his fingers, and one of the well-concealed side doors opened. Grant Rogers was the first to walk through, and Alina's eyes flashed angrily as he smiled at her. Then her gaze fell on the slumped figure held between two guards trailing after him.

Blane. Oh no. Oh no. Blane.

He was so beaten he could hardly walk on his own. One arm hung limply at his side, angled in a way that she didn't think was possible. She was afraid he couldn't even lift his head so his eyes would meet hers.

Blane. Oh, Blane.

He was brought into the center of the room near Black and was then released. She watched him battle gravity before he lost, falling to the ground with a sickening thud.

Oh, Blane.

"You see his pathetic and quite helpless state, Alina," Black purred.

Blane looked up at that moment, locking eyes with Alina. They held so much pain, yet there was strength in them. Strength he didn't have. For her.

Tears streamed down her face, and Black shifted his attention to Blane.

"It is a pleasure to once again be in your company, Mr. Burns. We didn't quite get the chance to end our first meeting the way I wanted. Well, no matter. Let's finish what we started."

Black nodded to his men, and they pulled Blane upward. His barely suppressed groan of agony reverberated inside her entire being.

Oh, Blane.

Deftly, carefully, Alina turned the lock picking tool in her hand. *Slowly. Gently.* She worked to fit the end in the keyhole of the handcuffs. *There.* Only by a miracle did the tool fit inside.

Alina had no idea what on earth she could possibly do.

God, please help me.

Her eyes were glued to Blane, and the men dragged him over to the wall to the right of where she was sitting. His arms were yanked upward as he cried out, and she watched in horror as his cuffs were hooked to a chain above his head, suspended from the ceiling. Her eyes were drawn to the keys as the guard slipped them into his pocket.

The chain was slowly tightened until Blane was upright, his toes barely touching the floor. A sharp cry of desperate pain as his shoulder wrenched. His cry. The excruciating, violent pain.

She was on her feet, almost forgetting to tightly clench the lock-picking tool still inserted in her cuffs. She was saying his name and trying to walk toward him. He needed her. So much pain.

Blane.

The men behind her dragged her backward, shoving her into her chair, and Black's face was suddenly inches from hers.

Such pale, lifeless eyes. Bulbous. Thin lips curled in a sneer. Hatred. All over his face. In every inch of his being. A monster. An ugly, cruel, despicable monster.

She glared at him with such venom he actually slapped her face. She bit back a cry of pain—she would not give him the satisfaction. As heat radiated from her cheek, she heard Blane shout and strain against his cuffs, but a severe punch to his stomach silenced him. She kept her eyes locked with Black's.

Black squeezed her face, and she held his stare with as much courage as she could. All she could think about was Blane.

"Enough of that defiance, Alina," he ground out. "As you can see, I'm liable to losing my patience. And we all know what happens when the time runs out."

He released her, and Alina gasped as her vision went fuzzy again. She knew he was talking about Ami.

"I need you to call Agent Moore. I know he has what I want. And he is looking for you, so I can only imagine he is close by."

Black was pacing now, his hands held by his sides.

"You will go to him, retrieve the vial, and come back for Mr. Burns. Then, depending on your cooperation, I may decide to let both of you live."

Alina chuckled, a sound which was magnified by the echoey room.

Black looked at her in surprise. "And the amusing part of this is…" he hedged, his hands curling into fists.

She could tell his patience was once again running dangerously thin.

"You are going to let us live?" she murmured, fixing him again with a fiery stare in a sudden burst of strength. "We've seen your face, we know who you are, and now we even have seen the inside of your—your lair. You think I believe you when you say you are going to release us? We would take you down. No. You are going to murder both of us."

Black's eyes got such a hard glint in them as she spoke that she felt light-headed. He looked like a madman. A madman still completely in control and holding all of the cards.

"You inept, stupid girl. You think you could destroy me?" He released such a bloodcurdling laugh that Alina nearly let her one loose cuff clatter against the chair. She felt cold all over.

Multiple countries are looking for this monster. He can't be invincible.

"You think I'm wanted all over the world for my crimes, dear one. But, in truth, they all want me on their side. And the fools too idiotic to realize I am of more value to their countries free than imprisoned? Their efforts are in vain. Nothing to convict me. They have got—" He leaned in close to Alina's face, and she stiffened, meeting his eye. She despised him. "Nothing," he trilled, causing the hair on Alina's arms to rise as if she had been electrocuted. "What I've built here…is invisible. Not one scrap of evidence until those bumbling FBI agents delayed operations at HAARP. But no matter. Nothing ties back to me. I am as innocent as the public will ever know. I never leave loose ends."

Those final, ugly words filled Alina with a cold rage. "Is that all she was to you?" she whispered, hatred coursing through her veins. "A loose end?"

"Ami?" Black questioned, a sickening grin spreading over his face. "That pathetic thing? She got too attached. And she could not do what was asked of her. She failed me. Ah, but she was a pretty thing. Very—"

"STOP!" Alina screamed at him. "You destroyed her life. You have no right to—" Another slap, this time even harder, snapped her head back, sending the world into a spinning, roiling mess. Black was standing still, breathing heavily, and then he glided over the floor to where Blane was hanging.

"Let's learn from Ami, Alina. You will do what I ask, or this man will suffer more and die because of you."

Black was standing, staring up at Blane, and Alina knew it was now or never. The cuffs were off. She moved quickly, darting across the room while reaching behind her to the hidden holster in the small of her back. The pistol that Blane had given her back in Washington was out, removed in one fluid motion. Held by shaking hands. And trained directly on the monster who had destroyed her life. And who was about to torture the man she loved. The two guards around her shouted and raced at her, but her clear, unwavering voice stopped them.

"I will shoot him if you move another inch," she ground out, steadily, carefully.

Black was staring at her, an impressed look spreading across his face. He held up his hand, and the guards stood stock-still.

"Well. An unexpected turn of events. My, my, dear—full of surprises. I specifically told my men to not interfere with you in any way. I shall have to readdress that command once you put your silly piece of metal away."

She was slowly getting closer, though she was sticking to the outside of the room. "Shut up, please."

Reviewing the plan Joseph had drawn out in her head. *I think this is a good place to stand.* She made brief eye contact with Blane, and his barely perceptible nod confirmed it.

Please, God. Please let them be here.

"What is your next move, dear one?" Black asked, staring her down. He was taking steps toward her. "You could never pull that trigger." He was coming, step by step. "You simply don't have it in you."

"And I hope I never do!" she burst out, holding his gaze. "But if you touch him, we'll find out for certain."

His eyebrows raised slightly as his eyes narrowed. She didn't look away. Stare for stare. Heart-stopping beat by heart-stopping beat.

Please, God. Please let them be here. Several long moments passed, and suddenly she was filled with a still, small voice.

"*Trust Me, My child.*" Something deep inside her was filled with peace at His words.

She knew they were there. She just knew it.

"I..." she began. *It's time.* "I am just the distraction." She fired twice into the air.

And then the miracle. One she was desperately praying for, over and over again. The opposite wall of the large room was suddenly a crumbled, groaning heap of rubble as a deafening explosion split the air. Everyone, including Black, stumbled to the ground, but Alina had been bracing for it. And she was ready.

280

She sprang forward, grabbing the keys to Blane's cuffs from the guard's pocket, and she darted over to Blane just as smoke grenades flew through the gaping hole of what used to be the stone wall.

Without thinking. Trying not to choke on the smoke-choked air. Working deftly. Trying not to scream as the first shots screamed out.

Miraculously again, the shots were not aimed at her or Blane. It was Joseph and others outside, shooting and receiving fire back. First cuff off, and Blane yelled in pain as he slumped down, jerking the still-suspended shoulder. A sickening crack resounded as the shoulder popped back into place. She just couldn't reach the second of Blane's cuffs to unlock it, though she was straining and trying and trying. She was apologizing. Over and over again.

"Oh, Blane I'm sorry. I'm trying. I'm so sorry." *God, please help me!*

The key turned just right, and Blane fell into her, sending them both to the floor.

Thank You! Thank You...oh, thank You.

And then she couldn't think... She was choking on the air, and her eyes were burning. But she ignored everything for a moment as they struggled to their feet. And in that moment, she was pulling Blane into her, hugging him as fiercely as she could.

A hand suddenly caught her hair through the smoke, and she screamed as someone started wrenching her away from Blane. With a roar he held on to her yet moved with her, punching into the smoke.

His fist must have found its mark as the hold on her hair loosened. Then he was clutching her to himself, and they were stumbling toward the door where he had been led out. And then she was half-carrying him as he nearly fell.

Oh no. I'm not going to let you fall. Adrenaline was coursing through her, and they were almost there.

They at last made it through the door, both coughing and desperately trying to wipe their eyes. Not able to see. Not able to breathe. But she could feel Blane. And that was all she needed.

They continued stumbling down a narrow hallway, and she handed the gun to Blane. Praise God for another miracle—the hallway seemed abandoned. Everyone must have been heading toward the cathedral room another way.

Now they were in a wider hallway, and Alina pulled them both to the ground as a Kratos agent abruptly ran past. Then she was pulling Blane back up, and they were stumbling along again. At least they could breathe now. And see! She glanced at the man she was dragging alongside her, but she felt her resolve crack and threaten to shatter at the pain on his face. And then she saw a gorgeous patch of…was it, yes, sunlight on the floor up ahead. Sunlight meant a door or window. Leading outside. Freedom was close.

"Come on, Blane, we are almost there!" she cried, and they kept moving.

Come on, Blane. We're almost there.

JOSEPH WAS BARKING ORDERS into his comms, trying desperately to see if they could stop the firefight. They needed as many alive as possible. And Black. He couldn't be killed. Joseph needed him alive. He was also pleading with everyone to keep their eyes peeled for Burns and Alina.

God, please help them be okay. Help them get out here. Keep them alive. I'm begging You.

He fired off a shot at a Kratos operative moving toward him, and the man crumpled to the ground. Joseph kept firing and moving around, surveying his people and looking for Alina and Burns. And then he saw them.

They had emerged from the complex a little further up, with Alina dragging Burns alongside her. They were getting closer and closer. Joseph's heart swelled with an inexplicable joy as he stood facing them, but he was suddenly knocked to the ground as a bullet struck the center of his bulletproof vest.

His gun clattered from his hand, and he watched the form of Grant Rogers walking toward him through a burst of smoke. His gun raised. And aimed. This time right at Joseph's head.

Before Joseph could reach for his gun, the man spoke. "Don't even try. Where is the vial, Moore? Give it to me right now, and this can all be over."

Joseph heard his voice answer, though he knew the agent would pull the trigger. "I will not."

A sneer distorted Rogers's face, his eyes full of hatred. "Then I will take it off your corpse."

Joseph rapidly rolled over and grabbed his gun, knowing that a bullet would tear through his brain at any second. But something stayed Rogers's hand.

Joseph glanced up to see blood streaming from a fresh wound in the agent's shoulder. He directed his gaze to trace the trajectory of the bullet, and Joseph saw Blane Burns standing through the smoke, pistol still raised. Burns had shoved Alina away from him, and he was shouting at Rogers. Joseph was on his feet in an instant, his gun trained on the agent.

"Give it up, Rogers," Joseph ground out. "It's over."

Rogers gave a hair-raising, triumphant snarl.

Burns was now standing about ten yards away, gun raised. Getting closer.

"Really, old man? Then you definitely won't see this coming." Rogers moved and fired twice, but the body that dropped was not Joseph's.

Joseph immediately fired, and Rogers collapsed on the pavement, dead. But Joseph's attention was on the agent's final victim. Burns was on the ground, and he wasn't moving. Joseph was starting toward him when he had to fire shots at two others approaching him. And then he was taking cover as a shower of bullets sprayed the ground near him. He risked a glance to where Burns had fallen, but a suffocating, blinding cloud of smoke obscured his line of vision.

Let Burns be alive, God. Please. Let him be alive.

He was remembering the bullets not tearing through him. As the fighting all around him intensified, Joseph kept replaying the wrenching moment in his head.

Of Blane Burns falling.

NO. HER EYES TRAILED him. His body falling. Her eyes watched him. The world blurring into silent chaos.

No, God. No.

Her heart pounded in her throat as she rushed to his side. Echoey yells and shots streaked around her, but all was meaningless except for Blane.

No.

His eyes were wide, and he was gasping for air. Blood blooming from his chest. Pouring from his arm.

No. Don't take him. Not him too, God.

"Please don't leave me here alone!"

Blood.

Oh, God, please. Blood everywhere.

She pressed her hands frantically to the wounds.

Stop the bleeding.

Hot blood covering her hands. Blane's blood.

Oh, God, please.

No.

She couldn't stop it. He was losing too much blood too fast.

I need supplies. An unexplainable calm overtook her and she knew exactly what she needed.

"Blane, I need you to help me. We don't have to go far."

Blood rushing in her ears, she shoved the pistol back into its holster before grabbing Blane's shoulders with both hands. He gasped in agony as she rolled him over. Dragging him to his knees, she pulled him over her shoulders. She stumbled to the ground, stunned and overcome by the weight. A scream burst from her, and she stood as adrenaline and a divine strength coursed through her body.

They were moving now. Another stumble, but this time, she stayed on her feet. Shouts streaking by. Men falling around them. But she just carried Blane on her shoulders as they reentered the complex.

Hold on, Blane. We're almost there.

She had glimpsed the room during their escape from the building minutes before. The infirmary. They were almost there.

Oh, thank You, God. There it is.

She clawed at the handle and strained against the door, finally crumpling under Blane. It opened miraculously, and they both fell through the open doorway.

Alina dragged him and herself away from the door, and she desperately kicked it shut. The chaos from the outside faded to nothing. Now only the labored breathing and gasping of the man beside her filled her ears.

She looked at him.

He was on his back, his eyes glazed as he clutched at the floor now stained with his blood.

Alina was on her feet then, frantically darting around the room. She knew what she was looking for. *WHERE IS IT?* She tore open the cabinets, the drawers, the carts. Gathering supplies as she went. *That's everything.*

She rushed back to Blane, carrying her supplies and dragging along a portable oxygen tank. She dropped to the floor beside him, immediately covering his face with an oxygen mask connected to the tank. Then she tied a tourniquet around his arm to slow the bleeding. Next, pressure dressings for his arm and chest. She applied them rapidly, even as the blood kept flowing. Without relief.

A wrenching groan from him, and then his eyes were closing.

"No, no, Blane, Blane, I need you to stay with me. Look at me," she begged, her hand tapping his face. But his eyes were still closed. His breathing still labored. She slapped him, hard. "I SAID STAY WITH ME, BLANE!"

His eyes opened again, his head turning toward her voice. Looking right through her. Seeing nothing. His face, his chest, everything cool and clammy to the touch. His pulse rapid and thready. He was gasping again.

Alina ripped at her hair, screaming in frustration. He needed blood desperately. Hemorrhagic shock. She was losing him.

God, what else can I do?

Suddenly, she went still.

Blood. He needs blood. And Alina knew where he could get it from. She was O negative.

She leaped up from him again with newfound purpose, and she nearly screamed when she came face-to-face with a startled older man coming through a side door. Her gun was out and trained on him in an instant.

"You," she said, slowly approaching him, "are you a nurse? A doctor?" His eyes, wide with apprehension, locked on hers as he nodded slowly. She kept a fierce expression on her face, and she kept the gun in her hand steady. "I need your help. You will help me with a blood transfusion, and I will not shoot. But we must hurry. Help me with this man!" Keeping her gun on him, she backed up toward Blane.

His eyes shifted to the body beside her before meeting hers again.

"I, I'm sorry," he began in a quiet voice. "I don't have any blood on hand—"

Understanding dawned on his face as he noticed her already rolling up her sleeves.

"I am the universal blood donor. You will obtain my blood and then transfuse him with it." The gun was still up, trained on him. Silence stretched between them, and in desperation, she cocked it.

He spoke again. "Please, I'll help you. No need for that." His eyes looked so tired. "I am a doctor. You do not have to force me to save someone… I am not here by choice."

Alina slowly lowered the gun. The desperation fading.

Together, they dragged Blane further into the infirmary and at last lifted him onto a cot in the center of the surgery. Alina switched him to wall oxygen and reinforced his dressings while the doctor quickly gathered supplies.

Alina pulled a chair near to Blane and sat. She just watched him. Only the faintest rise and fall of his chest. He was slick with sweat and blood. She couldn't even palpate a pulse anymore.

He's running out of time.

Before panic took hold over her, the doctor was beside her.

"You know how this works," he said.

He rapidly swabbed her arm and inserted an 18-gauge connected to a bag with tubing into her median cubital vein. All she saw was Blane.

Please, God. Let us not be too late.

Her blood flowed out through the tubing, bright and red and vital.

Her eyes. Focused on Blane's pale face. Willing him to pull through.

The doctor was deftly inserting a needle into Blane's cubital vein, and she watched as her blood in the bag began to flow into his arm.

Red. Life-giving. Blood. Flowing into him.

Please, God. Let this work.

Exhaustion overtook her. Her eyes slowly closed, and she leaned her head against the back of her chair. Only a few minutes. Her thoughts, swirling around each other. Focusing on one.

Blane.

She didn't know how long she was out before she was awakened by the gentle shaking of her shoulder. The old doctor stood over her.

"Miss, I have to stop it. You've already given more than I would have recommended."

She turned to look at Blane and saw that he was receiving fluids through another intravenous site. Tears blurred her vision, and she turned back to her unlikely ally.

"Thank you for helping us. I... I pray that God will bless you for your kindness."

A strange look flitted over the doctor's face just as the door banged open and Joseph burst into the room, his gun drawn. His eyes widened at the scene before him, eventually alighting on the bag of blood connecting her to Blane. In an instant, Joseph was by the doctor's side, asking what to do.

Alina just watched, sleepy and dizzy but filled with an over-whelming peace. Then Joseph was staring at her and yelling something to the doctor, but she drifted away.

Thank You.

JOSEPH CARRIED ALINA IN his arms to the nearest ambulance outside of the Kratos complex. He had felt such fear when she lost consciousness, but the doctor had known what he was doing.

Burns had already been loaded into one of the other ambu-lances on a stretcher; the paramedics and EMTs had arrived moments after the doctor stopped the blood transfusion. Everyone told Joseph that, without the transfusion, Burns would be dead. There was still a high probability that Burns wouldn't make it. But if the man pulled through, it would be because of Alina. And God only knew what Alina and Burns had been through before Joseph and the rest arrived. Before Burns was shot.

Joseph squeezed his arms tighter around Alina, hoping and praying. For her. For Burns. He was praying. Joseph had to smile in the midst of the darkness.

She has changed my life.

Joseph gently handed Alina to the emergency medical team, and after they loaded her into another ambulance, he climbed in after her.

FBI, CIA, MI5, Interpol. Agents from the four agencies were still actively storming the building, and he had left Davies in charge of overseeing the finale.

An eternity seemed to pass before they arrived at a hospital, and Burns was immediately taken for emergency surgery. At Joseph's question in English, the doctor simply shook his head. *No high hopes.*

Please let him live.

Alina was taken to an available room and laid on the bed. They ran some tests, and she was medically cleared.

Even so, Joseph was relieved she could finally rest. And he would stay by her side the whole time. He especially wanted to be there for her when she awoke. She was still so pale.

A few moments later, the girl stirred, and her eyes widened in severe panic until his face must have cleared in her vision. Relief relaxed her features, and then her eyes closed. Exhaustion and her weakness from the blood loss once again overtook her. *Poor girl.*

But so strong.

Please don't take another one away from her.

Joseph ran his fingers through his hair as he collapsed into a chair. Without thinking, he bowed his head.

Don't take another one away from her. I know You have the power to save him. Please, Lord.

He sat there for the longest time, praying. Just praying.

A sense of peace flowed through him, comforting him, telling him it would be all right. Everything would be all right.

Then Alina was talking to him. "Where's Blane?" she asked, brown eyes wide. "Is he through surgery? How long was I out?" Her hair was a tangled mess, hanging about her shoulders. Joseph told her he would check and that she should just lie still, but at her insistence, he supported her as she slowly pushed herself up and rose from the bed. She leaned on his arm as they exited the room and entered the hallway. Hours had already passed.

The English-speaking doctor told them that Burns was out of surgery and was recovering in the intensive care unit. Upon hearing the room number, Alina pulled away from Joseph and rushed in the direction the doctor indicated. As Joseph turned to follow her, the doctor put out a hand to stop him.

"Make certain she does not hope too much. The transfusion saved him, but the man suffered great blood loss."

On impulse, Joseph shook the doctor's hand. No matter what happened, he was grateful. They all were.

Davies, Donáll, and the Hernes were respectively pacing, brooding, and sitting patiently in the waiting room. Davies had debriefed him as soon as they had arrived, informing him that Black was not among the Kratos agents lined up for arrest. However, the Kratos doctor who had helped Alina save Burns's life was willing to testify. That was one of the few positive outcomes in the tragedy of the afternoon.

Rubbing his hand down his face, Joseph finally turned and followed in the direction Alina had gone. His thigh and the new bruising on his chest throbbed as he walked, his eyes trailing over each room number.

204. *To hundre og fire.*

At least Joseph was relatively sure that was how the number was said in Norwegian.

He shook his head. He was fixating on the insignificant, on the mundane. He knew his heart would break as soon as he entered the room.

He entered anyway.

Alina was kneeling next to Burns. Silent sobs wracked her as she clutched his hand, avoiding all of the tubes exiting his body. Tears streamed down her face, and Joseph had to turn away as she laid her head next to his.

The Scottish man's eyes were closed, and his face was brutally bruised. But he looked to be at peace, lying there.

He might die. Joseph was terrified he would die.

What on earth will Alina do then?

Joseph felt like such an intruder that he backed out of the room and sat on an empty cot in the hallway. Something wet trailed down his face. His own arsenal of tears—an arsenal he had always kept fortified with lock and key. Until the past few days. Now everything broke, and he was weeping. For her. For Burns. For Ami. For Jack. For all the good men who had died on his watch. For finding God again yet feeling so exposed. He wanted to be hardened and to get back out in the field. But all they could do now was wait for more reinforcements.

It was a miracle that so many agents had come to storm the complex, but they would need many more to actually dismantle the place and process arrests. Everyone all over the world wanted a piece of this man, but no one wanted to risk directly taking him on.

He was big. Untouchable.

And somehow he had slipped through their fingers.

Joseph hated him.

But Joseph wasn't sure that even hundreds of agents coming to help would do very much in the long run. Even if they were to take Draven Black, they had nothing on him. And his people would clear him out so fast...even Donáll was now locked out of Kratos's system, and it would take him weeks to break back in. But Joseph knew Kratos wouldn't move forward with *Azrael* until Black had the antidote. And at this point, he didn't.

Looking down, he watched as his own shaking hand pulled out the vial from his pocket. Davies had retrieved the antidote from a lockbox inside the plane that they had stored it in for safekeeping and had brought it back to him. The liquid inside was colorless. Thick. And worth countless lives.

Joseph's eyes were held captive by it. Mesmerized.

Countless lives.

Exhaustion hit him like a brick wall. The vial clutched in his hand, then returned to his pocket.

Joseph fought off the incoming blackness, though he knew it was a fight he was going to lose. He simply wanted to sleep. And sitting there, surrounded by busy Norwegian nurses and doctors, listening to Burns's heart monitor beeping soothingly, he did.

He was never aware of the figure crouching beside him.

CHAPTER FIFTEEN

"BOSS. BOSS!"

Joseph groaned, his mind resisting the sharp summons of Davies to return to the waking world. Then he jerked awake as his shoulder was frantically accosted, his eyes squinting against the sudden, harsh light.

"What? WHAT!" Joseph was on his feet, his hand instantly on his Glock 22.

Davies's distressed face came into view as Joseph shook his head, and the world at last stopped spinning. But his agent's next words set it on fire.

"Alina is gone. She didn't say anything to anyone. She just slipped out without any of us seeing her. She's gone."

"What?" Joseph blinked rapidly, running his hand over the full growth of beard on his chin. He stumbled past Davies and Lily Herne and peered into Burns's room. He was still out.

And she was gone.

The lights seemed too bright, the area too sterile. Alina gone. Missing. His heartbeat filled his ears and the room. He felt a firm hand on his arm, and he saw Davies staring at him.

"How about you sit down, Boss."

"NO!" Joseph roared, trying to fend off the echoing madness swallowing up his sanity. Joseph wanted to punch him, the wall, anything.

"Was she taken? Is Kratos here?" His heartbeat was a war cry.

"No, no, Boss, she left a note." Davies's voice was pleading with him, his wide eyes mirroring Joseph's desperation.

"What? Where?" He ripped the tiny note from Davies's hand.

I'm sorry for everything that has happened. I have to do this before anyone else gets hurt. I am going to make things right and finally end this. I love you all.

Alina

Joseph clutched the paper like his life depended on it. In truth, it did. It really did.

"Did anyone see her go? Is she on the security cams? Where on earth is she going? To 'end this?' What does she ever hope to bargain wi—"

Joseph's eyes grew wide. *Thump-thump.*

"Boss?" Davies's voice faded. *Thump-thump.*

"Joseph." Lily Herne. Brown eyes afraid. *Thump-thump-thump-thump.*

Joseph grabbed at his jacket. Checked his pants pockets. Tore off his jacket. Desperation.

"It's gone," he whispered, his palms slick with sweat. *Thump-thump-thump-thump.* "I'm such a fool." He took a weary breath. He was rubbing his hand up and down his chin. His blue eyes electrified by fear.

"She must have taken it. The antidote. I had it in my jacket's inside pocket when I fell asleep…" Joseph trailed off, horror and stress suffocating him. Gasps all around him. His team was reeling with the same confusion. The same confusion and terror.

"We have to go after her!" Davies shouted. "Is she meeting with him? Black? Why would she even consider going alone? Without backup? And we have more people coming—they'll be here in two hours!"

"I don't know! I don't know!" Joseph ground out, trying to take calming breaths.

She wouldn't give it to him. She knows his intentions. That vial is the only thing staying his hand from unleashing biological warfare across the world…from killing millions. What on earth is she thinking?

Suddenly, insight struck.

"Donáll!" he cried. "Activate her tracker! Activate her tracker right—"

"Already done," Donáll cut in, approaching them with an iPad he was gripping so hard his knuckles were white. "I'd say she's in a vehicle, and she's moving fast."

Joseph ran to the window and stared out.

Driving? She took my keys too. His van was gone.

The darkening evening cast shadows on the street as his eyes scanned the Norwegian traffic, vainly, hopelessly, for her.

"Is she heading back to the Kratos nest? But we reduced that cathedral to ruins, and the complex is still swarming with agents. Where else could she possibly be going?"

Joseph's beard may have been reduced to a stubbly mess with all the times he was rubbing it.

Donáll's response was amplified in his ears.

"Yes...no."

Nothing.

Donáll's silence was the final straw. Joseph lost his fragile hold on his red-hot temper.

"WHAT DO YOU MEAN NO—"

"DON'T YELL AT ME IT'S NOT HELPING!" Donáll cried, his fingers racing each other to scroll in on her movements. "It looks like she's driving toward...nowhere. AND DON'T YELL AT ME I'M TRYING THE BEST I CAN BUT IT LOOKS LIKE IT'S IN THE MIDDLE OF NOWHERE! THERE'S NOTHING OUT THERE!"

Joseph held up his hands in surrender. "Yep, yep, okay, okay, Donáll. Okay." Sudden shame filled him at the way he had just treated his loyal tech man. His friend. Joseph spoke again. "I'm sorry I yelled at you."

A beat. Donáll glanced in his direction, and a rapid nod confirmed that Donáll had already put it in the past. Though he tried his best to be patient, Joseph couldn't wait any longer. "Where is 'nowhere?' I'm going to get a truck ready—"

"But what about our reinforcements? I just got word that Interpol is sending more agents!" Herne cut in.

"They, they can, well, Herne, maybe you should meet them and, uh, apprise them of these...recent events. But I need Davies and your husband with me. We need to stop Alina before she does anything...drastic. DONÁLL!"

"Yes, yes, yes, I am GETTING THERE! She is driving far... It looks like she's heading into the Hamperokken range. Far into the range. Maybe approaching the cliffs—I can't really tell. I actually just lost her signal, all the way out there. But, uh, I will send you the coordinates and try to guide you in the direction she was heading..."

Joseph was already running down the hallway. Davies and Jason Herne were with him. Joseph quickly turned on his comms as they all clambered into one of the trucks.

"Davies, text Donáll and Lily Herne and tell them to turn on their comms."

He tore out of the parking lot.

Where are you going, Alina? God, help her. Alina, what are you doing?

Joseph shook his head again to stave off the panic threatening to make him career off the road.

Alina's words, playing on repeat in his mind. *"I'm sorry... I have to do this. I am going to make things right. I'm sorry. I have to do this. I love you all."*

"I love you all."

I love you too, Alina.

ALINA DROVE WITH TEARS nearly blinding her eyes. She couldn't shake the picture of Blane, bruised and hanging from the chain. His pain. His arm around her, protecting her.

Alina sucked in a gasp. His body falling to the ground. Bullets flying. So much blood lost. But then, hers was his. His face, pale and fading. And then so still, lying in that hospital bed. She let the tears trail down her cheeks, feeling only hollow emptiness. She hoped what she was doing would work. She was so tired...so tired of people getting hurt. She just wanted Ami back. And Blane to live.

Oh, God, please let him live.

The van slowed to a silent stop. She checked her phone one more time. Her lifeline.

She had arrived. At least, her GPS had said she was on the right track before it had lost signal. She gazed out of the window at the chilling sight, wrapping her arms around herself.

Her eyes traced a path of white snow, trailing upward until it was lost, swallowed up in jagged boulders. Boulders which soon took the form of cracked stone steps, tall and narrow and deadly. Her eyes continued up the curvature of the staircase, which disappeared into the cavernous opening of an ancient stone keep. Towers of stone, jutting out like daggers on either side. Competing with the height of the giant rocks surrounding its base, keeping it from being sucked over the edge of the snowy cliff.

Though the ruins looked abandoned, she knew.

This is it.

Black's hot whisper from the cathedral rang in her ears, his ugly words wracking her body with shivers.

"Bring it to me yourself, Alina. And no one else will get hurt."

He had told her of this place—an ancient lookout in the Hamperokken mountain range, neglected and long-forgotten. He knew she would come.

He knows I'm here.

Alina clutched the vial in her hand, studying its colorless contents.

This needs to work. Because I have nothing left yet have everything to lose.

She put the van in park and slipped the vial into her pocket. She felt numb. Palms slick with terror she knew was deep inside her, though the feeling was muted. Disregarded. This was her choice. Her fear of losing Blane overshadowed her fear of losing her own life. She couldn't bear to lose him—the man she loved with all of her heart.

She stuck her feet out of the van, and her sneakers disappeared in the white snow. She didn't mind the cold, even as the biting wind tore at her exposed skin. The winter coat Joseph had given to her was the only barrier between her and Norway's winter winds, but she was already numb, through and through. Her hair whipped around her face from the relentless wind as she walked with slow, deliberate steps. Upward. Following the path her eyes had traced moments before, her steps deep in the heavy, freezing snow.

Soon solid rock steadied the ground beneath her feet, and she looked up to see the stone staircase looming before her. Blackness beyond, seemingly defended by the howling wind threatening to push her to the ground and hold her there. She had no time to think. So she simply climbed. One foot in front of the other as she ascended the crumbling stairs.

Some steps were frozen over, with patches of ice glinting at her. Once, she slipped on one and fell, hard. Thankfully, she didn't slide back down; the rough stone of the stairs held on to her jeans, nearly tearing them. She only sat for a moment before she heaved herself upward, grabbing onto crumbling rock around her and scraping her exposed hands. She realized she felt very weak as she continued her climb. Maybe it was from her blood loss. Maybe it was the elements, shrieking and ripping around her.

Please, God. Give me strength.

She only had a few steps to go, and she suddenly was on level ground, blinking in the enveloping blackness inside the keep. Thin winter light filtered through cracks in the wall and ceiling, illuminating her breaths as they billowed out in front of her. Once her eyes adjusted to the darkness, she took halting steps forward.

The howling wind outside seemed to battle the stone, and she startled as she heard a dislodged rock crack against the frozen ground. She stared upward, seeing yet another curving staircase. She assumed it would take her to the lookout. Then she was climbing those stairs, resisting the urge to lean against the frozen, craggy walls closing in on both sides. She was almost there. Just a few steps more. With every step, her surroundings brightened.

I'm so close.

At last, she stepped on the floor of the uppermost level of the keep, where the walls opened onto the top of the cliff the structure was built on. It was an overlook, open to air and covered in ice and snow. Though the walls of the keep had sheltered her from the wind, she was relieved to be outside again. The echoey shadows that had taunted her during her ascent terrified her.

And there, beyond the icy edge of the overlook, was a wide, open sky. Darkness was falling, but sudden, brilliant streaks of green, purple, and blue were lighting up the black void stretching beyond.

The northern lights.

Her eyes hungry, Alina walked the final distance to the edge of the outlook. She stood still, the winter wind stealing her breath away as a few snowflakes spiraled downward. Even so, she drank in the beauty of the streaking colors contrasted against the black sky.

She thanked God for His handiwork. She imagined it was just for her.

I never thought I would see the aurora borealis when I die.

Her thoughts instantly dissipated in a puff of air that was sucked over the edge as she felt his presence beside her. And the numb fear returned as he spoke to her.

"Hello, dear girl. I am glad you came and that you safely made your way up here. I knew you would."

They stood in silence for a moment, both staring out at the purity of light and color against the darkness of the world.

But Alina knew she had to face him. So she did.

And as she did, she touched the new, round locket adorning her neck.

JOSEPH WAS DRIVING AS fast as he could as snowflakes swirled outside the window. He watched them with a growing unease. As if it wasn't already cold enough, it was going to get even colder.

She's going to freeze out here if Black doesn't murder her first.

His knuckles were white, and his fingers ached from his ice grip on the steering wheel. Each play Alina could possibly make kept running through his head, and each avenue she took ended with her death.

Then a high-pitched voice in his ear shattered his desperate thoughts.

"GUYS! YOU ARE NOT GOING TO BELIEVE THIS!"

Joseph waited for Donáll to elaborate, but silence resounded on the other end of the line.

We don't have time for this.

"DONÁLL!" Everyone jumped in the truck at Joseph's outburst, including Joseph himself.

"Oh, right. She's with him. Black. It looks like they are somewhere high up, and there's a lot of snow."

Joseph's head was reeling with worry, but the implications of Donáll's words didn't click until Davies spoke.

"How...how do you know that? Did Kratos hijack your system?"

"No, no, no, no! She's got a camera on her! Somewhere on her upper torso, judging from the angle of it. I don't know where it came from. I didn't give her one of those. But, yeah, she's livestreaming everything that's being said."

There was silence in the vehicle for a long moment as they processed this new development. Then Lily Herne spoke through their comms in a voice laced with excitement.

"He could confess to anything! We might get substantial evidence to bring him in!"

"Yeah, and keep him in a box somewhere that his corrupt government contacts will never be able to find!" Davies resumed, his words coursing with a thrill. He whistled. "She's incredible. Who can see the feed other than you, Donáll?"

Donáll sounded ecstatic as he spoke. "Me, and I hooked up with Crewe and Vlan so the FBI and CIA have eyes, and I am reaching out to Bauer in Austria and Interpol. I'm only sharing this with people I trust, but no one can alter the video, anyway. It's a live feed, so any of his Kratos people will simply be sweating in their suits, helplessly watching him confess to all of his crimes. No one can do anything to stop it. It's quite brilliant actually... Guys, you should really hear everything he's saying!"

"Something concrete? Tell us!" Davies continued, shaking his overgrown blond hair out of his eyes.

Joseph just drove, processing everything as a kind of hazy dream. He couldn't believe it. Hard evidence. A live confession. Not even Black's top dogs could shut it down… Donáll would make sure of that.

Alina had come up with a trap that could end this monster's game for good. Something that countless government agencies had been trying to do for years but had never come close to succeeding.

Jack would have been so proud.

But alongside his crazed relief, a deep dread systemically spread through every inch of Joseph's body, freezing the blood in his veins.

She's alone with him. And he doesn't know what she has done. But as soon as Kratos can notify him…he'll kill her. Right in front of our eyes.

Joseph gasped, sharply inhaling his next breath. *She knew what she was doing. She went into this knowing it's a suicide mission. It's only a matter of time.*

Joseph stepped harder on the gas, squinting through the snow and avoiding dangerous swaths of ice on the interminable road stretching before them. *God, help us get there in time. Protect her until we get there.*

ALINA PRAYED THAT DONÁLL was getting her video feed. She would not risk touching her locket again. She could only hope that it was working.

It had to work.

She would destroy this man who killed her mother and almost everyone else she loved. She was locking eyes with the materialization of her darkest nightmares. A slow, burning anger began to take root, deep inside of her.

I have to get him to start talking. And she would. Oh, she would.

"You look cold, dear niece," he purred, staring down at her. "I see you came alone, just as instructed. Now, where is it?"

"I need to know something before anything else happens," she began, trying to remove the waver from her voice. The task teetered on the edge of the impossible with his pale eyes sucking her breath away, trying to wither her resolve. But she pressed on. "Why did my mother have to die?"

With every word, her voice steadied. Her determination strengthened. And her fear faded to numbness and resignation within her. She knew how this would end. But if it meant that Draven Black would be locked away for the rest of his life, unable to hurt anyone else, it would be worth it.

At her question, Black's eyes clouded over with regret and longing. For the first time, he looked truly lost standing before her.

"Amanda. My little Mandy. She was my little sister, you know. I never knew I was capable of such love for another human being."

As he spoke, he reached up a hand to her face and carefully brushed her hair back behind her ear. She went still with revulsion, but the realization struck her. She had become Mandy.

"*Azrael* was close to its execution stage. In Alaska, you know. Mandy knew I was involved in something big, but I never told her about *Azrael*."

Alina risked a question. "The virus?"

"Yes, of course. I didn't want her to worry. She was so sweet and innocent. Then while her husband was deployed, she showed up in Alaska. Somehow, she knew where to find me." He laughed softly at some memory.

Keep going.

"It was impossible to hide it from her any longer. And I had to show her. How I desperately wanted her to see my life's work. My *Azrael*. My tool to become the most powerful force in the entire world."

Alina held her breath as he continued, his eyes wide and agitated at the flood of memories.

"I showed her everything. The lab. My *Azrael*. My legacy."

He was incessantly rubbing his hand. As her eyes dropped downward, she watched him slowly remove a glove. He didn't even see her anymore.

"She did not share my vision, though I couldn't see it then. I was blinded by my pride and my excitement. For her to know me. For her to be proud of everything I had built. I showed her my most invaluable asset last—the antidote. I told her that, without it, my work would be forfeit. Who can unleash a plague without the cure? The holder of the cure would control the world. *I* would control the world. It was truly my masterpiece."

He paused, seeing everything and yet nothing.

"We only had one prototype. The virologist team had to be eliminated, you see. One man became…disillusioned with the plan for the world, and he slowly poisoned the team against me, one by one. And so they died. This was it. My one vial of the antidote. When I showed her, she must have decided right then and there to take it."

His agitation increased, and his rubbing transformed into violent grinding.

"And she did. I had such faith and trust in her, and she stole it from me. She smuggled it out and hid it before I even realized it was gone. I was…distracted by the betrayal—her betrayal, and I relied on my most trusted agents to develop a plan."

Each of his words dripped with ice.

"Mandy went home to her child, Alina. A beautiful child. I let the matter go for a few weeks. I was convinced she would see reason and come back. She loved me, see? She loved me. She didn't want to betray me. But she…she never returned. So my agents arranged a little something."

Alina's knees went weak.

"I saw to it that her husband's military unit met with a tragic attack. I had a team follow them with land mines. No matter the route, no matter the path they took. Their deaths were inevitable."

Alina's breath abandoned her. It had been a rushed decision, an enemy's trap. But now it was all because of this man.

Joseph will know that he's not to blame.

Bile burned her throat, but she fought the urge to vomit. The anger that had been slowly kindling within her flamed into rage. He had taken everyone from her. Ami. Her mother. Nearly Blane. And now her father.

She hated him. With every fiber of her being, she hated him. When his confession took him down, she wanted him to suffer.

"She came to see me after that. I was in Pennsylvania, and she knew. She knew. Yet still she resisted. She refused to tell me where she had hidden it. So I threatened the only treasure she had left. Alina."

Alina's eyes snapped up to his face, expecting to meet his. She feared that he had come out of his reverie. But he remained trapped, a helpless observer in his own past.

"She left in a panic. I was...disappointed by her refusal to see reason. And I was angry. I was filled with such...fury, see? I loved her. But my...lieutenants misinterpreted my intentions. And they hated her. They pursued her."

Black's face had contorted. Transformed with poisonous, deadly violence. "I never gave the order to end her life. It was a mistake they paid for with their lives."

Alina saw her mother, terrified and alone, rushing home to protect her daughter. A daughter who had become her world entire.

"They caught her at her house. A beautiful, white house. And they opened fire. A bullet hit the gas tank, and it exploded."

Fire danced in his eyes, the flames climbing into his mind. Alina watched him, paralyzed. Hating him more as every moment passed yet hanging onto every word.

"She died. Instantly. But you see, I needed her alive. She alone knew where my vial was. I was wracked with...rage. I sent more of my men out to clean up the mess. Just like any other operation. Then, in a surprising moment of insight, they stole her daughter. The child had suffered a head injury from the explosion. She later exhibited retrograde amnesia, and she did not remember the incident or circumstances of her mother's death. Mandy's. My dearest little sister's death." His last words were a mere whisper.

"And the gunmen?" Alina dared to ask, her breath catching in her throat. She already knew the answer.

"Oh, I killed them. It was not a good death. I did it myself."

Alina's eyes dropped to his hand, and a violent shudder coursed through her at the scarring. Severe acid burns.

"It was what they deserved."

Suddenly, he was back. His pale eyes were bright with a strange danger, and he was staring at her.

"I've been...occupied with my memories, dear one. It is, in fact, you that we have met to discuss. I had you raised under close observation all these years while I waited for you to find where Amanda had concealed my vial. Now, I will only ask this once. One time. Where is my antidote?"

Alina pulled the glass vial from her pocket with a shaking hand. She held it out to him, and his face contorted with a savage desire as he snatched it from her.

"It's been so many years…" he began, and he sighed and smiled up into the snowflakes falling on them.

Alina had forgotten it was snowing. She glanced down. Her exposed skin was mottled, and her body was numb.

"I'm free-eezing," she whispered. She knew she was running out of time. "Malkovi-vich, Harris, and all the other men you've killed, did any of them know about this? The reason for the s-sudden halt in your plans?" She was risking exposure with this question.

"Some did, some didn't, but they are all dead now, so what does it matter, dear? I've ended their lives, and that is all we must say about…" He trailed off, silently drinking in every inch of the vial. His fingers, which had been gently caressing every inch of it, were still.

Deathly still.

He looked at her, a vehement and desperate gleam in his eyes. Then he was squeezing her face with fingers of ice.

"My vials have certain letters inscribed on them, Alina," he said, carefully, slowly. Biting out every word. "The 'X-K' is missing."

He was crushing her with his death grip, and when she cried out, he only grabbed tighter, cutting off her sound.

"You made a fake, didn't you." He swore and squeezed her face as hard as he could, his other hand grabbing her as she desperately struggled to pull away. "WHERE IS IT?" he screamed, releasing his grip as spittle flew from his lips.

She stumbled backward and fell in the snow, cold and freezing and paralyzed with terror. And yet, somehow, she was smiling at him.

It infuriated him.

He bent to lift her upward, and as he leaned toward her, his eyes fell on her locket. Her breath caught in her throat.

He knows. It's over.

"Burns," he muttered under his breath.

He ripped it from her neck and tore it apart, exposing the microphone and camera that had just broadcasted his confession to the world.

"Why you..." he began, swearing as he hurled the locket over the side of the cliff. He yanked her upward by her hair and struck her, silencing her scream. "You are going to tell me where the vial is, or I am going to kill you and then everyone left on this earth that you have ever loved. You have three seconds."

His hands curled around her throat and began squeezing. She only smiled again, searing him with the contempt in her eyes. "I w-will, ne-ne-never tell you."

"Fine," he hissed in her ear. "Say hello to your mother for me."

His arm wrapped around her neck, and though she clawed frantically, he did not release her. Instead, he was dragging her. Over the biting snow and stone. Toward the edge.

He was going to throw her over.

Instead of continuing to struggle, she held on to him with all of the strength left in her.

If I go over, I'm taking him with me. God, I'm ready.

Just as they neared the cliff's edge, his foot slipped. His grip loosened, and Alina took the moment to break free from him. She threw herself backward, grasping at the stones as the floor of the outlook itself shook and gave way beneath them.

With a scream of terror, Draven Black disappeared with the crumbling rocks over the edge.

Alina lay on her back, gasping for a long moment. She was cold. So cold. But then she heard it. Grunting and gasping over the side of the cliff.

Her blood ran even colder within her. *He's still alive.*

Inch by inch, she crawled to the edge. As she peered over, she saw Black clinging desperately to a rocky outcropping not far below.

Cold. Seeping through every inch of her. She wanted him to let go. The burning was back, and she wished desperately that he would lose his grip and fall. He deserved nothing less.

The man had stolen her entire life from her. He had killed her parents. Her best friend. And he had nearly killed Blane. With every wound he inflicted. Every ounce of Blane's blood that he stole. She didn't even know if Blane was still alive.

A breath, turning to ice in the air as she saw them. The bodies lying in the snow, far below. Ami was sprawled there, bleeding. And her mom and dad, crushed on the ground, their arms locked in a frozen embrace.

She moaned in anguish then, shoving her fists over her eyes.

"Oh, God, I want him to fall!" she gasped.

All at once, the meaning of her prayer struck her, and her breath choked off in a sob.

"What am I doing? What on earth am I doing?" she cried into the howling wind. She was clutching her face in her hands. And then she looked up.

Jesus was beside her, staring at her. Love shining in His eyes. Holding out His hand. And telling her to do the same.

Raw tears froze on her face, and with new strength coursing through her body, she made her decision.

She reached her hand down to the man dangling below her.

He stared up at her, a strange look overtaking the desperation in his eyes. He took her hand and began to climb up toward her. She was pulling him with impossible strength. When he reached the top, she scrambled away from him. But she wasn't fast enough. He grabbed her ankle and yanked her backward. As her body lurched back, the rocks and snow gave way underneath them again, and they were both falling over the cliff.

Falling.

Nothing to hold.

Ice cutting her face and snow swirling the world in white. Her body collided with a firm, snowy ledge, and though she rolled for a few earth-stilling moments, she stayed.

For several minutes, she lay gasping. Waiting for the world to stop spinning.

Her muscles screamed as she tried to turn, but she finally looked over the edge.

Draven Black's body was on the rocky, snowy ground far below, his neck at an impossible angle.

He's dead.

But she was alive. *I hope Blane's alive.*

The cold hit her; the numbness returned. She rolled onto her back, shivering. Shaking uncontrollably. Crying. But then she was peering over the edge again.

Her parents were still there, but they were alive. Her dad was holding her mother in his arms as they danced, swirling her around in the falling snow. They were so far below yet so close Alina thought she could reach out and touch them.

Alina heard her mother's musical laughter drift up to her in the wind, and though she tried to call out, her voice was only a whisper.

"I missed what you said, Alina," a voice said suddenly.

Ami.

Alina turned her head to see her best friend sitting beside her. Ami's hair was blowing around her in waves, and her white dress was shimmering in the soft light. Her friend's voice was gentle, yet strong. And her face was lit with a beautiful glow as she continued speaking.

"You gave me life, Alina. I wanted to tell you that. And you brought me to God. I love you so, so much."

Alina tried to speak back, but no words would come. Ami clasped her hand, and Alina felt a warmth slowly course through her. Chasing away the cold. Soothing her.

"It's okay, Alina. I'll stay here with you."

When she glanced back at the empty snow beside her, she tried to feel for Ami's hand again. She only grasped a handful of soft snow. She finally sank back down, and she closed her eyes.

God, I'm ready.

Her breaths, billowing out from her. Carried by the silent wind.

I'm coming, Mom and Dad.

I'm coming, Ami.

CHAPTER SIXTEEN

JOSEPH MOORE WALKED SLOWLY, CAREFULLY OVER THE FROZEN GROUND.

It was getting dark, though the aurora borealis lit up the sky enough that he could scour the ground around him. For her.

In one hand, he held the spotlight they had miraculously found buried in the back of the truck. In the other, he held his gun. And on his wrist, a tracker synced to her signal. Still silent. But his prayer was that it wouldn't be for long.

His mind kept replaying the moment when Donáll yelled that Draven Black was finished. No way for him to escape his own confession. Then the moment of dulled shock when he heard that the attack on his platoon had been at the hand of Kratos. That no matter what path he led his team down, they still would have been ambushed. But any sense of relief fragmented the minute Black was onto her, grabbing her and destroying the feed.

Lily Herne began speaking in his ear. The additional CIA and Interpol agents were finally here. Coming to join in the search.

Joseph beamed his searchlight on the snowy ground in front of and around him. The snowstorm had diminished to a light flurry, but any footprints had long been concealed. His freezing dread only grew as his gaze was drawn toward the edge of cliffs to his side. He wanted to crush the dread, to scream at it that it was wrong.

Please, God in Heaven, tell me she didn't fall.

He was walking. It was freezing.

Walking. Slipping. Sliding. Stumbling over a rock and falling. His bullet wound aching. The shrapnel in his knees. Piercing. Slowing him down.

Just then, his gaze was drawn to a towering structure, dark against the fading light.

Something inside him knew. He had to reach it. As fast as he possibly could.

As he neared it, he discerned that it was some old keep or fortress. The gathering night was blackest there.

Up the snowy path. Gritting his teeth against the pain. Nearly colliding with another structure, half-concealed in the dark.

And then he was running. And radioing to Davies.

The missing van. She was here. Oh, please, Lord. Let her be here. Let her be alive.

He vaguely heard Donáll's voice telling him to wait for backup. To be careful.

But a faint beeping from the tracker on his wrist shattered any thought of caution. *She is here.*

He ran blindly, forgetting the pain, the panic, everything. He was only thinking of her, alone with the devil in the dark fortress ahead of him.

The desperate picture in his mind pushed him faster than he would have dreamt possible. He had ascended the stone staircase before truly noticing its presence, and he only lost his balance once.

It appeared someone else had stumbled over the same step. There were deep imprints in the snow that the new layers had not yet obscured.

Alina.

He was climbing up another staircase inside the keep before his brain could catch up to his feet. Inhaling gulps of stinging, icy air. Running. To get to her.

Alina.

He reached the top level of the building, his gun out and ready.

But there was nothing. No signs of life. The outlook before him was empty, and Joseph was alone.

The shadows mocked him, and he shone his light frantically around him and out on the outlook. But there was nothing.

Joseph gasped for a breath, his gun shaking in his hand. He was too late. Black and Alina were gone. Despair overcame him, swallowing him whole in the ruins. Here, in a forgotten relic of the past, his future crumbled before him. He feared he would never see her again.

I'm too late.

His despair flamed into desperation, and he beamed the searchlight in the room again, and again outside on the outlook. If she wasn't here, Joseph could only assume Black had taken her somewhere close by, but he thought he would have at least seen fresh footprints in the snow blanketing the outlook up until the... His gaze froze, suddenly captured by the crumbling edge. It almost looked... like the whole outer edge had given out and fallen. His breath quickened. Blood rushed in his ears. Unless the stone at the periphery had fallen years ago, someone could have only recently stood on that edge, and the weakened floor could have collapsed beneath him.

Or her.

Joseph rapidly closed the distance between the tower room and the outlook, his steps pounding on the stone floor. As the icy wind once again slapped his face, he stopped. Dead in his tracks. Then he stared down in horror at the tracking device on his wrist. The beeping had intensified.

No. Oh no, please, Lord. No.

He rushed toward the edge, his momentum nearly sending him over before he caught himself, his hands scraping raw stone. His heart in his throat, he shone his searchlight downward. Fear and horror gripped him, chasing each other in his consciousness.

"No."

There was a body far below.

Only painstaking moments of careful staring finally stilled his pounding heart.

It was Draven Black, mangled on the ground.

He returned his firearm to his holster. Black couldn't hurt anyone anymore.

After radioing to Davies and to Herne's husband, Joseph stepped back from the edge, and he turned to face the crumbling ruins behind him.

Alina must be nearby.

He rapidly retreated back the way he had come, his searchlight sweeping over the rocks.

He froze.

The beeping had slowed like a dying heartbeat with every step he had taken. He doubled back to the edge, and he once again shone his light on Black's body far below. A gust of wind hit him, shifting his searchlight leftward. When he readjusted his grip, a shiver coursed down his body. The light had illuminated something that before had been beyond his circle of light. He aimed his light there, revealing a rocky ledge about five meters down from where he stood. Then a choked breath caught in his throat, and he was screaming for help into his comms. There was a body, curled up on the ledge against the cliff. Not moving.

Alina.

He desperately called to her, the howling wind his only reply. Then he was screaming for a mountain rescue team and for medical aid. He was screaming that Alina was stranded on a cliff ledge, not responding.

Davies answered. A rescue team was coming to his last known coordinates.

Tears froze on Joseph's face. He wanted to climb down to her, but that plan was folly. He paced, called out her name, ordered the team to hurry, shouted again for medical assistance. He looked down the precipice again. Black had not moved. She had to be alive. She would need warmth. Maybe oxygen. What else? To get warm.

Oh, God, please help her be alive. Please help her hold on. Hold on, Alina.

THE EMERGENCY MEDICAL CREW arrived and swiftly rappelled down the side of the cliff from the ruins. Within a few minutes, they had strapped her to a suspended litter and were now carefully lifting her to the top. Joseph hurried to her, but he was pushed aside as they carried her out of the fortress and once again to the white outside.

He followed, watching with heavy breaths while they stabilized her neck. Then they were rushing her to the waiting rig. He approached the vehicle, but he stopped and turned away as they cut off her clothing and drilled an intraosseous needle into her leg. He had seen those needles too many times in Iraq. Joseph called out to a member of the medical team, and the paramedic responded that she was alive but in critical condition. Her body was too cold, and she was unresponsive. But they said she was breathing. And holding on.

Hold on, Alina. Hold on.

When he at last glanced inside the rig again, he saw that they had covered her bare skin in blankets and that they were infusing fluid. Likely warmed saline in order to rewarm her core. He watched, his eyes held captive by the dripping of the IV.

Drip. Drip. Drip. Drip.

Then he blinked as a nurse reached up and opened the fluid wide.

Drip-drip-drip-drip-drip-drip.

A hand was on Joseph's arm, and a paramedic was talking to him.

"Sir, we must leave here immediately."

The man turned back to the rig before Joseph could respond, and Owen Davies was suddenly beside him, gently guiding him down the frozen path. But Joseph's eyes were locked on the ambulance doors as they swung shut. He couldn't breathe. Tears had overtaken his face, blinding his eyes as the screaming sirens of the ambulance deafened his ears. Then they were embracing him. His team. They all had tears of their own.

He loved her like his own daughter. He had never married. Had never had any children.

God, please don't take her from me.

They were in the trucks, slowly beginning their descent out of the mountains on treacherous roads.

She's in good hands. Have faith.

The promises lingered in the icy wind, in the bright colors still streaking through the sky. A sense of peace within him. And then he got a call.

"Moore." A pause. "Oh, thank you. Thank you."

Davies looked at him. "What is it, Boss?"

His peace flourished even more as he ended the call and returned the phone to his belt.

"Burns is awake. And he's rapidly gaining strength."

CHAPTER SEVENTEEN

BLANE BURNS SAT BESIDE THE HOSPITAL BED, HIS ARM IN A SLING STRAPPED TIGHTLY TO HIS CORE.

The nurse was not happy, but he had demanded it. He needed to be near her. His lass. Alina.

They told him that she would be dead if they hadn't found her when they did. It had taken nearly two days to slowly rewarm her; the doctor wanted to prevent her from experiencing heart complications and to give her body the time it needed to adjust. He had said the process had taken even longer because her red blood cell count had been so low.

Because she had given so much to me.

She was lying on the bed now, her exposed skin still deathly pale. Two fingers were missing on her left hand, amputated due to frostbite. Dressings covered her body, protecting the fragile skin that had begun to blister and peel from the damaging Norwegian cold.

By some miracle, her face had been spared. And she was beautiful, even as she slept.

So near to death.

He wiped at a tear trailing its way down his face, gritting his teeth against the white-hot pain shooting through his chest and the debilitating soreness of his arm. Of his entire body.

Blane glanced up to see Joseph Moore sitting a pace away, his hands steepled before him, his foot tapping up and down. His face, drawn and haggard with grief and worry. Blane knew there was nothing he could say. In fact, no words had been spoken between them since Moore had come into the hospital room. Moore had simply nodded at him and shook his hand.

Owen Davies had pulled Blane aside earlier that day, and he told Blane everything that Alina had done. That she had saved Blane's life at the Kratos base with her blood. That she had exposed Draven Black. That Draven Black was dead. And that Alina had ended up nearly frozen to death on a craggy ledge in the Hamperokken mountains.

His thoughts were interrupted as Lily Herne walked into the room. She smiled at Blane with such compassion in her eyes that he tried to smile back, but he could only manage a nod as pain radiated down his face.

She locked eyes with Moore, and with a final glance at Alina, he slowly got to his feet and followed her out.

Then they were gone. And Blane was looking at Alina again.

Blane stared at her face, seeing so much peace. Yet so little strength. So little color. He wanted to see her dark-brown eyes again. He needed to hear her laugh…to hear her voice.

A single tear. Then two.

He needed to hug her, to protect her. He couldn't protect her from this. He could only watch, and it was tearing him apart.

The tears were falling, raindrops in a heavy storm now. His grief overcame him as he gently, softly brushed a wisp of hair from her face.

Blane Burns had lost everything when his Isla and his Olivia were murdered on that road. Before he had the chance to say good-bye. He had lost everything: his family, his friends, his job. His life.

Then came the years of burning. The burning was all he had had left, the driving force behind him, fueling his rage at the world and at God. Blane Burns had been burning for so long. So long.

And then he had met her—this beautiful woman who had taken his broken heart with her hands and had slowly put the pieces back together.

He was sobbing, his finger caressing her cheek. He couldn't bear it if she would be taken from him, too.

God, please let it not be so.

Speak to her.

He needed to speak to her.

Blane pulled his chair closer to her bed, his muscles, bruises, and bullet wounds screaming at him. But he ignored them, and he took her delicate hand in his.

He sat there a moment, gently rubbing his thumb over hers.

"Oh, Alina," he finally choked out through his grief. "I, uh… I know you maybe cannot hear me, but I need to talk to you." He took a shaky breath and pressed on. "I looked up your name. Moore had said something about it on the plane, and I wanted to know what he meant. I looked it up. Your name means 'light.' Did you know that? Your name is light." He paused, shutting his eyes against the flood of sorrow threatening to send him under again.

"Alina, that's what you are. I don't, uh, I don't know if you know it, but you saved me. They told me you saved me after I was shot. But you saved me long before that. You saved my life back in Washington. The very first day we met."

Blane sat, lost in memories as fresh tears began the journey down his face.

"I was lost, you know. I was burning with…with rage and hatred. Everything black and dead. And then I met you. And you, sweet lass, you brought light back into my life. You saved me. You brought me back to God. You s-saved me, Alina. Oh, G-God, help me!"

Blane was too overcome to continue. His head fell against their clasped hands as he wept.

"I l-love you, lass. I love you. And… I cannot…b-bear to lose you. The light of my l-life. I cannot."

He was sobbing. He kissed her hand, wetting his own with a thousand tears. He didn't know if the tears would ever end.

He loved her. He loved her.

He wanted to take her place, to die instead. She was too selfless, too lovely, too good to die.

"Jesus," he said softly. "Jesus, I know Y-You are listening. I… I know You are always listening. P-please. Save her. I know You have the power. I know. I know. Please, Jesus, don't t-take her. Jesus. Please, Jesus. Help her."

Her heartbeat was the only sound echoing in the room. Its rate, too slow. He feared she was giving up.

Jesus! his soul cried out.

Head in his hands, listening to her heart. Beating slowly, so slowly. Nothing left.

And then the beeping increased. The beats of her heart, increasing.

He looked at her face. A pink glow upon her cheeks.

Fingers squeezing his.

Oh, Jesus. Thank You.

Her eyes opened.

ALINA FELT A BIG hand grasping hers, even before she opened her eyes. She knew it belonged to Blane Burns, and she clutched it tightly. Slowly, she opened her eyes. Through the blinding lights, her world at once focused on the one person she feared would be lost to her forever.

Thank You, God. Thank You, Jesus.

His eyes were wide and bright, and tears were trailing down his face. He was staring at her in wonder. She saw love there. In those eyes. In those midnight eyes that were now silver with tears.

Then he called out to someone, and she furrowed her brow.

Where am I?

She opened her mouth to ask him, but her lips were so chapped she bit back a groan. He was speaking to her, telling her she would be okay, telling her she was in a hospital and that she would be okay. And that he was not leaving her side.

As her senses returned, she became acutely aware of pain. Pain in her hand. Pain everywhere. She glanced down at her hand and saw a bulky gauze dressing where two fingers were supposed to be. She looked to Blane in confused alarm, and he was telling her something about frostbite.

As a medical team rushed in, she kept her eyes locked on Blane's. She never wanted to look away again. But she shifted her gaze when she heard a sob or a laugh; she wasn't sure which. Joseph was there, standing in the doorway. He looked so vulnerable and hesitant, standing on the periphery. She smiled at him, and he smiled back.

As the medical team bustled around her, she felt strength flooding her body. And she didn't feel cold anymore. All at once, her memories came rushing back. The meeting. The ruins at the cliff. And something she needed to know.

"J-Joseph," she began once the three of them were alone. He walked toward her as she spoke. "Did it work? Did you get my video? I used the special locket Blane had given me."

She struggled to sit up, but Joseph reached out and gently pushed her back down.

"Yes, Alina, we did, but you need to rest. You were so brave. It is such a miracle that you are alive. We thought… I thought…"

Joseph's blue eyes were full of tears, and she just looked back and forth between him and Blane.

After a moment, Joseph cleared his throat.

"But, Alina, where is the antidote? You took it?" Joseph asked.

She sifted through the fog of her memories.

"Yes… I did. I took the antidote. I saw you put it in your pocket, and I knew that I needed it in order to meet with him." The memories of the meeting hit her again, but she forced herself to continue.

"A nurse helped me find an empty vial here that was similar, and we concocted a solution inside that looked like the antidote. Before I left, I put the original vial back in the safest place I thought there was. Back in your pocket."

Joseph's face changed and panic suddenly gripped her.

"You…you don't have it?" she asked slowly.

The three of them stared at each other, and just as Joseph leaped toward the door, Donáll popped his head into the room.

After smiling happily at Alina, he addressed Joseph.

"Hey, Boss. In the craziness of the last several days, I forgot to give you this."

Joseph stared down in confusion as Donáll handed him a sleek metal key.

"What's this for?" he asked quickly.

"I just wanted to, ya know, let you know," Donáll began. "I thought it was plain idiocy that the antidote we've been fighting Kratos for this entire time was in a pocket. So...um. I took it, and I have it. It's in a safe place, all locked up."

Alina grinned at Joseph right before he charged at Donáll, his arms wide.

"Come here, smarty. I'm going to hug you! No, no come back!"

Donáll, who had been backing away from the older agent, now turned on his heel and fled the room.

Joseph pursued, cackling with glee. "I'll tell the others you're awake!" he called over his shoulder.

Alina and Blane looked at each other, and their collective sigh of utter relief filled the tiny hospital room. Then they were dissolving in laughter and simultaneously grimacing in pain.

At last, it sunk in that she and Blane were alone. She tried to sit up again, waving away his breathless protestations as he struggled to stop his wheezing laughter.

"I k-know what I am doing," she ground out, but she flopped back down onto the bed with a groan despite her best efforts. As Blane chuckled and tucked a pillow underneath her head, Alina couldn't help but smile.

Almost got him.

She finally managed to sit up. But before Blane took a few steps backward, she caught his hand.

Got him.

"Hey," she said.

"Hello, there," he replied. "Did you need me to get you something?"

"Huh?"

"You're sitting up when you should be lying back. Do you need something? Should I call for your nurse?"

"Nope," she said, and she gave him her broadest grin, lips chapped and all.

"I just wanted to hold your hand again."

CHAPTER EIGHTEEN

JOSEPH MOORE WAS SITTING OUTSIDE THE FBI DIRECTOR'S OFFICE.

He was scrolling through his texts, his missed calls, his emails, his updated case files from Abigail in the office. He sighed in weariness. Weeks gone, and the world moved on without waiting for him.

Joseph smiled to himself. But in that time, he had found his whole world. And he was never letting them go.

"Agent Moore," the new FBI agent walked out, looking at him. "Director Turne will see you now."

What's this guy's name? Flynn something? Joseph looked him up and down. *Yeah, I can get this one in shape. Put him on my team, and I've got him.*

"Excellent," Joseph responded, giving the younger man his most authoritative and intense stare as he rose from his seat. He was simply trying to build up his confidence. He knew whatever he would face next would not be…pretty.

Joseph took a deep breath as he entered the darkened office. Then he thought of Alina and Blane Burns, alive and well, and he was ready.

"Agent Moore."

Director Turne, forever a hulking and intimidating figure, was standing at his desk along with the man Joseph immediately recognized as the head of the CIA—Director Crow.

Joseph replied with his respectful "sir" and "sir," and then he waited, watching both warily.

"So you've at last returned from your unsanctioned operations in Alaska, Austria, and Norway," Turne began, fixing Joseph with his beady eyes.

"Sounds like you've been keeping close tabs on me and on my team's whereabouts, sir," Joseph replied, fixing him with his own contemplative stare.

"As well I should. HAARP is undergoing a massive and disruptive investigation, a privately owned residence in Norway has been reduced to rubble, and a man, a very influential and important man, is dead."

"You may also know, sir, that potentially catastrophic dealings in the back rooms of the HAARP facility were carefully and methodically uprooted, and their products and all traces were tracked down and destroyed by multiple agencies. You may also be aware, sir, that that private residence housed sensitive intelligence that has been confiscated and is currently being held by Interpol. And countless assassins for hire have been arrested from that facility, as well, thanks to the CIA and Interpol agents who, only eventually, I may add, made it to Norway. Some of which gave their lives to overtake the complex. And a brutal, evil, and allegedly untouchable criminal is dead, and only the tip of the iceberg of his crimes has been exposed, thanks to a well-timed confession straight from his own lips."

Joseph took a breath, his heart racing. Director Crow was eyeing him with guarded respect, and Director Turne was simply glaring at him. Crow eventually spoke up. "Well, we would like a full report on all of your actions, and we will need to correspond with Interpol with everything you have declared. Thank you, Agent Moore. It sounds as if you and your team have done well for your country."

Joseph nodded at him. *At least the CIA is in good hands. For now.*

As Joseph looked between them, they began conversing about agents they would contact and government officials to whom they needed to reach out. Eventually, Turne looked at Joseph.

"You are dismissed, Moore. We have a huge mess to clean up."

His pointed look almost drew a scoff from Joseph, but he held his peace and addressed them both again as "sir" before turning on his heel to leave.

At last, he was out of that stuffy, darkened room. But then he heard his name echo down the hall. Turning, he saw Director Turne hurrying after him. Joseph paused, every inch of him on edge.

"Moore," Turne ground out as he caught up to Joseph. He stuck a big, meaty finger in Joseph's face.

"I know exactly what you have done. What you are trying to do. But you know what happens when you cut off the head of a hydra, Moore. Two more grow back in its place." He leaned in close, but Joseph stood his ground.

"The monster only grows stronger," he hissed, and he turned and began walking away. "Watch yourself, Moore. Watch yourself very carefully."

Joseph called out, "Not when he burned them." Turne halted, slightly turning his head.

"What did you say?"

"The hydra. The heads didn't grow back after Hercules's nephew burned the necks. Then Hercules deftly and thoroughly...killed it."

Turne opened his mouth, lost his reply, and simply shook his head with a glance full of warning and thinly veiled contempt. As he continued back to his room, Joseph smiled and began his own walk back to the Transnational Crime Branch of the FBI.

He knew his job...maybe even his life...could be in danger. But he didn't think Turne or any of the other Kratos followers would expose themselves too quickly. Their leader was dead, and now someone would have to claw his or her way to the position. But everyone would be equally weak until someone managed to come out on top. And Joseph Moore, Owen Davies, Lily Herne, Lestor Donáll, and countless other agents all over the world would be there, waiting to strike when Kratos was at its weakest.

He smiled. Maybe even Blane Burns would return. He would need something to do after...well. After the next big step in his life. And he knew that Alina was planning to continue working as a nurse in Glen Allen.

As Joseph entered his office, he greeted each of his team by name.

"Davies."

"Hey, Boss."

"Herne."

"Good morning. How's that leg?"

"Feeling much better, thank you."

Joseph walked to the corner of the room, grabbed something, and then quietly walked over to his jumpy tech man. Donáll was sitting at his desk, furiously typing. When Joseph peered closer, it looked like he was playing some sort of game, crushing... *What is it? Candy? Hmmm.*

Joseph knelt down and brought his face beside Donáll's head. He was being cruel, but he was loving it. From the snickers he heard around the room, the others were loving it too.

After a beat, he murmured right in Donáll's ear, "Lestor."

Donáll startled with a yelp and a huge flurry of activity, as per usual. Coffee spilled everywhere; papers grew wings and enjoyed a short flight to the floor; and his colored pens, meticulously organized, scattered all over his desk.

"DUDE! Not cool. Not cool."

Donáll stared mournfully at the black coffee dripping slowly down his desk and puddling on the floor. He didn't even seem to care that his yellow shirt was stained. He was just missing his precious beverage.

Without a word, Joseph handed him a wet towel. Donáll took it without even looking at him. Then Joseph handed him a fresh cup of coffee. And Donáll took it without even looking at him. Joseph poked him. And then the little man let loose a yell, jumped out of his seat, and gave chase as Joseph sprinted away. Donáll soon overtook him, and the two fell to the floor, laughing. Joseph had never heard Donáll laugh quite like that before. It was such a cheery sound.

An hour later, the team was sitting around the conference table. Crewe and Shaw were there too. And Joseph stood up.

"All right, folks. We've got work to do, starting with all of the agents we arrested in Alaska. Right now, Kratos is weak. And we are going to take it down. Once and for all."

After Joseph finished and everyone scattered to their desks, he sat down and pulled his laptop toward him. They had done some good work. The virus was contained. The antidote was safe from greedy hands. The head of Kratos was dead. And now they would dismantle the organization, one corrupt politician and agent at a time. All over the world.

Joseph smiled, a sense of peace flowing through him. There was yet another mission he was choosing to accept. The mission where he would seek God again.

Joseph had ignored the Lord for so long…he had abandoned his faith the moment when Jack and his men had died on that fateful day in Iraq. But ever since, God had slowly and surely been drawing Joseph back to Himself. One miracle at a time.

Though they had never talked, Joseph knew the same was true for Blane Burns. Alina had truly saved them. And Joseph was looking forward to the journey ahead.

His phone buzzed. It was Alina, telling him that she and Blane were planning a trip to Lavallette Beach. His world complete.

Thank You, God.

ALINA STOOD FOR THE longest time before she knelt in the grass. A bouquet of purple roses in her hand. And tears slowly trailing down her cheeks. The wind gently kissed her face, and she closed her eyes as sunlight cleared the clouds and beamed down on her.

She was remembering, holding each precious memory in her mind before carefully storing it away. She was here not to say goodbye but to visit before Blane arrived. She planned to take this walk many times in the future.

She was back in Glen Allen and kneeling in Springfield Cemetery. Ami's gravestone was before her. It was such a pretty marble stone… It was such a beautiful place.

Wiping her tears away, Alina gently placed the flowers in the vase that was part of her best friend's gravestone. She smiled as the tears began afresh. The purple flowers would have been Ami's favorite. Alina knew she would have loved them.

"Ami," she said, gently reaching her fingers out to trace the smooth engraved letters of her best friend's name, "I miss you. I miss you so, so much. I… I want… I want you to be here…here with me. It's selfish, I know. There was no true happiness in your life here. And you're in such a better place." Alina pictured Ami meeting Jesus. He was hugging her and telling her she would never be alone again.

"But, Ami, I… I want you to know that I will never forget you. I'll be thinking of you until we meet again. I am so excited for that. I love you… I love you so much."

Soft tears, but with them a sense of joy. And then she heard someone walking up behind her and a gentle "Hello, there."

Blane was here. He was here, and he had said he would never leave her side. She loved him.

As she turned to him, still kneeling in the grass, he knelt down too. He closed his eyes, his lips moving in silent prayer. When he opened his eyes and looked at her, she allowed herself to become lost in their midnight blue depths. He reached out and brushed a tear from her cheek, and then it was her turn to close her eyes. After they listened to the soft wind and birdsong in the trees for a timeless moment, Alina finally spoke.

"I think I am ready to go now."

He looked at her and nodded, a small smile on his face. He was so handsome, and his accent was so wonderful. Blane helped her to her feet, and they strolled out of the cemetery. She didn't even realize it until they had reached his Toyota Camry.

They were holding hands.

He held open the door for her, climbed in, and then drove her home. At her request, he even walked in with her. It was too lonely being there by herself. Once they were inside, she grabbed her pre-packed bag.

"Let's go to the beach, Blane," she said, smiling at him.

As Blane drove, Alina watched the beautiful afternoon flash by outside of the car window. Eventually, she turned and peeked at him. Oh, she loved him. And she was so thankful he was here with her.

Thank you, Jesus.

BLANE BURNS WALKED WITH Alina along the beach, his eyes not truly taking in the colorful sea shells and wispy sea foam at their feet. Nor the beautiful sunset, sending streaks of vibrant color across the sky. Nor the deep blue ocean, sparkling with every wave that triumphed over the water for a moment before falling back down, all glassy and smooth.

No, his eyes were drawn to the beautiful woman walking beside him. She was wearing a soft-blue dress, and her wavy, brown hair was pulled back into a soft braid, allowing the tendrils to frame her face and to be kissed by the salty air. And every sensation in his body was tuned to the feeling of her delicate hand in his. He loved her. Oh, how he loved her.

Then the weight in his pocket drew his attention again, and the nervous feelings returned full force.

He felt Alina's hand squeeze his, and he looked up to see that they had reached her parent's beach house. He sensed her warring emotions of peace and dread.

She had told him she wanted to say goodbye, and this seemed like the right place to do so. But the memories of their first visit here were haunting her, and he squeezed her hand back. He hoped to replace those horrible memories with a new one. A beautiful new one.

They didn't go in, but they instead stood out by the ocean, taking in the peaceful scene. He watched Alina close her eyes, and he knew she was saying farewell to her parents. As they stood there, the moment seemingly frozen in time, the nervous feelings hit him again.

Then he thought of his Isla laughing at his nerves, telling him to get on with it. And he thought of his sweet, wee Olivia, and he treasured the memories he had of them as the breeze cooled his face. After an endless moment of precious memories, he returned his thoughts to the woman beside him.

And then he was pointing at imaginary dolphins bobbing along in the waves. And when she turned back around, he was down on one knee.

Joy coursed through him. And her eyes were full of it, too. They were also brimming with tears. She had such beautiful eyes.

Focus, Burns.

He pulled out the diamond ring. But her eyes stayed on his. "Alina, I love you. I am not one for many words, as you know, but I love you. I love everything about you. And with your say-so, I would like to spend the rest of my life with you."

Her smile was brighter than a thousand diamonds reflecting sunlight. "Yes! Yes, Blane Burns, my answer is yes!"

She was laughing and smiling. And she was crying. She stilled as he slipped the ring over her finger, and she was quiet as he stood.

He slowly reached out a hand and gently tipped up her face to meet his gaze. He looked into her eyes, searchingly, and when hers closed, he had his answer.

He kissed her. And when she kissed him back, he felt like dancing.

And he did, pulling her along with him as she laughed. Sand scattered up in the breeze as they stumbled around, and they eventually fell down to the sand, breathless. He jumped to his feet, pulling her with him, and they began the walk back up the beach, both taking one last glance at the beautiful house.

Alina turned and smiled up at him, and he wrapped his arms around her. Then they shared another kiss.

His heart was full. His world complete. And at long last, Blane Burns felt alive again.

Thank You, God.

EPILOGUE

ALINA STOOD IN THE DOORWAY, THE SEA BREEZE GENTLY TOUSLING HER HAIR.

Pale-pink clouds lined with gold floated effortlessly in the sky before her.

The smell of baking cookies reached her, and she walked carefully into the beach house to take them out of the oven. Leaving them to cool on the counter, she glanced up, seeing the pictures adorning the wall and the mantelpiece next to her.

Her wedding day, forever encased in silver frames. Alina's eyes trailed over each picture, the memories bringing a smile to her face. There was one of her, standing in her pearl-white dress and holding her bouquet of white dahlias, bluebells, silver-green leaves, and tiny purple rosebuds. Another with Keith, Sierra, and Becca.

Her gaze next shifted to the photo of her with a team of FBI agents. Her team of FBI agents. Joseph was standing directly beside her, his face shining with incandescent joy. Owen and Lily stood next to him, and she could see Officer Brady, his daughter, and June sitting in the pews behind them. She laughed as she once again studied Pete and Patch posing in the background, with Patch half-lifting Pete in his arms.

Donáll didn't make an appearance in any of the photos, as he himself had taken them. She vividly recalled him stalking around the tiny ornate church with a massive camera.

Alina picked up the final picture, her fingers tracing the silver flowers lining the frame. It was of her, Blane, and Blane's mother. Upon meeting her, Alina had at once understood where Blane's kindness and gentle heart had come from.

She set the frame back on the mantle, other beautiful memories flitting through her mind. Joseph's tears as he had walked her down the aisle. The memorial table that had held her parent's picture and a picture of Ami, accompanied by an additional bouquet. The way Blane's eyes had lit up when he saw her for the first time as his bride.

Four years had passed since that magical day. The day that had promised so many new beginnings and a life with Blane. And what an extraordinary life it was turning out to be.

Alina slowly walked back outside through the open door, eventually reaching the cushioned chair on the porch. She drank in the sight of Blane kneeling in the sand, holding out his arms as little Ami toddled toward him. When she started to fall, he gently clasped her arms and lifted her up before nestling her to his chest, her squeals of delight making him laugh.

Happiness enveloped Alina, and she rubbed her belly. Their second child was due in just a few months, and they were so excited for him to become a member of their family. At that moment, Blane looked up and met her eyes, and his smile made her heart flutter as warmth spread through her. Oh, how she loved him.

He was lifting Ami to his shoulders, and they began making their way to the beach house.

Her world complete.

Thank You, God.

ABOUT THE AUTHOR

Tenaya Metzler's passion for writing has followed her since she was able to hold a pencil. When she's taking a break from pursuing her career as a registered nurse, she enjoys acting, traveling, reading, and spending time with treasured family and friends. She resides with her family in the midst of rural Pennsylvania, and she highly anticipates trips to the beach where she can finally sit down with a good book.

CPSIA information can be obtained
at www.ICGtesting.com
Printed in the USA
BVHW040229040723
666615BV00006B/180